W9-BVV-834

One Mountain Away

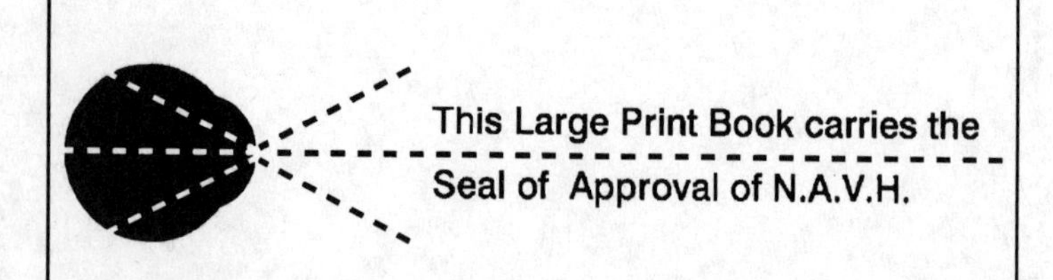
This Large Print Book carries the
Seal of Approval of N.A.V.H.

One Mountain Away

Emilie Richards

WHEELER PUBLISHING
A part of Gale, Cengage Learning

GALE
CENGAGE Learning

Detroit • New York • San Francisco • New Haven, Conn • Waterville, Maine • London

Goddesses Anonymous Series #1.
Wheeler Publishing, a part of Gale, Cengage Learning.

Wheeler Publishing Large Print Hardcover.
The text of this Large Print edition is unabridged.
Other aspects of the book may vary from the original edition.
Set in 16 pt. Plantin.

LIBRARY OF CONGRESS CATALOGING-IN-PUBLICATION DATA

Richards, Emilie, 1948–
One mountain away / by Emilie Richards. — Large print ed.
p. cm. — (Goddesses anonymous series ; #1) (Wheeler Publishing large print hardcover)
ISBN 978-1-4104-5269-6 (hardcover) — ISBN 1-4104-5269-7 (hardcover)
1. Real estate developers—Fiction. 2. Successful people—Fiction. 3. Life change events—Fiction. 4. Large type books. I. Title.
PS3568.I31526O54 2012
813'.54—dc23 2012026653

Published in 2012 by arrangement with Harlequin Books S.A.

Printed in the United States of America
1 2 3 4 5 6 7 16 15 14 13 12

For all the women who have reached
out to me throughout my life.
My very own anonymous goddesses,
too many to count or name.

CHAPTER ONE

First Day Journal: April 28

Today Maddie is wearing blue, the color of a summer sky. The choice is a good one. Any shade of blue probably suits her, but, of course, in the years before adolescence, most children look wonderful in every shade of the rainbow. At Maddie's age skin is flawless and radiant, and hair is glossy. I think her eyes are probably blue. This is an educated guess, based on the light brown of her hair, the rose tint of her cheeks and her preferences for every shade from royal to periwinkle. I bet somebody's told her how pretty she looks when she wears it. I remember how susceptible girls of ten are to compliments. Her mother certainly was.

This park is always filled with children. I come here to watch them play, while at the same time I worry they make learning personal facts too easy. I feel absurdly protective, so I make it my job to watch out for strangers who show too much interest or approach them to start conversations.

This is absurd, of course, because to the children, I'm a stranger, too. A stranger enjoying a glimpse back in time to a childhood she never experienced. A stranger scribbling in a journal she resisted for weeks until the lure became too great.

I'm calling this my First Day Journal because of a quote from the 1970s. When I first arrived in Asheville the words radiated in psychedelic colors from posters in every store downtown.

"Today is the first day of the rest of your life."

Ironically, during the time the saying was wildly popular, I was too busy to think about it. For me a day was just something to get through to make way for another. But now, every time I sit down to record my past and my thoughts, I'll need the reminder that every day brings a new start, whether we need one or not.

A shriek draws my attention. The boy laboring up the spokes of the metal dome with Maddie is named Porter. Apparently his mop of black hair makes it hard to see, because he continually shakes his head in frustration, or maybe just in hopes the strands will fly out of his eyes for the time it takes to lumber to the top. I know his name because the other children shout it loudly and often. Porter's something of a bully. Overweight, a little shabbier than the others, a little clumsy.

It's that last that makes the boy pick on Maddie, I think. Porter's figured out an eternal truth. If he makes fun of someone else, no one will look quite so hard at him. While this makes me angry, I understand. The world's filled with bullies, but at birth, not a one of them glanced at the next cradle and plotted how to steal the pacifier out of a baby-neighbor's mouth. It's only later they learn that knocking down other people may help them stand taller.

So while Porter's behavior upsets me, I feel sorry for him, as well. He's still just a boy. I want to take him in hand and teach him the manners he'll need to get by in the world, but Porter's neither my son nor grandson. I'm just a stranger on a park bench, watching children make mistakes and enemies, decisions and friends.

One of Maddie's friends is on her way to the dome right now to make sure Porter doesn't push her. This child, olive-skinned and lean, is named Edna, which surprised me the first time I heard another child call her name. Of course, names are a circle. They come into favor, then go. Today's young mothers probably never had an Aunt Edna who smelled like wintergreen and mothballs, and chucked them under the chin at family reunions. They find the name filled with music, the way my generation never did.

The child Edna is filled with music. She's a girl who dances her way through life. I think if she and I ever spoke she would sing her words. Edna certainly sings her way into the hearts of the other children. She's powerful here in a way none of the others are. Edna can rescue any situation. She's tactful when she needs to be, forceful when that's required and a mistress of the best way to avert trouble before it begins, which is what she's doing today. If no one beats her to the honor, Edna may well be our first woman president.

Edna waltzes her way up the metal bars with a quick, natural grace, and she's swaying at the top before Porter can work any mischief. From here it's obvious she's talking to him. Talking, not lecturing, because after a moment, I hear him laugh. Not derisively, but like the child he is. I bet Edna told him a joke, because now Maddie's laughing, too. Maddie's a courageous child, and she shows no fear. If Porter knocked her to the ground, she would pick herself up and start the climb again. I think Maddie refuses to let anything get in her way. Better yet, she doesn't seem to hold grudges or rail against obstacles. She simply finds a way to go around them.

I rarely cry. When I was younger than Maddie, I realized how futile tears were. But today my eyes fill as I watch the three children divide the world among themselves. Here's the future, right in front of me. Edna will lead, efficiently, carefully, fairly. Porter will try to disrupt everything around him, but if Edna can influence him, he may find a better place. And Maddie? Maddie will struggle with whatever life throws at her, but she will always prevail.

For the moment, though, the three are simply children, laughing at Edna's well-timed joke while I wipe my eyes on a park bench thirty yards away. When I look up, I see Maddie's grandfather, Ethan, start across the baseball diamond beyond us to fetch his granddaughter.

I turn away quickly to make sure he doesn't see me. I wonder, though, if he did, would Ethan feel a glimmer of sympathy? Would he understand why I'm sitting here, watching a child I've never spoken to? Would he join me on this narrow park bench and tell me about the granddaughter we share, the granddaughter we haven't discussed since that terrible night ten years ago when we stood at the window of a neonatal intensive care unit and broke each other's hearts?

As I gather my purse and sweater, and slip

my heels back into my shoes, I contemplate what to do next. I'm struck by how many possibilities confront us each moment, possibilities we rarely notice. We move on to the next decision by habit, then the next, and we never look around to see all the paths leading to other places, other lives. Right now I could meet Maddie's grandfather halfway across the diamond and ask him to talk to me, even to introduce me to the young girl who is so much a part of both of us.

As always there are too many choices to contemplate fully, but as I stand and turn in the other direction, I know I'm making the only one I can.

Chapter Two

Charlotte Hale tried to obey the law. She paid strict attention to street signs and rarely risked a yellow light. She drove in the passing lane on the interstate only if she absolutely had to. She was a decent enough driver, except for one flaw. She had never learned to park.

Knowing her limits, most of the time she improvised. She was guilty of lingering in no-parking zones, and leaving her car in a traffic lane with the blinkers on. If she was lucky enough to find a large enough space to park along the curb, she fed the meter well past the time limit, and even in less-challenging slots she often overshot the lines meant to separate her car from others. Consequently, despite being a perfectionist in every other way, she had learned to live with scrapes on her side panels and tickets on her windshield. Through the years she had paid enough citations to fund a personal meter maid.

Today, when she stepped out of her car and into the lot behind Asheville's Church of the Covenant, she saw she was taking up almost two feet of the space beside her. Since there were still plenty of other spaces available, she decided not to try again. She had no sense of entitlement. It was just better to stay where she was than risk a worse landing.

The late-afternoon breeze was as soft as azalea petals, and the only sounds were cars passing on the street and birds high in towering trees. She turned toward the church. Her heels clattered against the stone path, which looked as if it had been newly washed by their diligent sexton, Felipe. Apparently Felipe had also taken to heart the grounds committee's suggestion that the boxwood lining the path needed more severe pruning. This afternoon the hedge looked as if it had recently squirmed under the hands of a boot-camp barber.

Luck was with her. Felipe or someone had unlocked the front door and wedged it open, perhaps to let a touch of sunshine inside. She was heartened that she didn't have to go next door to the parish house to beg the key or wait for the secretary to unlock the door for her.

If the air outside was warm and mountain-meadow fresh, inside it was neither. As always, the sanctuary felt faintly damp and old smells lingered. Women's perfume, the moldering pages of hymnals, candle wax and Sunday's lilies from the chancel.

The sanctuary was voluminous, with massive ribbed vaults overhead and wide aisles flanking the nave. Sometimes the room felt like a cavern, sometimes a crypt. Usually, though, even Charlotte, whose head was normally filled with other things, felt a sense of peace, as if fragments of prayers that had been whispered for more than a century still fluttered overhead.

Today she just felt dwarfed by the empty sanctuary, smaller than a speck of dust. And while humility before God was important — and in her case, overdue — this afternoon she needed warmth and comfort, and hoped God wouldn't begrudge her either.

She found herself moving toward the side chapel, where light streamed through brilliantly colored windows, and she could hear the birds beyond them.

In a pew at the front she bowed her head. She hadn't stepped foot in a church in weeks, nor in those weeks had she mumbled even a prepackaged prayer. Since childhood, church attendance had always been a given, the need for it drummed into her by a grandmother for whom prayer had been the only barricade against defeat. Now, as she tried to formulate one and failed, she realized how odd it was that at a crossroads in her own life, when most people turned to God, all outward manifestations of her faith had simply vanished.

Charlotte closed her eyes, hoping to connect with something larger than herself, but instead she felt herself falling into a void as dark and limitless as a night sky without stars. Her eyelids flew open, and she could hear her own heart beating. Perspiration filmed her cheeks and dampened her hair, and even though her hands were folded in her lap, they trembled.

The stillness of the chapel seemed to close in around her, as if to ask why she was there. She couldn't find words, and her mind fluttered from image to image with no place to land. But there was something else the church could offer.

Some*one* else.

There were no confession booths at the Church of the Covenant, and Charlotte's minister was younger than she was, stylish and outspoken. They had butted heads on so many occasions that now Charlotte wondered if, deep in her heart, Reverend

Analiese Wagner would find pleasure in her turmoil.

Yet where else could she go? Who else could she talk to?

For a woman who had always had answers for everybody, she was surprised to learn how few of them really meant anything.

As she pulled into the church lot, the Reverend Analiese Wagner was thinking about food, which was not unusual. She always thought about food when she was worried, or when she had five things to do at once. Maybe that was why she was picturing double cheeseburgers in her mind, along with double scoops of Ben & Jerry's Chunky Monkey. This afternoon she was doubly stressed.

"If I make it through the memorial service, double cheese on my next pizza," she promised herself out loud, although she hadn't eaten pizza for years because it was as impossible to stop eating as salted peanuts. Even now, at thirty-eight, after years of adulthood as a willowy size ten, the fat little girl inside her was still clawing to get out. For the rest of her life she would be forced to watch every bite and exercise without mercy.

Someone had parked in the slot against

the side fence reserved for clergy. To be fair, the driver hadn't exactly parked *in* the slot. She — and Analiese knew it was a she — had parked beside it, but not well, so the silver Audi was actually taking up two places, one of them Analiese's. She recognized the car.

"Charlotte Hale." Mentally she thumped her palm against the steering wheel of her ten-year-old Corolla, the very same Corolla that Charlotte Hale had asked about several months ago, just before she handed Analiese the business card of a car dealer who could arrange a low-interest loan and a trade-in.

Analiese couldn't recall seeing Charlotte at services or meetings in the past month or so, but that was likely to mean that today Charlotte had a list as long as her arm of problems she wanted to comment on.

Analiese found another spot at the end of the row, but once she turned off the Toyota's engine, she sat quietly and closed her eyes.

"Please, Lord," she prayed softly, "help me mind my tongue, my manners and while we're at it, today please give me an extra spoonful of compassion, no matter how bitter it tastes." She hesitated. "A slice of no-cal pizza would be good, too, but I know better than to push."

Out of habit she put two fingers against the hollow of her throat to loosen her clerical collar — until she realized she wasn't wearing one. In half an hour she would be changing into her robe for the service she was here to conduct, so she was wearing a simple round-necked navy dress. Right now anyone who didn't know her would assume she was one of the mourners come to honor Minnie Marlborough.

There was nothing particularly ministerial about Analiese. Her nearly black hair was shoulder-length, and she rarely pinned it up so she would look older or plainer. Her regular features added up to something beyond striking. While no one insisted a minister be attractive, her first career had been in television news, where physical beauty had served her well.

She opened her eyes and continued to breathe deeply, staring at the building just beyond her parking place.

The first time she had been driven to this spot by a member of the ministerial search committee, she had sat just this way, gazing at her future. With its arrowhead arches and multispired north tower — not to mention imposing blocks of North Carolina granite and stained glass from the famous Lamb Studios of Greenwich Village — she'd been certain that Asheville's Church of the Covenant would withstand Armageddon and hang around for the Second Coming.

In any architectural textbook, the city's most influential Protestant church was just a yawn on the way to more impressive renderings of Gothic Revival glory. The church paled in significance beside the ornate Roman Catholic Basilica of St. Lawrence downtown, or the Cathedral of All Souls in nearby Biltmore Village, the seat of the region's Episcopal bishop. But Analiese had never quite gotten over that first punch-in-the-gut impression of the church to which she had later been called. Now, as then, she felt unworthy to be its spiritual leader.

One last deep breath propelled her out of the car. Before she locked it she reached into the backseat for the colorful needlepoint tote bag her oldest sister had made as an ordination gift. With the bag slung over her shoulder, she hurried toward the church, avoiding the parish house and, she hoped, the silver Audi's owner, as well. At the door, she saw Felipe had arrived first. For a moment she was glad she didn't have to wrestle with the cast-iron lock, which on a good day took the better part of a minute. Then, as she was about to slip inside, she wondered if Felipe had unlocked the door, or if someone *else* had borrowed the key and was waiting for her inside.

Someone she wasn't anxious to see.

Her brief burst of good humor disappeared.

She was happiest when the sanctuary was filled with people, and music echoed from the walls. Today the pews were empty, but that wasn't necessarily the end of the story. Cautiously Analiese found her way along slippery polished tile floors to the transept, following it to the cozier side chapel that had been added early in the twentieth century by an industrialist friend of the Vanderbilts.

Historically the chapel had been a place for quiet contemplation, but most often these days it was used for children's worship services. Felt banners made by one of the Sunday School classes hung between two narrow stained-glass windows of contemporary design. Stylistically wrought jewel-tone doves and olive branches vied with off-center renditions of the Star of David, the Taoist yin-yang and multiple Buddhas, both smiling and glum.

The woman sitting in the front row staring at the banners was neither, but then Charlotte Hale was not a woman who often showed emotion. In the ten years of her ministry here, Analiese had learned that the Charlottes in a congregation were the members an alert minister should most fear.

She debated what to do. She couldn't believe Charlotte had come for Minnie's memorial service. Beyond that, the service didn't start for almost an hour, so mourners could attend after work.

Analiese almost turned away, but something told her not to. Maybe it was the way Charlotte was sitting. Maybe it was the stillness in the chapel and the sanctuary beyond, plus the fact that Charlotte had entered this quiet place alone.

She walked through the doorway, making enough noise to alert the other woman. Charlotte was not dressed for a memorial service. She wore a casual lightweight turtleneck with three-quarter sleeves and a skirt of the same mulberry. Her auburn hair was windblown, and she hadn't bothered with jewelry except tiny gold studs in her earlobes. She looked as if she'd run out for milk and bread and forgotten her way home.

"Charlotte?"

Charlotte turned to look at her. Her expression was blank, her cheeks pale, and she looked exhausted, which was unusual. "Reverend Ana." She nodded, but she didn't smile.

"I'm not sure what to do," Analiese said. "Offer comfort or silence. You look like you might need both."

"I was just thinking about these banners."

Analiese didn't sigh, but that took effort. "I'm afraid our first and second graders aren't at their artistic peaks," she said, but not as an apology. "They don't know it, though. They get such a thrill from seeing their work hung here for a week or two."

"Then you're planning to take them down?"

"Only because the other Sunday School classes are making more, and they all want their turn."

Charlotte turned back to the banners. "I hope all of them are as funny as these. The Star of David on the left has seven points. Did you notice? And that Buddha —" she pointed to a thin stick of a man "— looks like he's been on the South Beach Diet."

Analiese was minimally encouraged. "He's probably historically correct. The *fat* Buddha is actually based on the folktale of a Chinese monk named P'utai, who was eternally laughing and happy, not to mention well fed."

"And the children and the rest of us are learning these stories from you in church every Sunday."

"It's a very small world, and we're all neighbors."

If Charlotte disagreed, at least she had the grace not to say so. "I was glad to find the front door unlocked. When I was a girl . . . about a million years ago . . . I used to wish I had a quiet spot like this to come and sit."

Analiese didn't know Charlotte's age. There were a thousand committed members here and many more who simply showed up on holidays. She had long ago given up trying to memorize every biography. She guessed Charlotte was only in her late forties, perhaps early fifties. Most likely well-executed surgery had given back a portion of the perfection age had stolen, so she was an attractive middle-age woman who knew how to make herself even more so. It was odd to hear her refer to herself as old, but today her shoulders drooped and her face looked drawn, as if she was trying to live up to her words.

Analiese made an attempt to crack open the invisible door between them. She dropped down beside her, making sure to leave enough room so Charlotte would feel comfortable. "You needed a place to think?"

"I was on the Council Executive Committee the year we decided to keep the building locked unless there was a service taking place, but I've regretted that every time I've wished I could slip inside, sit in a pew and stare up at the rose window. We were worried about vandalism."

"It's a valid concern."

"I thought so at the time, yet here I am." She turned to gaze at Analiese. "Because the door was open. Is there a reason?"

"There's a memorial service in an hour. Felipe probably propped it open after he cleaned, or he didn't bother to lock up after the florist delivered the arrangements."

"I noticed them. Very sweet, like somebody went to an abandoned farmstead and picked everything that was blooming."

Analiese thought just how fitting the flowers must be, then, and how Minnie's many friends had planned it that way. "I haven't seen the arrangements. I was just on my way up front to check and make sure everything's set up correctly before I robe."

"I didn't know about a memorial service. Is it a church member?"

"Not a member, no. But a church as large as ours was needed to hold this one."

"Somebody important, then."

Analiese nodded. "Yes, she was important." She paused, then plunged. "The service is for a woman named Minnie Marlborough."

Charlotte's expression didn't change, but she was suddenly still, because certainly the name was familiar to her. "Minnie Marlborough died?"

"Last week."

"I'm sorry, I've been out of town for a while. I didn't know. Had she been ill for long?"

Analiese couldn't figure out how to answer that. From the moment she had seen Charlotte's car, she had known this conversation might be necessary, although she hadn't been sure Charlotte would remember Minnie. Now she was just as confused about the direction to take as she had been before she murmured her prayer in the parking lot.

"I don't know how to answer that," she said after a long pause. "I don't know what you want me to say. I can tell you the truth, or I can tell you some version that's easier to hear."

"I remember the first time I heard you speak in our pulpit — I was overwhelmed by your honesty." Charlotte paused, but not long enough to allow Analiese to respond. "But I was also fascinated."

"Were you?"

"At the time you had to know you were destroying your chances of being called as our pastor, but that didn't stop you from telling the truth, exactly the way you saw it."

"Here I am, anyway," Analiese said, "ten years later, and both of us completely baffled about how it happened."

"I voted against you."

"I assumed."

Charlotte rubbed an eye, a gesture that was out of character for a woman who gave the impression she wouldn't flinch under torture. "So do what you do best, and please tell me the truth."

"Minnie never adjusted to life in town."

Charlotte waited for more, but Analiese shrugged. "I'm sorry, it's that simple. Her little farm, her animals? They were all she had. When they were gone, she didn't have anything left to live for. At least that's what her friends say."

"You blame me for that." It wasn't a question.

"I'm your minister. It's not my place to blame you, Charlotte. I wasn't even sure you'd remember her."

"And what about the woman Analiese Wagner. Does *she* blame me?"

"I wish I could separate the two that easily." Analiese turned the question around. "What about the woman Charlotte Hale?

How does she feel?"

Charlotte spoke slowly, as if she were putting memories together. "Minnie Marlborough's farm was needed for a retirement facility that would benefit hundreds of seniors and has. Her neighbors wanted to sell when they heard our terms. We thought everyone would come out ahead. The city's richer for the taxes the facility pays. The road's been widened and improved, so residents in the area benefited, too."

We, Analiese knew, was Falconview Development, of which Charlotte Hale was the founder, president and CEO.

She thought carefully before she spoke, struggling to be fair. "I know you or someone at Falconview found her an apartment where she could have some of her things —"

"I knew how much she loved those animals. I got the owner to lift the restrictions on pets so she could bring the two cats she'd had the longest," Charlotte said, although not defensively.

"And found homes for almost all the rest who were healthy. I know."

"Did you ever see her house? Ever walk around the grounds? Every penny Minnie Marlborough had from Social Security and savings went to those animals she took in.

And she was such an easy mark. Somebody's cute little kitten started clawing the furniture and suddenly Minnie found a new pet on her doorstep. She could never say no, and everybody knew it. I was told the house was falling down around her. I doubt she ate as well as the animals she fed."

Analiese thought carefully before she spoke. "I think the hardest decisions are the ones where we'll reap benefits from only one of the outcomes. How can we remain objective?"

"I guess you're saying I didn't."

"I've been told Minnie had friends who went to that house every day to help. They brought food and took animals to the vet, and helped her find homes for everything from iguanas to llamas. I'm told that for every person who took advantage of her, there was another who reached out to help. She wasn't a hoarder. She was poor, overworked, but she was happy. She had friends, purpose, the animals she loved, the home she'd lived in all her life."

"You *do* blame me."

"Right now I'm more concerned about how you'll feel if you stay here much longer. You accused me of an abundance of honesty, but I think you need to know. There will be people coming through those doors in a little while, and some of them will be unhappy to find you here."

"I was here for . . ." Charlotte stopped and shook her head. "Don't worry. I'm not planning to stay." She put her hand on Analiese's arm when the minister slid forward to rise. "You really are expecting a crowd, then?"

"That's the guess."

"She had that many friends?"

"SRO." She saw Charlotte hadn't understood the showbusiness term. "Standing room only," she clarified.

"All those people . . ." Charlotte dropped her hand.

"A tribute to a life well lived." Analiese got to her feet. She had delivered her message, and while she'd been unsurpassingly blunt, she thought she'd done Charlotte a favor. Grief had turned to anger for some of Minnie's friends who blamed Minnie's decline and death on Falconview and everyone connected with it. Charlotte would not be welcome here today, and Minnie's friends would probably make certain she knew it.

"It was a complicated situation," Charlotte said, still seated.

"I know. We specialize in those in this building."

"Are they taking memorial donations?" Charlotte reached for her purse.

"Don't." Analiese spoke so sharply the word echoed off the stone walls and could not be retrieved.

Charlotte looked startled, then she tilted her head in question. "I just thought . . . maybe the animal shelter? I can write a check."

"Minnie Marlborough never asked for a handout in life, so I doubt she'd want one in death. She was a woman with her hand outstretched to help, not to ask. That's what people loved about her. That's why they're all coming today."

"You're giving a sermon, and I'm the only one here."

Analiese knew Charlotte was right, but she couldn't apologize. "A hazard of the profession."

"How many people will be at *your* funeral, do you suppose?"

"I'm sorry?"

"When you die, how many people will come to say goodbye?"

Analiese had never asked herself the question. "Why do you ask?"

"Maybe it *is* the measure of a life well lived."

"Only if people attend because they want to."

Charlotte's smile warmed and softened her face, like a light going on inside a room at dusk, and even though the smile was sad, she looked more like herself. "You mean well-dressed businessmen checking smartphones don't count?"

"It wouldn't be fair to ignore them completely. Say . . . three businessmen equal one faithful mourner."

"Maybe I'd better reserve this little chapel for my own funeral. Or the sexton's broom closet." Charlotte smiled again, almost as if in comfort.

Analiese wasn't sure how to answer. "I'm afraid you'll have to take a number. The broom closet's been booked for months."

As exit lines went, that and the smile accompanying it would do, but Analiese didn't leave. She could hear a clock ticking inside her head, and still she couldn't go without offering something better. As odd as it seemed, she felt as if Charlotte had just tried offering something to her.

"I don't think we should worry," she added. There's probably time for both of us to cultivate a few more mourners. Unless we take matters into our own hands, only God knows the hour of our death."

Charlotte looked surprised. "How strange you should say that."

"Why?"

"I was thinking about that exact phrase, right before you walked in."

"Cultivating mourners?"

"No, that only God knows the hour of our death. A long time ago I heard those same words in a very different place, and I've never forgotten."

Chapter Three

Early in his granddaughter's life Ethan Martin had learned that his major role — next to doting uncontrollably — was to give Maddie the confidence she needed to become an adult who took the hand life had dealt her and played it with skill and daring. This meant that while he never lied to her, he also never quite leveled, at least not when she scared him to death. Which she did frequently.

She was scaring him now, swaying at the top of a piece of carefully engineered climbing equipment like a pirate searching the seas for ships to plunder. She was with two other children, and he recognized one, Edna Ferguson, whose mother, Samantha, was a long-time friend of his daughter's. Sam wasn't far away, on a bench typing on a laptop, but he caught her eye. She nodded, then gave a barely perceptible thumbs-up sign that told him Maddie was fine, but she had kept his granddaughter in her sights just in case. All was well.

"Hey, kiddo," he said, when he got close enough that Maddie could hear him. "We're having an early supper tonight, remember?"

"Papa!" Maddie swung lower until she'd reached a height that no longer frightened him. He judged all heights the same way. How far could the girl fall without hurting herself? At what point was she risking a broken bone? A concussion? He was never sure, but he *was* sure it wasn't his place to hamper her. Maddie and her mother had worked out rules, and so far Maddie had been good about obeying them, most likely because they were few and sensible.

She launched herself into his waiting arms, the way a younger child might. But Maddie was small for her age, and delicately boned. He caught her easily and swung her to the ground.

Ethan ruffled her hair. "See the Blue Ridge Parkway from way up there?"

"I wasn't paying attention. Edna was telling us about a movie she saw on television. Where's Mom?"

"Making dinner. She's teaching a class tonight, so you'll have me all to yourself."

"Cool!" Maddie's blue eyes danced. "You're eating with us, too?"

"I even brought dessert."

"Cookies?"

"Chocolate chip."

Maddie yelled goodbye to the other children. Then she waved at Samantha, who glanced up as if she'd just realized Maddie was there and smiled in response.

As they crossed the park they chatted about school. Although she was ten, Maddie was only in fourth grade, which wasn't uncommon. Parents often held children with summer birthdays back, even if they were officially able to start school a year earlier. But Taylor, Ethan's daughter, had decided Maddie should start later because, among other things, she had been more than two months premature at birth.

The street where Taylor and Maddie lived was eclectic, modest one-story homes mixed with more expansive ones. The architectural styles were eclectic, too, and it pleased Ethan, an architect himself, that the homes weren't cookie-cutter copies. Most were well taken care of, but some, particularly the obvious rentals, needed paint or simple landscaping.

Taylor's own landlord was, for the most part, invisible, because Taylor only contacted him when something major needed repair. He, in return, never asked for an increase in her modest rent. Ethan hoped nothing changed in the near future. The house spelled independence, something Taylor badly needed.

They were still two houses away when he smelled charcoal. They cut across Taylor's yard, bordered with swaths of daffodils and grape hyacinth in full bloom, and rounded the house. His daughter was just putting burgers on the grill in the center of a postage-stamp patio, paved in salvaged flagstone she and Maddie had laid themselves. A confirmed vegetarian, she'd fashioned the burgers from black beans and quite possibly baked the buns herself. They would be delicious, he knew, but as he smacked his lips in appreciation, he would still think longingly of USDA prime.

"Hey, sweetie," Taylor called to her daughter. "Can you get the salad out of the fridge? Just put it on the picnic table. Then get the lemonade. These will only take a few minutes on each side."

Maddie grumbled, more as if it was expected than with conviction, and climbed the back steps.

"She do okay?" Taylor asked softly.

Before he spoke Ethan took a moment to admire his daughter. Taylor was medium height and deceptively slender, deceptive because the narrow hips and long legs didn't project the strength within. She wore her dark brown hair as short as a boy's, but cut in feminine wisps around her face and nape. The cut emphasized heavily lashed brown eyes, which were a mirror of his own, and the delicate lips of her mother. She was already dressed to teach her yoga class in a green tank top covered with a gauzy scoop-necked shirt and leggings. She wore no jewelry except gold hoop earrings. Taylor spent little time on her appearance, but the effect was striking, anyway.

"She was up at the top of the jungle gym when I got there," he said. "But Sam had an eye on her. You don't think Maddie knows Sam's there to watch out for her?"

"She knows, but it's the kind of world where parents have to keep an eye on their kids, isn't it?"

"Did you tell me Sam's looking for a new job?"

"And she got one. She's so excited. She wanted something where she could have a bigger impact on patient care, and now she'll be the nursing supervisor at a maternal health clinic. She's the kind of person I wanted watching over me when I was pregnant with Maddie," Taylor said.

"The way she was watching over her today."

Taylor lowered her voice to match his. "There are only so many excuses I can invent to go to the park myself. And she's been free of heavy-duty seizures for three full months. I have to let go. I'm not going to hold her back from anything if I don't have to."

Three months without a major seizure was a new record, and Ethan, like his daughter, was cautiously hopeful. Several times a day Maddie experienced swirls of light or odd sensations in her stomach. These were manifestations of simple partial seizures, but she didn't lose consciousness, and usually only those who knew her well could tell anything out of the ordinary had just occurred.

While children born prematurely suffered from epilepsy more often than full-term children, there were no easy answers as to why Maddie was one of them. Her seizures had begun at age three. From that point on she had experienced frequent complex partial seizures, classified as such because she lost awareness of the world around her, and sometimes experienced spasms, which caused her body to jerk uncontrollably.

Maddie's neurologist was a cautious older

man, long experienced in managing epilepsy. Right from the beginning he had taken time with Taylor, questioning her carefully and listening to her answers. Although he was a highly trained specialist, in personality he was more the legendary family doctor who was never too busy to take a phone call. Three months ago he had placed Maddie on a different drug regimen to manage her seizures, which had become more frequent and severe, carefully adjusting and weaning her off prior medications. Taylor was confident her daughter was in the best of hands, and confident that the new treatment would finally give her daughter a better life.

So far, she seemed to be right.

"She had a good time today," Ethan said. "And the exercise was good for her."

"Next week, if all's well, I'm going to let her ride her bike to the park." Taylor must have seen the question in his eyes, because she added, "She needs to believe she can conquer the world, and the only way to make sure of that is to let her try."

He knew better than to protest. Maddie wore a helmet when she rode her bike, required by the state of North Carolina for children, anyway. If she had a seizure and fell, she would be like a million other kids who tumbled off bikes to the sidewalk. She would climb back on as soon as she could and pedal away.

"I appreciate you staying with her tonight," she went on. "She has a lot of homework, so she'll be better off here. They give them so much these days. She has to write a poem about spring, read a chapter in her social studies textbook and look up something she finds interesting on the internet to get more information. Plus they're already doing geometry, if you can believe it, and she has worksheets."

"I remember how much you loved geometry."

"That's funny, I don't." She smiled conspiratorially, because Taylor's disdain of math was legendary. Ethan had always been the go-to parent when it came to the subject. Charlotte had never . . .

He cut that off as quickly as the thought occurred to him. Not thinking about Taylor's mother was one of the things he did best.

Taylor flipped the burgers, before she crooked her neck to see if she could spot her daughter, or at least her shadow in the kitchen behind them. "I wonder what's taking Maddie so long."

"She probably had to hit the little ladies'

room first," Ethan said. "I'll go check on her. I can grab the lemonade."

"Great, I'll set the table."

Ethan let himself in through the screen door and called to Maddie, but there was no answer. No salad adorned the counter, nor lemonade, so he figured his guess had been right. He took out both, the salad a glistening medley of leafy greens and finely chopped vegetables, the lemonade with lemon slices floating on top inside a cut-glass pitcher. Taylor liked to make dinner a special occasion when he shared it with them. She thought, incorrectly, that her father didn't eat well enough when he was alone, and he didn't put much energy into convincing her otherwise, since it meant meals like this one.

"Maddie?" he called again. There wasn't a corner anywhere in the tiny house where she couldn't hear a booming male voice. For the first time he began to worry.

Taylor stepped inside, frowning. "She didn't answer?"

"Not yet . . ." Ethan started through the house, Taylor close at his heels. They didn't have to go far. Maddie was on the floor outside the bathroom. Her eyes were open, then they rolled back and her body arched, and she began to convulse.

■ ■ ■ ■

An exhausted Maddie cuddled on the family room sofa with Ethan and picked at her dinner. After what he had recognized as a grand-mal or generalized convulsive seizure, he had carried her here to nap, and she still hadn't left. Taylor had called Dr. Hilliard to describe the ferocity of the event. Not only had the long string of seizure-free weeks ended, the girl seemed to have passed into a new land. Ethan knew a lot about his granddaughter's condition, but now there would be new language to describe what had happened, new theories why and surely new or additional medication as she traveled her lonely path.

In the meantime Taylor would need to go into school and tell Maddie's teacher what to do if Maddie experienced a similar seizure in class. The other students knew she had epilepsy. She'd had seizures in school, but they had been milder in comparison, not as frightening to witness. Even Ethan, who had seen many, had felt angry and helpless during this one. There'd been so little to do. Move things out of reach. Get a cushion under her head. Stay right there so that when she regained consciousness, they could comfort and reassure her, or turn her to her side as she slept off the effects.

Maddie played with the medical alert bracelet she always wore, sliding it up and down her wrist. "The teacher explained to my class. She said it's like a lamp cord. Sometimes the wire has a short inside it, wires that rub together or something, and when somebody moves the cord, the lamp will blink or even stop working. Then, if they move it back to the right place, it works just as well as it ever did."

"How did you feel when she said that?"

"I guess it was okay. Kids asked me what a seizure feels like. I told them I don't know, that I can't remember. They thought that was weird. One boy said maybe if I didn't move my head, I'd never have another one, like not moving the lamp cord. I don't know how to do that, though."

"It wouldn't help," Ethan assured her, "because you're not a lamp."

"Mom thought the new pills made me all better. But they make me feel funny. Like I'm not me."

"What do you mean?"

"Like I'm somebody *watching* me."

Ethan didn't know what to say. Taylor had gone through a brief period when she'd refused to medicate Maddie. She'd adjusted her daughter's diet, trying a hard-line no-carb approach that seemed to help some children, then she'd switched to vitamins and nutritional supplements. She had instructed Maddie in yoga and meditation, and taken her to chiropractors and naturopaths.

Reluctantly Taylor had finally admitted that her daughter's seizures were milder and fewer when she was on drugs, even as imperfect as they were. That was when she'd discovered Dr. Grant Hilliard, who had restored Taylor's faith in traditional medicine.

"Do you think you can do a little homework?" Ethan held up Maddie's social studies textbook. "I brought my laptop. After you read the chapter, you can use it to find more information on the internet."

"In a little while." Her speech was slower, and she still seemed a little dazed. He knew better than to push to get her started. Maddie wanted to do well in school, but while she was a smart child and determined to learn, she was also handicapped by the medication, which sometimes made her drowsy, by evenings, like this one, when it was unlikely her assignments would get finished, even by "absence" seizures during class, when she was deaf to all instructions and information.

Then there was the teasing and ostracism by her classmates, which dogged children who were "different" in any way.

Ethan cuddled her closer. Although television had never triggered one of Maddie's seizures, Taylor had a firm rule that the set not be turned on right after one. "Why don't I read to you? We can start a new book. We never finished *The Chronicles of Narnia.*"

Before Maddie could respond the telephone rang. Ethan reached around her to grab the receiver. He made a guess that Taylor's class was doing warm-ups and she was quickly checking in.

Instead, the voice on the other end was male. Ethan recognized it at once.

"Hello, Jeremy." He felt Maddie stir against him and push away.

"Is it Daddy?" she asked.

Ethan nodded. "I'm babysitting," he said into the phone. "Taylor teaches on Thursdays now."

The twang of country music was a pleasant background to Jeremy Larsen's drawling baritone. Ethan guessed he was taking time from a rehearsal of his band.

"Sounds like she's got a full plate."

Ethan never knew what to say to Maddie's father. Jeremy and Taylor maintained a cordial relationship so they could be better parents to their daughter, but the road wasn't easy. Their history was troubled. Maddie had been conceived when Taylor was only sixteen and Jeremy just a year older. Their high school romance had been stormy and brief, the baby a postscript. They had few if any happy memories to build on.

Ethan was never sure where Jeremy's questions or even casual remarks were leading. Was he merely making conversation? Was he implying Taylor was too busy to be a proper mother? Was he hoping to throw a wrench into the finely tuned machinery of their custody arrangement?

"Taylor manages everything like a pro," he said pleasantly.

"Maddie still up?"

"It would be a rare evening if she was asleep this early," Ethan said. "I'm putting her on."

Maddie was sitting taller, and she flipped her disheveled ponytail over one shoulder. "Daddy!"

Ethan went into the kitchen to give his granddaughter privacy. While technically Jeremy and Taylor shared custody, Taylor had Maddie with her most of the time. Jeremy spent time in Asheville with his daughter whenever he could, but Maddie had never visited him at his home in Nashville. Ethan wasn't sure if Taylor had convinced him their daughter was better off in familiar surroundings, or if Jeremy didn't want to learn what he needed to know to care for her. Whatever the truth, Maddie adored and missed her father.

Taylor hadn't been able to get to the dishes, and now, as Ethan stacked the apartment-size dishwasher he'd given her for Christmas, he hoped his daughter had gotten to the studio in time. She taught eight classes a week at Moon and Stars, and the owner was understanding. He just hoped Taylor hadn't tested the woman's patience tonight.

By the time Ethan had finished cleaning the kitchen, Maddie was still chatting with her father. He stood at the sink and stared out at the yard beyond. He was a shadowy reflection in the double-hung window — long face, pointed chin, high forehead — a man still attractive to women, judging by the offers of dinner and more he received from women at least a full decade younger than himself.

Beyond his reflection the faint outline of a

crescent moon hung low in the still-bright sky, just visible beyond the neighbor's tree line. A wisteria-scented breeze through the screen door ruffled his silvering hair. He was just fifty-six. Charlotte had been twenty-five when she had given birth to Taylor, and Taylor had just turned seventeen when Maddie was born. But this evening Ethan felt older than the mountains.

Spring was a time of renewal, of flowers bursting into bloom, of birds mating and building nests. He was twice divorced, but now his first wife, Taylor's mother, was on his mind, and so was the spring right before they met.

He had only been twenty-five, an intern at a local architectural firm and still a stranger to the city that was now his permanent home. With few contacts and no real friends, he had begun jogging after he returned home in the evenings from the office. He had often parked in unexplored neighborhoods and jogged along residential or downtown streets to learn more about the Blue Ridge community where he'd landed.

Now he remembered one such evening, twilight just beginning to thicken around him and the same haunting fragrance in the air. He had chosen Montford for his jog, a historic neighborhood with a satisfying mixture of architectural designs, some shabby and in need of renovation, but many that were still prime specimens of another generation's craftsmanship. He'd begun on Montford Avenue, then veered off on a side street to avoid traffic.

He had been lost in thought about the blueprints for an office building he'd been asked to comment on, just aware enough of his surroundings that he didn't stray into traffic or run behind a car backing out of a driveway. He'd dodged a woman walking two identical yapping poodles, stumbled over a loose chunk of concrete.

Funny the details he still remembered.

He had just been ready to turn the corner and circle the block on his way back to his car when a woman on the next block caught his eye. Back then, as now, Asheville had been filled with young women. He had been as appreciative as any twenty-something heterosexual man of the opportunities, but having just moved away from a failed love affair, he had also been wary.

This woman, seen at a distance, was more vision than flesh. A ruffled skirt floated just above her ankles, a scoop-necked blouse bared a long, graceful neck. Her hair curled over her shoulders, shining and hinting that it might be red, although in the dying light, he couldn't tell for sure.

Something about the way she hurried tugged at him. She was willowy, bending into the breeze like a sapling at the edge of a mountain stream. He liked the way she held herself. He liked the curve of her hair, of her jaw, of her breasts. He liked the graceful yet determined way she moved up the sidewalk, as if she had all the time in the world and none of it to spare.

He'd wondered then whether the vision-made flesh would be less than this fleeting glimpse. Would he be disappointed, sorry the dream was eclipsed and replaced with reality? He remembered that he had been torn between speeding up or slowing down, and before he could decide, the vision had entered the ground floor of a funky old Tudor and vanished behind the door, never to be seen in that place again, despite more frequent and increasingly desperate jogs.

Charlotte Hale, his twilight vision, who months later would spring to life in a university classroom, and who had not, at least for years, disappointed at all.

Charlotte, who, as it turned out, had been best enjoyed from a distance.

Charlotte, who, this afternoon, unless he was mistaken, had abandoned a park bench as he approached, just thirty yards from the climbing dome where their granddaughter had been playing with her friends.

Chapter Four

First Day Journal: April 28

"Only God knows the hour of our death!"

I'm sitting in a coffee shop not far from Biltmore Forest, because I'm not ready to face my empty house for the evening. I'm writing in this journal with hopes those words will stop revolving in my head once I commit them to paper. Reverend Ana spoke them this afternoon, with no idea of their impact. But the first time I heard them was on a day I wish I could forget. In far too many ways that day defines me.

Maybe in real-time it's April of my fifty-second year, but in my mind it's August, and counting backward I think the year must be 1970. I'm ten years old, Maddie's age, and I'm sure I've been sitting in our little country church for at least a century. But, of course, at ten, so much feels that way.

Ten yards in front of me the preacher slaps his Bible against our pulpit, one my grandmother is particularly proud of, since her own father carved it from a fallen black walnut tree. When I was six Gran pointed out the stump of the "pulpit" tree in a wooded clump not far from her kitchen garden. Sometimes now I go there to think, especially when Hearty comes home drunk, which is most of the time.

I'm startled by the slapping noise, and only Gran's withered arm across my chest keeps me from diving under the pew in front of us.

"Lottie Lou, you sit up now, and no more dozing," she whispers to me as she hauls me closer. "Else you'll end up being the 'zample in this fool's sermon, you get my meaning?"

The preacher screeches the same words again. He's a guest in the pulpit of our church, the Trust Independent Baptist Church, because the regular preacher, equally loud but less given to repetition, is hauling a truckload of hand-harvested burley tobacco to Raleigh. Preaching is something he does on the side, for the sake of the Lord.

The guest preacher farms tobacco, too, but his is as sorry as his sermons, so it isn't likely he'll need a truck or a trip any time in the near future. He's as scrawny as a cornstalk in a drought, and he drools when he shouts, so now his chin glistens.

I wriggle on the unpadded bench to get blood flowing to my backside. The service started with hymns, then the preacher demanded we stop singing so he could preach — which he's been doing forever. I worry we'll be here another hour or more.

And while we listen to Preacher Pittman's substitute fumble with words, what will Hearty Hale be doing?

It's as hot inside as it would be if we were standing full in the sunshine. All week the church is closed up, and it takes more than half an hour to suck out the heat before services. The building sits to the side of a country road, and there's no electricity for fans, although we have a woodstove for winter. Windows dot the walls to let in what breeze can be had, but we have no screens. Wasps fly in and out and circle the freshly washed heads of worshipers.

I have nothing to do except think about the words that brought me so fully awake. I can't picture a God who not only knows when everybody on earth is going to die, but keeps track of the information, too. I wonder if He makes notes, or if He can just snap His fingers and call up whatever He needs in an instant.

I imagine God pointing and shouting, "You over there, your day'll be July 17, 1977, and not an hour later! And if I was you, I wouldn't bother taking out pork chops when you get up that morning. You won't be needing them."

When I giggle, Gran pokes me with her elbow. I look for something else to occupy my mind. I settle on a girl who's two years ahead of me in school and two rows in front of me now. She has white-blond hair, wispy and fine, and she's pulled it back from her face with a black velvet hair band that has a bow on the side, anchored with a cluster of rhinestones. Her name is Sally Klaver, and she lives not far away, in a brand-new house, brought in by truck and set right down on a slab of concrete. The house is the color of a creek bottom, with a porch in front, just big enough for a pot of flowers and a doormat with Welcome printed nice and proper on it.

The old house, where Sally used to live, is still standing back behind some trees, but it's boarded up now, and most likely full of mice and hornets' nests. Sally's daddy runs cattle and fattens more from his acres of corn. Mr. Klaver grows more tobacco than anybody else in the vicinity. I wonder what that would be like, having a house nobody else ever lived in, having enough cattle to eat beefsteak every night, having money to just walk into a store and buy a velvet headband whenever I felt like it.

I'm not just tired of sitting, I'm tired of worrying, too. This morning our neighbors, Bill Johnston and his wife, picked up Gran and me as we walked down the road on our way to church. Gran squeezed into the cab, and I settled myself in the back of the truck, making a little nest on an old piece of canvas to keep my dress from getting dirty.

I was glad to sit in the open. As we bumped over the dirt road I watched out for my father, but I never saw a sign of his truck or him. I'm not worried something's happened to Hearty. I'm not even hoping it has, at least not while I'm sitting in church, because it's possible God listens a little harder here, and wishing your father would keel over dead might get you in trouble.

Right now I just want to know where Hearty Hale is this morning, and whether he's going to make Gran or me that much more miserable later.

The preacher finally wears down and stops, slamming his Bible one more time against the pulpit as he shouts "Amen." The girl who's playing the piano leaps to her feet and throws herself across the bench, as if she's afraid he might change his mind.

In a moment we're all singing "On Jordan's Banks," and the preacher is exhorting sinners to come forward and make a commitment to Jesus. I figure everybody's as hot and cranky as me, because today only a few straggle forward, as if afraid the preacher will keep shouting until supper time if they don't.

After the last chorus I shake down my skirt and admire the lace adorning the hem. My grandmother added the lace by hand to "prettify" my dress, something she made over from one my own mother wore as a girl.

When I was younger I might have been thrilled at this connection to Thalia Hale, but now I'm not so sure. My mother died of pneumonia just one month after giving birth to me, her only child, and with ten years to consider it, I've decided it's likely Thalia thought the best way to get away from Hearty and her squalling baby girl was to cross the river Jordan as swiftly as possible.

I wish that weren't true, but even Gran admits she indulged the sickly young Thalia shamelessly, and forever after Thalia did exactly what she pleased. Gran's told me pretty stories of baby birds my mother rescued, poems she learned and songs she sang, but nobody else has ever said a good word about Thalia in my presence. And I've been paying close attention.

Around me now people are moving into clusters, most pausing near windows or the door, catching up on the week's gossip while they try to catch a breeze. Gran will linger. Despite the sorry state of the Sawyer farm — which is what everybody in Trust calls our home place — and the sorry state of her son-in-law, the local people respect Gran and wish her well. As far as they can, they do whatever they're able to be neighborly, just as long as it doesn't involve helping Hearty Hale.

"Lottie Lou . . ." Sally Klaver of the velvet headband rounds the corner of her pew and heads straight for me. "Weren't that just awful? Him going on and on like that? I wish we'd gone over to Marshall. They got air-conditioning at the church there, but my daddy says we have to come here sometimes, too, so people don't forget who we are."

I figure nobody will ever forget Sally's family, because the Klavers will always be sure to hang their good fortune right out where everybody can see it, like a bedsheet flapping in the wind.

"That a new dress?" Sally asks, smiling a little as her gaze drops lower.

Despite myself I stand straighter. "My gran made it for me."

"I guess she made it big, so you'd get lots of wear out of it."

I can feel the heat rising in my cheeks.

"But green's a good color with that red hair of your'n," Sally continues. "Of course, you got to be careful what you wear with hair like that. I'm lucky anything goes with mine. That's what I told Ma when she brought this brand-new dress home from Charlotte. 'Get me anything, 'cause it'll look good on me, I reckon.' " Sally holds out the short skirt of a black-and-yellow-striped dress that looks exactly like a man's undershirt.

I wish with all my heart that I had one, too.

"It's real pretty," I say. "And I guess she bought it big 'cause one of these days you'll fill it out real nice."

Sally has narrow eyes, a little too close together, and at that, they narrow even more. "How's that daddy of your'n? Thought I saw that truck he drives down yonder by the creek." She flips her hand carelessly over her shoulder. "He fishing while you get right with Jesus?"

I wonder if there's any truth in Sally's claim. "Could be. Hearty doesn't answer to me."

"You call your father Hearty?" Sally tries to look surprised.

"Everybody calls him Hearty." I've never called my father anything but, although it's only a nickname he got as a boy on account of his last name, barrel chest and wide shoulders.

"He didn't tell you anything before he left home this morning?" she probes.

I haven't seen my father in two days, but I'm not about to report that. "Your daddy tell you where he's going every minute?" I ask with a toss of my head. "Seems like he'd be awful busy for that, but maybe he's got all the time in the world to account to you."

Sally just repeats the sly smile that matches her eyes. "He don't, on account of how hard he works. But even if he only worked an hour a week, that would be more than your daddy works in a month."

I can hardly argue. I wait for the next blow. Church is no different than school, where I'm an outcast because I come from one of the poorest families in a poor county. I've learned to fight back a little, but I've also learned it doesn't help. There's nothing I can say or do that will change anybody's opinion. I am Lottie Lou Hale, daughter of Hearty Hale, whose reputation is as troubled as nearby Spring Creek in a winter storm.

"You oughta come over to our house sometime," Sally says. "Get that daddy of your'n to drive you, if you can find him." She smirks and turns away, lifting her hand in a careless wave. Anybody watching will think we're friends.

I go to find my grandmother, who's up front talking to the real preacher's wife. Mrs. Pittman is as tall as any man in the place, with skin that's seen too much sun and eyes that have seen too much sorrow. Years ago the Pittmans lost their two children in a house fire.

She claims her faith got her through it, but to look at her grim mouth and tired eyes, I'm not sure it's done the trick.

"Mrs. Pittman says she'll take us home today," Gran tells me. She waits for me to add my thank-yous.

"That's mighty nice of you," I say dutifully. "It's a long walk for Gran, with her arthritis and all."

Gran's arthritis, which cripples her once-sturdy legs and twists her arms, is, in my view, worse than having a drunk for a father and a mother who died rather than face her unfortunate choices. Gran's had enough problems trying to make do with nothing, trying to raise her granddaughter and keep her husband's family farm from being taken for taxes or sold off by her greedy son-in-law.

Unfortunately, my grandpa never made a will. He died suddenly, so the farm was divided by the state, one half to Gran, and one half to my mother, their only child. When Thalia died without a will, her half was divided again, half to Hearty and half to me. This means Hearty only owns one-quarter of the property, but he wields it like a hatchet. Any time he's unhappy, he threatens to sell his portion along with mine and leave Madison County forever.

So it isn't as if Gran hasn't had plenty of

trouble. But she holds her head as high as her aching neck will let her and just keeps going. She's old, though, and the arthritis wears her down. She is increasingly grateful for any help and says pride is a luxury a woman like her just can't afford.

"We'll go in a few minutes," Mrs. Pittman says. "Preacher Pittman asked me to check on two people before I leave. You know which car is ours. You can go ahead and get in if you like. I'll be quick as I can."

I wonder if Mrs. Pittman calls her husband "Preacher Pittman" when they're alone together, eating dinner or plowing their garden.

"Right nice of her to offer," Gran says, after Mrs. Pittman strides off to find the objects of Preacher Pittman's concern. "I weren't sure I wanted to walk home after all that sitting."

"Sally Klaver said she saw Hearty by the creek down yonder." I point in the direction of the back of the church.

"None of them Klavers knows a truth from a lie. That's how come they came into so much land. Her grandpa cheated a brother out of his inheritance, just like Esau and Jacob, and took it for himself. Me, I take anything any one of them says with a grain of salt."

I feel a little better that I'm not the only one in the church with no-good relatives. "He could be back there, sleeping by the creek," I warn.

“It’s the kinda thing he’d do.”

“If he is, he’ll wake himself up when he’s good and ready. You don’t need to worry about Hearty.”

I’m still standing in church, so I know better than to risk the Lord’s wrath by admitting how little I worry about my father. I lower my voice. “I was worrying he might wake up and come wandering up here.”

“We’ll be gone soon enough.”

But we aren’t, not nearly, because when we walk through the door to get into the preacher’s car, Hearty is staggering up the road, his shirt wrinkled and unbuttoned, his belt unbuckled and his pants sagging down around his hips. I see he is dirty and unshaven, and his hair, which hasn’t been cut in months, looks like a tangle of fishing line.

More than half the worshipers are still standing in the shade of dogwoods heavy with creamy blossoms to chat with friends. As if they are one body, they turn to watch Hearty’s approach.

“You go down and see if you can head him off,” Gran says softly. “I ain’t got the strength to do it myself, and I’m not fast enough.”

“What’ll I say?”

“I don’t rightly know. Maybe something about his truck. Maybe somebody told you he’s got himself a flat tire. Tell him you'll go with him to see."

Hearty does love his old truck. When he's sober, which isn't often, he spends hours under the hood, and even though he's too lazy to pick fights for no good reason, he can flare into a rage if the truck gets scratched or dented. The sheriff has slapped him in jail a time or two for truck-related attacks.

I head quickly toward my father, my cheeks blazing with embarrassment. I keep my head high, although what I want most is to look at the ground and not at the faces turning toward me. I hear somebody snickering, and see Sally Klaver with a small group of kids around her age, watching and pointing.

"Didn't I tell you I saw him down by the creek?" Sally calls. "Ought to have gone and looked for that ol' drunk before he came callin'."

I just lift my head a little higher and move my feet faster.

I reach Hearty before he gets to the parking lot.

"Hearty!" I call. "Where you going?"

He squints at me as if he's trying to recall where he's seen me. Once he was handsome enough to steal my mother's heart, despite all warning from my grandmother. Now his belly hangs over the top of his pants, like a woman in her final months of pregnancy, and his skin is slack and sallow. I haven't inherited anything obvious from my father except his auburn hair, but today Hearty's is the color of Georgia mud.

"Came to get money . . ." He stops, as if trying to remember what he was just saying. "That grandmother of your'n," he finishes, after a long moment during which he sways from side to side, as if considering which way to fall.

"Gran doesn't have any money, Hearty. Her check comes next week, and there's nothing left of the last one." I remember what my grandmother has told me and change the subject. "Listen, while you're here, one of those girls up there said she saw your truck, and you got a flat tire in the front. I'll go back with you. Maybe we can wrestle it off together."

"You . . . come with me?" He snorts. "Since . . . when you want to be anywhere I am?"

"You want help with that tire or not?" I ask.

"Ran out of gas." He stares beyond me, as if looking for my grandmother so he can plead his case.

Hearty works in the woods cutting and hauling lumber, but he rarely has money. When he manages to gather a little he buys gas and liquor, in that order, since this is a dry county and he needs the first to get the second. I doubt he's really run out of gas, but I bet he's run out of liquor.

I hear a noise behind me and turn. Mrs. Pittman is coming toward us. Her dress has red-and-white checks, like a tablecloth Gran uses in the summertime, and the skirt snaps angrily against her calves.

"That . . . ol' scarecrow . . ." Hearty spreads his hands in some odd sort of illustration, and the motion nearly sends him careening into me.

"What's happening here?" Mrs. Pittman asks in a voice that says she already knows.

"Nobody . . . ast you for a 'pinion," Hearty says.

"You owe this child better than showing up in public looking the way you do," Mrs. Pittman says. "You're embarrassing her and your mother-in-law."

"Don't care." Hearty waves his hands again. "I need money. You got some you want to rid yourself of, I'll take it . . . and be gone."

"You're lower than a rattlesnake, Hearty Hale. You ought to get down on your knees and beg the Lord for forgiveness. You've tried the patience of the rest of us for too long. He's all that's left."

Hearty spits on the ground at his feet. "Somebody here'll give me money."

"Not as long as I'm standing here. Now you

go back the way you came, you hear?"

By now I want to throw myself off a mountain ledge. I know everyone is watching, and a glance over my shoulder shows two of the men from the service are coming up behind Mrs. Pittman, one of them the morning's preacher, the other Sally Klaver's father. I realize that most likely they are spurred by embarrassment that a woman has been forced to lead the charge.

Hearty sees them, too, and realizes they aren't coming to help him. With a snarl, he falls forward. I'm not sure if he propels himself in Mrs. Pittman's direction, or if he merely loses his precarious balance, but without thinking I sidestep quickly and just in time. In a moment my father is sprawled on top of Mrs. Pittman, pinning her to the ground.

The men launch themselves forward to drag Hearty away. As drunk as he is, he fights back, slugging the preacher in the stomach with a fist, kicking out at Mr. Klaver with the toe of his worn work boot. It's all over in a moment. While sober he might have held his own, now he's slow and uncoordinated. The men grab him under the armpits and haul him off Mrs. Pittman, who sits up, then manages, with my help, to get to her feet. By then Gran has joined us.

Hearty is blinking hard, as if trying to remember what's just happened.

"You hurt, Mrs. Pittman?" Mr. Klaver asks, shoving Hearty to one side. "He hurt you?"

She looks a little dazed, but she shakes her head and begins to brush off her checkered dress. "He wants money."

"You don't give a man like this money." Mr. Klaver looks at Gran. "What are you going to do about him? Why'd you let him come here, anyway?"

I want to weep, but Mrs. Pittman intervenes. "What are you saying? She's an old woman. There's nothing she can do, but the men in this community might consider forming a plan. She and that girl need protection, not accusations."

"Hearty's never hurt either of us," Gran says. "He just drinks."

"And lies and steals," the preacher says. "Don't pretend he don't. He'll take anything that's not nailed down and claim he didn't, so he can buy himself more liquor. People 'round here pretend they don't see, because they respect you. But one of these days he'll go too far, and somebody'll come after him with a shotgun."

"I'll take . . . my shotgun to them first," Hearty says, just before he bends double and vomits at the preacher's feet.

"You'uns leave us." Gran shakes her head

as her son-in-law retches and heaves. "We'll get him out of here. But we'll have better luck doing it without you. I'm sorry it's come to this."

"No," Mrs. Pittman says sharply. "These men will walk him back to wherever he came from. I'm taking you home myself. You got stuck with Hearty Hale when your daughter made a foolish decision, but you don't have to be stuck with him today. Now come along."

I hope my grandmother will refuse, that the command in the other woman's voice will anger her enough she'll stay right here. I don't want to walk back to the preacher's car and face the knots of churchgoers again, not as long as I live. But Gran looks the way a dog does after he's been whipped. She doesn't have the strength to refuse. Instead, she starts hobbling after the preacher's wife and beckons for me to join her.

The walk back through the lot and over to the preacher's car is the longest I've ever made. I can feel every eye staring at me, particularly Sally's, and I know what everybody is thinking.

If I ever harbored hope that someday people might overlook the man who fathered me and see me for the person I am, now I know that hope was foolish. I will always be Lottie Lou Hale, the daughter of no-good Hearty Hale.

And as long as I live in Trust, North Carolina,
my future has already been decided.

Chapter Five

The coffee shop where Charlotte had settled to write in her journal had been recently remodeled. Now it was officially a bistro, with a newly painted sign announcing it had evolved, but it was still called Cuppa. The Orange Peel, a music venue down the street, was probably awakening for a long night and beginning to attract patrons, and she was glad she had arrived early enough to find parking.

Cuppa had a row of tall windows looking over the street and fancifully trimmed topiaries between each set. Ferns hung in the window, and the hostess stand was flanked by trios of potted palms. Once past the hostess stand, though, Charlotte had seen just how casual the little restaurant was. Denim ruled, and several patrons had set up laptops on their tables. More were talking on cell phones with nothing in front of them except steaming mugs. A coffee bar jutted from one side of the room, and two young women stood there chatting and waiting for the barista to supply their order. Maybe the owners had added space for more tables and real food, but at heart the place probably hadn't changed much.

When she had asked for a quiet table, a young man in a green T-shirt had led her as far away from the hubbub as he could without pushing her through the emergency exit, and for a long time she'd had the area to herself. But now that she was finished writing in her journal, it was dinnertime, and a family with two squabbling preschoolers was divvying up a pizza at the table beside hers. A middle-age couple, who looked as if they'd either had a bad day or engineered one for everybody else, had just been seated steps away from both tables, and the man, in his early forties, was squinting at the menu as if it had been salvaged from a shipwreck.

Charlotte knew she had taken up her table for too long, ordering coffee, then an untouched pastry, out of guilt. Now she was finally hungry and knew she should probably try to eat something before she left for home. Cuppa wasn't exactly her usual, much more casual than the places she frequented with friends and colleagues, but the atmosphere was upbeat and the pizza at the next table smelled wonderful.

She studied a menu snuggled alongside a brief wine list between the sugar dispenser and the salt and pepper shakers. The selection was simple. Pizza, salads, wraps, a variety of sandwiches and a few Italian specialties. As ordinary and ubiquitous as the choices were, the ingredients seemed innovative. The Cobb salad had pea shoots and shiitake mushrooms, the Greek wrap featured baby spinach, fire-roasted red peppers and sun-dried tomatoes.

She had sat there long enough for a shift change. Now a tall young woman approached, dressed in another of the restaurant's dark green T-shirts paired with an ankle-length khaki skirt. She had long sun-bleached hair pulled back in a low ponytail, masses of freckles and eyes rimmed with sandy lashes. The all-American, girl-next-door essentials were marred by a gold ring in her nose and the winged edges of a tattoo just visible on the right side of her neck. Charlotte thought the image might be a fairy or a dragonfly.

Green eyes flicked to the menu in Charlotte's hand, then back up again, before the young woman spoke. "Hi, my name is Harmony, and I'll be happy to get you anything you'd like." She smiled shyly to show slightly crooked teeth.

"You know what, the eggplant provolone pizza sounds wonderful," Charlotte said. "Is it as good as it sounds?"

"I like it."

Charlotte ordered the pizza and a salad, and asked for a bottle of sparkling water to go with them.

The young woman took her order, then moved to the couple who had just arrived and introduced herself to them, as well.

"Harmony?" the man asked loudly enough that half the restaurant could hear him. "I bet that's not what your mother named you."

The young woman looked puzzled. "Harmony No-Middle-Name Stoddard, right there for all the world to see on my birth certificate. May I get you something to drink before I tell you our specials?"

"I bet you were born in Asheville."

Charlotte was trying not to eavesdrop, but it was impossible, since the couple were so close. She knew not everyone held their mountain community in the highest regard. Some of her colleagues thought Asheville was outdated and outclassed, a frontier hippie outpost with a redneck contingent that barely kept it from tumbling off the left side of the universe. Luckily most of them kept such unpalatable sentiments to themselves, at least in public, but this man had either had too much to drink already, or too many frustrations.

The waitress looked perplexed, and the man's companion, a frumpy brunette who looked only marginally more pleasant, intervened. "My husband's just saying it's not as uncommon a name here as it is in other places. He's making an educated guess."

"Harmony, Serenity, Moonbeam, Sagittarius." The man picked up the wine list and waved it as if he were shooing flies. "Do you sell wine by the bottle?"

"I was born in Kansas, and no, we only sell by the glass. What would you like?" The young woman looked composed, but wary, as if she understood she'd been insulted and was hoping to get beyond it.

"I'll have a glass of red wine," the woman said. "Cabernet?"

Harmony nodded. "And for you?" she asked the man.

"Whatever . . ."

"Then shall I bring you the cabernet, too?"

He gave a curt nod.

Charlotte knew all too well what the

young server was probably feeling. Years had passed since she'd waited on tables herself, but it wasn't a time in her life that was easily forgotten. When a restaurant wasn't too busy and customers were friendly, the work was tolerable, even enjoyable. But when customers were rude, like this man, then a shift could last forever.

Harmony returned with Charlotte's water and promised the pizza would be ready in about twenty minutes. Then she gave the couple their wine and set ice water in front of them, too. "Would you like to hear our specials?" she asked them.

"Not if they're low-fat, whole grain and heaped with vegetables." The man sneered.

"You've pretty well described it. You might like the pot pie, though, our chef —"

"It's an exaggeration to call anybody who works in this place a chef," he said. "We'll split a large eggplant-provolone pizza."

"I have to apologize," Harmony interrupted, "but the *chef* just told me he used the last of the eggplant on another order. Could I interest you in our pissaladière? It's a white-onion pizza with thyme, rosemary and feta, and —"

"Unbelievable."

Charlotte frowned. The girl looked pale, as if having to deal with the man's bad humor was taking its toll.

The woman poked her menu in Harmony's direction, as if to forestall more of her husband's bad temper. "We'll split a large one, and bring us two green salads, please. I'll have the raspberry vinaigrette on the side. He'll have the specialty mushroom blue cheese."

"Out of eggplant?" he said loudly, after Harmony had left and after he'd taken a long sip of his cabernet.

In a few minutes Harmony returned with salads on a tray. She gave Charlotte hers first, then placed the woman's in front of her. Just as she was about to set the man's on his place mat, one of the children at the next table screamed and launched herself off her chair, slamming into the server, who dropped the ceramic salad bowl. Salad flew over the table and into the man's lap, and the bowl bounced against the table edge and shattered when it struck the floor.

"I'm so sorry," the mother at the next table said, clearly horrified at what her daughter had done. She grabbed the girl's arm and hauled her back to her chair, while the man leaped to his feet, eyes blazing.

Harmony, who could not have avoided the accident even if she'd been an Olympic gymnast, tried to apologize, anyway, but he was furious. Dressing splattered his pants and sport coat, and lettuce tumbled to his shoes.

"You need a new profession," he said. "Who told you waiting on tables was a good career move? Get the manager. Now!"

The young woman's eyes glistened, and her freckles stood out in sharp relief on pale cheeks. "She . . . she's stepped out. I'll send her right back when —"

He stopped dabbing at the stain with his napkin and threw it on the table. "You think we're staying?"

"Let me take your number, and I'll be sure she calls —"

"*You'll* be sure?" He sounded as if he was sure she wouldn't get *that* right, either.

The young woman looked down at the vegetables and crockery covering the floor at their feet, the dressing oozing into a chunky cheese puddle dotted with green, and suddenly her face drained of all color. She closed her eyes, covered her mouth with her hand and took off toward the coffee bar.

Charlotte could remain silent no longer. With one smooth motion she pulled a pad out of her purse, stood and held it out to the man. "Do us all a favor and put your number there. You can leave it on the way out. And maybe you can add an apology."

He had the grace to look ashamed, or maybe he was just worried Charlotte was going to continue. "Never mind." He stood and motioned to his wife. "Let's get out of here."

He rounded the table and started toward the door, his wife close behind him.

Charlotte started to sit back down, but she realized what little appetite she'd had was gone now, and she was too upset to eat. Instead, she took out her wallet and dropped two twenties on the table before she started toward the door, too.

Harmony was nowhere to be seen.

In Charlotte's opinion, her house was the finest example of Colonial Revival architecture in upscale Biltmore Forest. Built from salmon-tinged brick with imposing white pillars and decorative woodwork, it ruled over its neighbors from a rise in the center of a two-acre lot.

The house was much too large for a woman alone, which hadn't stopped the newly divorced Charlotte from snapping it up when it came on the market ten years ago. She'd had her eye on the house for years, had even tried to buy it once before when she was still married. So when it had come back on the market a second time, she'd made sure she was first in line.

Since then, despite a sagging economy, the house had increased in value, thanks to her constant attention to maintenance and landscaping. Of course, even though she was free to gloat, there was nobody who cared. The house inspired one of two undesirable reactions. The first was awe, often tinged heavily with envy. The second was worse, something she could only tag as dismay. The house clearly sucked up money and resources without mercy or discrimination.

The house in Biltmore Forest had been a dream, a symbol, a satisfied "yes" at the end of a long, torturous road.

Or so she'd thought.

This evening she turned into the driveway with groceries tucked into the passenger's seat. After leaving Cuppa she had stopped at Earth Fare to stock up on fresh salads and baked goods, because her refrigerator was as empty as the rest of her evening promised to be.

Right now all she wanted was to put the bags in the refrigerator without even bothering to unpack them and fall asleep in her bedroom, fully clothed. She was so tired every cell in her body had shriveled from fatigue.

She didn't bother with the garage. She pulled into the stone-paved parking area hidden behind a bower of English ivy and turned off the engine.

"Okay, now you're getting out," she said out loud, then forced herself to follow her own orders.

Inside, she put away the groceries and told herself it was good to be home. But once she'd made herself a cup of hot tea and a slice of toast, she lay exhausted on the living room sofa, staring at the ceiling. In the end, as the grandfather clock tolled ten, she rose, smoothed wrinkles from her clothes, closed the front door behind her and headed back to Cuppa.

After being forced to park several blocks away on a side street, she stood outside the restaurant once more. She doubted Harmony Stoddard would appreciate reacquainting herself with a witness to her unfortunate dinner-shift encounter, but Charlotte wanted to be certain that the bad-tempered man hadn't complained. And if someone else had spoken to the manager, the mother at the next table, perhaps, or another server, Charlotte wanted to be sure Harmony wasn't blamed for something that was certainly not her fault.

Inside, the hostess stand was empty.

Farther in a few people sipped coffee, but one of them was packing up her computer. A muscular middle-age man in one of Cuppa's signature shirts stopped Charlotte as she continued toward the back.

"We're closing," he said. "Did you need something?"

"By any chance are you the manager?"

"She went home early. I'm in charge."

"I was here earlier. I was sitting in the back, and a child at the next table slammed into my server and sent salad flying all over a man at another table. I just wanted to be sure the server didn't get into trouble. I was right there, and it was absolutely not her fault."

He looked surprised. "You came all the way back to tell us that?"

"And to make sure she's okay." She decided to level. "The man behaved badly. He didn't apologize. I thought somebody ought to."

"You know how rare that would be?" He ran his hand through short-cropped hair. "Who was it? Harmony?"

"Uh-huh." She wondered how he knew.

His mouth twisted into a wry smile. "She had a bad night. I didn't know why."

"Is she here? Maybe I could make it a better one."

"She left about half an hour ago, after she finished her shift."

Charlotte felt a pang of regret. "Maybe I could write her a note?"

"Sure. Just leave it on the coffee bar. I'll make sure she gets it."

Charlotte wandered over and sat on a stool. She penned a few lines on a sheet of notebook paper and signed it. Then, on a whim, she added her business card and circled her cell phone number, although she doubted the young woman would call.

With nothing else to do she left the note and trudged to her car. The air was cool, and while the street wasn't deserted, she felt utterly alone. On the street, in the city, on good old Mother Earth. She thought of the memorial service where she had not been welcome. She thought of the wary expression in her own minister's eyes.

She thought of her granddaughter climbing to the top of a jungle gym, unaware that her grandmother was sitting just yards away watching her.

She slowed her pace. She had nowhere to go except home, and nothing to do there but think.

If she hadn't slowed she wouldn't have glanced into the car parked in front of her. Under the light of a streetlamp the sedan looked like something General Motors had long since discontinued. Rust etched wheel hubs. The rear door had been badly dented and someone — clearly not a professional — had tried to hammer it back into shape. Most important, as Charlotte drew even with the car, what she saw inside made her stop and stare.

The woman in the backseat, head pillowed on a blanket and another blanket drawn up around her, was all too familiar.

Charlotte debated what to do. She'd come to find Harmony Stoddard, but not like this. Before she could make herself continue along the sidewalk, Harmony's eyes opened, and the two women stared at each other.

"I'm sorry," Charlotte said, since only a pane of glass separated them. She started forward, then she stopped and went back. "Are you okay?"

Harmony was sitting up now, and she wiped her eyes before she moved over to the door and opened it, swinging her long legs over the side to face Charlotte.

"What are you doing here?" She didn't sound angry.

"Well, right now I'm on my way to my car, but I was just at Cuppa to find you. I wanted to apologize. That man behaved so badly, and I wanted to be sure you weren't in trouble for anything he did or said."

Tears glistened on Harmony's cheeks, and she rubbed them away with her fist before she spoke. Charlotte was reminded of her daughter as a toddler. Taylor had always done exactly that. Taylor, the daughter she hadn't spoken to for almost eleven years.

"You didn't have to come back. It was okay." Harmony got out of the car and stood with her back to it.

"It wasn't okay." Charlotte debated what to do or say next. Part of her thought she ought to continue to her car. But suddenly the conversation wasn't about a stranger's bad manners anymore. It was about so many other things.

"You're not okay," she said. "Are you sleeping in your car tonight?"

"No . . ." Harmony bit her lip. "Not for the whole night, anyway."

"Just part of it?"

"I'm . . . I'm staying with a friend."

"You can't get in? You don't have a key?"

"That's not it." The young woman seemed to debate with herself. "She's got a date. I don't want to be there when . . ."

Charlotte understood. "Oh, right, I see." She hesitated. "It's a small place, I guess?"

"Like a closet, and I'm crashing on her sofa until I can find something better. I —"

She shook her head.

"You've been there awhile?"

"You don't want to hear all this." Harmony smiled a watery smile. "This isn't your problem, right?"

"Absolutely not. Not one bit." Charlotte smiled, too. "So tell me, anyway."

Harmony started to cry. Charlotte wasn't sure what to do, but before she could decide, she'd put her arms around the girl and pulled her close.

"When was the last time you ate?" she asked, as Harmony, bending at the waist, sobbed against her neck. She felt the girl's shoulders hunch in answer.

"Will your car be okay here tonight?" Charlotte asked, making a decision.

"I . . . I guess. But I don't —"

"You're coming home with me, and don't worry, you can call your friend and tell her where you are. You'll be safe. I'm not a serial killer."

"You don't have to do this."

Charlotte was afraid she did. She was afraid no one needed to do it more.

Chapter Six

Living in Asheville was a trade-off for Taylor Martin. At first, after Maddie's problematic birth, the city of Taylor's own birth was the only place she *could* live. Without her father's help, both financial and emotional, she would never have been able to support herself and care for her daughter.

Jeremy's parents, who also lived in town, had helped, as well, and despite Taylor's disdain for her daughter's father, she couldn't dislike the senior Larsens. From the beginning they had stepped up to the plate, insisting that Jeremy acknowledge the baby, then offering financial support. After Maddie's birth they had put their son through college, or tried to, but they had also made certain Jeremy understood that once he was earning a living, they expected him to take over the child support payments.

The Larsens were now only part-time

Asheville residents, migrating to Florida for the coldest months, but when they were in town, they were enthusiastic babysitters, available at a moment's notice. While nowadays Jeremy paid his own child support, his parents paid all the health care extras insurance didn't cover.

Taylor knew she should consider moving to a city with more and better jobs, perhaps one with specialists making their mark in neurobiology. But nowhere else on the planet would she have the support system she had here, and nowhere else would Maddie be surrounded by so many people who loved her.

This evening she reconsidered that conclusion. Classes at Moon and Stars were physically grueling, and in addition to yoga, she also taught Pilates at a local gym. For this she was paid enough to keep body and soul together, but not much more. She had a degree in Health and Wellness promotion and had hoped to go on to something in the medical field, but earning one degree had been difficult enough, even with a network of friends and family.

Asheville was short on jobs and long on people with the same kind of skills she had. At times like this she found herself imagining a less exhausting way to survive. The truth was, she was lucky to have the jobs she did. Her employers at both the gym and the yoga studio understood that sometimes Maddie needed Taylor more than her students did. That benefit was impossible to beat.

This evening, when she pulled up in front of her house, she stared up at the crescent moon rising overhead. She knew Maddie was all right or her father would have called. Her daughter was probably sleeping off the effects of the most serious seizure Taylor remembered in years, what her doctor had called a "breakthrough" seizure on the phone, since it had been an escalation of symptoms. She'd been so sure they had finally gotten the medications right. Dr. Hilliard had been cautiously optimistic, as well. And now they might have to start all over.

She got out of the car and only then noticed that her father's Acura was no longer in front of her house. His spot had been taken by a familiar yellow Volkswagen bug.

The front door of the house was unlocked, which was no surprise. Taylor locked up at bedtime, but the neighborhood was quiet, and the neighbors on both sides had great-grandchildren and time to watch the world go by outside their windows. Her neighbors were another reason she didn't want to move to a better job in a faceless city.

She closed the front door loudly so her guest would know she was home. The house was so small she was through the living room and kitchen in seconds, then beyond to the family room that was just large enough for a small television and sofa. The television was off and Samantha Ferguson was curled up on the cushions, but if she'd been sleeping, she wasn't now. She smiled, arms out and fists clenched as she stretched.

"You're not my father," Taylor said. "He's older, and his hair's turning gray."

"I forgot you were teaching this evening. I popped by on my way back from Mom's, so I told him I'd wait for you. He looked tired. I think he was glad to go."

Taylor felt a twinge of guilt. Her father adored Maddie, but she wondered if she was taking advantage of his devotion. By drawing constantly on his support and help, was she keeping him from finding a woman he could share his life with?

She tossed her backpack on the coffee table and flopped down beside her friend. "Where's Edna?"

"Mom's got her. Tomorrow's a field trip to a local farm, and Mom's on spring vacation, so she said she'd chaperone."

Taylor lowered her voice. "Maddie's already asleep?"

"For a good hour. She was exhausted."

"Dad told you what happened?"

"He said she had a generalized tonic-clonic seizure."

Samantha's medical training made it so easy to talk to her. Taylor was always grateful not to have to mince words. "Maybe it was an anomaly," she said.

Samantha nodded. "It's hard to know."

Normally Taylor might have treated herself to a glass of wine after a long day, but Samantha didn't drink, and the two women were such old friends that if Samantha had wanted anything else, she would have gotten it.

"She seemed okay?" Taylor probed.

"A little disoriented. I don't think she got much homework done."

"I'll have to call her teacher. They try not to give homework over the weekend. Maybe Maddie can make up whatever she didn't do on Saturday."

Samantha was half lying, half sitting, with her dark hair spread against the back of the old sofa. She was of mixed ancestry, as if the continents of the world had huddled together at her creation. Her father had been half Korean, half African-American.

Her mother's heritage was unknown but likely European. Samantha's face was long and elegant, her huge eyes slightly tilted, her hair wild, her complexion the color of almonds. She wasn't classically beautiful, and *exotic* was too charged a word to describe her. She was distinctive, extraordinary. At twenty-nine, she'd already lived harder and faster than most people twice her age.

"Maddie told me she talked to Jeremy," she said.

"Did she tell you what they talked about?" Taylor didn't even try to mask a grimace.

"She told him about the seizure. She said he asked a lot of questions."

"He's good at questions. It makes him feel involved, like he's actually participating in her life."

"By my standards, sweet pea, he's Father of the Year. He pays child support, and puts money aside for her college."

There was something to be said for that. Samantha refused to even discuss Edna's father, who she claimed was completely out of the picture. In contrast, last year, after one of his songs had sold to a recording company, Jeremy had sent Taylor an unexpected bonus check to sock away for emergencies. Taylor had to give the man some credit.

"Getting checks is great," she said. "But he's around just enough to remind Maddie that she has a father, and gone just enough to make her yearn for a real one."

"What would you do if he was around all the time?" Samantha asked. "Would you really like that better?"

Taylor shrugged that off. "Not worth worrying about, since it's never going to happen. He's got Nashville in his blood, and that's where the money is for the band. I'd better hope he doesn't move here, or he'll be writing ballads about being too broke to support his baby girl."

The phone rang just in time to prevent Samantha from answering. She got up and ambled into the kitchen to give Taylor privacy. "I'd love some tea," Taylor called after her, before she picked up the telephone.

The male voice was unmistakable, but he identified himself, just in case. "Taylor, Jeremy."

It might be relatively early, but she was tired, and she wondered if he knew it. Jeremy wasn't a bully, but he was a master at figuring out how to get what he wanted. He called that talent the ability to size up a situation, something that had helped him wedge open the door of the country music scene. It hadn't helped him enough to make him a star, but his band, the Black Balsam Drifters, was now opening for big-name acts, and the songs he wrote and sang were being heard by significant players in the business.

"It's been a long day," she said, hoping honesty would throw him off his game. "I just got home, and I'm beat. Can we make this short?"

"Maddie and I had a nice talk."

"Sam told me."

"How is Sam?"

"Waiting in the kitchen while we *finish* this," she said.

"Maddie said she had a whopper of a seizure this afternoon."

"That's how she said it?"

"She described how she was feeling at the moment, and I guessed the rest. Maybe I'm wrong?"

"No." She sighed. "She'd been doing really well. I hoped the new meds . . ." Her voice trailed off.

"How bad was it?"

"Bad enough."

"You called the doctor?"

"No, I sent her out to play in traffic." She

could have kicked herself the moment the words came out of her mouth. "I'm sorry. It really has been a long day."

"What did he say?"

Jeremy was almost always rational, and he rarely engaged in sniping. Usually she was at least polite. She attempted to continue that tradition.

"He told me to keep an eye on her and bring her in on Monday. If anything significant comes of the visit, I'll let you know, I promise."

"Taylor, I know this is a bad time to bring this up. You've made it clear you're whupped. But I think we can do better than Dr. Hilliard. I know you like him —"

"Like him? Before Dr. Hilliard, Maddie was just a name on a chart. Half the time I don't think the doctor of the moment even read her case history. If I have a problem, he calls me back. He's doing everything he can to get the medication adjusted, so we don't have more events like the one we had at dinnertime."

"But it's not working."

"This is not a sinus infection. If epilepsy were simple to treat, I could go to the drugstore and grab something over the counter."

The silence went on so long, she began to

wonder if they had been disconnected. Then he spoke.

"Not the right time for this. And it's not a criticism, Taylor. But I worry. You're right there, you can watch and make decisions based on what you see. I don't have that . . ."

"What? Luxury? Is that what you were going to say? You think it's a *luxury* to be right here watching her go through this?"

"I don't have that *information,*" he said. "I need more time with her."

"You know where we live. You send her support check to this address every month."

"I want her to come to Nashville this summer."

This time the silence was on Taylor's end. "Did I hear that right?" she asked at last. "You want her to come to *Nashville?* And then what? You get a gig out of town, drag her along and stow her backstage? Or what, she stays at your apartment with a babysitter who doesn't know jack about how to help her if she needs it?"

"None of the above. Look, there's no casual way to tell you this. I'm engaged. Her name's Willow, and she was our promoter on the last tour. She loves kids. I want her to get to know Maddie before we get married."

Taylor took a moment to recover. "Well,

that's completely out of the blue. Does Maddie know?"

"Willow and I have been together awhile, but I didn't see any point in telling Maddie if it wasn't going to work out."

"Thanks for that."

"I do think about what's good for her."

"Why don't you just bring Willow to Asheville to meet Maddie?"

"I don't want her to *meet* Maddie. I want her to *spend time* with Maddie. Real time, two weeks at the beginning of summer. And Maddie's been asking to come to Nashville. Willow has a little house with some land outside the city, and it's a great place for a kid, so we'll stay there. The band's going to hunker down and put together our next CD, so there's no chance we'll be out on the road. I want to introduce them here, where there's no pressure from anybody else."

"Nobody here's going to pressure you, Jeremy. But I think it would be better if you introduce the two of them where Maddie feels comfortable and safe. Her doctor's here."

"She needs to be here with me, without *you,*" he said pointedly. "She needs to be away from Asheville to give Willow a real chance. We have good doctors in Nashville, and I'll get copies of her records. Our custody agreement allows for this."

There was no threat in his tone, but the threat was in the words. Custody agreement. Papers they had signed. Choices they had made when they were still teenagers.

"We have time to talk this over," she said at last.

"We have time to make the arrangements," he countered. "I'm not going to change my mind. I didn't mention it to Maddie, because I wanted to warn you first, but I *will* tell her the next time we talk."

Warn, not consult. She heard the difference.

"Anything else?" she asked. "New and better bombshells?"

He spoke slowly and with surprising feeling, as if he had rehearsed what came next. "We've done surprisingly well through all this, you and me and the kiddo. Not the best start, not the best circumstances, but we've muddled through and grown up along the way. I know you've had the major burden, while I got to go out into the world and live my dreams. But it's time for me to take some of the day-to-day stuff on my shoulders, and time for you to have a little flexibility and freedom. This isn't going to be a one-time thing, Taylor. It's the beginning of a new phase for all of us. Let's make it work for Maddie, okay?"

"I always want what's best for her."

"Then we're on the same page." He said good-night and hung up.

Taylor stared at the wall until Samantha came back in, carrying two bright red mugs of tea.

As she handed a mug to Taylor, peppermint and chamomile scented the air. "It can't be that bad."

Taylor told her just how bad it was.

Samantha flopped down on the sofa beside her. "Well, what do you know about that?"

"Very little, as a matter of fact. He hasn't given me a single hint this was coming."

"The two of you never talk about anything personal. Why should he?"

"Because he's giving my daughter a stepmother. Doesn't that seem like something he'd mention?"

Samantha waved her free hand in emphasis. "In your eyes Jeremy can't do anything right. You do see that, correct? I mean, a few minutes ago you were dissing him for not spending more time with Maddie, and now you're after him for wanting to spend a couple of weeks of quality time with her while he introduces somebody who's going to be important in her life."

Taylor considered that, but not for long. "See, there was this day, oh, eleven years ago, give or take a month or two. I went to him, sobbing, and told him I was pregnant with his baby. And you know what he said to me?"

"Something stupid? Like any seventeen-year-old boy with a noose around his neck?"

"Maddie is not a noose."

"You know that, and so does he. *Now.* But his whole life changed in that moment, and he was still just a kid. Both of you were."

"Eleven years ago he told me my baby wasn't his problem, that I was the one who was pregnant, and I'd better leave him out of it."

"And you've never forgiven him."

Taylor hadn't. At times she'd come close. She realized that nobody should be judged by something he said when the world as he knew it was collapsing. Later, when confronted by his parents, Jeremy had not denied that the baby was his. Of course, denial would have been futile, since a paternity test would have proved him a liar.

"You remember how it went," she said. "We'd broken up. He was already dating somebody else when I realized I was going to have his baby. Later he told me he thought I was just making up a pregnancy to get even with him."

"I can see that."

"Really? I can't. He knew me better than that."

"Maybe not. He was the class bad boy. Your mother wouldn't let you date him, right? Whenever you saw him you were sneaking behind her back. How well could you know him? How much time could you spend together?"

"Enough to make a baby." Taylor shook her head. "I guess we've worked things out well enough, considering our start. There's no love lost between us, but both of us love Maddie. Now, everything's going to change."

"Particularly if you don't lose the attitude."

Samantha had been her friend for so long that Taylor couldn't be offended. She just reached over and socked her on the arm.

"I don't think it's Jeremy," Samantha said, unperturbed. "I don't think you want to share Maddie. And you're wondering what you'll do without her for two weeks. Part of you wants her to have a closer relationship to her daddy, and part of you probably hopes she'll get along with her new stepmother. But another part of you hopes the whole thing will blow up, and she'll never want to leave you again."

"If that's true it sounds pretty squirrely."

"No, it sounds pretty natural. I don't have that problem, since Edna's father was never in the picture. But if he showed up tomorrow and said he'd been searching for us all this time, I'd probably feel the same way you do. Like he was the enemy clambering over my castle walls, an invader trying to stake a claim to a piece of *my* daughter."

"And people think the hard part of being a single parent is not having anybody to share childrearing with."

"The hard part of being a mother is knowing when to let go and when to hang on."

For no good reason, Taylor thought of her own mother. As always, she was sorry she had.

Chapter Seven

First Day Journal: April 29

I've spent most of my adult life trying to forget my past. Maybe I thought if I changed myself into someone else, the past would fade away with my Appalachian accent and one day a country girl named Lottie Lou Hale would cease to exist.

Now I know how much time I wasted. No matter how hard we try to lock memories away, they break free, sometimes taking on new life because we witness others with the same struggles, like the young woman sleeping in my guest room this morning. Just like Harmony Stoddard, I was once nearly homeless, with no one to help me and nothing to fall back on.

It's not a memory I recall with fondness. But this morning, while I wait for my guest to wake up, I'll take it out again and examine it here.

Almost exactly seven years after Hearty's Sunday morning appearance at the Trust

Independent Baptist Church, I am sitting beside him on a bench in front of the pulpit, and this time no one is trying to persuade him to leave.

In the past year someone has donated screens, and someone else convinced the county to run an electric line so that now floor fans blow channels of steamy air over the mourners lucky enough to be sitting close to them.

I'm not one of those. I'm sitting in the front row, close enough to my grandmother's coffin to wish I could hop up and brush away the flies that entered the church with the mourners. I know better than to make a scene. I am seventeen, newly graduated from high school, and now I'm a woman. None of my grandmother's friends gathered today would appreciate even a pause in Preacher Pittman's words. Those attending came out of respect, but I know that no one wants to sit in the heat a moment longer than necessary. Fans or not, the temperature has to be close to ninety and climbing as the sun rises higher in the sky.

"Would anybody out there like to speak?" the preacher asks at last.

I turn to my father, who wears a clean shirt and pants and is, for once, freshly shaved. Even Hearty Hale realized he had to show up at his mother-in-law's funeral or risk losing whatever shred of credibility is still attached to his name.

Do not get up, I mouth.

He narrows his eyes, as if trying to make sense of that. I realize saying something about Gran has never occurred to him.

From behind us a neighbor stands and begins to speak, detailing the kindness my grandmother showed his family, the food she brought when his wife was sick, little gifts for his children when Gran could hardly afford bacon and beans. Someone else remembers how hard she worked and the way she held her little family together after her husband died, even giving her son-in-law and granddaughter a place to live. The unspoken message, of course, is that anybody who put up with Hearty all those years is already sitting at the feet of the Lord.

I know my grandmother earned her neighbors' respect one thoughtful act at a time. I also know that now that Gran has finally succumbed to the torment of her twisted body, respect for anyone at the old Sawyer farm will be buried right beside her. The locals will feel sorry for me, of course, sorry I've been left to cope with my alcoholic father and his debts and antics, but they'll stay as far away as possible, lest they get sucked into the drama of my life when their own are already difficult enough.

I gather my courage and stand when it's clear no one else intends to speak.

"My grandmother was the only mother I ever knew," I say, my voice strong and clear, despite the lump in my throat. "She was a God-fearing Christian, and she practiced every principle anybody ever preached from that pulpit. I think she held on to life just long enough to see me graduate, but I'm glad she's gone now, because she suffered. A whole lot." I clear my throat. "I just want to say thank you for those of you who were kind to her and to me while she lay dying. She would have wanted me to say that."

I sit down, and the preacher nods. A hymn is sung, a prayer is said and the service is over.

We all stand as four of the deacons come to the front to shoulder Gran's pine coffin and carry it outside.

I follow, and in a moment my father stands to follow behind me. I hope he doesn't stumble or worse. It will be a testimonial to my grandmother if Hearty can make it to the graveside without creating a scene.

Gran asked to be buried at our farm, in the family cemetery next to her husband and my mother. Outside, I glance at my father, who is leaning against a tree, his eyelids drifting closed. I wonder if he's sober enough to remember where he parked his pickup to drive himself home.

The coffin is loaded into a hearse, and I sit beside the driver and wonder how many mourners will accompany us. I glance behind me and see a dozen cars, headlights bright, and I know what a tribute this is to my grandmother.

The trip takes just minutes. On our hillside cemetery the grave has already been dug, and the ceremony there is blessedly short. Mrs. Pittman, dressed in a black skirt and blouse, with her graying hair pulled back in a tight bun, comes to stand beside me. She puts her hand on my arm once I've thrown the first handful of dirt on the coffin that holds the only person who ever loved me.

"Why don't you come home with us now, Lottie Lou?" she asks, turning me so I won't have to stare at the coffin disappearing under clods of dirt thrown by the rest of the mourners. Men from the church will finish filling the grave once the others leave, but my grandmother's friends are doing their parts with gusto.

"Preacher Pittman can drive you home after supper." Mrs. Pittman bites her lip, as if the thought of my returning home without my grandmother to protect me is disturbing. Normally the neighbors would go up to the house after the funeral. Food would be served and memories exchanged, but no one is about to go to our house, knowing Hearty Hale will be the one waiting there.

A few other mourners are closing in to mouth their condolences, and I must speak quickly.

"You're very kind, but I made other plans." I hesitate, then lower my voice. "I'm going to Asheville. Bill Johnston's taking me. He's got flowerpots to deliver this afternoon, and I guess you could say he's delivering me right along with them."

"Asheville?" Mrs. Pittman sounds puzzled. "Do you have family there? Friends?"

"I have some money Gran saved for me. I'll find a job. I just can't live here no — anymore."

Mrs. Pittman clears her throat. "Are you afraid to be alone with your father?"

I know what she's worried about, but I shake my head. "Not like what you mean."

"Then don't you think you ought to wait until you have something lined up? Maybe we could help find you —"

"I can't stay another minute," I say. "I already packed, and my stuff is in Bill's truck. He picked up my suitcase when he took me to the church. There's nothing keeping me here.

It's time to move on with my life."

"Your father —"

"Is a worthless no-good, even when he's sober. And there's nothing I can do to change him, but he'll drag me down if I stay. Gran warned me he would, and she was right."

Mrs. Pittman doesn't argue, because what is there to say, even for a preacher's wife? "What about the farm?"

"I guess he's welcome to it." The people waiting impatiently on the sidelines begin to move in.

"Does he know?"

"He'll find out soon enough."

Soon enough comes sooner than I expect. When just about everyone else has gone, after Preacher Pittman has silently pressed two twenty-dollar bills into my palm along with his phone number, I turn and see Bill Johnston pull his pickup around so he's headed down our driveway. I know Bill hoped to get an earlier start into the city, and the time has come to leave — and quickly. But before I can get in the front, I see my father staring into the bed of Bill's pickup, squinting at the small suitcase that once belonged to my mother, one he clearly recognizes.

"What's that doing there?" Hearty claps a hand on my shoulder as I try to pass.

I had hoped to simply tell him that Bill

Johnston was taking me to a friend's, but I can't think of any lie that involves the suitcase, too. I decide the time has come for the truth.

"Mr. Johnston's taking me down to Asheville." I shrug off Hearty's hand. "I'm leaving."

"Leaving?" He seems unable to comprehend the word.

"That's right. I'm going to start a new life."

"With what?"

I ponder that a moment. I'm leaving home, setting out for an uncertain future, and Hearty has only zeroed in on what for him is the crucial question. How have I gotten enough money to make this escape, and how can he get it away from me?

"I'll miss you, too, Hearty," I say, leaning close. "Thanks for the good times and good wishes."

His eyes narrow. "Where'd you get the money to leave?"

"Gran left me just enough to get away from you. She did the best she could."

"How much?"

I shake my head. "Don't matter. You aren't getting a cent of it."

"Who's going to take care of things?"

The switch is so sudden, it takes me a moment to catch up. "Things?"

"The farm? Get me dinner when I'm home?

Take care of things!"

"I have no idea. Maybe you'll figure that out."

"You aren't going anywhere."

"Try and stop me." I hear Bill's door slam and his footsteps as he rounds the cab.

"It's your job to stay and take care of . . . things!"

I see Bill come up behind my father. "Can we leave now?" I ask.

Bill is a substantial man, outweighing Hearty by fifty pounds and topping him by at least four inches. Right now I'm glad for all the years and pounds of his wife's deep-fried country cooking.

"You can't take her," Hearty says.

"I don't want a fight," Bill responds. "But the girl's going where she wants to."

Hearty considers that. I can almost see him weighing his options. Winning a fight with the well-fed Bill isn't one of them. He turns back to me.

"You leave now, I'll give my share of this farm your grandma loved so much to one of my drinking buddies when I die. You won't be able to get your hands on my piece of it."

I shrug because I'm fairly sure that Hearty will destroy the farm before it comes to that, burn down the house, whatever it takes.

"Or that ridge land of mine, neither," he says, when he sees I'm not impressed enough. "You won't get a square inch of it."

From his own family Hearty has inherited land too steep for anything but logging, something Hearty does when he absolutely has to earn money. The more valuable Hale land was left to his four sober sisters, who stayed away from Hearty and, by extension, me, as if what ailed their baby brother might be catching. The ridge land was a blessing, because when he was there hauling out trees, Hearty was gone for days.

"You're welcome to everything," I say. "I don't want to lay eyes on you again. Not ever. You can drink yourself to death, or sober up and change your ways. Makes no difference to me."

I glance at Bill and see that the last part of my speech dismayed him. I know I sounded heartless, so I sigh and add, "Of course, for your sake, Hearty, I hope you can change."

"I want some of that money your grandmother gave you. Right now." He holds out his trembling hand, palm up. "I deserve it."

"The girl's heading for a new life, and you want to steal her money?" Bill asks.

"If she's got money, it came from this farm. I own part of the farm."

Bill shakes his head, and this time he shoots me a sympathetic glance. "We're going now." Bill reaches around Hearty and takes my arm.

I skirt my father and step up to the running board. Bill's wife, Zettie, moves over to the middle to make room for me, then she leans over and opens the door. "You get inside, Lottie Lou. And don't you give that man one red cent."

I slide inside, but Hearty holds on to the door. "You got nothing for your father?" he says.

"That's what you gave me my whole life." I have to force the words past a sudden lump in my throat. Hearty Hale is my father, and while I despise him, he is my blood and my past. Suddenly the future looks very frightening, more frightening than I had anticipated.

"That's what you'll get if you leave me," Hearty says. "I'm warning you."

Bill has already circled the truck, and now he slams his door shut and starts the engine. Without another word he starts forward. I grab the door handle, and when my father loses his grip on it, I slam the door shut.

A part of me knows I ought to turn my head for one more look at the man who sired me. I will not come back. These will be our final moments together. But I don't turn. I hold tight to the door handle all the way down to Asheville.

Chapter Eight

Harmony awoke in a strange bed, and for a moment panic filled her. She had been dreaming of home, of the muffled footsteps of her mother wearing the slippers Harmony had given her as a birthday gift. Before that, no matter the season, Janine Stoddard had tiptoed around the house in her bare feet, because she had been afraid of prematurely waking Harmony's father.

Harmony's childhood had been all about walking on tiptoes, about muffling laughter or tears, about apologies. The dream was no surprise, but this bed and this room startled her into stillness. She was afraid to move, afraid to cry out. And whose name would she call, anyway?

Slowly the events of last night came back to her. Her shift at Cuppa, the man who had succeeded in making her feel small and stupid. The chunks of salad spread on the floor with dressing pooling beside . . .

She wouldn't think of that now.

Charlotte Hale, who had witnessed everything, had found her lying in the backseat of her Buick. Her cheeks burned at the memory. She had been afraid to park on a darker side street until it was okay to go back to Jennifer's. Instead, she had parked far enough away from Cuppa to feel certain no one would spot her. When she'd returned to the car after her shift, she had stretched out in the back as best she could, an army blanket rolled under her head and another pulled over her.

She had wondered where Davis was at that moment — and with whom. She had wondered exactly why she was alive.

Then she'd opened her eyes to see Charlotte Hale staring down at her.

Now she was in the woman's mansion, because Harmony could think of no other word for this house. It was a home beyond any she had ever been inside, with a front hall as large as Jennifer's entire apartment. She had been stunned as they walked to the kitchen, scuffing her soles over rugs as soft as pillows, winding through rooms with sky-high ceilings. She had been unable to stomach more than a glass of milk, and as she'd sipped, she had gaped at what *had* to be a place where food would be smart enough, confident enough, to cook itself without interference.

Charlotte — because that was what she insisted on being called — had seen how exhausted and upset Harmony was, and she had led her here, to a green-and-yellow bedroom with polished cherry furniture and a bathroom Harmony would be content to live in. Charlotte had returned with a nightgown that was inches too short but otherwise perfect, told her where to find a new toothbrush, soap and anything else she desired, then abandoned her.

Now, gazing up at the ceiling, Harmony was once again amazed. Even the ceiling was extraordinary. It was high, like all the ones she'd noted last night, but the center was marked by a plaster medallion that would look at home in a palace. She thought she identified grapes and the faces of cherubs. The ceiling curved down into sage green walls, and where it did, there was more adornment, plaster ivy, flowers, birds. In another era artists might have labored for months creating these scenes. Now she imagined there were shortcuts and factory-produced enhancements that could be quickly added by construction workers, but she was still awed by the time and expense, if not by the art itself.

She only moved her eyes. She didn't move her head. In the past week she'd learned that lesson. When she awoke it was important not to move quickly, to let her body adjust and prepare. Then she could get up by degrees, swinging her legs over the bed in slow motion, pushing up an inch at a time until she was sitting on the edge. If she was lucky she'd remembered to put her purse beside her, and packs of saltines from Cuppa's vast supply waited there for nibbling. If she didn't move quickly, if she took her time slowly eating a morsel at a time, she would not have to run gagging to the perfect marble bathroom with its multi-nozzle shower and spa tub.

She wondered if there would be time for a shower after she finally rose. By now Charlotte would surely be asking herself why she had invited a stranger to her home. One look around had proved there was so much here worth stealing. The house was filled with valuable art; even this room had china figurines that were clearly not from the Wal-mart housewares department. Of course, Harmony had never stolen so much as a toothpick. Even the saltines in her purse were courtesy of her manager.

Fifteen minutes later she was on her feet and holding steady. The saltines had, as she'd hoped, calmed her roiling stomach. She debated a shower, and in the end, she couldn't resist. Inside the marble-tile enclosure three separate sprays pummeled her from behind. The showerhead itself had more settings than Davis's state-of-the-art flat-screen television, but the warm water made her nauseous, and she didn't stay long.

She dressed in yesterday's rumpled skirt and Cuppa T-shirt, which were all she had until she could get back to Jennifer's apartment to rummage through her suitcases for something clean. She pulled her wet hair back from her face and fastened it with the same band she'd used last night. Then she went to find Charlotte.

She realized it was possible her hostess might still be asleep. Harmony had always been an early riser. She'd never had an opportunity to be anything else. As a child, if she wanted time in the family bathroom before school, she'd needed to get up at dawn, because once her father and brother, Buddy, were up, the house and everything in it belonged to them. In the summer she'd been required to get up by six to help Buddy bag newspapers for his route.

Since leaving home she hadn't lived anywhere she could be comfortable sleeping in.

Even when she had lived with Davis, she'd felt obligated to cook an early breakfast before he left for his office. He had never told her she had to, but he'd made enough snide jokes about "kept women" that she'd known better than to become one.

Charlotte's house was easy to get lost in. Harmony paid attention as she tiptoed through the hallway looking for her hostess and still ended up in a mahogany-paneled study by mistake. She left that quickly, and later, the dining room, although she could swear she'd also seen a dining room off the entry way. A house with two dining rooms perplexed her. Separate dinner parties? Would the guests realize they had competition for their hostess from the other side of the house?

She found the kitchen at last, guided by the smell of coffee brewing. While she'd given it up, the smell was enticingly familiar, and her stomach behaved. She stepped in and saw Charlotte wearing a fuzzy bathrobe and standing at the stove.

"Good morning," she said tentatively.

Charlotte turned and smiled at her. The smile was so welcoming that Harmony felt her tension ease.

"I hope I didn't wake you while I puttered around in here," Charlotte said.

"This house is so big, I think you could drill for oil and I wouldn't hear you." The moment she said it, Harmony wondered if she'd sounded critical, but before she could apologize, Charlotte laughed.

"On top of that, the builder did everything he could to soundproof the rooms. Maybe he thought it was destined for a large noisy family."

Harmony moved closer, then took a seat at the island when Charlotte waved in that direction. "It's an amazing house. Really."

"I could say you don't know the half of it, and I would be right. It goes on and on and on, and you haven't even been upstairs. If you were wearing hiking boots, I'd give you a tour."

Harmony relaxed a little more. "I really can't thank you enough for —"

Charlotte held up her hand. "It was so little, Harmony. Were you comfortable?"

"More than comfortable. That's the most wonderful bed I've ever slept in."

"I'm glad to hear it. I think you might be the first person to try out the mattress."

"It's new?"

Charlotte hesitated just a moment. "Just unused. I don't have many guests." She held up a coffeepot. "Ready for some of this?"

Harmony shook her head. "I . . . I don't

drink coffee. I mean, at least not right now."

Charlotte nodded. "Tea?"

Harmony wasn't sure that she should have tea, either. In fact, she wasn't sure what she was supposed to drink. "I . . ." She shook her head.

"Orange juice, then?"

"Oh, that would be perfect. But I don't want to be any trouble."

"Now if you'd been here yesterday morning, you might have been. My refrigerator was practically empty. But not today, so I'm delighted to share. Let's figure out what we should eat. I have bread for toast, fresh berries, yogurt. I almost never cook anymore, but I can do that much."

"This kitchen never gets used?" Harmony couldn't believe it. She was a Food Network groupie, and she was pretty sure Giada, Rachel and Paula had never seen a kitchen better equipped than this.

"I know. It hardly seems fair, but I'm afraid it's used only rarely," Charlotte said. "And then mostly by caterers if I'm putting on a dinner party. The rest of the time I eat out or snack."

Harmony realized she was actually hungry. In fact, she tried to remember when she'd last eaten. Yesterday afternoon, she thought. A Cuppa wrap purchased with her employee discount. She was going to have to do better — and fast.

"Everything sounds good," she said.

"Wonderful. It sounds good to me, too. Let's eat everything in one fell swoop."

"Have you ever wondered what that means? Have you ever seen any swooping fells?"

Charlotte's laugh was low, almost sultry, and somehow didn't fit with her uptown bearing. "Not lately. Swooping fellows, maybe, in singles' bars, but I haven't seen any of those in decades."

"They're still there, only now they come with their latest blood test clutched in one hand and industrial-strength condoms in the other." Harmony realized what she'd said and wondered if she ought to just take a vow of silence.

"Then I'm guessing that's not how you got pregnant," Charlotte said, after a brief pause.

Harmony hung her head. "How did you guess?"

"Well, I have a daughter. And while I had her a long time ago, I've never forgotten the thrill of morning sickness all day long. I figured it out last night."

"No, I didn't meet the father in a singles' bar." Harmony cleared her throat. "We were living together, but I moved out when I realized I wasn't the only woman he was sleeping with."

"And I'm guessing this was recent, and the reason you're sleeping on a girlfriend's sofa?"

Harmony nodded. "Three weeks ago. I . . . I didn't know I was pregnant until last week, at least not for sure."

"This must be a confusing time for you. And it probably doesn't help that you don't have your own place."

"One of the baristas at Cuppa might know of a room for rent. She promised she'd check for me."

"Networking, huh?"

Harmony looked up and made a wry face. "She's not very reliable, but Jennifer's lease runs out at the end of June, and she said if I haven't found something else by then, maybe we can rent something bigger together."

"So you're making plans."

"It will work out."

Charlotte didn't answer. She got food out of the refrigerator and turned down Harmony's offer of help. She put bread in the toaster, then dished yogurt into bowls and washed berries to go with it, setting things on the island as she worked.

Harmony watched closely. Charlotte Hale was a stranger, but there were clues as to what kind of woman she was. She was middle-age, with hands that were well-cared for and hair that was probably touched up but naturally that deep shade of red, since it fit so perfectly with the creamy tones of her skin. Jennifer worked at an expensive salon, and she was always pointing out things like that.

Charlotte was probably around the age of Harmony's own mother, but she looked much younger because she had time and money to take care of herself, and a belief that she had the right, something Harmony's own mother lacked. She was probably from somewhere in the South, although Harmony guessed her educated drawl hadn't come from here, but perhaps from someplace less "mountain," like Atlanta or Charlotte. The latter would even explain her name. She moved with grace, but slowly, as if she wasn't certain her body was up to the tasks she'd set for it this morning.

She was clearly rich. Unless she was the housekeeper for the real owner. Harmony smiled, because she was pretty sure that was not the case.

Charlotte closed the refrigerator. "Would you like to eat here? In the breakfast room?"

"Here's great," Harmony said. Her stomach was rumbling now, and the breakfast looked perfect.

"Oh, good. My choice, too." Charlotte slid everything closer to her guest, and motioned for her to take a plate and dish up.

"When we finish, I'll leave," Harmony said, in case that hadn't been clear. "And I'll find a way back to my car. You don't have to worry. Jennifer can —"

"There's no hurry. Unless you have an early shift at Cuppa?"

"No, I go on at four. I just need to go back to Jennifer's and change clothes before I go in." Harmony dug into her breakfast, which couldn't have tasted better.

"This is none of my business . . ." Charlotte had settled beside her and was dishing berries over a small dollop of yogurt as she spoke.

"You want to know about the baby, right?"

"Only what you want to tell me."

Harmony wondered if Charlotte was part of one of those organizations that made it their mission to talk girls like Harmony out of abortion. She wondered if that was why Charlotte had invited her here, because she had guessed Harmony was pregnant and possibly alone.

That all made sense, although Charlotte

wasn't pushy, the way Harmony had imagined someone with that agenda would be. Somehow it didn't really fit, because she didn't seem to be selling anything.

"I wasn't planning to get pregnant," Harmony said. "I was pretty careful. I guess pretty careful wasn't careful enough."

"I've been there. I understand."

Harmony thought maybe there was a sisterhood of "pretty careful" women who had been faced with decisions like hers. She was afraid to ask Charlotte's story, although she wished she knew.

"Davis doesn't know. I haven't told him yet."

"I'm sure you have a good reason."

Harmony found herself relaxing again. "I guess I don't want him telling me what to do. He likes to do that. When I lived with him, I let him. His place, his rules. But all my life, other people have told me what I should do, and now, well, I need to figure this out myself. Because this baby won't matter nearly as much to anybody else as it will to me. So that means I have to be the one to decide things."

"That makes sense to me, although you sound pretty certain the baby won't matter as much to Davis."

"He doesn't like children."

"So you're pretty sure what he'll say when you tell him?"

"He won't be happy."

Charlotte reached over and rested her hand on Harmony's. "There's good news. He can't make you do anything you don't want. Nobody can."

"It's just . . . well, it's just going to be a little crazy for a while. I just have some hard thinking to do."

"Right. Without interference."

Harmony was glad to hear those last two words. "I've been thinking about making a list. You know, of things I need to do and things to decide. Maybe then I could figure them out faster. Check things off . . ."

Charlotte passed the plate of toast, and Harmony gladly took another piece. The bread was wonderful, and Charlotte had put real butter on it. She tried to remember the last time she'd had real butter on toast. Davis had insisted on olive oil spread because he wanted to live forever.

"What's going to be at the top of the list?" Charlotte asked. "Have you gotten that far?"

"Finding a place to live."

"Sounds like you have definite priorities."

"That's number one, for sure. I've still got to save up a little more, even if Jennifer and I get a place together. I've been working extra shifts, and I saved some money when I lived with Davis, but then I had car problems, and there was a month when Cuppa closed down while they finished the renovations." Harmony wondered why she was telling Charlotte all this, and decided it was because Charlotte was listening. She couldn't remember the last time anybody had really listened to her.

"I like the way you think," Charlotte said. "You've got important decisions, but I'm guessing you want to be settled before you get too much further."

"I need a better job, too. Something with regular hours and insurance. The baby deserves that. And once I have to pay for child care . . ." Harmony shook her head. "But one step at a time, right?"

"I imagine this is scary, isn't it?"

"Sometimes."

"May I tell you a story?"

As nice as it had been to have somebody listen to her, Harmony was glad to be out of the spotlight. "About you?"

"About me, yes. Because when it's finished, I'm going to tell you that the guest room where you stayed last night, or any guest room in the house, is yours as long as you need time to figure things out." Charlotte held up her hand to stave off Harmony's protests. "Let me tell the story first, then we'll get back to that. Okay?"

Harmony couldn't say no. How could she refuse such a small thing, when in the past ten hours Charlotte Hale had made her feel like a whole person again?

Charlotte watched her houseguest's expressions as she recounted the story of her grandmother's funeral, the same one she'd written in her journal that morning before Harmony woke up. After finding Harmony in the car last night, that day had been very much on her mind, and sharing it with the young woman now seemed natural, although in her whole life she'd only told it to one other person.

Ethan.

"So you left home? You just drove away?" Harmony asked, after Charlotte finished.

Charlotte pulled herself back to the present and nodded gravely. "We just drove away."

"You were terrified. I know you were."

Charlotte decided not to take Harmony's comment at face value. "I'm guessing something like that may have happened to you?"

Harmony bit her bottom lip. Then she nodded. "I left home, just like you. I . . . I couldn't stay. My father didn't drink, but he's not a nice man."

Charlotte sat quietly and waited, but Harmony didn't go on, so she said, "A bad father should make us appreciate the good men in our lives when we find them, but we're not always able to without practice."

"Sometimes I still believe the things my father said about me."

"If I had to guess, I'd say you're reconsidering them."

Harmony smiled a little. "What happened next? After you got to town?"

"It was pretty awful." Charlotte glanced out the window at the expansive lawn stretching away from the house, at the dogwoods in bloom, the magnolias in bud. She hadn't gotten this far in her journal, and it was hard to find the right words. It had been awful. She still felt a stab of fear when she thought about it, even though she had worked so hard in the intervening years to put that day behind her.

"I didn't know anybody. I didn't have any place to go." She turned back to Harmony. "Was it that way for you when you arrived?"

"I had a friend from middle school who had moved here. That's why I chose Asheville. Her family gave me a place to stay for the summer, but they're gone now, living in California. Still, they helped me get on my feet, find a job and car, make some new friends. . . .”

Charlotte didn’t point out that Harmony’s security net was still full of rips and tears. No one knew that better than the girl herself.

“I had a little money,” Charlotte said, “but not much. What the preacher gave me, the little my grandmother had been able to save. It was late by the time we got to town. Bill and Zettie took me to a cheap hotel, and they paid for a week, even though I hated that, because I knew they couldn’t afford it. They told me to call if I couldn’t find a job or a place to live, and they would come and get me. But I knew if they did, I’d never come down from the mountains again, that I’d never find a different path.”

“You must have found one,” Harmony said, looking around, because Charlotte’s house spoke for itself.

“It was the end of the week, and I had one more night at the hotel. I’d walked everywhere, talked to everybody. I bought a loaf of bread and a jar of peanut butter on sale, and that’s what I ate every day until it was gone, then I bought more. Nobody wanted me. Nobody needed me. I didn’t have any experience. I didn’t have the right kind of clothes. I was desperate, but what does that mean?" She looked at Harmony. "Call the preacher or the Johnstons and admit I'd failed? Rob a bank?"

The last got a smile out of Harmony. "It kind of looks like you did," she said. "That would explain things."

Charlotte was glad her story was helping, and telling it was easier than she'd expected. "I was sitting in a café, reading the paper, hoping I'd missed something, some job I could apply for, some lead, anything at all. Two women came in and sat next to me, and ordered breakfast. I'd ordered the day's special. One egg, a slice of toast, a cup of coffee. Ninety-nine cents. Do you believe that price?"

"Where *is* that place?"

"Closed, I'm sorry to say. The women ordered these huge breakfasts. Bacon and sausage and French toast. I was so hungry I wanted to steal the food right off their plates." She saw that Harmony understood, and she reached over and touched her hand again. "You know, I've never told anybody that part before."

"Not everybody would get it."

Charlotte patted her hand. "I was close to tears, so I started listening to them to keep my mind off my future. One of the women was in her thirties, and I realized she was complaining about how she needed a live-in babysitter for the summer, but nobody wanted a low-paying job like that. Her friend laughed and said that maybe the problem was they didn't know what to do with two active boys. It would take somebody young and energetic. And stupid, the other woman said, and they both laughed."

"Nothing like a hard sell, huh?" Harmony said.

"So I stood up and leaned over. And I said, 'I'm not stupid, but I am looking for a job for the summer and a place to live.' They looked me over like I'd just crawled out of a tunnel. I knew I had thirty seconds to sell myself. So I told them I had references, that I was from the mountains but I had a high school diploma and, more important, that I really needed the job and the place to stay because my grandmother had just died. I said if that mother hired me, she could be sure I wasn't going to up and leave — that's how I said it — because I really didn't have any other place to go, no matter how much trouble her little boys were, and besides, I had helped my gran teach Sunday School for years, so I knew kids."

"It's like somebody put that woman in your path."

Charlotte considered that. Maybe at the

time it had felt that way, but in the years afterward she'd convinced herself that people made their own luck — probably so she could be even prouder of herself for what she had achieved.

"That's the definition of faith, isn't it? I honestly don't know whether I believe that, Harmony, but I do believe this. If life hands you an opportunity, you grab it and hold on to it the way you hold on to a child who's squirming to be set free. That's what I did. Mrs. King was never sorry, not for one moment, that she grabbed her own opportunity and hired me. I stayed with the family a couple of years, and by the time they moved away, I wasn't afraid anymore. I knew I could make it, and I did."

"Lottie Lou?"

Charlotte felt herself smiling. "My mother's idea, and I'll tell you a secret. It's not even a nickname. It's the name that was right there on my birth certificate. I changed it legally the moment I had the money to do it, but Charlotte Louise Hale is a fraud."

"Never a fraud. You're a kind woman. And all this, this part of your past? That's why you're offering me a place to stay?"

Charlotte thought of all the reasons why she had offered, so many more than she could tell the young woman. She had already made herself uncharacteristically vulnerable, and that was enough for one day.

"That's the reason," she said. "Because I know what it's like to need a safe place to get back on your feet. I was homeless. I know what it feels like to worry about where you'll sleep and whether you'll be safe. I wanted you to know that I really do understand."

"Wow." Harmony's eyes filled with tears. "But that woman at the restaurant gave you a *job,* Charlotte."

"Harmony, you have a job. You don't need another one."

"No, you worked for what you got. I'd just be living here and taking up space." She brightened. "I could cook for you. And clean."

Charlotte saw that earning her way made all the difference to Harmony. "I have a housekeeper who comes in part-time to clean, but she doesn't cook. Do you like to cook?"

"I love to when my stomach cooperates. But I'm a vegetarian. I don't cook meat. And I'll have to fix things early in the day if I'm working the dinner shift. Would that be okay?"

"Better than okay. I have a small appetite, so I won't need anything fancy. And I'll pay for all the groceries."

"May I do the shopping? You can tell me what you like, and I'll make sure we have it in the house."

Charlotte reached over and held out her hand, palm up. "That would be such a big help."

Harmony slapped the outstretched hand with her own. "You've turned things around to make me feel better about this. We both know *you're* helping *me.*"

"Trust me when I say it's mutual, okay?"

"What could you need that you don't have already?"

Charlotte tried to smile. What did she need? A thousand "first days" to fix all the mistakes she had made? Her daughter and granddaughter safe in her arms? A chance to tell Ethan she was sorry she had so easily discounted the life they had shared?

"I'll get back to you on that," she said. "For now? A friend and a cook."

"May I look around the kitchen? You know, to see what's here?"

"I'm officially turning it over to you."

Harmony looked as if Charlotte had just given her a present. "You won't be sorry."

Charlotte wasn't sure about much in her life, but she was sure she wouldn't be sorry she had made this offer. No matter how it turned out, what did she have to lose?

Chapter Nine

If Analiese had one complaint about the Church of the Covenant, it was the migraine-producing administrative tasks that fell to her. The meetings, the committees, the pledge campaigns, even her association with Covenant Academy, the private school affiliated with the church. On the day that she had heard the call to ministry she had envisioned a different life, filled with prayer and the spiritual needs of her flock. Instead, too often she combed through budgets, fiddled with mission statements, coordinated volunteers and staff alike. Even their competent church administrator couldn't save her from the worst of it.

During her first week she had realized she would burn out quickly if she allowed her days to be swallowed by paperwork. So she'd made rules. Except for emergencies, Thursdays were devoted to the Sunday service, the sermon and liturgy, and whatever research they required. Fridays were devoted to pastoral calls and counseling.

Usually Fridays were her favorite day of the week, but today she awakened with a vague feeling of dread.

She made two hospital visits before stopping for sandwiches downtown with the new chairman of the finance committee. The young CPA had recently gotten a divorce, and instead of budgets and endowments, they talked about how well he was coping. Well enough, she decided, when he admitted his biggest concern had been who would get custody of their collie. Analiese hoped he would wait a few years before he tried married life a second time, but she was glad he'd ended up with the dog, if not the wife.

After he left to go back to work, the afternoon stretched in front of her. She had two counseling appointments in the early evening and plenty to do at church. But she had one more person to see before she went back to the relative peace of her office.

A vision of Charlotte Hale sitting in the chapel had nagged at her since yesterday. It had bothered her all through Minnie Marlborough's funeral and later that night at the monthly council meeting. When she got out of bed this morning, she had realized she had to see Charlotte again.

She didn't want to call her at Falconview or meet her there. She had been to the Falconview headquarters once on church business. There was nothing wrong with the modern office building on Hendersonville Road, with its sleek surfaces and smoky glass windows, except that words seemed to echo and disappear in Charlotte's office. At the time she had wondered if that was intentional. After all, Charlotte was not particularly fond of listening to anyone else.

Now she pulled out her cell phone and called Charlotte at home to leave a message. She planned to ask if she could drop by that evening. Instead, she got Charlotte on the first ring. She was so surprised it took her seconds to form a different plan.

"I'm sorry," she said. "I thought I'd be leaving a message. I was calling to see if I could stop by for a visit this evening, but if you're home now and up for it . . . ?"

Charlotte sounded weary, but she told Analiese to come ahead.

Half an hour later she pulled up in front of Charlotte's house. Sitting in her car and reluctant to go inside, she looked over the serene landscape. She'd been here several times, and it never ceased to amaze her that one woman lived alone in a house that was large enough for three generations.

Several years ago Charlotte had volunteered this house for a mission fundraiser, and a hundred people had fit so easily inside and around the light-bedecked swimming pool that Analiese had been sorry the committee hadn't tried to accommodate twice as many.

The fundraiser had gone off without a hitch, organized down to the final slice of cheesecake by Charlotte herself. It had all been so perfect, but no one had lingered, or talked too loudly, or eaten more than his share. No one had taken off pumps or wingtips, rolled up hems and dangled feet in the twinkling turquoise pool. By ten the caterers had disappeared, and Analiese and the others had gone home, oddly sober despite an abundance of fine wine and a bartender with unlimited abilities.

She wasn't sure what she was going to say. *I'm sorry I snapped at you when you were trying to make amends? I can't shake the feeling you might need to talk and I might need to listen? I'm worried about you even though you're a woman who discourages such a thing?*

Without a firm plan she got out of the car and walked to the front door. Sometimes it was just best to see what was needed. Anyway, it was entirely possible that Charlotte would politely and firmly boot her back out the door before she had a chance to probe.

She rang the bell and listened to the electronic Westminster chimes resonate through the foyer and up the curving staircase. Charlotte took her time, but she answered the door herself. She opened it and stood back to let Analiese inside. She wasn't smiling, but she didn't look as if she regretted the intrusion.

"I have iced tea," she said. "And juice. Why don't we get something to drink and sit out by the pool? It's turned into a beautiful day, hasn't it?"

Analiese agreed but asked for iced water instead. In a few minutes they were sitting on a flagstone patio with the kidney-shaped pool sparkling just beyond them.

"Is this how you get your exercise?" Analiese asked. "With the weather getting warmer, swimming must be something to look forward to."

Charlotte played with her glass of tea, rubbing the accumulating moisture with her palms. "I hate to say this, but I almost never use it. I used to swim every single day when I moved in, but over the years . . . ?" She shrugged.

Swimming was a communal activity for

Analiese. She couldn't remember ever being in a pool alone, and she wondered if that bothered Charlotte, too.

"How did the memorial service go?" Charlotte asked, before Analiese could think of a way to say what she needed to.

"The best services leave people feeling better because they can start to put the life and death in perspective. I think we began that yesterday. The stories about Minnie went on almost an hour. There was a lot of laughter. That's always good."

"I never met her."

"I didn't think you had."

"When Falconview realized we had to have her property, I sent other people out to talk to her. They brought back reports. They did all the legwork. I only saw the house once, just before it was torn down. I never saw . . ." She shook her head, staring at the pool. "Do you ever look back at your life and wonder how you could have been so wrong when you were so sure at the time you were right?"

Analiese didn't know what to say. She had known Charlotte Hale for nearly a decade, but this was *not* the same woman.

She realized something personal was called for. "You know I used to be in television news? I can't tell you the number of times I pushed people to reveal something on the air that I knew would come back to haunt them. I told myself the public had a right to know the truth. That's what we always told ourselves, but when I look back on it now? It doesn't seem to help."

"You're being kind."

"I'm being truthful."

"I have so many regrets."

Analiese felt as if she'd stepped into another dimension.

Charlotte turned to look at her and saw her confusion. "And now you're wondering if Charlotte Hale's been the victim of body snatchers."

"No, I'm thinking that I'm glad I'm sitting here with you. Being here today won't be one of the things *I* regret."

Charlotte sighed. "I'm dying."

For a moment Analiese wasn't sure she'd heard her right. She leaned forward and rested her fingertips on Charlotte's arms. "What do you mean?"

"Maybe I'm being dramatic. I have leukemia, an acute form, which means the news is very rarely good. I got sick a couple of months ago — in fact, I nearly died. The doctors say it's still theoretically possible I won't die at all. Not from leukemia, anyway. But even the most optimistic say it would have improved my chances to make an earlier diagnosis. I let myself get right to the point of no return because I was too busy to pay attention to the way I felt. Too busy changing the Buncombe County landscape. Too busy making money and trying to get the world to see things my way." She smiled a little. "Too busy to wonder why I never recovered from what I thought was a drawn-out winter cold."

"I am so sorry."

"You and me both."

"But you could beat it?"

"I did a serious round of chemo at Duke and I'm in remission, waiting for my strength to improve and my counts to go up high enough to start the next phase. But while the bone marrow looks good, the counts don't, so my doctors are being cautious."

"How did you pull this off without people knowing?"

"I told anyone who mattered that I was in Europe with a group of investors, then off to Saint Martin on a well-deserved vacation. Trust me, chemo was no vacation." She touched the top of her head. "I didn't lose too much of my hair, so that was a bonus, and I could afford a good haircut and products galore to make it look thicker.

I'm trying to gain back some weight."

"Why didn't you tell me *then?* Was there somebody . . . ?"

"To help? No, you're the first person I've told, and maybe the only one for a while. The last thing I want is anybody to feel sorry for me. I don't want anybody trying to be nice because they don't want to feel guilty when I die."

Analiese already felt this secret weighing her down. All the things she knew that might help wouldn't, not unless Charlotte was willing to let people know she needed their support.

"Why are you telling *me?*" she asked at last.

Charlotte laughed a little, and to Analiese the sound seemed real, not a bit forced. "You mean you don't think I need you to absolve me of all my sins?"

Analiese smiled in response. "I would, if that were in my power."

"I know. You take your job very seriously."

"I'm afraid it's a serious job."

"Especially at moments like this one."

"Not my favorite part."

"Do you feel burdened?"

"Who's helping whom?"

Charlotte was quiet for a moment, as if she needed to put her words in order. "You know, if you were some kindly older man, with thirty years of ministry behind you and a beatific smile —"

"This would be easier," Analiese finished for her.

"That's actually not what I was going to say. No, I was going to say this would be impossible."

"Really?"

"Here's the truth, and I've given it a lot of thought. No matter our differences, I know I can trust you. And I know you're going to give helping me your best shot. You're going to be sensible and thorough, and you're going to dig deeper than somebody who thinks he has all the answers at his fingertips because he's too tired to look for more."

"That may be the nicest thing anyone's ever said about my ministry."

"And now you're waiting for the punch line."

"Something like that."

Charlotte set her glass on the table and wiped her hands against her beige capris. "I should die more often. It makes for great repartee."

"I'd rather you didn't."

"I think you mean that."

"I think so, too."

Charlotte was silent again, and Analiese

sat quietly.

"I said I have a lot of regrets," Charlotte began at last. "Here's one of my biggest. When I heard the diagnosis, in the moments right before I zoomed off to Durham? I felt such a rush of relief." She had been looking out at the pool, but now she turned. "Even though I was terrified, I thought, 'It will be good to die and get this over with.' "

Analiese realized her concern must have shown, because Charlotte hurried on.

"I would never, never take my own life. You have to understand that. But when I realized living a long full life was probably out of my hands? I just wanted to close my eyes and wait for the end. My grandmother used to tell me death was the last mountain we have to climb, and just before she died, she opened her eyes and looked toward the window in her bedroom as if she were viewing a miracle."

"That must be a good memory."

"When the doctor told me my diagnosis? I thought about that day and about the look on her face, and I found myself hoping that she hadn't really been looking at the gates of heaven, that there really wasn't anything waiting for any of us except eternal sleep. That's when I realized what a loss my life has been."

When she didn't know what to say, Analiese knew not to say a thing. She was almost certain this was *not* the moment for reassurance, although it felt wrong not to give it.

"I have to change things," Charlotte said at last. "I realize whatever time I've been given, whether it's months or years, I can't die knowing I've made so many mistakes and never tried hard enough to set them right. I realize dying's not about what comes next, because no matter how great or poor our faith, we really can't know what's waiting, or at least *I* can't. For me it's about what came before. The impact we had. The love we gave. The hearts we left intact . . ." She cleared her throat, and her eyes filled with tears. "Or broken."

"I hope you aren't saying that you've done nothing important with your life until now. Because you've given generously in many ways."

"Too often for the wrong reasons." Charlotte held up her hand to stop Analiese from continuing. "I realize nothing's that cut and dried. I've done things because I knew they were important and right, and sometimes they were. But I've done so many things that seemed right and were terribly, terribly wrong. Like moving poor Minnie off her land. And here's how I know. When I found out I was dying, I realized there wasn't one person in the world who would really care. That I've lived fifty-two years, and while some people will feel conflicted, or even a little bit sad, no one will really miss me. Not because people are cruel, but because I haven't given them a reason to."

Analiese would have given almost anything to be able to contradict her, but not only wasn't that the right approach, she was afraid what Charlotte had just said was true.

Who would miss Charlotte at the Church of the Covenant? The council and committee members whose opinions she had too often ignored or overlooked? The staff who winced whenever she approached with a new list of jobs or, worse, helpful advice on how to do their present ones?

And what about the rest of Charlotte's contacts? She was said to have an iron grip at Falconview, with an annual exodus of staff who fell out of favor or disagreed with her one time too many. She'd served on boards all over town, but despite the advantages she brought of insight, financial support and prestige, she routinely tried the patience of administrators and board members alike.

Then, of course, there was her family, who

were never mentioned, despite the fact that they lived right here in Asheville.

"Why haven't you?" Analiese asked. "Why *haven't* you allowed anybody to get close?"

"That would take longer to tell than we have now."

"But it sounds like you understand, at least a little?"

"I had nothing but time when I was hooked up to those IVs at Duke. Everybody should be shut up alone in a room for weeks, with nothing to do but reconsider their lives."

"And it wouldn't hurt to have an actual death sentence to urge them on."

"It's quite the motivator."

Analiese felt for the right words. "I admire you. I admire *this* — this desire to set things right, to reevaluate, even though your life could be nearing its end. But, Charlotte, are you trying to make a bargain with God?"

"No, I think God's better than that."

"This is a lot to admit to, especially to someone you've butted heads with in the past."

"That's what makes you perfect, Analiese. Because if you ever had anything to lose by being honest with me, you've lost it already. So I think I can count on you to continue being honest, to pull me up short if I go off half-cocked, to help me live out whatever time is left in a way that won't come back to haunt me on my deathbed. That's what frightens me most. That one day in the not so distant future I'll have only moments to look back on my life and nothing I'll see will give me comfort."

Charlotte leaned closer. "I know I'm asking a lot, more than I should. You've probably already guessed one thing I want to try to set right before I die."

"Minnie? You tried to give me money for the animal shelter. . . ."

"When I got home that night I wrote a check in her honor and sent it off, anyway. But you were right, that's not what *she* would have done. It's a worthy cause, and I'm glad I did it, but she would have acted in a way that mattered personally, reached out without thinking about the consequences. So I'll be looking for more ways to do that myself. To honor her."

Analiese took Charlotte's hands. It felt natural, although before today she could not have imagined touching Charlotte Hale spontaneously and with affection. "Do you want me to look for ways to help?"

"I don't think so. Not yet, anyway. I think I'll know the right things when I see them. I just wanted someone to know what I'm feeling. And I guess I just needed to say this out loud."

Analiese nodded, but she gripped Charlotte's hands a little tighter and felt them soften in hers. "What else can I do?"

"Will you let me tell you about my daughter?"

Chapter Ten

First Day Journal: April 30

Each day at the park is like a human lifetime. Early in the morning everything sparkles with promise. Dew glistens on blades of grass; the sidewalks are empty pages sneakered feet have yet to write on. The air is still, as if a puff of breath from an angel's lips is needed to set the day in motion.

As morning progresses, the park begins to waken. Birds sing on branches, and young lovers walk hand in hand. On benches like mine, coffee's consumed, newspapers unfolded, cell phones pulled from pockets for casual conversations. Two mothers push strollers and chat. The sun peeks through the leafy canopy.

By afternoon balls whiz through the air and children shout commands. On the playground, mothers keep careful eyes on preschoolers who beg to swing higher. The climbing dome becomes a spaceship, the monkey bars an obstacle course over teeming pools of barracuda. The sun beats down on baseball caps and the open pages of books.

When evening comes, stragglers take their time departing, as if sorry to move on to other things. Some scoop up trash and toss it in bins. Others scuff feet in newly planted grass, as if making sure to leave their mark. Darkness is kept at bay by strategically placed lights.

In this way only is a day at the park different from a lifetime. No one and nothing can keep our darkness at bay, no matter how hard we try. I learned this in the hospital from a woman named Gwen, a powerful and uninvited lesson that haunts every step I take.

It's morning now, and I've been waiting an hour. Maddie isn't here, although she often comes to the park on Saturdays. I wonder how many friends she has. Are other children frightened of her seizures? Do they shun her to avoid the possibility of witnessing one?

Edna is here with her mother, who is typing on her laptop from a bench closer to the jungle gym. Her mother's name is Samantha, and I came here for days before I realized exactly who she was. I knew her when she was a teenager. That this eluded me so long is a surprise, because Samantha is striking enough that even more than a decade later, I should have known her immediately.

In fairness to me, the girl I knew always carried herself as if she was spoiling for a fight. The woman smiles and moves with extraordinary grace. She laughs easily and clearly adores her daughter. She doesn't seem to be watching Edna and her friends, but I know from watching her that she's always aware. The transformation is so complete that I wonder what brought it about.

I wonder, too, about Samantha's mother, Georgia Ferguson, once the Covenant Academy headmistress, where Taylor and Samantha, even Jeremy, Maddie's father, went to school.

At the end of an hour Samantha gets up and approaches me. There's no place to go without drawing attention, so I look away. She stops in front of me until I'm forced to glance up.

"She's not coming today," she says.

I don't pretend not to understand. Instead, I thank her, and she nods and motions for Edna, who reluctantly follows her up the hill.

I wonder how long she's known that I come here to watch my granddaughter. I wonder why she, of all people, cares enough not to expose that secret to my daughter. She hasn't told Taylor, or I'm sure I would know. Although we haven't spoken in years, Taylor would find and confront me.

My visit to the park has ended in disappointment, but I think I've discovered a friend, even though I don't deserve her.

CHAPTER ELEVEN

After leaving the park, Charlotte found herself driving aimlessly before she thought about where to go. Since she had instinctively headed toward town, she parked near the center and stopped by the City Market, something she hadn't done in years.

After a cup of coffee and some self-scrutiny, she wandered through the stalls, buying a pound of fresh red pepper linguine she knew Harmony would like, along with honey and eggs. The last vendor was selling woven baskets, and on impulse she bought one and filled it with another vendor's fragrant handmade soaps, which bore romantic names like Moon Lady's Ocean and Ginger Grass and Silk. She was glad she had come, because she knew exactly who to give the basket to, if she dared.

She pulled out her cell phone and got Samantha's address by calling Falconview and asking the receptionist to scout directories.

Five minutes later she was on her way.

Ten minutes after that she pulled up to a tiny brick cottage not far from the street where Taylor lived. The house was substantially smaller than those around it, with a front yard gobbled up by a circular driveway and what looked like a complete absence of yard in the back. Now Charlotte understood why Samantha and Edna spent so much time at the park.

A yellow Volkswagen was parked in the driveway, and Charlotte thought she'd probably found them at home. Before she could think too hard, she took a deep breath, tucked the basket under an arm and made her way to the front door to ring the bell. Laughter spilled out through open windows, and in a moment Edna answered the door.

"I've seen you at the park," she said in greeting.

"Yes, you have," Charlotte said. "My name's Charlotte." Up close the child was even prettier than she'd expected, but of course, her mother was stunning. Edna had green eyes set off by her coffee-and-cream skin, and her shining black hair fell in curls to just above her shoulders. Tiny hoops adorned her earlobes, and her smile was beyond magnificent.

"I brought your mother a present," Charlotte said, "but I bet you'll enjoy it, too." She handed the basket to Edna, who rummaged through, picking up the first bar of soap to sniff it.

"This smells good!"

"I liked it, too."

"Mom?" Edna shouted. Samantha, who probably could have heard a whisper in the tiny house, came out wiping her hands on a dishtowel. She stopped when she saw who their visitor was, then she smiled.

"Come in, Charlotte."

Edna ran over to show her the basket, while a relieved Charlotte stepped inside and closed the door behind her.

"This is lovely," Samantha said. "Edna, why don't you put the basket in the bathroom? And choose a soap you'd like for your bath tonight."

Edna turned, basket in hand. "Thank you," she told Charlotte. Then she took off.

"Thank you from me, as well," Samantha said. "But you know —"

"That I didn't have to do it?" Charlotte found herself relaxing. "I know, but I wanted to. I think you've gone out on a limb for me, and for no good reason I can think of."

"Except that I understand how much you probably wish you could know Maddie.

Come sit down. Iced tea or hot?"

"Whatever's easiest."

Charlotte made herself at home on a comfortable slipcovered sofa and took a glass of iced tea when Samantha returned with a tray. She added lemon and a packet of sugar before she spoke.

"I think I've put you in an awkward situation. I take it you and Taylor are friends? And you haven't told her about seeing me at the park?"

"We've been friends since the Academy. Of course she was younger than I was, but a kindred spirit. Neither of us was comfortable there. Now, of course, we have daughters in common."

"I love watching Edna at the park. She's quite a diplomat, in the best possible way."

"I only recognized you last week. How long have you been coming?"

"At first just on and off. Then . . . Well, a lot recently."

"I haven't told Taylor."

Charlotte wasn't surprised, given Samantha's kindness so far. "I want to talk to her, Samantha. Do you think she might listen?"

Samantha was silent for a long time. Charlotte watched as she doctored her tea. She wore a purple T-shirt with sequins sprinkled over swirls of violet, and denim shorts that showcased her long legs. Her movements as she lifted the cup, added sugar and lemon, were like waves in a gentle ocean. Charlotte understood why Edna was so graceful.

"I don't think she will," Samantha said at last. "And I'm *sure* it won't help to have anyone else plead your case."

"I would never ask you to do that, but this can't go on. Nobody should have to keep secrets for me. I never meant to involve anybody else."

"You must feel so frustrated."

"That's the least I deserve."

Samantha was silent, and Charlotte was glad the younger woman didn't deny it or make excuses for her.

"This has gone on so long, this trouble between the two of you," Samantha said at last. "I know time can heal, but sometimes it can magnify pain. I'm afraid that's what's happened with this."

"Do you have a suggestion?"

"Did you know they're back to square one on medication for Maddie's seizures? That's why she wasn't at the park today. So this is a stressful time for Taylor. Maybe not the best moment to pop back into her life."

Charlotte wanted every detail, but she knew she had no right to information. Still, she had to ask. "I appreciate the warning, but is there anything at all you can you tell me about Maddie's condition? Without feeling like you're betraying Taylor?"

"You probably already know she has temporal lobe epilepsy and they're on a roller coaster ride. They're looking for the perfect combination of medications to halt the seizures, but from the reading I've done in my nursing journals, I'm not sure it's that easy. Taylor and her doctor are determined, though."

"You're a nurse, Samantha?"

"Sam. I just got my dream job at Mountain Medical. The clinic over on Martin Luther King? I'm the nursing supervisor in charge of the Child and Maternal Wellness program."

Charlotte congratulated her as she filed away that information for Harmony. "So you're not sure a perfect combination of medications is just a matter of trial and error?"

"Maybe, but often if a child doesn't respond well to one combination, it means there's a good chance that trend will continue."

"That doesn't sound promising."

"Taylor's sure they'll beat the odds."

"How frustrated she must feel. I can only imagine." And it was true, because that was all she was *able* to do. Imagine. Worry. Wallow in regret.

"Maddie's a wonderful little girl, well-adjusted, happy. . . ."

Samantha had been surprisingly forthcoming, but Charlotte suspected Taylor's friend wouldn't be comfortable offering more detail. Once upon a time she wouldn't have let that stop her, but that was then.

She bit her lip, trying to figure out how best to change the subject to one that was just as difficult. Finally, she simply did.

"You actually have a couple of reasons to dislike me. One is Taylor. The other's . . ." She paused for a moment, and Samantha filled in the blank.

"My mother?"

Charlotte nodded.

"People change."

Charlotte waited, but Samantha didn't go on.

"They do," Charlotte said tentatively. "But sometimes it takes a long time."

"Taylor's probably my best friend. We have a lot in common, but that's one way we differ. Second chances? Well, she's not big on them, and you should know that. I can look back at my own life, at who I was and who I am now, and I can say, yeah, people change and here I am, a prime example. I came this close to destroying my own life." She held her index finger and thumb so close together it looked as if they were touching.

"I know you had a hard time in high school."

"If only it were that simple." Samantha smiled easily and did so again. "I drank. A lot. I partied all the time. You probably know that."

"Just the basics."

"Short of chaining me to the bed frame, my mother tried everything to control me. Then one night I got out of the house and into a car with a guy I hardly knew. We went to a kegger out in the country, and halfway home I decided to drive because he came close to passing out at the wheel. Of course I was in no shape to drive, either, and the car was weaving back and forth. I thought it was hilarious. A cop spotted us. I thought I'd see if I could lose him, so we had a ten-mile race up and down mountains until I ran off the road into a ditch and nearly killed us both."

Charlotte also remembered what had come next. "And after that, I used your arrest to convince the other board members at Covenant Academy to fire your mother as headmistress."

"I think you said if Mom couldn't control me, then she couldn't control anyone else's children."

Charlotte didn't point out how poorly she had later controlled her own daughter. They both knew.

This time Samantha didn't smile, but she spoke matter-of-factly, as if what she had to say had been said many times, in many crowded rooms, with many listeners.

"And the thing is? As awful as it was, Mom being fired was probably the thing that saved me. Because when I recovered enough to see what my actions had done to her, that she'd lost her job and maybe even her standing in the community because of my selfishness, then I began to figure out that I had to clean up my act. That and the courts, a great probation officer, AA, of course, and later, Edna. They all brought me back to earth. Oh, and the real threat of prison if I messed up again."

Charlotte didn't know what to feel, because even if firing Samantha's mother had resulted in unintended positive consequences, it still had been terribly wrong.

"You were young, a mixed-up kid. I was an adult, and I had no excuse. Your mother and I never saw eye to eye on the way she ran the Academy. She wanted the students to have more freedom and control, and I just wanted her out of there. I used your personal tragedy to make that happen. You have no idea how much I wish I hadn't."

"I have to say, this is weird. I know people change, but I honestly never envisioned us having this conversation. I'm sure Mom never did, either."

Charlotte leaned forward and told her the truth, because what would be the point of pretending now? "Taylor learned to hold grudges by watching *me.* Do you know how much space they take up in your heart? When you let go of your grudges, you're practically empty inside."

"So you go looking for something else to fill the space. And I think you want your granddaughter and your daughter right here." Samantha touched her chest with her fingertips.

Charlotte felt a lump growing in her throat. "I'm not sure it can happen. I think maybe I stepped over that line, the one that you didn't. You pulled yourself back from your personal precipice, Sam. I may have fallen over mine."

"Don't quit five minutes before the miracle."

Charlotte tilted her head in question.

"I learned that in AA," Samantha said.

"You have to keep trying, because if you stop, you might miss something extraordinary, something that's right around the corner. I think you're going to have to find your way to Taylor by yourself, Charlotte, because you're the only one who can recognize the right way to turn when you see it. But I promise, I'll be rooting for both of you."

Charlotte wasn't sure of much, but she *was* sure this extraordinary young woman meant every word she said.

Not only was Saturday Harmony's only day off, it was also payday. While she made most of her income in tips, the small checks were a nice addition. She immediately put them in the bank, and eventually she hoped to have enough to rent her own apartment. While she hoped she and Jennifer could share quarters once the other woman's lease ran out, she was no longer counting on it. Jennifer didn't know Harmony was pregnant, and noisy nights with a screaming baby wouldn't be much of an attraction for a roommate. Harmony needed to find something she could afford by herself, and with the expense of child care, the tally was going up and up.

Today the worst of that weight was off her

shoulders. She was going to pick up all her belongings at Jennifer's and move them to Charlotte's house. She had toured the upstairs that morning and settled on a room at the far end of the house.

The room, which had a luxurious connecting bath, was airy, with half a dozen windows, and she could hear the fountain in the swimming pool when she opened them. Best of all, the bedroom wasn't downstairs, where she would be constantly underfoot. She liked the butter-colored walls and the embroidered white bedspread over pale lilac sheets. She liked the Van Gogh–style watercolors of sunflower fields and lavender. From her mother she'd learned to tat, and she thought she could afford enough thread to edge the pillowcases with handmade lace as a thank-you gift when she moved on.

She wondered what she had ever done to receive such a gift herself. To have a wonderful room where she could rest, save and prepare for the future was almost beyond imagination. Today, after she picked up her check and her belongings, she was going to shop for dinner with the crisp twenty-dollar bills Charlotte had given her.

She remembered that her benefactor had ordered the eggplant provolone pizza at

Cuppa. She thought Ray, the chef, might give her the recipe so she could make it tonight as a surprise. Charlotte's kitchen had everything, including vented pizza pans that still had the stickers on them. She was going to have such fun.

She parked down the street from Cuppa and smiled at the customers sitting at outside tables. Inside she spotted Ray talking to Stella, her manager. Unfortunately, halfway across the room, on the way to join in their conversation, she also spotted Davis. Or rather he spotted her, because suddenly he was right there, his lanky body blocking her progress.

"Hey," he said.

Her ebullient mood vanished. Almost immediately her stomach dived for her toes, giving credence to her theory that stress magnified morning sickness times two.

"What are you doing here?" she asked.

"What do you think? I came to find you. I know you always pick up your check on Saturday mornings."

"Should I be impressed? It's not exactly remembering to be faithful, but it's something."

"Harmony . . ." He shook his head. "Please don't be sarcastic."

She felt the sting, but she thrust her

shoulders back. "Don't make this *my* problem, Davis."

"Can we sit and talk? I'll buy you coffee, lunch, whatever you want."

It was on the tip of her tongue to blow him off, but she suppressed it. As a matter of fact, she was hungry again, and eating might actually help her roiling stomach. She wouldn't be sorry to have one of Ray's blueberry scones with a decaf latte.

A smile lit his long face when she agreed. Without a word she found a table in the corner and watched Davis step up to the coffee counter. She hoped the barista took his time on the latte. Davis was notoriously impatient, and when they'd lived together, she had always taken on situations like this one. She'd stood in line to get the food, while he sat at tables with his smartphone or his portable computer and transacted business.

Today she didn't lift a finger. Instead, with pleasure, she watched him shift his weight from foot to foot.

She hadn't expected Davis to come looking for her. The moment she'd learned he was sleeping with the new hygienist at his dentist's office, she had packed her belongings and moved to Jennifer's. A week later he had come here to Cuppa to admit that, yes, he had been having an affair, but it was actually more like a one-night stand that had gone on for a few weeks, and it was over now. He was sorry, but it really hadn't meant a thing, and Harmony should come back.

She hadn't. She knew she had very little backbone. She'd grown up in a home where a woman's role was to grovel, and while she knew that was wrong, old habits died hard. Still, there were limits. She would not tolerate physical abuse, and she would not tolerate infidelity. Or maybe she was able to hold that line because she didn't really love Davis. For a time she'd thought she did, but since moving out, she had wondered if all she'd loved were the bonuses that had come along with him. The sleek condo that she'd cleaned until it sparkled. The well-equipped kitchen that had been such fun to cook in. The soft king-size bed where their baby had been conceived.

Their baby.

She watched him lean over the counter and give the barista their order. Davis was thin but well-proportioned, wide shoulders, narrow hips, long muscular legs. And sitting here, the rear view wasn't half-bad. He kept his brown hair CPA short, and he was attractive, with his serious, bordering-onbrooding face with its prominent nose. He looked good in suits and usually wore them, although today he had on khakis and a pale blue sport shirt. Even his casual clothes were starched and ironed to perfection.

He came back to the table with a fruit salad as well as a scone and set both in front of her. "I know how much you like cantaloupe."

She nodded her thanks, and he left, to return a moment later with the largest size latte for her and orange juice for himself.

"Decaf?" she asked, then took it when he nodded.

He seated himself across from her. "How have you been?"

"Busy."

"Do you have big plans for your day?"

"I'm not planning to run for president, but I have things to do."

"I'm heading into the office in a little while."

She wondered why he thought she cared. Davis worked for one of Asheville's oldest accounting firms. His plan was to become a partner and eventually a top dog, and to that end, he scrutinized everything in his life for its possible effect on his future. He had a long list of certifications to work toward, and he put in extra hours every day just to prove he had the right stuff. No surprise he was heading into the office, unless he was heading for some other woman's bedroom.

"Are you still living with Jennifer?" he asked.

"I'm staying in Biltmore Forest."

He looked surprised. "Seriously?"

"It's temporary, but it's a lot better than Jennifer's sofa."

"What kind of room? Who's house?"

She took her spoon and began to stir her latte, beating the foam into submission. "Exactly what gives you the right to ask, Davis?"

"It's just so out of the blue. Who do you even *know* over there?"

"You mean who could somebody like me know in the poshest part of Asheville? Somebody without talents, resources, education —"

He reached over and covered her hand. "I didn't say any of those things."

"It's none of your business," she said, looking down. She wondered if he had covered her hand out of affection or because the stirring had annoyed him. Davis was easily annoyed.

"Fine." He lifted his hand. "I was worried, that's all."

"A little late, this worrying thing, wouldn't you say?"

"I made a mistake."

"You got that right."

"I know you're pissed. You have a right to be. I don't know what I could have been thinking."

"I'm not sure *thinking* had anything to do with it. You wanted something, and you went after it. End of story."

"When you moved in with me, that was a commitment. I guess I just didn't get that. I didn't see it through your eyes. I was still thinking like a single guy."

She looked up. "Thank you for breakfast. You can leave anytime."

He leaned forward. He had dark eyes and heavy brows, and he used the eyes to his advantage now, pleading soulfully. "Can we start again?"

She was pregnant with his child. Since he hadn't mentioned it, she figured he didn't suspect the truth. Whatever had possessed him to apologize and win her back was something different. Could he possibly miss her, or did he miss her attentions to his apartment, her cooking, the way she had tried so diligently not to irritate him?

"I don't think people ever really start again," she said. "We started and stopped.

A relationship is not a stalled engine. There's no road service on the highway of life."

"I've missed the way you express yourself. I've missed waking up with you."

"And the way I washed your underwear and did the grocery shopping and entertained your colleagues. I even took your cat to the vet to have him put to sleep because you were too busy."

"You volunteered because Paws was suffering. I was going to do it the next day."

He'd had meetings when the going got rough for Paws, so, sobbing, she'd taken the poor animal in by herself. She wondered what kind of father Davis would be. Would his job take precedence over a child's needs? He'd told her he didn't want kids, that he was sure he wasn't the right kind of person to have them. She was afraid he was probably right.

"So we can't start again," he said, and this time he covered both her hands, although neither one was fidgeting. "Not without some garbage behind us on that highway of life, but once we're around it, maybe we can put some distance between it and us. Can we try?"

She wanted to say no, but why, exactly? To hurt him? Possibly. Because she knew he wasn't the right guy to hook up with long term? Possibly. Because even with all the anxiety of leaving him and trying to find her way, she hadn't really missed him?

Despite all of the above, she was carrying his child, his son or daughter. And breaking all ties now made little sense. Eventually, if she continued the pregnancy, Davis would have to know, have to participate, if only to provide child support.

"What are you proposing?" she asked at last.

"We can start slow." He grinned. "We could go out on a date. I'll take you to Zambra. You love it there. We can take our time and talk over tapas. That's all, I promise. We can see how it goes, then decide what to do next."

"When were you thinking?"

"What's your next night off?"

"Tonight, but I'm busy."

"Doing what?" He held up his hand before she could reply. "I'm sorry, never mind. What's a good night for you?"

"Next Saturday."

"A whole week?"

"Anticipation is a good thing, on a par with denial."

He didn't look happy, but he nodded. He really did hate to wait. "Okay, let me know where to pick you up."

She didn't want Davis to come to Charlotte's, but she wasn't sure why. "We can meet at the restaurant."

"Thank you, Harmony. I promise things will be different."

He had no idea *how* different. She just gave him a thin smile as he stood. "I'll see you about seven on Saturday."

He bent over and, before she could stop him, kissed the top of her head. She watched him leave and tried to figure out how she felt.

Hungry, she decided, and she turned her attention back to the food in front of her.

CHAPTER TWELVE

First Day Journal: May 1

I'll confess I began this journal reluctantly. A therapist on my cancer treatment team recommended I keep one. She told me to look back at what I've done, what I've gained, what I've lost. I was supposed to find ways to say hello and ways to say goodbye.

I was certain a journal was silly. I was at Duke to be cured, not changed. When I told her that, she asked what I wanted to be cured of? My cancer? My anger? My denial that death is inevitable?

After I reluctantly agreed, she suggested I write as if I were reliving events. She said this would deepen my understanding and make them immediate once again.

Once I began, I found I couldn't stop.

The most important things are the hardest to write about. My leukemia. The weeks of treatment. Facing the truth. Taylor and Maddie.

It's past time to write about Ethan, because after seeing him at the park on Thursday, he's entered my dreams again. In dreams I'm young, and so is he. The world is standing right before us. All we have to do is reach out our hands.

As a country girl, I find adjusting to life in Asheville is anything but easy. After convincing Mrs. King to try me as her summer nanny, I move into the family's house and befriend their two active school-age boys. In the beginning the city frightens me. I have a room in the third-floor attic, and the house isn't far from the Biltmore Estate, where the boys and I hike and bike. The woods and paths remind me of home, and I spend as much time with them there as I can. At the end of the first summer, the Kings invite me to stay on in exchange for occasional babysitting and light cleaning, an arrangement that continues for years.

Grateful to be rescued once more, I quickly find a second job serving lunches at a small Biltmore Village café with clientele who tip well. More important, they're the people I want to become. Being near them is instructive, and I watch closely and practice becoming someone new.

Two summers pass, and I save enough money to attend community college part-time.

I spend what free time I have alone. I'm surrounded by men and women my age, but we're all rushing toward a better life, and we have no time to enjoy the one we share. At the same time the feeling that I'm poised on the edge of a precipice lessens. While I occasionally run into people who knew Lottie Lou Hale, most of the time I'm free to work toward a different future.

My life centers on achievement. I have so much I want to leave behind that I have little time to think about what comes next. I need money for everyday living. I need education. Respect and prestige are my goals. I never want anyone to look down on me again. I want to be in charge, to be looked up to. I want all the good things I see around me.

I don't want to stand on the outside looking in.

So important is this that I spend hours poring over plans. First community college. Then, with financial aid, one of the excellent state universities. Perhaps a degree in business, although I want more than to manage an office or shuffle papers. Nothing feels grand enough. Unlike my father, I don't want a trip down easy street, but whatever street I travel, I want my destination to be worth the journey.

I learn a lot about my new home. After our city fathers faithfully paid back all debts incurred before the Depression, our sleepy little mountain town woke up. With an economic cloud overhead, nobody had any reason to bulldoze our architectural heritage in the name of development, so almost accidentally, we now have much to offer. Retirees are stepping up the pace of their mountain moves. There's a new feeling of optimism in the air. I want to be a part of it.

In the meantime I date, but only a little. I'm afraid I might make my mother's mistake and bind my life to a worthless man. As part of my attempts to change Lottie Lou into Charlotte Louise, I study clothes and styles, hair and makeup. At work and in the Kings' home, I observe the wealthy, the way they sit and walk, their table manners and conversation, their vocal inflections and accents. I'm careful not to put on airs, as Gran would say, but slowly I leave the mountain girl behind.

During my fifth summer in Asheville, Ethan walks into my life, or rather my classroom. I've just completed my first year and a half of coursework, and the Kings have decided to move to Rhode Island.

The hours I devoted to the boys are snapped up at the café, and I make enough money to afford a sunny room in a big house in Montford. That summer I sign up for only one course, a humanities survey. The professor is enthusiastic about guest lecturers. We hear musicologists and artists, and one day we hear Ethan Graves Martin, who shows a historical slideshow of European architecture, and the way each building and site is connected to the centuries that came before.

Ethan is starting his architecture internship with a local firm, and he and my professor know each other from the lacrosse team at the University of Virginia. Ethan is twenty-six to my twenty-three, with warm brown eyes, longish brown hair with just a hint of curl and a lanky, athlete's body. The best thing about him, the thing that sets him above the ordinary, is his smile, eyes crinkling, lips turning up naturally, a smile that says everything about who he is. He clearly loves his subject, and transforms us from students marking time to participants with opinions. Ethan is mesmerizing.

I remember everything. I'm wearing a brand-new sundress I found in a consignment shop, a peachy floral with a short green jacket and green sandals. My hair is long and layered, and I wear most of it pinned on top of my head with tendrils curling around my face. It's a style I favor because it's easy.

During class Ethan focuses on me. Since there's no harm, I flirt shamelessly. At the end I'm sorry Ethan's tenure as guest lecturer is over, because I have never been this intrigued. The young professionals I meet are either on the prowl or taken. I'm never sure what to talk about with them. My present life is boring, and I don't want to share stories of my childhood. I don't know anybody who wants to talk about the things I'm learning or my hunt for a path that will bring me wealth, respect and security.

Afterward I gather my purse and notebook, and when I look up, Ethan is right there. I see his gaze drift to the ring finger on my left hand. "Not," I tell him, in answer to the unspoken question, "and don't want to be. How about you?"

Up close, his smile is even better. My heart, which has remained firmly in my chest all the years of my life, plunges to my toes. He asks me to go out for coffee. Instead, we settle on a casual breakfast the next morning.

The next morning is anything but casual, and we're in bed before noon, where Ethan introduces me to all the amazing pleasures of sex with a considerate man. I tell myself I deserve this interlude in a life filled with work and determination. As he slowly removes my clothes, piece by piece, and desire replaces honesty, I invent the lies I'll tell myself over and over in all the years that follow.

Ethan doesn't fit into my plans. He is an architect, but he wants to make a difference more than he wants to get ahead. Even then, at the fledgling beginnings of sustainable design, Ethan wants to plan and build in ways that don't harm the environment. The firm where he has just begun his internship is cutting edge. His goal is to leave behind structures that won't harm the earth, and train and encourage others to do the same.

For the first time since leaving home, I'm sidetracked. I tell myself I deserve a little happiness, and that when the differences between us become truly evident, Ethan and I will be relieved to end whatever we found together.

One thing I've learned about myself in the past months. I have always been deaf to the throbbing of the human heart. Never more than I was then.

CHAPTER THIRTEEN

Since Thursday afternoon Ethan had debated what to do about Charlotte. His first inclination had been to do nothing. He certainly hadn't wanted to report her presence at the park to Taylor. As mature as his daughter was, and as responsible, she became a child again whenever Charlotte was mentioned.

Maybe Charlotte had simply been in the neighborhood and taken a seat on a park bench to make phone calls or page through email. Wasn't it possible she had been sitting there unaware that one of the children playing on the jungle gym was her own granddaughter?

Unfortunately, there were many things he could say about his ex-wife, but never that she was clueless.

He was left with two options. Ignore what he'd seen, or gird himself for a confrontation.

By the time he woke up on Sunday morning, he had chosen the latter. If Charlotte frequently visited the park, eventually she would run into Taylor. Ethan needed to warn his ex that their daughter would react badly if she thought Charlotte was trying to establish a relationship with Maddie. He doubted Charlotte really understood the depth of Taylor's anger.

After his shower he fortified himself with a second cup of coffee and pulled on a comfortable shirt, khakis and scuffed loafers. He looked more like a workman hired to fix a sink or a roof leak than the ex-husband of one of Biltmore Forest's finest, but he wasn't trying to impress Charlotte's neighbors. Clearly he'd already proven he couldn't impress *her*.

The drive to Charlotte's house took just minutes, and he parked in front and sat for a moment, remembering.

The last time he'd been here, Charlotte had been intent on convincing him the house would solve all their problems. By then their marriage had been on the skids, their daughter verging on uncontrollable. Charlotte had been sure that buying a house in Biltmore Forest, *this* house in particular, would change their lives. She would be so much happier living in a grander home, and together they could join the country club, where they could establish even more professional contacts. Taylor would be exposed to better role models, girls with important prospects and connections.

Ethan had hated the house on sight. In his opinion it sat on the lot like a cancerous mole on the curve of a beautiful woman's hip. If he had designed a house for this lovely rolling landscape, he would have sited it for views, passive solar design and practical sustainability. He would have designed hallways and doorways to serve as part of the ventilation system. Simplicity would have been his watchword, and the result would have been elegant but not austere.

As he had silently followed her through rooms that seemed to have little purpose, he had realized, step after step, that their chance of a future together was bleak.

Finally they had stood together gazing over the swimming pool that Charlotte believed would catapult their daughter into the popular crowd at Covenant Academy, and she had turned to him. "It's our dream home, Ethan," she had said with complete sincerity.

He had gazed into her eyes and realized that at last they had reached crisis point. "I thought our dream house was supposed to be one I designed," he'd said. He had, in fact, begun designing a house in the country as a birthday surprise, although lately he hadn't been particularly inspired.

She'd had the grace to look chagrined. "I mean dream house for *now,*" she amended. "Until the day we can build up in the mountains."

In that moment he had known what he hadn't wanted to admit to himself for far too long: that he and Charlotte had never shared the same dreams and were never likely to.

They had not bought this house together. He had refused to sign papers, citing multiple factors, including its ridiculous size, and Charlotte had been crushed. After their divorce the "dream" house had come back on the market, and she had snapped it up. The house that had been too large for three was now inhabited by one.

This morning he didn't bother to look for changes. He was sure Charlotte had made them. After all, she was a woman who put her stamp on everything she touched. For all he knew she'd added a wing so she could have more empty rooms to rattle around in, or a second pool so she could choose where to swim during those rare moments when she had time.

He got out and slammed the door of his SUV with unnecessary force. He still wasn't sure how he was going to broach what he had to say. Asheville was a small enough city that he and Charlotte had been in the same room more than once since he'd walked away from their marriage. They had been cordial, perfectly aware that others were watching, and he'd even introduced her to his second wife, Judy.

Afterward Judy had said she understood Ethan's attraction to Charlotte but, even more so, their divorce. He still missed Judy's casually blunt opinions. She lived in Chicago these days, and they talked occasionally, but as befit their altered status, her honesty was tempered.

At the pansy-flanked door he rang the bell and waited. The welcome mat had script initials, with the *H* curlicued almost beyond recognition in the middle. These were Charlotte's court-amended initials, not the ones she'd been born with, which was no surprise. Too, although they had been married for seventeen years and she'd built her reputation in Asheville real estate as Charlotte Martin, she had changed her surname back to Hale immediately after their divorce, as if sharing even that much with Ethan and Taylor was an unwelcome reminder of a careless mistake.

A young woman answered the door, dressed in denim shorts and a tank top that revealed a tattooed fairy with gossamer wings. She had a gold hoop in her nose and wheat-colored hair that fell to the bottom of her rib cage, some strands braided, most not. Her smile was lovely, refreshingly imperfect and genuine.

"What can I do for you?" she asked.

"I was hoping to see Charlotte. Is she home?"

"I'd better tell her who's asking."

"Please tell her Ethan's here to see her."

She left the door cracked, as if certain he was trustworthy, and returned a few minutes later. He figured it had taken that long just to walk to wherever Charlotte had installed herself.

"I'm sorry you had to wait," she said. "Charlotte's cutting flowers out in the garden. Do you know your way back there? It's just beyond the pool."

Ethan had thought he might have a fifty percent chance of finding Charlotte at home, but he would never have expected to find her gardening. During their marriage she'd made a point of not working outside, citing years of doing just that as a child. Instead, she had landscaped with rocks, mulch and evergreens, and twice a year professionals had come in to spray and trim.

"I can find my way," he said.

"I'd guide you, but I've got to shop for groceries. . . ." She squinted up at the sun. "I'm probably not going to beat the after-church crowd, am I?"

"You might if you hurry."

She smiled and waved, squeezing past him to head in the direction of the garage. He gave up wondering who she was well before he managed to find his way outside to the pool and around it. He'd made a point of not investigating as he went, but one thing was clear. When she moved to this house Charlotte had started a brand-new life. He didn't recognize one painting or piece of furniture, not even a dish, from their marriage.

The Brits used *garden* for *yard,* and Charlotte imagined that Ethan expected to find her on an expanse of green grass, trimming a few tulips or daffodils planted around a tree trunk. He wouldn't expect a real garden, but once he navigated the route through her house, that was where he would find her. Four raised beds sat at one side of the yard, so they weren't part of the view from the back, but they had been built here at her request, to grow flowers for cutting. She was sure Ethan would find that odd, since she hadn't pulled a weed or planted a flower in all their years together.

Had she known he was coming, she would have tried to make a better impression, although she wasn't sure why. Ethan had seen her at her worst. When she had the flu. When she had been up all night with their colicky infant daughter. Even during childbirth — although he'd had to fight her for that privilege. The sight of her in jeans, a bright butterscotch camp shirt and a wide-brimmed hat, with clippers in one hand and a straw basket in the other, wouldn't send him away.

She wondered if he would also see how terrified she was. It was more than just confronting an ex-husband. If she handled this encounter the wrong way, it might permanently destroy any chance she had to reconcile with Taylor.

She was bending to reach the bottom of a parrot tulip so dark a purple it appeared to be black when she heard footsteps behind her. She straightened slowly, flower in hand, and turned.

"I'm not sure how these got here, but Harmony just saw them and fell in love. I'm making her a bouquet."

"Harmony?"

"The young woman who let you in."

She imagined he wasn't here to ferret out details about her life, but Ethan did look curious. Curious was better than furious, and she built on it.

"She has unusual tastes," Charlotte said with a smile she dredged up from deep inside her. "Which is good, since I don't know what I'd do with these otherwise. I'm almost sure the package said the bulbs were early doubles, pink and white. Life's full of surprises."

"*You* planted them?"

"A couple of years ago I got tired of paying exorbitant prices for fresh flowers. Gran always said if you can't grow something yourself you should do without. Which meant I never tasted an artichoke or an avocado until I married you."

She clipped another tulip to join the ones in her basket. Then she slipped the clippers into a holster at her waist, with hands that weren't quite steady. "But you didn't come here to talk about my garden, Ethan. How are you?"

He didn't seem to know. He seemed more interested in examining her.

She was ten years older than the woman he'd divorced, and yes, she looked every year of it. Her skin was no longer as smooth as the petals of one of the tulips in her basket. There were lines around her fatigued blue-gray eyes, she was too thin and her neck was no longer tight and perfect. But considering everything she'd been through, Charlotte thought she still passed muster for a woman of fifty-two.

"This feels odd," he said. "Being here at this house so many years later."

Although the morning air was cool, she knew perspiration was beading on her forehead and her hair was growing damp. The slightest exercise tired her, and she knew better than to let it.

"Let's sit. I've been out in the sun too long."

Ethan followed her to a bench set beneath an expansive maple. Charlotte lowered herself to the cushion and leaned against the slatted wooden back, removing the hat and using it as a fan.

"You must have known you were taking a chance, showing up here without calling," she said as she fanned.

"If I'd called, would you have invited me over?"

"Absolutely."

He looked as if he didn't believe her. "I'm glad I found you in."

"Well, that's good, because who knows how you'll feel by the end of the conversation. I'm sure this isn't a social call."

"I saw you at the park on Thursday."

She was silent so long he must have realized she wasn't going to answer.

"It *was* you?" he asked.

"I was there, yes."

"You were watching Maddie."

She wanted so badly to explain, yet the words eluded her. "Yes, and Sam's daughter, Edna, and a boy named Porter, who's well on his way to becoming a bully, except that Edna's trying to change him and very well might."

"I gather that's your way of saying it wasn't your first visit."

She turned to look at him. She saw the same changes he must have noted in her, but Ethan was aging well. The years stripped away nature's most lavish flourishes, but they left the essence of a man behind. Ethan's bone structure would still serve him well at eighty, but his eyes, a golden-brown that took in everything around him and didn't judge, would serve him best.

Those eyes served him well now, although she thought that on this rare occasion, they were not judgment-free.

"She's a beautiful little girl." Charlotte

turned away. "Well worth watching."

"You're not one to do anything without thinking it through. So what do you think will happen when Taylor finds out what you're doing?"

"I don't know for sure, Ethan."

"Then I'll tell you. She's going to be furious."

She wasn't surprised — after all, Samantha had made that clear, as well — but somehow, stupidly, she had hoped otherwise. She nodded, but the nod hid a wealth of feeling.

"I was hoping that wasn't going to be your answer, but Sam agrees. She says it won't be easy."

"Sam Ferguson?"

"We've talked. She recognized me at the park."

He looked surprised that Samantha had been willing to talk to her. "How could you think Taylor would feel otherwise?"

"Time changes things, and people, too. I guess I hoped . . ." She realized she was still wearing garden gloves, and she began to slowly strip them off for something to do, because she couldn't go on.

He had no such problem. "Taylor had to grow up quickly when she realized she was going to be a mother, and she's done an admirable job. But she hasn't gotten past her anger yet."

"Yet?"

"I hope it will come."

"Do you keep it alive?" She made certain the question didn't sound like an accusation. She really wanted to know.

He didn't look happy, and his answer was as distasteful as the question. "We don't talk about you at all. She won't allow it. But if we did? I would try to point out that in your own way, you were trying to protect her."

"In my own way . . ." She folded the gloves and placed them in the basket. "In my own way I *was* trying to protect her, Ethan. I was sure I knew what was best for her. Knowing what was best for everybody was something I was good at. I prided myself on it."

"What to do about the pregnancy was *her* decision. Without more pressure than the situation already called for."

"Of course it was."

He seemed surprised she hadn't argued. *She* was surprised their conversation brought back such vivid memories of the day Ethan had walked away from their marriage. She had known it would, and yet the ferocity of her feelings made her close her eyes for a moment.

"I want to find my way back into Taylor's life," Charlotte said, when he didn't respond. "And I want to know my granddaughter. I need to find a way. Asking you to help is the definition of audacity, I know, but here you are, sitting right beside me. If we can say anything conclusive, it's that I never miss an opportunity."

"Audacity doesn't cover it."

She turned so she was looking right at him, and this time she was sure her feelings were plain. "I'll grovel. I'll do anything it takes. I made a terrible, terrible mistake, and I want to rectify it for their sakes."

"Do you? Or is this all about *you* and what *you* need?"

"It's both and everything. Taylor needs a chance to put this behind her, and I think Maddie might need her grandmother. I need my family. I need to do the right thing. I love Taylor. I never stopped."

"I can tell you what your daughter will think, because it's the same thing I do. You'll try to run things. You'll want to do this for Taylor and that for Maddie, all things that you think need to be done and have nothing to do with what she wants."

She took a moment before she spoke, as if she was thinking about what he'd said, although she really didn't need to.

"I understand why you feel that way, but I can assure you it won't be true."

"Maddie has seizures. You know that?"

She nodded.

"Taylor makes all the decisions about Maddie's health and treatment. She doesn't want advice, and she doesn't want interference."

"Does she need them?"

"It doesn't matter," Ethan said. "Maddie is her daughter, and she has the right to do what she believes is best."

"And Jeremy?"

"He loves Maddie. They got off to a rough start, and Taylor's never quite forgiven him for not wanting the baby at the beginning, but he did step up to the plate. And his parents have been great."

"I'm so glad."

Charlotte was sure that wasn't the response Ethan had expected. She had despised Jeremy, who in high school had played in a rock band called Insidious Pagans and challenged any and all authority. She had forbidden Taylor to see him, guaranteeing that not only would Taylor sneak behind her mother's back, but that she would also find Jeremy even more attractive and succumb to his charms.

"I don't know what I can do for you,

Charlotte."

"Or what you *want* to do."

"That, too."

She knew she had little time left to convince him. She tried to make every word count. "I can imagine how you feel. I can even imagine how you feel about *me.* Please, just know I have such deep regrets, starting well before that final terrible fight. I can't change the past, but maybe I can change the future. At least a little?"

They sat that way for a full minute. She fanned herself and waited. Her hands were trembling.

"She won't appreciate a go-between," he said at last. "I can tell you that for sure. Taylor takes no prisoners and wants no mediators. If you stand even the smallest chance of making amends, you'll have to do it directly."

"Sam said the same thing. What would be the best time, do you think? When she's not feeling harried or worried?"

"I'll get back to you." He stood, and she did, too.

"Will you?" she asked. "You're not blowing me off?"

"Would it do any good?"

"If you don't want to see or talk to me again, I'll understand. Why would you? Why *should* you?"

"Because we share a child, even though she would rather forget that. And a grandchild, too. At least we did that much right."

She smiled a little at his admission, and he returned it. Despite herself, she felt the warmth curling inside her like wood smoke drifting skyward on an autumn afternoon. "You look well. Are you happy?"

"Does it matter?"

"I want you to be."

"Are *you?*" he countered.

"I may be finding my way in that direction, even if I lost the map a long time ago. It's a path over mountains, isn't it?"

"A very steep climb."

She touched his arm. Briefly, gently. "Thank you for this, Ethan. For coming, for listening, for thinking it over."

He nodded, then he started back toward the house.

She wondered if he would walk through the kitchen, the shortest route to the front. Framed on the wall beside the refrigerator he would see three familiar finger-paintings, the first Taylor had done as a preschooler. They had been framed to hang in the home their family had shared together. She imagined he hadn't thought about them since the divorce.

But Charlotte had never forgotten.

Chapter Fourteen

First Day Journal: May 4

Ethan and I have lived apart nearly eleven years, but for a few moments today while he was here, I almost felt we had never parted. Marriage demands a level of intimacy that permanently changes us. In some ways it feels as if Ethan left an imprint on my heart. All those years ago, that's exactly what I was afraid might happen. I tried to prevent it, but love will find a way.

In my memories I am twenty-three again, and my relationship with Ethan seems impossible, yet impossible not to continue. He calls me Lulu and drags me to bluegrass bars or south of the city to sliding rocks and waterfalls. I take him bicycling through the Biltmore Estate on paths the King boys and I called our own.

At Christmas we go to his home in Roanoke, Virginia, and my guesses about his family and upbringing are confirmed. He and a younger brother are the products of private schools, of summer camps in New England and special tutors when their grades are less than perfect.

I'm welcomed with interest. His physician mother makes time to have tea, and shows me Ethan's childhood photos and portraits of ancestors rooted deeply in Confederate aristocracy. His attorney father brags about Ethan's golf game.

We attend a Christmas Eve party at their country club, and Mrs. Martin loans me a silver fox stole to wear with my perfect consignment shop dress. Ethan, of course, asks me to leave the stole at home, since he doesn't approve of fur — nor, for that matter, of his parents' country club, which is segregated.

The next morning there are gifts for me under the tree, and his family seems genuinely pleased with my small gifts to them. Still, I sense his mother watching and judging, as if she can see past my thin veneer to guess that I'm not good enough to bear her grandchildren.

All conversation in Ethan's house is surprisingly tepid, as if anything of interest is purposely omitted. I ask Ethan if they're being particularly polite, and he says no, what I've seen is his family with their hair down.

He sneaks into my room late that night, and

we make love with surprising passion. Suddenly I understand that while his home and family seem perfect to me, they have never seemed perfect to him.

This is the first time I realize that Ethan and I aren't going to simply drift apart, that we've created a bond that will be messy to sever. Is it possible to have a long-term relationship when we want such different things? I want the life he lived as a child, the one his parents still live and he disdains. If Ethan and I marry, can't we have everything?

That winter and spring I take classes, and work dinner and lunch shifts. Although Ethan begins to casually mention marriage, I'm just glad to be with him, to cook a meal or nap while he does. At least half our nights are spent in my bed or his. He, too, is working hard, and for the moment we're content just to be together when we can.

Summer is pivotal. His mother arrives unannounced on her way to Highlands to visit a friend, and I'm at Ethan's having supper. She seems surprised we're still together, although she covers it quickly. The next morning she takes me to her favorite Asheville boutique. She knows so little about me, she says, as she probes for details. I know she's hunting for confirmation of her suspicions.

I tell her only a little more, that my ancestors settled in the mountains generations ago and I was raised by my grandmother. I tell her that life in Madison County was never easy, but my family worked hard and prayed harder. I don't mention Hearty. Even Ethan knows little about my father.

As we shop she subtly corrects most of what I say and do, looking vaguely sympathetic, as if she realizes she's wasting her time. At the end of the morning, as I say goodbye, I'm fighting tears. Then, surprisingly, on the way home, I'm fighting nausea.

A week later my suspicions are confirmed. I don't have the flu, I am going to have a baby.

CHAPTER FIFTEEN

On Thursday afternoon Taylor Martin juggled prescription slips, along with samples and literature about Maddie's newest medication, and still managed to smile at Dr. Hilliard's nurse, a woman who had been with his practice since the day it was established. Rhonda had once told Taylor she was ready to retire, but loyalty to Dr. Hilliard kept her from taking the final plunge. He was that kind of person. Inspirational, compassionate, involved. Taylor wasn't sure what she would do when he, too, decided it was time to call medicine quits.

"Maddie, you're growing so fast," Rhonda said. "Your mother must be feeding you all the time."

Maddie didn't smile. She hadn't been sleeping well, and although she hadn't had any more full-blown seizures during daylight hours, Dr. Hilliard thought it was possible her sleep was being disturbed by smaller ones. After the grand-mal seizure on the day of the cookout, he had changed one of her medications, and today he'd added another. He was hopeful this new combination would give her more rest. So was Taylor, although she was afraid that once she looked over the new drug's potential side effects, she was going to feel less so.

"She hardly ever lets me have dessert," Maddie said, with an uncharacteristic whine in her voice.

Rhonda, a woman who looked as if dessert might be her first course, shook her finger playfully at the girl. "Whatever she's doing is working. Next time I see you, you'll be a foot taller."

Taylor ushered her daughter into the overly air-conditioned hallway, then the elevator. She hoped Rhonda's prediction was true, but as often as she and Maddie came to this office, she suspected her daughter wouldn't have grown a millimeter.

Outside the building Maddie scanned the cars parked diagonally along the curb. "Papa's not here."

Taylor checked the time. "We finished early. Cut him some slack." Her father had agreed to do transportation today while she got new tires on her car.

Ethan could be relied on to be where he said he would, *when* he said he would, but it didn't come naturally. Growing up, Taylor's mother had always been the punctual one, tapping her foot like the ticking of a clock if anybody kept her waiting. Back then Ethan had been the dawdler, the creative spirit who lingered in front of every unfamiliar house to imagine how space was divided or whether a no-talent remodeler had installed fake ceilings and slapped white paint on precious mahogany paneling.

Now Ethan was punctual, too, but only because he knew Taylor and Maddie counted on him. Sometimes Taylor thought he was trying to be both father and mother, the best part of each.

The whine hadn't left Maddie's voice. "I don't want to go back to school. The day's almost over, and everybody will look at me."

Taylor had saved good news, just in case Maddie needed cheering after her appointment. "You don't have to go back. Since it's so warm this afternoon, Papa's taking us for ice cream."

"Really?"

"Then over to Pack Square, so you can get good and wet. It *is* too late, and your teacher gave me your homework assignment, so we're playing hooky."

Maddie held up her hand, and they slapped palms. Just then Ethan drove up, avoiding cars and effortlessly squeezing into a small space just in front of the office. Maddie scrambled into the back as Taylor got in beside him.

"Everything go okay?" he asked.

"He's cutting down one med and adding another. And thanks for getting us. The garage called, and my car's ready, so if you don't mind, after the park you can drop us off there."

They chatted until he pulled into Ultimate Ice Cream Company, one of Maddie's favorites. They dithered over flavors, discussing the pros and cons, but Maddie was the first to make a decision. After ordering one Moon Pie cone for her, lemon-mint sorbet for Taylor and goat cheese and cherry for Ethan, they made the short trip to the center of the city and Pack Square Park.

No matter where they were, Ethan always found a parking place. Taylor was never sure quite how he did it. She'd finally decided his karma was just good, and today it was stellar. Half a block from the park he pulled into a spot with a broken meter, so they didn't even have to dig for quarters.

"You're sure you don't mind getting wet?"

he asked Maddie. "You're pretty dressed up."

She flung her door open. "I'm just wearing jeans and a T-shirt."

"But you look so pretty."

She flashed him a smile before she went skipping toward Splasheville.

Pack Square Park was part of Asheville's history, but a recent expensive and innovative update seemed destined to make it the heart of the city. Streets had been closed and the area expanded. The park was now divided into sections, with Roger McGuire Green, where they headed, directly in front of and between the extraordinary Neo-Classical Revival courthouse and equally extraordinary Art Deco city hall. The designers had made lavish use of native trees and shrubs, and constructed a fifty-foot stage, adorned by beautifully wrought ceramic tiles. For children they had also constructed an interactive water feature, with jets shooting intermittently from a circular tiled basin.

Taylor let her daughter run ahead. It was a pleasure to see Maddie come back to life. She'd been groggy and out of sorts since they'd started on the new medication, and Taylor hoped that the changes Dr. Hilliard had made today would make all the difference.

"She looks happy," Ethan said.

"Ice cream, playing hooky and now this." Taylor watched her daughter edge slowly into the spray. "She deserves to be happy."

"So do you."

"One follows the other. If I can get her life on track, mine'll follow. Right now I need to get her stabilized before her stay in Nashville. I can't imagine what will happen if Jeremy has anything major to deal with."

They settled on one of the stone benches along the side and watched Maddie behave like the child she was, darting in and out of the water, and splashing with other children.

Taylor kept her gaze glued to her daughter. It seemed easy to slip in the water, but for most children the odds of staying upright were good. At least Maddie knew that if she began to feel different in any way, she was to quickly sit. She wasn't always able to tell when a seizure threatened, but when she could, even in a place like this, she knew better than to stay on her feet.

"I've always loved this space," Ethan said, "but never more than now. It's a visual feast. Have you ever been to Pack Tavern?" He nodded toward the brick building at the corner to their right. "More historic architecture. Do you know it was a speakeasy during Prohibition? They say tunnels linked it to other downtown businesses, a great way to ferry illegal booze from one place to another."

"I'm afraid I'm a big fan of their fried pickle chips. *Those* ought to be illegal."

"It used to be Bill Stanley's Barbeque and Bluegrass. Do you remember? A real honky-tonk, and the place to be if you liked either. When we were dating, your mom loved to go there."

Taylor pondered how odd it was to hear "your mom" on her father's lips. "I can't imagine my mother in a place like that."

"Ribs, beer, some of the best fiddle music you've ever heard. She knew how to clog, at least the rudiments. She'd tap her feet like she wanted so badly to get out there with the dancers, but I could never convince her it was okay."

"It's strange to hear you talk about her." Taylor realized she was chopping off words, spitting them out, as if they tasted foul. "You never do." She was afraid the rest was clear from her tone. *And I never want you to.*

"Taylor, Charlotte and I were married a long time. And the three of us were a family for a long time, too. There were good times, more than you let yourself believe. Maybe we need to remember that."

"You're right about one thing."

He turned to examine her. "What?"

"When it comes to my mother, I really *don't* believe in the good times."

CHAPTER SIXTEEN

First Day Journal: May 7

Harmony hasn't shared many thoughts about her future. I think she's afraid that if she does, I might disapprove. She doesn't know how wrong she is, because when I tried to tell my sixteen-year-old daughter what to do about her pregnancy, I lost her, possibly forever.

Nor does Harmony know that many years before that, I, too, was faced with the same life-altering decision that she must make soon.

All too well, I remember how it feels to be twenty-five. I am older than Taylor and Harmony when I find I'm pregnant with a baby I haven't planned. Ethan wants children, but when I've thought about it, I've seen a baby in the distant future, after I've settled on a career path. If we marry I want to establish myself and nudge Ethan toward a firm with clout and money, perhaps in bustling Charlotte or even Atlanta. I want to give any child of ours all the things I never had and separate myself from the past forever.

Frantic, I debate what to do. Since I've gotten pregnant while using birth control, surely a planned pregnancy in a year or two will be easy. With limited success I tell myself the fetus is just a speck, less than a tadpole. I can travel to a clinic out of town, and Ethan will never have to know. Later, if we marry, if we've considered the question of a child at length and carefully planned, then we can start our family.

I visit a doctor to confirm what I already know. He examines me carefully, then he tells me I've surprised him. I have severe endometriosis, which often causes fertility problems, and the fact that I've gotten pregnant is something of a miracle. He said I should carefully nurture this pregnancy, since it's entirely possible it may never be repeated.

My entire world is turned upside down.

That night I finally tell Ethan the truth, unsure how he'll react. First I tell him about my morning with his mother, about her almost palpable fear that I'll destroy his chances for a promising future.

"And membership in the best country clubs," he reminds me, with a remarkably straight face. "Don't forget, Lulu, you may destroy that, too, because on weekends I'd much rather be in bed with you than out on the tenth fairway."

"I don't know how much time we'll have in bed," I tell him, tears welling. "I'm afraid we're going to be changing diapers."

His mother may not believe I'm good enough to marry her son and conceive his children, but Ethan lays all my doubts to rest. In the history of the world, no man has ever been more thrilled to learn he's going to be a father. No woman ever loved a man more.

Almost eight months later, having been married by a justice of the peace in a ceremony Ethan's family attends with strained good grace, we become the parents of a baby girl. Ethan chooses the name Taylor in memory of his Taylor grandparents. I agree, hoping it will lay all his mother's doubts about our marriage to rest. I miss the first week of my baby's homecoming because of an emergency hysterectomy.

My doctor was prophetic. Taylor will indeed be our only child. I was prophetic, too. I'm not ready to be a mother. By the time I arrive home, our baby is a stranger to me, but not to her father.

Chapter Seventeen

On Saturday harmony and Charlotte had breakfast in the smaller dining room, because Harmony liked the light cherry dining set with the delicately curved legs. She had pulled back Charlotte's heavy curtains to let the sun burst through multipaned windows to dazzle the table, and used cut-glass goblets for the orange juice.

When she had finished drizzling honey on her oatmeal, Harmony looked up with some unease and decided now was as good a time as any for an announcement. "Charlotte, I've decided to have the baby."

She wasn't sure what she would see on Charlotte's face, joy or dismay, but, with relief, she saw neither. Charlotte looked interested, even supportive, but if she had an opinion about Harmony's decision, she didn't show it.

"I've thought about it a lot . . . well, actually I haven't thought about anything else,"

Harmony continued. "And even though it seems like I'm not ready to have a baby, I'm even less ready to have an abortion, you know? I went to a clinic and talked to a nurse there, just to understand my options, and five minutes into it, I knew that wasn't the answer. Because I'm already imagining what this baby will look like, whether it'll be a boy or a girl, and I'm pretty sure that's not what most of the other women were thinking. They were thinking they needed to close that door behind them, and fast."

"And you want to leave your door open?"

Harmony liked the way Charlotte asked. There was no hint of judgment in her voice.

"I do," Harmony said. "That doesn't mean I know what I'll do after the baby comes. But that's one choice out of the way."

Charlotte reached for the pot of tea Harmony had put in front of her and poured a thin stream into a delicate white cup. Harmony liked to set the table with Charlotte's china, and today she had chosen dishes so thin they were almost iridescent in the sunshine. Charlotte had four sets, and Harmony had free rein to use them any way she chose, so she mixed and fussed and set unnecessary pieces, just because she could. She was like a little girl giving an elaborate tea party for her dolls and best friends, but she didn't care. Her childhood hadn't included many hours of play, and one of the bright memories was her mother pouring tea for them from her grandmother's teapot.

"I . . . I just wanted you to know," Harmony said. "Do you think I'm doing the right thing?"

Charlotte set the pot back on an embroidered doily discovered in a drawer overflowing with beautiful linens. "I think you're doing all the right things. You're taking your time, giving it a lot of thought, consulting professionals. I think you have a good head on your shoulders, and you use it to make good decisions."

Harmony realized she was having trouble taking that in. It seemed so wrong. "I made a whopper of a bad decision. I got pregnant, and I'm not ready to be a mother. That's not even in question."

"You are in excellent company." Charlotte didn't go on.

"It wasn't easy to figure out the baby thing. I grew up in a family where everything was black and white. There was no room for interpretation. Our church was very strict, and my father was even stricter. Especially with my mother and me."

"It sounds like you might have a brother or sister?"

"I *had* a brother."

"So now you're trying to find different ways of making decisions," Charlotte said. "Ways that aren't quite so cast in stone."

"Maybe the other way's easier," Harmony said, thinking of all the decisions that still faced her.

"But not half as fruitful."

"Fruitful?"

"Because every time you make a decision, good or bad, you learn something. Right? If you just do what you're told, you don't learn a thing."

The telephone rang, and Charlotte went to answer it. Harmony finished her oatmeal and thought of her mother, who'd never had a chance to think for herself. Then she thought about Davis, who, like her father, had definite ideas about the way other people should live.

If *she* could change, could *he?* Did men like Davis ever turn themselves into good husbands and fathers? She was afraid that might take a magic wand, and despite a plethora of New Age stores downtown, that was something she didn't have in her possession.

Charlotte returned just as Harmony was

about to reheat the older woman's oatmeal, and sat again, but she didn't pick up her spoon. "It's your day off, isn't it? Are you busy?"

"I'm going out for dinner, but nothing before then. Is there something I can do for you?"

Charlotte reached over and put her hand on Harmony's. "Be my friend. Would you like to spend a day in the country? I promise we'll get back in time for your date."

Charlotte wasn't sure why she had asked Harmony to come along today. But, of course, she *did* know, she just didn't want to admit it. She had asked Harmony to join her not only because her young friend needed support but also because Charlotte herself needed some.

Harmony clearly believed in destiny, and Charlotte thought that had to be the most plausible explanation for this trip. She had two reasons to drive up Doggett Mountain on this glorious Saturday, and she was too practical not to see how aiming one stone at two birds might pay off in the long run.

"So, why are we going up a mountain?" Harmony had dressed for the occasion. Faded jeans hanging low on her hips, a long-sleeved shirt tied just under her breasts, a gold chain belt that drooped over the bare skin of her waist, which didn't yet show the pregnancy.

Charlotte put off answering the question. "You're sure you're up to this? It's going to get steep for the second part of the trip, and it might be tough to turn around."

"I never get carsick."

"Not even when you're pregnant?"

"I've never been pregnant before."

"I rest my case."

"If I get sick, you can laugh all the way home."

"Only if you don't get sick in my car."

"It's warm, so I'll hang my head out the window."

Charlotte laughed, and the laughter felt good. That was another reason she'd brought Harmony. The girl made her feel young and silly herself.

They were quickly in the country, since metropolitan Asheville was small by city standards. They passed mobile homes on hillsides, and businesses in ramshackle buildings fronted by haphazardly parked pickup trucks. Expensive newer homes dotted the landscape, as well, along with a few refurbished Victorians from another century, and everywhere land had been plowed for gardens. The road dipped, turned and switched back, but Charlotte knew that the real climb lay ahead.

"We're almost at the first stop, I think," she said, after she checked her odometer. "We're supposed to look for a barn —"

"That'll be easy. I mean, who has a barn in North Carolina?"

Charlotte tossed her a smile. "It's on the left, with diagonal slats, which are unusual. There's a pond to the left of that, and the road's got new gravel. Typical North Carolina directions. We turn and follow the gravel about a mile and a half before we turn off on a dirt road. The farmhouse is about a hundred yards beyond the turnoff."

"Is this something you're doing for your job? Don't you sell real estate?"

"Not exactly."

"I've noticed brochures in your den. Falconview Development, and I saw your photograph on the front."

"We do sell real estate, but more often we develop it." Since a glance showed Harmony was interested, Charlotte continued. "We buy land either for our own projects or those of investors, and we do the necessary work so we can improve it for other uses. Siting, permits, architectural renderings, for example."

"What kind of projects?"

"Shopping centers. Office complexes. Housing communities. Institutions like schools or banks. Sometimes we do the construction, but sometimes we just do the groundwork, make improvements and sell the property for others to build on."

"The economy's in the toilet. People are still developing land around here?"

"Not so you'd notice." Charlotte realized she didn't even feel frustrated when she thought about all the housing communities that had never been finished, all the ground that hadn't been broken. A serious illness changed everything. She no longer cared whether she was making money hand over fist. Now, more than anything, she felt sorry for all the people who hadn't been as lucky with their own investments as she had, and she wished she could help.

She glanced at her companion again. "We're hanging by our fingernails, but we'll hang on until things improve. We had the foresight to get out of some deals and sell property that would have dragged us so low we could never have recovered. Some people thought we were crazy, because we took large losses, but they aren't shaking their heads anymore."

"I can't imagine how you learn something like that."

Charlotte was grateful to spot the barn in question, because talking about Falconview made her uncomfortable. She had changed from a hands-on executive to an absent one, turning over most of the jobs she normally did and the decisions she usually made to others. She showed up most mornings, but only for brief periods, and she avoided probing questions and explanations. She knew her disinterest in the company she had founded was the talk of the office. She also knew it might well breed a power play she was no longer strong enough to thwart.

She slowed to make the first turn and turned the conversation to something more important. "Right now, I want to tell you what we're doing here."

She waited until they were on the gravel road, glad she'd taken her Jeep Cherokee instead of the lower-slung Audi. Stones pinged against the undercarriage, and she had to drive slower. There had been a time in her life when a gravel road like this one would have seemed the ultimate luxury.

"There's a woman who lives down this road, a dog breeder named Marilla Reynolds," Charlotte said. "She specializes in service dogs."

"Armed services? Like attack dogs?"

"Friendlier than that. Most of her puppies

go to agencies that train them to be helpers. I've been reading. Dogs can assist the blind or the hearing impaired, even people with mobility issues. Anybody who needs the help a trained dog can provide." She paused. "Even people with seizure disorders."

"How's that work?"

Since the gravel was thundering louder under the Cherokee, Charlotte slowed even more. She didn't want to shout. "A variety of ways. First, the dogs stay with somebody having a seizure. They can even lie beside them to cushion them so they don't get hurt. They can alert others so they can come to help. At night they can pull pillows and covers off the bed to reduce the chance a child having a seizure might smother."

"Wow, that's amazing."

It *was* amazing. "I forgot to tell you. The road we turn on has weeping willows on each side of it and a sign that says Capable Canines."

"I'll watch."

"The other thing only some of the dogs can do? They can actually sense a seizure coming on. It's uncanny, but real. Those dogs can warn their owners and let them know what's ahead, so they can lie down or get to a safe place. Dog owners noticed it first, on their own, and started telling their doctors. Researchers have done studies, and they've proved it happens."

"Is it possible a dog alerting its owner to a seizure could cause one?" Harmony asked. "You know, like if somebody says you stepped in poison ivy you start itching, even if it's a false alarm?"

Charlotte never doubted how bright Harmony was, but she enjoyed the daily proof. "That's a good question. Researchers actually learned that seizures diminish in numbers with a seizure response dog. Having a dog companion helps with relaxation. Plus the dogs are ice breakers and encourage socialization. Anyway, the owner becomes more comfortable and secure, and that helps."

"So the dogs put a wagging tail on a serious problem."

Charlotte smiled. "I love the way you express yourself."

Harmony looked startled. "Davis said something like that last time we were together, only it's not true. He's happiest when I don't express myself at all."

Charlotte knew better than to interfere, but she couldn't help her next remark. "A lifetime of that could be tough."

"I lived one already. Take my word for it."

Charlotte saw the willows and sign up

ahead, and slowed even more to turn. Harmony changed the subject before Charlotte could add anything else.

"You didn't tell me why you're interested in these dogs."

"Someone I'm close to . . ." Charlotte realized how far from the truth that was, ironically so. She sighed — audibly, she was afraid. "Someone I'm *not* close to, but wish I were, has seizures. The dogs are very expensive, thousands and thousands of dollars by the time they're trained. And they're hard to get. The thing is, there's no real way of knowing if a dog will actually be able to sense a seizure. Trainers can hope, but it's a unique skill, maybe inborn. They can train for everything else, but they can't guarantee that."

"Are you going to buy a dog today? For your friend?"

"It's my granddaughter."

"I didn't know you had a granddaughter. Those must be her paintings in the kitchen."

"No, those are her mother's." A house loomed before them as they followed the driveway into a steep curve. It was an old North Carolina farmhouse, the real thing, not a copy, painted a dark blue-green with white trim. Hydrangeas bloomed against a lattice-trimmed porch, and a swing set adorned a side yard in front of a two-story garage.

Charlotte had expected to hear dogs barking when she turned off her engine, but except for the angry cawing of a crow, the property was eerily quiet.

"Her name is Maddie," Charlotte said. "Her mother's very angry at me, and we haven't spoken since Maddie was born. I've never met my granddaughter, even though she lives in Asheville, too."

"Oh . . ."

Charlotte thought how much one syllable could say. "It's hard to understand. I don't really understand it all myself, except that the fault's mine."

"Is the dog . . . Is this a way back into her life?"

Charlotte opened her door. "I think her mother might see it as a bribe. But it's . . ." She tried to express exactly what it was. "It's just a gift. No strings attached. If I can make it happen."

"How could she not be happy, or at least happier, with you afterward?"

They were both outside now, walking up the path toward the house. Charlotte tried to explain. "I suspect from things you've said that you have a problem with your mother?"

Harmony grunted. "No, my mother and I have the same problem. My father."

"What if you needed something, and your father magically produced it for you. Would you suddenly trust him? Or would you assume there were complications or pitfalls you couldn't see?"

"I'm afraid that's easy."

"You see my problem."

"I see the part of it you want me to."

Charlotte gave her a quick, one-armed hug. "Thank you for coming today. This is easier with you here."

"I'm glad."

On the porch, Charlotte rapped on a screen door adorned with decorative fan and spindle woodwork from another era. As they waited, she wondered if anybody was home. At the least she had expected a canine chorus, but the house was suspiciously silent.

"How'd you find out about this place?" Harmony asked.

"My minister told me. That's who called during breakfast. We talked about Maddie recently, so she knows the story. She was doing a wedding last night, and somebody in the wedding party fosters puppies from this kennel. She thought I might want to check out what they do, maybe get on the list for a dog, if that's how it works."

"Fosters puppies?"

"These people are the breeders. Some helping dogs come from shelters, but this breeder is trying to perfect a line of goldendoodle puppies from parents that have been particularly good at detecting seizures."

"What's a goldendoodle? You're not kidding?"

"It's a cross between a poodle and a golden retriever. Once the pups are weaned, they pass them to families to be fostered. The families do basic obedience training, get them used to differing environments and make notes about their progress or lack of it. Once a dog's matured and been evaluated and accepted, it goes into professional training, then training with its new owner, and finally, it goes to its new home."

"Your minister told you all that?"

"I did a little internet research before we left this morning."

"Enough to find out if they're still operating?"

Charlotte was trying not to feel disappointed. "There were directions on their website, but when I tried the phone number, their answering machine clicked off before I could leave a message. I thought at the least I could leave a note if they weren't here."

"You might want to get out your pen." Harmony went to the edge of the porch and looked beyond the house. "We could try the barn. Maybe that's where they keep the puppies? Maybe they're out there now."

"Let's do that before we give up. I just hope none of the dogs are loose. They might feel territorial."

"Dogs usually like me. I'm not sure why, but I seem to attract them."

Charlotte followed her down the steps and along a worn dirt path toward a small unpainted barn. She could see sunlight streaming through the open center, but nothing else.

"Did you have a dog as a child?" she asked.

"Dogs are messy. Mess was forbidden in our house. And noise. And confusion."

Charlotte felt a stab of anger at a family she didn't even know. "That's a hard way to grow up."

"If everything was exactly the way he liked it, my father was actually pleasant. He would bring my mother flowers, tell her how happy he was that she made his life so easy. Once he bought me a gold necklace because he said nobody had ever had a better daughter. That night he slapped my mother so hard she hit her head on the kitchen counter and had to have six stitches. I don't remember what she did to make him angry, but the blood made him angrier. He accused her of landing against the counter on purpose. While they were at the hospital, I flushed the necklace down the toilet."

"I don't even know what to say," Charlotte said, which was true.

"She never reports the abuse. Maybe if he was hateful all the time she would get the courage to leave like I did. But the kindness, the flowers, the compliments? The uncertainty keeps her rooted to the spot. Now every time I call, her voice seems farther away. I think she'll fade away one day and nobody will notice."

"I'm so sorry, Harmony, but I'm glad you left."

"Sometimes I think I should have stayed to protect her. But she helped me pack and bought my bus ticket." Harmony hesitated. "I dumped that on you, I'm sorry. I don't know why."

"I hope you aren't really sorry, and I hope you know you can't protect her until she's ready for help. She wanted you to have a better life."

"I've always thought she named me Harmony because that was the only way she was ever going to have any in our house.

She used to have a great sense of humor. It helped."

Charlotte noted the use of the past tense. "It's a lovely name. You do it justice."

"You're so nice to me."

They had reached the barn, and since it was the standard gabled crib barn, stalls on each side with a wide roofed opening between, they could easily walk right in. They found it empty, although it still smelled like horses.

Harmony pointed out the back door. "That's where the kennel is."

They kept walking until they were outside again, where they started toward the kennel, a long, one-story building with a chain link fence bordering a grassy slope. Everything Charlotte had seen so far was neat and well kept. No peeling paint here, no trash or sprawling weeds, but something was amiss. The place felt more like a graveyard than a working farm.

They rounded the fence, got to the door and knocked. Charlotte didn't expect an answer. In fact she was beginning to feel like a trespasser and was ready to give up for the day. Just as she was about to say so, a man threw the door open and stared at them through red-rimmed eyes.

Their host looked as if he might have just

gotten up from a nap. He was at most in his mid-thirties, wearing straw-dusted overalls covering what was probably a college sweat-shirt. His chocolate-brown hair needed cutting, and he needed a shave, which he seemed to realize, because his hand went to his chin.

"I don't get many visitors all the way out here," he said in greeting.

"I'm so sorry," Charlotte said. "We just took it on ourselves to see if anybody was home. We were about to leave."

He opened the door wider and gestured them in. After a brief hesitation, Charlotte preceded Harmony into a cheaply paneled office with a metal desk against one wall, file cabinets and a bulletin board against the other.

"You caught me at a bad time," he said, "but at least you caught me. You wouldn't have in an hour. I'm on my way out of town."

Beyond them was a large room divided into sizable partitioned areas that opened into attached runs along the back of the building. Here, too, everything was clean and neat. Only there were no dogs in sight.

Charlotte held out her hand and introduced herself, then Harmony. He wiped his palm on the side of his overalls before shaking hands with both of them. "Brad Reynolds," he said.

"I think we've not only come at a bad time, we've come to the wrong place," Charlotte said. "I'd heard you bred goldendoodles for seizure-response dogs, but it looks like you got out of the business."

With fingers spread wide, he swirled his hair off his forehead. He still looked half-asleep. "Right place, wrong time," he said. "We're shut down for now. Breeding was my wife's project, and she was in a car accident three weeks ago."

"That's awful," Harmony said. "Is she okay?"

"She's going to be, after a few hard months of therapy. For the next two weeks she's at a rehab center in South Carolina, where her mother's a nurse, and she and my father-in law are keeping our two kids. I'll be on my way down there to see them in a little while."

"We won't keep you," Charlotte said. "I'm so sorry. May I leave my card for later, when things get back to normal?"

"What happened to the dogs?" Harmony asked, before he could respond. "Even if you don't have puppies, you must have the mothers?"

"We were between litters — well, except

for one mother who's about to whelp. Friends are keeping the rest of them for us, along with our horses, but nobody's ready for a litter of pups."

"What will you do with her?"

"I don't have many choices. The organization we sell the puppies to is closed for a couple of weeks, off on vacation somewhere, and I can't reach them to see what they can rig up. They're in Indiana, so they wouldn't be much help, anyway, not until the puppies are old enough to transfer to local families to be socialized and trained."

He hadn't answered Harmony's question, so Charlotte persisted. "So what will you do?"

"Tonight my sister's coming down from Johnson City, and she'll take Velvet to her vet. She'd keep her, but she's got a couple of territorial females who won't accept her. So the vet's agreed to take her, and when the time's right he'll find good homes for the puppies and make back his investment. Unfortunately, we won't be able to afford to pay his fees if we try to get them back." He looked surprised he had told them so much. "Look, I —"

"They won't be trained as seizure dogs, then?" Charlotte asked.

"Probably not. The logistics are just too

difficult. Rilla, that's my wife, had real hopes for this litter, too." He glanced at a clock on the wall. "I —"

"Couldn't a volunteer raise the puppies? At least until they're old enough to go to the right homes to be trained?"

He looked frustrated and flipped his hands, palms up. "I don't know *anybody* like that. I've cashed in all my chips with friends and family, even my own vet. Everybody's already taking care of something."

Charlotte thought about Minnie Marlborough, who would have stepped forward without a second thought. They needed Minnie right now, or somebody like her. Analiese had told her about all the people who had helped and loved the old woman. She thought about the large check she had written the local animal shelter as penance.

"I could take them," she heard herself saying. "No charge, of course. Until they're old enough, I mean. The mother would come back to you?"

He looked as if he was trying to make sense of that. "She could, although Rilla was going to retire her after this litter. We're not a puppy mill. We don't wear out our breeders, and we were probably going to find her a family once the pups were weaned. Do you have —"

"Experience?" Charlotte shook her head. "I'll be honest, not a bit with raising puppies, but I grew up on a farm farther up Doggett Mountain, and I know animals backward and forward. I have money for vet care and advice, and resources —"

"And she has me," Harmony put in. "I'm good with dogs. They trust me, and we could learn anything we need to really fast."

"Why?" he asked.

Charlotte admired the young man for going straight to the point. "Because my granddaughter has epilepsy, and one day soon I'd like her to have a trained dog. If these pups have potential to be particularly good with seizures, then they shouldn't be wasted. And with luck maybe we could even end up with one from this litter. I know you can't guarantee we'd get one, that's probably up to the organization that trains them, but maybe you could put in a good word."

He was waking up now. Charlotte imagined the days since his wife's accident had been all about reorganizing and making decisions. Sleep had not been a priority.

"Someone will vouch for you?" he asked.

She opened her purse and took out her card. "This is me. You can call my office for a start. They can give you a long list of Asheville's finest who will promise you the puppies will be in good hands."

He thought for a moment. "You have a place for them?"

Harmony took that one. "You ought to see Charlotte's house. Every puppy could have a private room with a bath. Not that they will. Will the mother be okay with this? Living indoors? Strangers?"

"Velvet's lived in and out of our house, so that's not an issue."

Charlotte could imagine his dilemma. The offer sounded too good to be true, but if it *was* true, it solved so many problems for him.

She added a bonus. "If it doesn't work out, we'll get in touch and bring them back here. Or even take them up to that vet in Johnson City, if that's still the only answer. But at the very least this will give you some time to work out a better plan. When are the puppies going to come?"

"Sometime next week."

"We'll be ready. We'll take good care of Velvet."

"I have a friend, Glenda, who works as an assistant to a vet in East Asheville," Harmony said, as if she'd just remembered. "I bet she'll come and stay with us, to be there when the puppies are born."

That seemed to be the final piece of the

puzzle for Brad. "Mind if I make a few calls?"

"Of course. May we see Velvet in the meantime?"

"Sure. She's been out here keeping me company. She's probably still snoozing in that last kennel." He gestured to the room beyond.

Charlotte followed Harmony, who took the lead. The space was divided into six cubicles. There was only one dog in sight now, an amber-colored retriever asleep on a bed of clean straw in a kennel with an open door. Charlotte wouldn't have been surprised to learn that Brad had been napping on the straw beside her when they knocked.

"That's a goldendoodle?" Harmony asked.

"No, Velvet looks like a golden retriever, so the puppies' father must be a poodle. According to their website, a first-generation cross of the breeds is supposed to be the best. Isn't she gorgeous?"

The dog lifted her regal head and stared at them, but she didn't bother to get up.

"Boy, don't I know how she feels?" Harmony squatted beside the dog and offered her hand to sniff. Then, when it was accepted, she began to pet Velvet's neck. "She's a beauty."

Charlotte joined Harmony closer to the

ground, offering her hand as the younger woman had done. "I don't think we're going to make it up the mountain today, after all."

"Where were we going?"

"A place called the old Sawyer farm. Velvet would love it there, but we'll have to go another time. We need to take her back to the house and settle her in. If Brad decides we're reliable enough."

"What will your references say when he asks if you're sane enough to take the dog?"

"They'll think he's joking. Then they'll think I've lost my mind."

"Maybe you have."

Charlotte stroked Velvet's ears. "If I have, I won't be looking for it anytime soon."

Chapter Eighteen

Harmony loved trying this and that, so tapas were her favorite and Zambra her favorite restaurant. She hoped she and Davis could eat in the courtyard, with its parallel rows of tables against caramel stucco walls. She loved the fresh air wafting through the keyhole-shaped doorway and the snatches of conversation as people strolled the side-walk beyond. It seemed Davis was going to spare no expense to get her back in his bed and in front of his stove.

He had no idea just how cheap dinner was going to be in comparison to the child sup-port the court would probably order him to pay next year.

She considered not dressing up. Asheville was a casual town, and she knew Zambra's patrons would be dressed in everything from denim and shorts to flowered sun-dresses and dress shirts. Her wardrobe was perfunctory at best, but in the end she donned a lime-green layered skirt that fell almost to her knees and a paler green tank top. She covered the top with an oversize white shirt from the men's rack at Goodwill, and rolled the sleeves up to her elbows. Beads, hoop earrings and hair down her back, she was on her way.

"You're sure you'll be okay with Velvet?" she asked Charlotte.

"We're already friends." Charlotte was lying on the living room sofa with a book, and the big golden retriever was curled up on the floor beside her. On a pillow, Harmony noticed. Or possibly two, from the bedroom she'd occupied that first night.

"I'm not going to be late," she promised. "It's just dinner."

"You've got a key. Have a good time."

Harmony wondered where Velvet would sleep that night. They had made the dog a bed of folded blankets in the laundry room, but somehow she didn't think the dog would spend much time there.

Outside, she turned her car in the driveway and started into town. After a turn around Zambra she ranged farther afield and found parking a couple of blocks away. The day had taken its toll, and she was ready for a good night's sleep, not a hike uphill. She was also hungry, or at least she thought that was what her roiling stomach was trying to tell her.

As she'd dressed, she had asked herself if she should tell Davis about the baby tonight. While she had considered the possibility, she didn't want to. Of course, even though she was going through with the pregnancy, she still had options. If she decided to give the baby to adoptive parents, she'd learned she could choose a family, interview them, see their home, even communicate regularly and reunite with her child some day in the future.

At the library she'd discovered a website with photos of happy couples just waiting to give her child a home. She appreciated their struggle and desire, but the website had made her uncomfortable, as if these smiling people were vultures poised to tear the flesh from her bones. All she had to do was say yes, choose the pair with the sharpest beak and the widest wingspan, and her baby would be stripped from her arms.

She figured maybe choosing parents from a website wasn't going to be a good solution, either.

Davis wouldn't be any help. He was nothing if not practical, and a baby out of wedlock was a bad career move for an up-and-comer in a conservative firm. He would probably pull out his calculator, punch numbers while he mumbled things like "private school, formula, diapers — do you know how much diapers cost, Harmony?" Then he would show her the final screen, with some astronomical figure even a Saudi sheik couldn't afford, and shake his head sadly.

No, she wasn't going to tell Davis tonight.

When she got to the restaurant, he was waiting out front. He wasn't even staring at his watch, which was good, since she was five minutes late, something that always annoyed him. He wore a charcoal sport coat over a casually styled white shirt and designer jeans. This was Davis trying to be cool.

Actually, he'd managed cool. For a moment she saw beyond her own anger at his fling, her recognition of his impatience and perfectionism, and just saw the guy she'd been crazy about once upon a time.

"You look great," he said, leaning over to kiss her.

She turned her head so he just caught her cheek. "You don't look half-bad yourself," she said, sorry it was true.

"I asked for an outside table. I hope that's okay? It's so pretty out tonight."

She knew he had done this for her. He

absolutely hated retrieving napkins that blew off the table. She had to silently give him a point for trying.

Once inside, the host led them to the courtyard. She noted they were escorted to the same table where they had celebrated her twenty-first birthday. That time she'd asked for an outside table, and Davis had fidgeted and brushed imaginary dust particles off the surface through the entire meal. Tonight, though, he pulled out her chair before he seated himself across from her.

"Think it's warm enough for sangria?" he asked. "Or is that a summer thing?"

He was suggesting sangria to please her, too. Only she wasn't drinking these days, not even something watered down with fruit juice and sparkling water.

"I'm not really in the mood," she said. "But I *am* thirsty. Maybe some club soda and lime." She hoped it would settle her stomach, which apparently had chosen dinnertime tonight to misbehave.

"You don't want me to order a bottle of wine? They have a great wine list."

"It's been a tiring week. You don't want me falling asleep."

"Not here," he said, raising a brow provocatively.

"Don't get any ideas. I'm going straight home. One dinner doesn't make up for everything you've put me through, Davis. Not even at Zambra."

He reached across the table and took her hand. "Whatever it takes, Harmony. I mean it."

Child support for the next eighteen years? She slid her hand out from under his and picked up her menu.

"So what happened to tire you out?" he asked.

Egg met sperm, did a little dance, cozied up to the rhythm of a beating heart and found a place to settle in for nine months. And the little duo had asked her to play hostess.

But she couldn't say that. She told him about work, then about the trip out to Capable Canines.

Their server arrived and introduced herself. The woman was just a little older than Harmony, and curvier, with artfully layered black hair that swung over a round face when she leaned against the table. Harmony watched Davis, but he seemed oblivious. He ordered her club soda and a glass of pinot noir for himself, and waited until the young woman left.

"So your friend Charlotte just scooped up

this dog and took it home?"

"The owner checked her references, and said it was a go. He sent us off with five pounds of dog food and the name of his vet. It's a really lovely little farm, Davis. He showed us around on our way out to the car. They have a big garden area, a couple of horses, chickens. They have a two- and a four-year-old who'll be staying in South Carolina while his wife recuperates. They're waiting for the insurance companies to stop squabbling and pay up, so they can make plans for the future. But first she has to get out of rehab."

She realized she'd lost him. She was talking about strangers, and he wasn't interested.

"The whole thing sounds strange," Davis said. "This woman lives in Biltmore Forest, but she's willing to take a bitch who's about to whelp, and pay all the vet bills and clean up the mess?"

"She has her reasons." Harmony didn't plan to go into them. Charlotte had told her about her granddaughter's epilepsy in confidence.

"I'm not sure that's a good place for you." He was bent over the menu, studying the night's offerings. "She sounds flaky as all get-out. Have you checked her out?"

Harmony didn't answer until he noticed the silence and looked up.

"You will not criticize my living situation," she said. "Got it?"

"I'm just worried, that's all."

"You're worried that I'm living in a private suite in Biltmore Forest with a woman who stretched out a hand when I needed one and hasn't asked me for one thing in return? That worries you? The same man who wasn't worried that sleeping with the woman who scrapes plaque off his teeth would upset me?"

"You're going to bring that up and bring that up, aren't you?"

"I get so much pleasure from the memory."

"Harmony, I'm trying to make it up to you. Have you noticed? And what's wrong with expressing concern? I want you to be safe and happy."

"Then you're in luck." She lifted her menu so she could no longer see his face.

The server arrived with their drinks and a lovely smile, and Davis asked Harmony what sounded good to her. The sad truth was that tonight nothing did. They had already settled on ordering several tapas each, but she was having problems selecting anything that didn't make her stomach churn. She decided on an egg dish, which she thought she could handle, and a wild-mushroom concoction that under better circumstances would have made her salivate in anticipation. She remembered that she'd liked the fried tofu the last time and finished with that.

Davis ordered veal sweetbreads and char-grilled octopus, along with a special lamb taco. His meal sounded like something an interrogator would threaten to feed little-old-vegetarian-her if she refused to co-operate. She couldn't think of one secret she wouldn't give up to avoid his meal.

When the server left, Davis held up his glass in toast and, reluctantly, she brushed it with her own. "To better times ahead. Tell me more about work."

"Same old, same old. Ray's going to give me some hours in the kitchen. I'd like to learn some of his techniques and recipes. I'll just be doing prep work, at least at first, but he promised to teach me as we go."

His expression said he thought that was a bad idea. "I wish you'd let me help you find a real job. What are you going to make in the kitchen? Minimum wage?"

"I work hard, and I get paid. Isn't that the definition of a *real* job?"

"My insurance guy said he might need

somebody in his office. Filing, answering phones. You could probably learn the business from the ground up."

The suggestion was beyond awful. Not only was Davis trying to settle her into a position that sounded more important — at least to the people he hoped to impress — the idea came with more personal baggage than a flight to Australia.

She leaned forward, so he wouldn't miss the significance of her words. "My father sells insurance. Do you honestly think I want to follow in his footsteps?"

"Your father sells insurance to truckers, right? This is hardly the same thing. It's a white-collar job. You wouldn't be scrambling around truck stops knocking back brewskis with the boys."

"My father has an office, Davis, with his own secretary. And he doesn't drink, smoke, use drugs or even celebrate holidays. He's rigid and hateful, and for fun, he beats the women in his family to help set them on the right path. And no, the sickness in his soul has nothing to do with selling insurance, but you can see, if you try, why I might not be inclined to wend my way along the same career path."

If Davis picked up on the emotion in her words, he didn't acknowledge it. "You're overreacting, but just listen to yourself, to the way you said that. What you really ought to do is go to school. You're so smart, Harmony. If you move back in with me, you can go to AB Tech and get a couple of years behind you there. You can afford it on what you make if you aren't paying for rent or food. I'll help. I'd like that."

She wasn't warmed by the offer. She thought Davis probably *would* like that version of her life. If he was more or less supporting her, wouldn't that give him more power?

And besides, wasn't all this just so much smoke in the wind? A baby was on the way, and everything was destined to change.

Their server arrived, and she was saved from answering. The pretty brunette delivered the mushrooms to Harmony and the octopus to Davis. She focused on her own plate and began to eat. The mushrooms were succulent and subtly flavored. She took a piece of the bread Davis had ordered for both of them, and ate slowly and carefully. Her stomach began to calm.

"How's work?" she asked.

"They're pleased with me. I think I've exceeded their expectations. I'll be promoted as soon as they're sure I plan to stay and invest myself in the community."

"What does that mean?"

"I'm not sure. I think they're watching a couple of us for proof we're not planning to take better offers in bigger cities."

"Why *don't* you take a better offer somewhere else?"

He smiled seductively. "Because you're here."

"Sure," she said with no conviction. "And what else?"

"I'm settled. Weather's good. Real estate's not crazy expensive anymore, and I'll be able to afford a house before too long. I'd rather be at the top of a firm here than hanging out in the middle of one in Atlanta or Chicago. Good schools, pretty scenery. Great restaurants. Mostly, though, I'm settled. Why pull up stakes when this meets my needs?"

She had singled out one phrase. "What do good schools have to do with anything?"

"Businesses don't move into communities where their employees don't want to live. If the schools are bad, they look elsewhere. Bad schools equal a lousy economy. More local governments should figure that out."

For a moment she'd been hopeful.

Their server arrived with their next selections. She set the plates on the table and promised she would be back in a few minutes.

Harmony took the one closest to her, the egg dish that looked less like an omelet than eggs and sauce scrambled with a variety of vegetables and herbs. She took a bite, and while it wasn't what she'd expected, it wasn't exactly unpleasant, either. Just different.

"I thought you didn't eat veal," Davis said, looking up. "Aren't you all animal-rights-vegetarian? I can't believe you're eating sweetbreads, of all things."

His words took a moment to sink in. Then she looked down with horror at the plate and shoved it toward him, her stomach erupting like a dormant volcano. "I thought —" Suddenly there was nothing else to think about. She jumped up from the table and ran toward the doorway into the restaurant.

Ten minutes later, pale and shaking, she found her way back to the table. She wasn't sure what she would find, but Davis was still sitting there, although the plates looked untouched. His wineglass was full, though, and she knew he'd made decent headway on his first glass before she left. She wondered if this was glass number two or three.

"Hey, don't apologize," he said, when she

sat. "Not for getting sick. Maybe for not telling me you're pregnant, though."

She didn't deny it.

"*Were* you going to tell me?" His tone was even, but cool, the way it might be if he was interrogating a client who'd been cheating on his income tax.

She was cringing inside, the way she'd cringed as a child when she knew her father was growing angry — a situation that never ended well. She tried to sound strong. She told herself she'd done nothing wrong. But she felt both weak and guilty.

"When I decided the time was right," she said.

"How would you know? When the time was right, I mean?"

"First, when I knew what I planned to do. Second, when I knew what I planned to do about *you.*"

"You have lots of choices, Harmony, but what to do about me probably isn't one of them."

She inclined her head regally, as if that was not unexpected.

"I assume I'm the father?" he asked.

"Was somebody else in our bed? Besides the woman who found the cavity in your upper left molar?"

"I can't say. I don't know what you were

doing when I was at work. Maybe you were getting it on with the *dentist.*"

Since the dentist was pushing seventy, she knew he was just being hateful, but she was suddenly furious. This time she worked to keep her tone even for a different reason. "Let me put your mind at ease. In what free time I had between shifts, I was cooking, scrubbing, taking your clothes to the cleaner, having your oil changed. Unless one of those activities leads to pregnancy, we can assume you're the father. Something a paternity test will prove."

"If you're talking tests, I gather you're not having an abortion?"

She reached for her beaded clutch purse, a dollar purchase at a garage sale, and stood. "I'm not having an abortion, I'm having a *baby.* And I may be young and stupid, which this whole episode proves beyond a reasonable doubt, but I'm not so stupid I'm going to forego child support. The baby deserves it. So put that in your budget, along with your toilet paper and the internet. I don't care what else you contribute, but this child is going to have the things it needs most."

When he didn't reply, she turned and hurried out to the sidewalk. By the time she reached her car, her stomach was in turmoil again. But she was safe. There was nothing left inside her to expel except anger.

Chapter Nineteen

Velvet had a cold nose and a warm heart. While most dogs in her situation would have waited impatiently at the door to go home, Velvet was smarter. She'd immediately taken stock of her new situation and realized she had two women ready to do anything she wanted. Introduced to her new quarters in the laundry room, she had daintily pawed the blankets, then looked up as if to say, *Well, it's very nice, but I think you can do better.*

She had been marginally happier with an expensive suede cloth bed, placed in the butler's pantry, which was closer to the action. But a week later she was even happier, because her new sleeping quarters were in Charlotte's bedroom.

The master bedroom suite had his-and-hers walk-in closets, and Velvet was now sole resident of the "his" closet. The few things Charlotte had stored there had been moved to a guest room. Velvet had a water dish in Charlotte's bathroom, and a bowl of kibble in case she felt like a snack. In truth, though, at night she slept on the priceless Flokati rug beside Charlotte's bed. In fact, Charlotte was pretty sure if the dog hadn't been about to bring a litter of puppies into the world, she would have been happy to leap right up onto the Egyptian cotton sheets and make herself at home.

On Saturday morning Charlotte arrived for breakfast with Velvet leading the way. Harmony was making whole-wheat pancakes topped with fresh fruit. Charlotte might have protested all the work, but the young woman really loved to cook, really loved the kitchen with all its gadgets and cookware, and really loved to please. Charlotte knew she was lucky.

Halfway through the one and only pancake she could eat, Charlotte put down her fork. "Have I mentioned that with my calling plan, phone calls are free? Unless you call Beijing or the North Pole, there's no charge to me."

Harmony looked up from her third pancake. "Thank you. But I don't have anybody to call."

Charlotte debated. There was a line between helping too much and too little, and it was never easy to find. Harmony hadn't confided in her since Saturday, when they had brought Velvet home, but the girl had been quiet, clearly considering something, or feeling the weight of her new burden.

"Okay," Charlotte said, after a brief hesitation. "But if that changes, now you know you're welcome to call anybody you'd like to."

"You think I should call my mother, don't you?"

Charlotte laid down her fork. "It's not my decision. I just thought you ought to know you can if you want to."

"What do you think I should say? 'Hey, Mom, I'm pregnant, and I'm not married. Can I come home?' "

Harmony hadn't said this with anger, she'd said it as if she really wondered.

"From everything you've told me, I don't think going home's an option," Charlotte said carefully. "But I also suspect you miss her."

"I hate that she's there with *him*. I hate that she doesn't know she's going to be a grandmother."

"You'll know what's best for you and your baby. And you know best how the news will be greeted. I just didn't want money to stop you."

"Having money's important, isn't it?"

Charlotte knew everything in the house showed how important she had believed it to be. "Having enough so you don't have to worry about every penny's important. I remember what it felt like when I didn't. I remember all those years when a long-distance phone call was as elusive as a mink coat."

"It's going to be more important with a baby. I see that."

"So much to balance, right?"

"Right." Harmony smiled, but as if she'd been forced to excavate it from someplace deep inside her. "I'm working on it."

"And you're going to figure it all out."

Harmony looked down at her plate as if the secrets of the universe could be found there. "What do you have planned for your day?"

Charlotte knew a change of subject when she heard one. "I thought I'd hit the pet store for kibble and those rawhide treats Velvet's so fond of."

"You really love that store."

Charlotte also loved the fact that the store wasn't far from the park where Maddie went to play. If Maddie were there today, Charlotte wasn't going to stay and watch, but she did hope her granddaughter's condition had improved enough that she was able to go again. She just needed to know.

"I'll be back in an hour or two," she told Harmony. "You don't have to stay if you have things to do. Nell will be in for a little while this morning, and she'll call me if Velvet starts acting like her litter's on the way." Nell was her part-time housekeeper, who thankfully loved dogs.

"Glenda's car is toast, and she's riding her bike everywhere until she can pay for the repairs. I told her I'd pick up her things and bring them here while she's at work. She's moving in tonight, and she'll stay with us until the pups are born, just in case."

Harmony had brought Glenda by earlier in the week to meet Velvet. The girl had buzz-cut hair dyed an incongruous blue, and tattoos of snakes winding up both arms, but she was politely soft-spoken, and her eyes, behind octagonal ruby-rimmed glasses, sparkled with humor. Best of all, Velvet had adored her from first sniff.

As Charlotte rose to clear her place, she told Harmony how great the meal had been.

Harmony looked skeptical. "You don't have much of an appetite. You're not trying to lose weight, are you? You're already kind of thin."

Charlotte was afraid to weigh herself and see. She'd been ordered to gain weight, but she'd lost her appetite during chemo, and it had never returned.

"I'm not on a diet," Charlotte assured her. "And I'm sure you're going to fatten me up. I just don't eat a lot at one sitting."

"These'll heat up great, only you shouldn't use the microwave. Use the stove. You don't want deadly radiation pinging all over the house."

Charlotte tried hard to sound concerned. "I certainly don't."

"No, I'm serious. I read an article about it, or somebody told me, I can't remember which. But I never use your microwave. I don't take any chances."

"You're doing a wonderful job of cooking without one." Charlotte was moving a little slower than usual. She hadn't slept well last night, and for the past two days she'd been achy right down to her bones, as well as chilled. She hoped the warmer weather on its way would help. She would lie out by the pool and soak up the sunshine until she felt more like herself.

"I'm making a stir-fry with organic vegetables tonight. If I'm not here when you get hungry, all you have to do is warm up the rice in one pan and the veggies in another."

"Only not in the microwave," Charlotte said.

"You got it."

Fifteen minutes later as she drove toward the park, Charlotte thought about all the poisons that had drained through her system during her month of intensive chemo. Harmony would be horrified to know that Charlotte saw lethal chemicals and radiation as ways to prolong her life, even though the experience had nearly killed her. There was more chemo ahead, but by then Harmony would have to know.

She parked next to a curb on a side street with no other cars nearby and no maneuvering. The park was only two blocks away, but she walked slowly, the way she'd once imagined she might at eighty. She had rushed through her life, and she told herself slowing down and paying attention were gifts that had been forced on her by the leukemia.

There had been others. Her roommate in the ICU had been the most important. Charlotte had been angry at having to share her room, the unfairness of being forced to give up her privacy warring with the humiliation of having a stranger witness her struggle to hold on to life. But Gwen had saved her. Gwen, with her calm, resolute manner, her soothing words, her questions — always questions, never answers.

Gwen, whose bed had been rolled away one night as Charlotte slept, not to return again. Gwen, whose fate Charlotte had never learned, because she had been too cowardly to pursue it.

Once she reached the park she crossed the path leading to the tennis courts and started downhill, slowing her steps even more. She didn't want to get too close, just close enough to see.

She paused under a clump of trees. At first she couldn't find Maddie among the other children, then the little girl burst out from behind the concession stand, running toward the climbing dome with Edna right beside her.

Maddie felt well enough to be here, and that was another gift, one that brought tears to Charlotte's eyes. Maddie kept up with Edna, although her legs weren't nearly as long. She swung her arms with abandon, as if every swing would propel her faster and farther. Edna could have outdistanced her easily, but didn't. Charlotte wondered if Samantha had ever considered writing a parenting manual.

They reached the dome at the same moment and began to climb. Samantha was sitting just beyond, at an angle, but Charlotte saw her glance up and check the situation before she went back to her book.

She told herself she could leave now. She'd learned exactly what she needed. Maddie was doing well enough to be here with her friend, running like any other child, climbing the dome and racing Edna to the top.

As she allowed herself just another moment of her granddaughter's company, Maddie stood hands-free near the top, pumping her fists in the air in victory.

"You tell them," Charlotte said softly. "No matter what, sweetheart, you're a winner."

For a moment, it almost seemed as if Maddie had heard her, because the child stiffened and her head swiveled in her grandmother's direction. Then, as Charlotte watched in horror, Maddie arched backward, and with her feet catching between bars, toppled in an arc and fell headfirst, snapping her head against the bars as she went, until she was a boneless heap on the ground, thrashing uncontrollably.

Before she realized it, Charlotte was racing toward her granddaughter. She reached her well after Samantha, who was trying unsuccessfully to cushion the child's head with a folded sweatshirt. With horror Charlotte saw that the sweatshirt was already red with Maddie's blood, which was seeping from somewhere at the back of her head.

"Call 9-1-1," somebody shouted from the sidelines, and somebody else said she already had.

Charlotte knelt beside Samantha in the mulch at the bottom of the dome. "What can I do?"

Samantha didn't look at her. "Make them stand back."

Charlotte got to her feet. Most of the onlookers were children, as she would have expected if she'd had even a moment to think. She started at one end, gently shooing them away. "There's nothing you can do," she said. "We need privacy."

Edna was at the end closest to her mother, and she looked stricken. Without thinking, Charlotte put her arm around the girl. "It's not your fault," she said. "She was having a wonderful time with you."

"But we were running!"

"Honey, these things are unpredictable. It's really, really not something you did, I promise. Now, can you get the other children away?" She ended by glancing back to Samantha and Maddie, sure that Edna would do as asked, or at least try.

One of the adults joined Edna and helped her herd the children toward another area of the park. Another woman moved to stand beside Charlotte.

"Who lets a child with that kind of a problem run loose on a playground like this one?" She looked to be in her mid-thirties, hair neatly held back by a thin gold band, pink and white clothing perfect for a charity picnic.

Charlotte felt fury building inside her. "A mother who knows how important a normal day is to her little girl."

"Well, it backfired, and now all the other little girls and boys have had their day ruined." She stalked off, as if Maddie had done this solely to annoy her.

Charlotte was already back at Maddie's side. The seizure seemed to be winding down. It wasn't the first she'd seen. Hearty had experienced seizures when he couldn't get enough to drink. Once he'd been so down on his luck he'd tried to drink rubbing alcohol, with disastrous results.

Up close, it was clear this seizure was a bad one, but most frightening was the darkening stain on Samantha's sweatshirt. "Where's the blood coming from?"

"I can't tell yet."

Maddie had stopped moving, and Samantha gently turned her to one side, sliding the sweatshirt under her cheek to cushion her. "Do you have anything I can use to stop the bleeding?" she asked.

Charlotte had already slipped off the cardigan she was wearing over a sleeveless shell. She folded it and handed it to Samantha, who pressed it against the back of Maddie's head.

"Try emergency again," Samantha said. "Find out how long they'll be."

With shaking hands Charlotte pulled out her cell phone and punched in the numbers. She explained where she was and what had happened. "It's my granddaughter. Please, we need somebody right now."

She answered the dispatcher's questions, then put the phone in her lap. "She says we should hear the sirens in a moment, they're that close."

"She's not coming around," Samantha said. "It was a bad fall."

"She's been doing better?"

"She's been champing at the bit to get back to the park. Taylor finally gave in. Usually Maddie can sense a seizure coming on at least a few seconds before it arrives and protect herself a little. But this time . . ."

"She was having such a wonderful time."

Charlotte realized she was crying. She stretched out her hand to stroke Maddie's bangs off her forehead, the first time she'd ever been close enough to touch her granddaughter.

"Taylor's teaching a class."

"Does she have a cell phone?"

Samantha gave her a number, and Charlotte punched it in. She planned to hand the phone to Samantha, but no one answered, not even voice mail.

"No answer," she said.

"She's probably out on the floor with a student. Do you have Ethan's number?"

Charlotte didn't, but she called directory assistance and got his home number, then she waited as she was connected.

There was no answer at Ethan's, either, but this time she got voice mail. She left a brief message, telling him what had happened and that an ambulance was on the way. Before she hung up, she left him her number.

Sirens were audible now. "Thank God," Samantha said.

Charlotte hoped there was an even better reason to offer thanks. She prayed her granddaughter wasn't badly injured.

In minutes the ambulance had pulled in as close as possible, and the EMS team was doing an initial assessment while they tried to stabilize the bleeding. A woman took Samantha's brief statement, as a man finished examining Maddie.

"We're going to take her to Mission," the woman said, after she and the man conferred for a moment and she had called in to the hospital. "You can meet us there."

"I want to come, along with my daughter," Samantha said. "I'm in charge of her."

"I'm sorry, but not unless you're a relative," the young woman said, not without empathy.

"I'm her *grandmother,*" Charlotte said.

"Then you can ride along."

Charlotte looked at Samantha, who nodded. "I'll get Edna. We'll meet you there."

"I'm sorry," Charlotte said. "I'm not trying to take over, but I don't want her —"

"You go. It's a good thing."

Charlotte stepped back as the two paramedics quickly and professionally readied Maddie for transport. She knew how misleading, how wrong, this was, but at the moment she didn't care. She didn't want her granddaughter to wake up in the ambulance surrounded by strangers. Because even though she was a stranger herself, she was a stranger who loved her.

■ ■ ■ ■

Ethan's workshop was his little slice of heaven. It also made a significant contribution to his livelihood. After divorcing Charlotte and severing ties with Falconview, he had purchased a small house with a large outbuilding, which he had converted into the office and workplace where he was now finishing kitchen cupboards built from recycled hickory flooring.

The cupboards were one of the finishing touches on six loft condos designed to fill a space that had once housed a bottle factory. Martin Architectural Design consisted of Ethan, a part-time project manager and an architectural designer, who was full-time when needed. They were a small firm, specializing in sustainability and adaptive reuse, and they hired other professionals when needed. He could afford to stay small and work on projects that interested him, because the lump sum he had taken as severance from Falconview, along with a decidedly unlavish lifestyle, made both possible.

As a boy he had enjoyed working with his hands, but only after the divorce had he taken up carpentry again, finding that in bringing old, tired materials back to life, he found new life himself. Now he made a point of handling whatever finishing touches he could himself, a plus during an economic downturn, when time was the one thing he had plenty of. The bottle factory was his to convert any way he chose, but real estate sales were slow, and he was hoping one of the units would sell soon, so he could begin work on the final one, where he planned to live himself.

A house was meant for a family. The final unit of the old bottle factory was designed for a single man who was tired of yard work and housekeeping nobody else appreciated. The condo that would be his was to be the simplest of the six, with a small bedroom for Maddie when she stayed overnight and a larger one for himself. The rest of the renovation would be open and airy, stripped down to nothing except lovingly recycled materials and surfaces he could wipe down in minutes.

As he turned off the electric sander he heard his phone ringing, but by the time he picked up, the ringing had stopped. He checked caller ID, but the number was unfamiliar. Curious now, since the call had come in on his home number, he waited a moment and picked up the receiver to see if the caller had left a message. Moments later he was on his way to the Moon and Stars yoga studio.

Taylor was just finishing up a class in a long room with mirrored walls when he walked in. He knew enough yoga to recognize the posture of her students as Savasana, the "corpse" pose used for relaxation at the end of a class. When she saw him in the doorway, she went perfectly still, then gave the class some final instructions before she hurried over to greet him.

"Maddie?" she asked softly.

"She had a seizure on the playground and fell off the climbing dome. She's at the hospital. Sam's with her." He hesitated.

She knew him too well. "What else?"

"And your mother is, too. She happened to be there. She called me."

"What are you talking about?" She honestly seemed lost.

"Your mother was at the park when Maddie fell. She called me. Sam tried your cell phone and couldn't get you."

"She was at the park?" Taylor held up her hands. "Don't! I don't care. How badly was Maddie hurt?"

"I don't know, honey. I missed the call. I just got the message, and when I tried to get your mom, I got voice mail."

"Let me get my things."

Once they were in his car he offered Taylor his phone. "Try calling your mom again. I programmed her number into my speed dial before I left. She's number four. See if you can find out what happened."

Taylor didn't take his phone. Instead, she pulled out her own and hit several buttons. "Sam called. It's right here in the call history. But there's no message because my voice mail's been screwed up. It takes forever for them to fix anything. I've tried and tried!"

Ethan waited impatiently at a light. "I'd like to know what's going on, wouldn't you?"

"It won't help to know. We just need to get there."

"It would help me."

"What was she doing there, anyway? Were they holding a charity tennis match? Somehow I don't think so. Has she been stalking Maddie?"

"I don't know what she was doing there today. I didn't talk to her." His mind was racing in circles, but all of them ended and began with the truth. He couldn't pretend otherwise.

He took a breath, because he knew what was coming. "I saw her from a distance at the park when I picked up Maddie a few weeks ago. I went to see her afterward, and I asked her exactly what you just did. She's never approached Maddie or told her who she is. But she goes there sometimes just to see her."

"Damn!" Taylor hit the dashboard with her palm. "She has no right!"

"She's Maddie's grandmother."

"No, she is not! She gave up the right to be *anything* to my daughter."

"We're going to have this conversation later. I can't drive safely and have it now, Taylor."

She began to cry and tried to fight it. He glanced quickly at her, and saw both the tears and the fury. Everything inside him twisted into knots.

"If she hadn't been there," he said, because somebody had to, "if she hadn't had the presence of mind to call me and ask me to find you, we wouldn't even know what had happened."

Taylor cried silently beside him.

The trip to the hospital seemed to take forever, but it probably only took minutes. At the emergency entrance the paramedics capably and quickly got Maddie inside. She hadn't regained consciousness. She had never known for even a moment that the grandmother she'd never met sat beside her the entire way, holding her hand.

Once they arrived, Charlotte knew better than to try to assert herself. While she had been required to turn off her cell phone in the ambulance, she knew Ethan might already have gotten her message and could be on the way to the hospital with their daughter. The last thing Taylor needed to see when she arrived was her mother conferring with hospital personnel about Maddie's treatment.

She was spared explaining when the hospital staff whisked Maddie away to be examined without her. Some minutes later, as her legs were about to give out from pacing, a nurse returned to say the doctor on call had ordered an immediate CT scan, and since she was still unconscious, they preferred that Charlotte take a seat in the emergency waiting room until she was needed.

Charlotte lowered herself to a chair in an empty row and rested her head in her hands. Part of her knew she should leave now, before Taylor arrived. Another part thought she should stay, so she could tell whoever arrived first exactly what had happened and what was being done about it.

She was so shaken she couldn't make a decision, and so drained she wasn't sure she had the strength to go outside where she could finally turn on her cell phone and call a taxi.

Before she could decide, she looked up and saw Taylor jog through the emergency room doors, heading straight for reception, which was only about twenty feet from where Charlotte sat.

"Let me check," the woman at the desk said calmly, after Taylor told her why she was there. "You're the mother? Do you have identification?"

"You need proof?" Taylor asked angrily. "At a time like this?" She riffled through her purse and began to slap cards on the desk.

Charlotte saw that Ethan had followed their daughter inside, and now he put his hand on Taylor's shoulder. "We're worried and upset," he said. "I'm sorry. I'm Maddie's grandfather."

The woman ignored Taylor. "Your wife was with her, but I think they've taken your granddaughter for a CT scan. The doctor will be out as soon as there's something to tell you. You'll need to present your insurance card and fill out the paperwork over there." She pointed to a window just beyond reception.

"I want to be with my daughter," Taylor said, punching every word for emphasis. "Now."

The woman looked her over, then her gaze softened. "I'll see what I can do. Why don't you sit over there while I find somebody who can talk to you?"

She pointed to the row of nearly empty chairs where Charlotte was just getting to her feet. Charlotte hadn't been sure she could feel worse, but now, at the fury in Taylor's eyes, she knew how foolish that had been.

Ethan took Taylor's arm and edged her away from the desk. It looked as if he was trying to talk to her, his voice low, but Taylor shook off his hand. She focused on Charlotte standing at the end of the row, and for just a moment she looked stricken. Then, before Ethan could say another word or Charlotte could move in her direction, she strode toward her.

"Why?" she demanded, when she was facing Charlotte. "Why were you watching my daughter? Why were you *there?*"

"I knew she'd been having a hard time, Taylor," Charlotte said quietly. "I just wanted to see how she was doing. I thought —"

"You *thought?* You have no *right* to think about Maddie? What gave you the right, Mother? You didn't want her, or rather, you didn't want *me* to have her. You wanted me to have an abortion, or, barring that, you wanted me to give her away. And when I said I wouldn't? You told me to get out. I was sixteen, pregnant, and you told me to get out of the house unless I did what you wanted!"

Charlotte's eyes filled, and the tears spilled over. She said the only thing she could. "I wish I could take back that day, Taylor. You have no idea how badly I wish I could."

"And I don't care. Because when I had her too early, when she was fighting for every single breath, you said if I had only done what you wanted me to, my poor imperfect daughter, my brave little girl fighting for her life, would never have been born! And wouldn't the world have been a better place, Mother? One less imperfect child."

Ethan put his hands on Taylor's shoulders. "Stop it, Taylor. This isn't the time or place."

"There is no time. There is no place."

Charlotte felt as if somebody had sucked the air out of her lungs. For a moment she struggled to breathe. When she could finally draw a breath, she faced Ethan and managed to speak. "You told her what I said that night? You told Taylor what I said just to *you* outside the intensive care nursery the night Maddie was born?"

Taylor gave a bitter laugh. "Nobody told me! I overheard you. I was there. I'd gotten up to see her, but neither of you knew it."

Ethan looked sick, but before he could say anything, Charlotte did.

"Taylor, I was devastated. She was suffering. All I could think about was —"

"Stop!" Taylor stepped out of her father's grasp. "Leave, okay? I'm going to see if I can find out what's going on here, and when I come back, I want you gone. Just the way you've been gone for my daughter's entire life. Just the way you were gone for most of mine."

She turned and strode toward the reception desk. Charlotte closed her eyes and swayed.

Ethan reached out to grab her. "Sit," he said.

She tried to shrug off his hands. "No, I'd better leave. I'll call somebody to pick me up."

He looked doubtful she was capable of either. She knew her cheeks were as colorless as air, and with his hands locked on her arms, he'd probably determined how thin she really was.

He dropped his hands at last and stepped away.

"Will you let me know . . . ?" Her voice trailed off.

He nodded, although they both knew that if Taylor found out he'd been in touch with Charlotte again, she would be furious.

"I'm not going to be anybody's pawn," he said. "Not yours or our daughter's. But I'll let you know. You deserve that."

She felt behind her to find her purse. "Maddie never opened her eyes in the ambulance. I held her hand, but she never saw my face."

"I'll call you."

She moved away, still unsteady on her feet. She skirted the reception desk, where Taylor was once again arguing with the woman behind it, and disappeared through the doors.

Outside, she leaned against a pillar and tried to breathe slowly. She told herself she had done everything she could for Maddie, and that riding in the ambulance with her granddaughter had been the right thing to do. But her profound sense of loss was all too familiar. It was the same feeling she had experienced on the day that Ethan and Taylor had walked away from her forever.

Chapter Twenty

First Day Journal, May 14

It's not easy to look back at my life and see when problems began and solutions fell by the wayside. Yet at the time I believed the patterns were forming without my help. I was there, like an actor repeating my lines, but I never realized I was also the playwright.

Now I am there again.

Taylor is not an easy baby. Even after our week of separation I try to nurse her, but she screams for more, and formula never quite agrees with her. We walk the floor together at night, but even when she is between bouts of colic and earaches, she seems dissatisfied, as if I should know how to comfort her and she holds me accountable.

My years and experience with the King boys have no impact on a baby. She prefers Ethan, who's less worried about how to please her. She will sleep in his arms, while in mine she stiffens and screams.

Since I feel like such a failure at home, I go back to school in the fall and take a heavy load of classes. The wife of one of my professors offers child care, and Taylor loves it there. No one else finds her behavior discouraging. Experienced and relaxed, they keep her happy and entertained, and sometimes when I retrieve her at the end of my day, she cries to stay.

I finish my classes on Taylor's first birthday. My baby girl loves the gifts we've chosen, and my homemade cake dissolves in a pool of crumbs and slobber on her high chair. For once I fulfill my role as her mother exactly as I'm supposed to, and I am encouraged. As my graduation present Ethan buys tickets to Hawaii. His parents agree to babysit for the week we'll be gone.

The trip is a second honeymoon. Without school, work or our baby, we're lovers and friends once again. Ethan has been unfailingly supportive as I learn to be a parent. He seems born to the job.

We talk about our future. I'm torn between spending the next year at home and finding a place for myself in the world. I have my education and degree, but neither is as important as my ambition. I have a new reason to succeed. Now I desperately want to provide Taylor with all the things I never had, hoping, I think, that it will make up for my lack of mothering skills.

Ethan wonders how we'll manage two busy schedules and a baby. He's considering his own future and looking for employment. To my disappointment, he's only looking in the Blue Ridge, determined to stay in the mountains he loves. The firm where he interned wants him to remain, but I think his career will be better served in a larger one where he can make his mark and still design the structures he most loves. He agrees, but reminds me we might need to move as far away as Tennessee. What's the point of my beginning a career in Asheville, he asks, if I'll just have to leave? Why not begin once we're settled?

I love being with him, and I'm beginning to relax. Now that she isn't colicky, Taylor's easier to mother, and Ethan seems to thrive on my love. Maybe I can settle into a simpler life.

We return home to find that Ethan's mother has completely rearranged our house and Taylor's schedule. She's sweetly apologetic, of course, but she hints that since I have little experience with babies or keeping a house for a professional man, she's given me the benefit of her superior breeding and knowledge. An angry Ethan tells her we don't appreciate the changes, but her message is clear. I'm not good enough to be married to her son, or to be the mother of her granddaughter, and as much as it pains her, she's been forced to set our shabby little world to rights.

By the time she leaves, the peace and serenity of Hawaii are forgotten and I am, once again, confused and unsure. A terrifying incident shatters what little confidence I have.

Ethan leaves town for a job interview in Knoxville, and for three days I'm alone with Taylor. She's unusually fussy, but at first I discount it. I assume she misses her father, who's better at soothing her. When I'm the only one available to put her to bed, she can't be consoled. She wakes twice during the night, and the second time I let her fuss. In the morning she sleeps later than usual. I assume the fussing has worn her down and she's making up for it now.

By nine, when she still hadn't awakened, I check on her and find she's feverish. The pediatrician's office is overflowing with children, and on the telephone they tell me there's a virus making the rounds. They suggest I keep my daughter at home, away from other children, and explain what to do, as well as what to watch for.

Since the job interview's an important one, I decide not to call Ethan, and I certainly don't call his mother, who would make it clear that I have failed my daughter by allowing her to get sick. I spend the day bathing Taylor in cool water and giving her the over-the-counter medicines the pediatric nurse has suggested. By evening she seems better, and I'm encouraged, though worn out by her demands.

That night she sleeps fitfully, but she doesn't seem worse. We have another day that's much the same. By then it's Friday, and Ethan's due home the next afternoon, so when he calls, I tell him what we've been through but assure him we're coping. I put Taylor to bed early because she falls asleep in her high chair. She's quiet, and doesn't seem as hot.

I don't know what wakes me at midnight. Maybe she cries out, or maybe it's just a mother's instinct, but when I check on her, I find she's burning with fever and unresponsive. I leave a message on the pediatrician's emergency line. I call Ethan, wake him at his hotel and tell him I'm taking her to the hospital. He promises to drive home but reminds me it will take several hours. Somehow I manage to dress us both and get my limp daughter into her car seat for the race to the emergency room.

The waiting area's nearly full, and I'm lucky to find a chair. There's been a car wreck on the outskirts of town, and the injured are taken care of first. An hour of pacing passes before a nurse takes us back into a cubicle to take Taylor's history.

The woman looks familiar, although I'm hardly paying attention. She takes Taylor's history, shaking her head, then she does a quick examination before she leaves us alone. She returns with a resident, who does his own exam. They question me closely about why I've waited so long to have Taylor seen by a doctor. I explain the situation, what I've done, what I was told by my pediatrician's office, but they wave my words away. Taylor's very sick, something I should have seen, and now they must admit her right away.

The doctor leaves to make the arrangements, and the nurse faces me. Only then do I finally realize who she is. The woman is Sally Klaver, grown and educated. She asks if I've been drinking. I realize immediately she's recognized me, as well, and assumes I've followed in Hearty's footsteps. I tell her of course not, that I've hovered over Taylor since the first sign of illness.

"Children don't get this sick so quickly," she says. "You were negligent." She goes on to tell me she's going to call social services and have them look into Taylor's safety.

I'm stunned, then mortified. Sally knows nothing about me except my family background. Tonight I grabbed the first thing I could find to wear, jeans and a wrinkled shirt. In her opinion, I am still white trash.

Upstairs no one will tell me what's happening. Repeatedly I'm told to wait at the end of the hall, and hours later the resident finally comes to find me. He's spoken to my pediatrician, who's on the way to examine Taylor. The resident is perfunctorily apologetic. My pediatrician has confirmed that Taylor is a regular patient with two educated, involved parents who consult him frequently and pay close attention to her welfare.

Ethan arrives as the young man begins the apology, and when he finally says social services won't be notified, my husband explodes. I've never seen Ethan so angry. He demands to know why anyone thought they might be needed, and the resident admits that he and the nurse made an error in judgment.

Only I know the reason why.

Taylor recovers. She isn't the only child who has taken a quick turn for the worse with the same virus, and the pediatric ward is quickly filled to overflowing. I don't see Sally Klaver again during Taylor's stay, but years later I sit in on interviews for a coveted position as the head of nursing at an upscale retirement community. Sally is the top candidate until I, a respected board member, arrive to vet the finalists. During that interview, if she recognizes me, she doesn't say so.

She doesn't get the job.

The incidents with Ethan's mother and the staff at the hospital change me, or maybe I just use them as the excuses I need. Gone are all thoughts of a quieter life or a slower start up the career ladder. I vow never to allow anybody to look down on me again. Not Ethan's family, not prior acquaintances. I want everyone in my path to bow and scrape. I want power, control, status, all the things that will set our little family apart and protect us, and since Ethan isn't interested in any of them, it's clearly up to me.

Taylor's recovery takes weeks. Mine takes a lifetime.

Chapter Twenty-One

Ethan waited at the hospital with Taylor until Maddie regained consciousness, and Dr. Hilliard, who had arrived quickly, assured them there was no cause for alarm. Maddie had suffered a concussion, and a gash to her head that was now sutured. She had also broken her collarbone and dislocated her shoulder, which, with luck, would not require surgical intervention. They were still doing tests, but so far none of them indicated a more serious injury. She would be in the hospital at least a day or two, though, just to be safe.

Throughout the ordeal Taylor was shaken, grim, uncommunicative. Ethan tried once to explain why he hadn't told her he'd seen Charlotte at the park weeks before, but she held up her hand to stop him.

"I can't deal with this," she said, and he realized it was true. Taylor, who was mature beyond her years in almost every way, who was a marvelous mother and teacher and all-around human being, was a child again when it came to Charlotte.

"Do you want me to stay?" he asked, after he'd been allowed to pop in and say hello to a groggy Maddie.

"They'll make up a bed for me in her room. We'll be fine. They want her to get as much rest as possible."

"Call if you need anything."

She hugged him, but she held her body stiffly, as if she was already withholding part of herself. He hadn't realized how important it had been for Taylor to view him as her fully committed partner in the battle against her mother. Now she sensed disloyalty. He wondered how much he had fed into her perception.

He'd promised Charlotte a phone call, but he knew he owed her more. Not only had she been there for their granddaughter when she was most needed, she had absorbed Taylor's fury without returning it. Both efforts had taken a toll. He'd seen how pale she was, and noted for the first time how fragile she seemed. Still, she'd borne both the accident and the rage without collapse.

For that, she deserved a full report.

Without phoning first, he drove to the

house in Biltmore Forest. He hadn't eaten lunch, and now it was dinnertime. He was exhausted, hungry and badly in need of a few hours alone. But this was more important.

He parked where he had the last time and knocked. The same young woman — he couldn't remember her name — answered the door. This time she didn't check with Charlotte. She just opened it wider and ushered him in.

"Look, I don't know what happened today," she said in soft tones, "but Charlotte looks like somebody hit her with a semi. If you're here to make things worse, please don't, okay?"

He admired her for getting straight to the point. "I'm here to relieve her mind about something."

"Then she's out by the pool. I have to leave in a few minutes to do an errand. I don't think she ate lunch, and I know she's not going to eat dinner unless somebody makes her. Will you stay and eat with her? The food's in the fridge, all ready to go. It just needs to be heated up."

Despite everything, his stomach growled. He nodded. "I can do that."

"Great. The dog's about to have puppies, and I have to help my friend — she's a vet's assistant — move in so she's here when it happens."

"Dog?"

"We're taking care of somebody's dog as a favor. Charlotte volunteered."

This was more than Ethan could take in. During their marriage every discussion about having a dog had ended in a stalemate. Dogs were messy, unpredictable and time-consuming. And according to Charlotte, Taylor wasn't old enough to be responsible. By the time she was, Taylor had lost interest.

"I'll find my way to the pool," he said.

"Good. I'm leaving in a few minutes."

He wound his way through the house and out the back by a slightly more direct route. Charlotte didn't turn as the door closed behind him. She wore a hat with a brim wide enough to shade her neck and shoulders, even though the sun was well on its way to meet the horizon. He saw she had what looked like a notebook on her lap and a telephone beside her, probably waiting for his call.

As he walked toward her, he spoke her name. Only then did she turn. She looked wary, as if she was steeling herself, and closed the book.

"She's okay," he said, when he was close

enough to be easily heard. "They're keeping her, probably for a couple of days, but she's going to be fine."

He saw relief steal over her features, and she seemed to go slack with it, shrinking before his eyes.

"Thank God," she said, and now he was close enough to see her eyes were filling with tears.

Without being asked he took the chair beside her. "They let me see her. She's awake, but pretty lethargic. They'll be watching her closely." He outlined the problems. "If we're lucky, she'll recover quickly," he finished.

"It was an awful fall. She'd just gotten to the top, and she was pumping her fists in the air in victory. Then . . ." She shook her head. "I was too far away to do a thing. Kind of the story of my life."

"I'm sorry Taylor was so brutal."

"Taylor never kept her feelings to herself. Not from the beginning. Remember the year she was three and we bought her . . ." She laughed a little, but it sounded forced. "Now I don't remember what it was, but she told us clearly she was disappointed. She'd told us what she expected, and we had failed her. I think she said it just that way."

"She's gotten a bit more tactful in the past decade, but apparently not enough."

"She has every right to be furious with me. And now I'm skulking around spying on her daughter. At least that's how it looks to her, I'm sure." She turned to watch him. "I'm glad you didn't tell her what I said that night in the hospital. I'm sorry she overheard us all those years ago, horribly sorry, but I'm glad it wasn't you."

"Do you think I would try to make my own daughter feel worse when *her* daughter was barely holding on to life?"

"No, not when I think about it. You've never been cruel."

He didn't say what he was thinking, because he wasn't cruel, either — or tried not to be.

She turned away. "I know I sounded cruel that night," she said. "I'm not defending myself. How can I? But there I was, looking at that poor little preemie, tubes going everywhere, a machine breathing for her, a prognosis so grim it was horrifying. All I could think about was how much pain she must be in, what a terrible introduction this was to life and how little she might have to look forward to if she survived. So yes, I wished out loud Taylor had taken my advice and ended the pregnancy quickly, so Maddie wouldn't have suffered that way. I felt like every one of those tubes was draining the life from her sweet, innocent little body. And I knew if I'd been a better mother, someone Taylor could have talked to before she slept with Jeremy Larsen, I wouldn't be standing there. We would be off looking at colleges or having pedicures, or shopping for her senior trip."

It was a long speech for a woman who had always chosen her words with precision, but it said so much. The events in question were the same. He'd witnessed them, so there was no way to alter that. But the slant was so different.

"That's not the way Taylor heard it," he said after a moment. "She heard 'I told you so.' She'd heard it before, only this time it was her baby's life at stake."

"I've been thinking about this so much lately. Taylor and I got off to a bad start, right from the beginning. And I compounded that by trying so hard to give her the childhood I never had. If you boil down our relationship, at least from my end, there it is. But while we were living it? I couldn't see a thing. When I threatened to kick her out of the house if she didn't do what I knew she ought to, I was just taking our long history to the logical conclusion. I wanted what was best for her, and I was willing to do anything to make it happen. I was absolutely certain she was going to destroy her life."

"Your life, not hers. The one *you* wanted for her."

"Right."

He waited for recriminations, because wasn't this exactly the moment when she could have pointed out that during their years together he hadn't helped the situation? That early on he had allied himself with Taylor and slowly shut out Charlotte? That he hadn't tried hard enough to help his wife see what was happening, or demanded they go to a counselor? That he hadn't stood up to their daughter — or to *her* — when it was really needed?

But the recriminations didn't come.

"I made mistakes, too," he said at last.

"It's amazing, isn't it? That two people who want nothing more than to raise a happy child can go so easily astray? And now look where we are. I think the only thing I can do is back off for good. I don't want to compound my mistakes or her misery. If I try to make myself heard, she'll only shout louder."

"Then write her a letter."

This time she turned her chair so she

could really see him. "Do you think she would read it?"

"I think she *might.* She's usually more reasonable than she was today. I'll ask her to keep it for the moment when she's ready to find common ground again."

"It seems so cowardly."

"No, it's just a first step. If you do meet face-to-face again, Taylor'll let you know what she thinks and how she sees what happened. It won't be fun. But this might get you to that meeting."

"Let me think about it. I just don't want to make another mistake."

"There are years ahead, Charlotte. You have time to get this right."

Her face was in shadow from the hat brim, but she looked sadder at his words. He supposed that for somebody like Charlotte, who was used to making things happen on her own schedule, potentially waiting years, or even months, for results was particularly hard.

"It was good of you to come," she said, but not in her lady-of-the-manor voice. She sounded sincere, as if she realized what this had cost him. "And your advice is welcome, Ethan. Let me just think about what to say and how to say it."

"The young woman living here? I forgot

her name."

"Harmony."

"She offered me dinner, and I haven't had anything since breakfast. She says there's enough for both of us."

"You're staying for dinner?" She sounded surprised. "You must be completely exhausted."

"I'm hungry more than I'm tired. What say we fix that?"

She rested her fingertips on his arm. "You were born to take care of people. You spent the day taking care of your daughter and granddaughter, and now you're worried about me?"

"Not particularly. I'm just curious what kind of dinner Harmony made you."

She looked exhausted and her color was almost ashen, but a smile brightened her face. "She's a vegetarian. I'm becoming one by default, but she's a wonderful cook."

"Taylor's a vegetarian, too. I always leave her house with a full stomach and a yearning for pulled pork."

"I'm so glad you said that. I've been dreaming about pulled pork, too."

He laughed; she smiled again.

He told himself to be careful.

If Charlotte had known Ethan was going to

stop by, she would have combed her hair, changed her blouse, done something about her face. Instead, she just removed her hat and fluffed her hair with her fingers. But maybe that was one of those unheralded benefits of divorce. She and Ethan had already proved they were unsuited. What was the point of putting best feet forward? A fresh coat of lipstick wasn't going to change a thing.

She pulled dishes out of the refrigerator and handed them to him. Different fridge, same man, same ritual. Early in their marriage, one or both of them had tried to cook pots of this or that on weekends, so they could eat leftovers for the first part of the week. Before Taylor charged full tilt at adolescence, she'd often wandered into the kitchen to be with them, and chopped and sautéed. Charlotte had passed on some of her grandmother's favorites, but if Taylor was a vegetarian now, it was unlikely she was making chicken and dumplings or red-eye gravy.

Anyway, who was she kidding? By the end of her marriage, the only time Charlotte had made it into the kitchen was when she had to cross through it on the way to some place more important.

"Remember your venison meat loaf?"

Ethan asked.

She straightened, the last container on the counter now.

"I can't believe *you* remember," she said. "I'm the one who dared you."

"For some reason you never quite got that I'd been raised in the land of hunters. My father was usually too far gone to hold a rifle, but anybody who wanted to hunt on our land had to share their kill."

"It was the best meat loaf I ever ate."

For a moment she didn't know what to say. Twenty-some years ago Ethan had brought home neatly wrapped packages of venison from a hunter friend at his firm, and for some reason he'd expected Charlotte to balk. Instead, they'd dined like royalty for the rest of the month.

She busied herself taking off lids. "Harmony wants to put in a vegetable garden. I haven't picked a tomato or a green bean since I left home. Maybe it's time again."

"Tell me about her."

"What do you want to know?"

"Who is she?"

"Just a young woman who needed a friend and a place to stay. Our paths crossed, and now she's here."

"Why?"

"I have the room, and she's a joy to be

around."

"I know the economy's a mess, but you're not the boardinghouse type."

"No?" Now that he'd mentioned it, she thought the idea was charming. "Maybe that's what I'll do with my future. I have enough bedrooms, that's for sure. Harmony could cook and garden, and I could just enjoy all the new faces around my table."

"She's very protective of you. She asked me to stay and make sure you ate."

She felt a ridiculous slap of disappointment. "So that's why you stayed. Here I thought you were hungry."

"She didn't have to twist my arm." He added in a lower voice, "Not at all, actually."

She knew better than to ask why and risk another slap. It was enough just to hope her company was at least a part of the reason.

"This is strange, I know," she said. "Us, together, doing what we used to do when we were married. And it's all brand-new, at least for *me*."

"But not for me, because I was married again in between?"

"Probably not the best thing for me to bring up."

"My abysmal record? It's not all that painful. I married Judy on the rebound, and she did the same. We were great friends who got married because it was convenient, at least until she decided she wanted to move back to Chicago. Now we're distant friends who aren't married anymore."

"I expected you to marry a younger woman yearning for babies so you could start a second family."

"And I expected you to find an oil tycoon to give you all the things I never did."

She got plates down and set them in front of him. In spite of Harmony's warning, the microwave was about to take a beating.

"We're doing pretty well so far, Ethan, don't you think? Even without a lot of practice. We aren't yelling at each other, or blaming each other, or gloating. I'm sorry your marriage to Judy didn't work out. I wanted you to be happy, even then."

"Really?" He lifted a brow, which gave his face the devilish cast she remembered well.

"Okay, not so much." She handed him a plate and gestured to the containers. "Not right away. But later. And maybe not happy, but I wanted you to find the things I hadn't been able to give you. I thought you deserved that much."

"My thoughts about you weren't that pure."

"No?"

"I wanted you to have everything you'd ever wanted and finally realize none of it mattered."

She waited until that stopped tearing at her. "You always were good at expressing your feelings."

"I'm sorry."

"No, sometimes it hurts, but I've missed it. I live in a world where people say one thing and mean something else. I used to think that was sophistication, and now I know it's just another way to distance yourself. Keep everybody guessing. I never had to guess with you."

"I think maybe we're getting too close to recriminations, and you've had enough of those today."

She began to dish up the meal. She scanned the possibilities, filled a plate and held it out to him. He looked down at it.

"You skipped the sweet potatoes," he said.

"You don't like them." She paused. "Or you never did before."

"You'll want white wine with dinner because it's seventy-six this afternoon. If it was seventy-four, you'd be drinking red."

She smiled, because despite the pain of all this, she still could. "While we eat, will you tell me about Martin Architectural Design?"

"If you promise not to tell me how much

more successful I can be if I just branch out."

"I promise. It won't even cross my mind."

Chapter Twenty-Two

By Tuesday the puppies still hadn't arrived. In the morning Charlotte, Velvet, Harmony and Glenda went to the vet, who declared the dog to be fit as a fiddle, and the puppies ready for their journey. The women worried him more, since they were considerably more anxious. He predicted the wait would be over later that week and sent them home.

Harmony didn't want to miss the big event, but neither did she want to lose her job. So late that afternoon she parked her car and sped toward Cuppa through the warning drops of an oncoming thunderstorm. Stella, the forty-something manager, greeted her with one eye on her watch and one hand reaching for a wad of napkins.

"You ever hear of an umbrella?" Plump no-nonsense Stella looked and acted like the mother of three she was, a little harried and a lot maternal.

Harmony grinned and mopped her

cheeks. "At least I remembered to put my Cuppa shirt in my purse. I'll change in the ladies' room."

"Take your time. You're early. Warm up with a cup of something first."

"Actually . . ."

Stella waited as Harmony fumbled for the right words. "I . . . I need to call somebody, but it's long-distance. Could I use the phone in the office? You can take it out of my pay."

"No problem. Keep it in the country and it doesn't cost us anything. You go on and make your call, but take some coffee back with you."

A few minutes later, steaming hot chocolate in hand, Harmony stared at the telephone. The office was really just a storeroom, and it smelled like the coffee beans piled in bags in the corner. A battered metal desk was shoved against a wall, and the top was scattered with papers weighted in place by a photo of Stella's preteen sons, an industrial-size stapler and a telephone with an intercom and two outside lines. Harmony lowered herself to an equally battered desk chair and considered what to do.

Her father bowled on Tuesday nights in a Chamber of Commerce league. He wore a royal-blue shirt with the name of his insurance agency emblazoned in bright red and yellow letters, and once he had knocked Harmony's mother to the floor because she hadn't noticed a button was missing when she'd carefully ironed the shirt that morning.

Janine Stoddard never went to watch him bowl. Harmony's father claimed she made him nervous, plus the wives of his teammates were bad influences. They drank beer and wore too much makeup, and every one of them made jokes at her husband's expense. The lone woman on his team was even worse, although her sins were undocumented. Harmony suspected the woman, another agent, probably talked back to the men, a behavior her own mother might find perplexing or, worse, encouraging.

When Harmony was living at home her father had never returned after work to change. He always changed at the office and went directly to the bowling alley, stopping first to pick up Buddy, Harmony's brother, after football practice, in the days when Buddy was still in high school. Tuesday nights had been the highlight of Harmony's week. Without her father or brother to supervise her, she and her mother had cooked whatever they wanted for dinner and watched whatever they wanted on television.

She had no idea if her father still followed the same routine, although she did know, from searching the internet, that he was still bowling on the Chamber league. Even though Buddy was no longer alive to cheer him, most likely her father still didn't invite her mother to watch. And really, if her mother wasn't at home, what was the harm in letting the telephone disturb the silence?

A utilitarian clock ticking loudly on the wall insisted Harmony's shift was about to start. She lifted the receiver and punched buttons until the telephone was ringing in a Topeka suburb, in a house so scrubbed and sterilized that nothing, not germ, not human, could happily live here.

The phone rang three times before Harmony heard a familiar tentative voice.

Harmony gripped the receiver the way she might grip a life preserver in a choppy sea. "Mom? It's Harmony."

"Harmony?"

"How are you?" Harmony asked. "Are you alone?"

"Not for long," her mother said, as if she was preparing to be interrupted.

"Daddy's not bowling tonight?"

"He comes home . . . to change now. The restroom at work . . ." Her voice trailed off.

Harmony guessed. The restroom wasn't

clean enough, or it had a mirror that showed too clearly the expanding paunch or receding hairline. Whatever the reason, she couldn't have cared less.

"Mom, I'd better tell you quickly, then. I'm . . ." She squeezed her eyes tightly shut. "I'm going to have a baby. You're going to be a grandmother."

Silence greeted the announcement.

"I'm not married," Harmony went on, getting the worst over quickly. "The baby's father and I broke up. But I'm going to have the baby, and I'm going to be a good mother. You could come here to be with us, Mom. You really could. You could help with the baby, and I'd take care of you both. We could rent a little apartment —"

"Oh, Harmony, what have you done?"

Harmony swallowed a sob, and no answer occurred to her except the obvious.

"Your father . . . your father will never forgive you."

"I don't care. Why should I? He's a bad man, Mom. You know it. Deep inside you can feel it, I know you can. I got out of there to start a whole different life, and you can, too."

Her mother continued as if Harmony hadn't spoken. "You can't visit now." Then she began to cry.

"Mom, I wasn't going to visit. I'm never coming back there. I want you to come *here,* where you'll be safe, where he won't be able to hit you anymore."

Janine Stoddard didn't seem to hear. "Your father . . . He'll never understand this. You can't come home now, Harmony. Don't you see? And if he finds out the truth and knows you've been calling . . . You can't call anymore, either. He asks me every night if I've heard from you, and I have to lie to him whenever I have. If he finds out . . ."

Harmony didn't know which of her sins might enrage her father the most. That she'd dared to call? That she was having a baby out of wedlock? That she'd tried to convince her mother to leave Kansas? That she hated him so much that if she ever saw him lift his hand in anger again, she might well kill him?

"You can't call anymore," her mother finished.

Harmony gently hung up the telephone, put her face in her trembling hands and let the reality of how alone she really was settle over her like a shroud.

By the time her shift was up, Harmony was exhausted. Midweek wasn't Cuppa's busiest time, but several large, rowdy groups had descended simultaneously, and at the last minute another server had called in sick. Harmony and an eighteen-year-old named Matt, who was still in training, had handled all the tables, and by the time the last dishes had been cleared away, both of them were dragging their feet.

"It's pouring out there." Matt squinted into the darkness through the front door. A few people had trickled in for a final cappuccino or smoothie, but the kitchen was now closed and counter service reigned. They were done, tips tucked in their pockets.

"Stella loaned me an extra umbrella. Need shelter getting to your car?"

"Got a friend picking me up," Matt said. "We could drop you at yours."

Harmony considered. Stella's loaner was small and flimsy, and the way the wind was blowing, she wasn't sure the umbrella would last the necessary block.

Then the wind blew someone through the door whom she hadn't expected to see.

When he saw her standing there, Davis barricaded the doorway with his body, as if he expected her to dart into the rain just to get away. "We need to talk," he said.

"You go ahead," Harmony told Matt. "I'll be fine."

Matt, who weighed a good fifty pounds less than Davis, looked him up and down first, as if assessing her risk. Then he shrugged. "Whatever."

"You did a great job tonight," she said, warmed by his obvious concern. "See you tomorrow."

She waited until he was gone before she squared her body to look Davis in the eye. "The place closes in about fifteen minutes, at which time I'm heading home."

"Then let's find a table fast. Can I get you anything?"

A better handle on men? A different childhood? Mimicking Matt, she shrugged with the same lack of conviction. "Not a thing."

They took a table by the window, empty of all condiments and still damp from her own dishcloth. She tilted her chair on its hind legs to ease her aching back. "Fourteen minutes and counting."

"I'm not here to try to convince you to have an abortion. You're acting like I'm some kind of selfish jerk."

She just lifted a brow and waited.

"I admit I've been less than a perfect boyfriend."

"You think?"

"I got into our relationship for the wrong reasons. I thought it was temporary, fun for both of us but not long-lasting."

She wondered if, at the beginning of their relationship, she'd even given the substance of it *that* much thought. Davis had been older, secure in a good job, and she supposed she'd thought that meant he was also wise and mature. She'd been so flattered by his attention that she'd fallen into bed without thinking about the future. Getting through each day had been her main concern. Unfortunately, that was still the case.

"I guess I thought the same," she said, struggling to be fair.

"I didn't realize what a gem you are. Not until you walked out on me."

No one had ever called her a gem, and just for a moment, she let Davis's flattery work its magic. She sobered quickly. "If by that you mean I waited on you hand and foot, I was a five-carat diamond."

"I don't mean that, Harmony. I mean you're special. You're funny and smart, even if you haven't been to college yet, and you're good to people, even if they don't deserve it. And I didn't see that clearly enough. I guess I figured us together wasn't real, just kind of a passing phase, and so nothing I did was going to really hurt either of us."

She wondered how hurt she really was. Was she hurt, or angry, or just scared now that she was on her own again? Really on her own, something her mother had certainly confirmed. Then there was the baby.

"So where is this leading?" she asked. "Because Cuppa's about to close."

"You're making this pretty hard." He wasn't scowling, not exactly, although Davis's normal expression was a cross between perturbed and cynical, and this was more the first than the second.

She tossed her braid over her shoulder and grasped the end, brushing it over the back of her hand. "Apparently I forgot to remind myself when we were together, but it's *not* my job to make your life easy."

"I want to do the right thing."

"And what would that be?"

"I think you should move back in with me. I think we should get married."

She dropped her braid in astonishment. "What?"

"It *is* the right thing. You shouldn't face this alone, and I need to be responsible. You didn't get pregnant on your own. I had everything to do with it, and the baby's mine. It's the best scenario for both of you. I checked my policy. You'll be covered by my insurance. You'll have a good, safe place to live. We'll get you a better car, one you can count on, and when the baby's older, you can go back to school and earn an associate degree. You don't want to work at Cuppa the rest of your life, do you?"

She thought of Stella, the mother of three who was doing just fine working here, although she was far from rich.

Oddly, that was the only thing she could think of. She couldn't seem to wrap her head around anything Davis was saying. He wanted to marry her? She was young and romantic, but never, even during the best part of their time together, had she actually thought he might want to tie the knot. It wasn't a daydream she'd indulged in. She certainly hadn't gotten pregnant to make it happen.

"Marriage?" she asked at last.

"That's what I'm talking about." His expression lightened. "I thought about doing this with a ring. Then I thought maybe you would rather choose one together, and I wasn't sure you would give me time to pull one out of my pocket tonight, anyway."

"Davis, one minute you're furious Mother Nature and I collaborated to make this happen, and the next you're offering to marry me?"

"Not exactly one minute. You sprang this on me, Harmony. One minute we're having dinner, and the next you're racing to the bathroom. I didn't really have time to think it over at Zambra. And let's face it, you didn't even tell me. Not in so many words. I was busy trying to figure things out. But I've had more than a week to consider it. It seems like the thing to do, don't you think? Have the baby, be a family."

"You don't like children. You've told me you don't."

"I don't like other people's children, no. But my own'll be different."

She thought about her father, who had never allowed noise or commotion in their home. Even his beloved Buddy had tiptoed around on the worst days. Would Davis be that kind of father? For better or worse this child belonged to him, but creating a child and living with one were very different.

"You're not exactly jumping for joy." His expression darkened again. "I thought you would be pleased once you heard me out."

"It's a lot to think about." That much was true. "I'm going to need time to decide what's best for the baby and me."

"And what about me?"

She could think of many ways he might have said that. Teasingly? Lovingly? But under the words she heard the faintest whine. *What about me?* Was that going to be the primary question in their marriage? *If* she married him?

"You're a big guy," she said. "You know, sometimes you just have to sit back and let things unfold."

"So what? Now you consult the tarot or something?"

"Think about it, Davis. You might have an entire lifetime of me doing things like that. It could drive you crazy."

He surprised her and smiled. Then he leaned over and took her hand, and wove his fingers with hers. "If that's the worst, I can live with it. Just think about me when you shuffle the deck. Remember all the good times we had? At some point during one of them we created that kid inside you. And we had fun doing it. Don't forget *that* when you lay out the cards. I'm just the guy who wants to take care of you and our baby."

Every day of her hospitalization, Ethan had brought Maddie presents. A new electronic Scrabble game. Colorful hair clips. Sequined flip-flops. Today he'd really lucked out at his favorite rare bookstore and found an autographed copy of *Because of Winn-Dixie,* a book Maddie loved. She was going home in the morning, but she would have to stay quiet for a while, so rereading a favorite novel would be just the thing.

Maddie was still nearly as pale as her pillowcase, and her freckles seemed to dance wildly on her cheeks when she spoke. She thanked him for the book and hugged it to her chest. She smiled, just the way she knew she was supposed to, but her blue eyes still looked sad.

"It's great, Papa. I'll read it all over again."

"You're getting out of here in the morning. Are you excited?"

"Everybody's nice, but I miss my bed."

"I bet. How about school? Miss that, too?"

"I guess. I can catch up on the work. I've already started. Mom brought me a bunch last night."

Ethan had expected her to be more excited that life was returning to normal. "Don't forget, you're going to be good as new."

"I've never been as good as new."

He didn't have to ask what she meant. "I know the seizures are hard to deal with, especially after what you've been through. But I hear you're on new meds, and your doctor's optimistic they'll help."

"He's said that before." She sounded very adult, as if she was the one who needed to bring reality into the conversation. "He always hopes they'll help, but they never really do."

"It takes time to get this right."

She nodded, as if she didn't want to worry him.

"What are you looking forward to?" he asked to change the subject. "If not to going back to school?"

"Going to Nashville."

In the midst of this crisis Ethan had nearly forgotten that Jeremy planned to bring Maddie to Nashville to spend part of the summer with him. Now he realized just how much this trip meant to her. Normal children of divorced parents — something that was almost the norm itself these days — went to visit their noncustodial parents wherever they lived. This was not only Maddie's chance to be with her father, but to do what other children did. Leave town. Go somewhere different. Find out what was waiting there.

"Do you think he'll take you to the Grand Ole Opry?"

"You bet! He promised."

"Are you going to take your guitar and let him teach you some new chords?"

"If there's room in his car. He's going to pick me up here and drive me to Tennessee."

Ethan knew better than to outstay his welcome. He stood and bent over to kiss her forehead, glad to leave on a happier note. "I'll come see you tomorrow once you're home. You sleep tight."

"I can't wait to show Mom my book."

He ruffled her hair, then left the room and started down the hall. He hadn't seen Taylor, who'd been off having a sandwich, but now she was coming toward him. Once they were almost on top of each other he gave her a quick hug. She looked tired but resolute. She also looked older than twenty-seven, maybe a lifetime older.

"Just left Maddie." He told her about the book.

"What a perfect gift." She glanced at her watch. "And just in time. Visiting hours are almost over."

"She seemed a little down, but she cheered up as soon as she started talking about the trip to Nashville."

Taylor shook her head. "Why did you talk to her about that?"

"I asked her what she was looking forward to, and she said the trip. She brightened up right away."

"I wish you hadn't started that particular conversation."

Ethan considered just letting it go, but instead he pulled her to the side of the hallway so an orderly pushing a bed could get past. “Why not? Looking forward to this trip makes her feel like everybody else. All the other kids go on vacations.”

“Because she can’t go. I can’t believe you don’t see that, Dad. She’s in the hospital because she had a seizure and got hurt. Badly hurt. Do you think Jeremy’s up to handling something like that? He hardly knows her, and he sure doesn’t know anything about handling emergencies.”

“None of us *handled* it, Taylor. The paramedics handled it. Jeremy can dial 9-1-1 just the same as anybody else.”

She took a step back, either out of surprise or in assessment, he couldn’t tell which. “And when she came to, I was there. You were there. She trusts and loves us. I’m not going to let my daughter end up in the care of people she hardly knows.”

Jeremy was Maddie’s father. He’d been involved in her life from the start. He was, by nobody’s measure, a person Maddie hardly knew. But as Taylor kept her gaze locked with his, Ethan knew that he couldn’t say as much. Taylor was certain she was right, and from the very beginning, she had made it clear that Maddie was her child and her responsibility. She loved her father. She needed his support.

But she did not want his advice.

"I wish you luck when you explain that to her," he said at last. "She's counting on this, Taylor."

"I'm not going to say a thing until she recovers, so please don't mention it, okay? I'm hoping Jeremy will come here for a good long visit. That'll soften the blow."

He nodded, although he didn't want to. "Do you need help getting her home tomorrow?"

"We'll be fine."

He leaned over and kissed her cheek. "Just let me know when she's there, and I'll stop by tomorrow after work. Okay if I bring her some ice cream?"

"She'll love it."

They chatted for another moment, then said goodbye, and she continued down the hall. He wondered, if he seriously questioned his daughter's decision, whether she might begin shutting him out of her life, the way she had shut out her mother and Maddie's own father.

This was a side of Taylor he wished he had never seen. Or, perhaps more accurately, this was a side of Taylor he wished he had never recognized.

Chapter Twenty-Three

First Day Journal: May 23

Taylor is almost two when my father dies of exposure in the front yard of my grandmother's farmhouse, unable to find his way out of a snowstorm. With effort I've continued to pay the annual property taxes, using a post office box to avoid Hearty's arrival on my doorstep. Two weeks after his death I find a letter in the box from Bill Johnston, our helpful neighbor, who's tracked me down through a courthouse clerk. I can only mourn the man my father never was, and when Ethan insists on accompanying me to pick up and deal with Hearty's ashes, I agree.

An aunt I've seen only once has made arrangements for a cremation, since hers was the only address the authorities found in the house. To her credit, she cleans before we arrive, making neat piles of Hearty's belongings for me to go through. She tells me the family is sorry they haven't gotten to know me better, but they felt every contact with Hearty was like diving into quicksand.

I understand only too well.

Because Ethan and Taylor are with me, I see my family home with new eyes. The house is in desperate need of repair, but Ethan crows over the chestnut logs, the fieldstone fireplace, the setting with its view of far-off mountains. He says it was built by true country craftsmen, and thinks it can and should be saved.

Since real estate in the area is selling for very little, Ethan suggests I find a renter with carpentry skills who can do the work under his tutelage. He feels sure the arrangement will be appealing, since the forty acres surrounding the house can be put back into production by someone with energy and enthusiasm.

On a warm afternoon with Taylor in a backpack carrier, we take my father's ashes to scatter them on the mountain land he logged, because burying them in the Sawyer family cemetery is out of the question. By then my aunt is gone, leaving me with addresses of the family who are and will forever after remain strangers. While I understand their desire to sever ties with Hearty, it does not make me love them.

We drive most of the way and hike the rest

on a logging path. The land looks so different. Many of the grand old trees are gone, and what was an impenetrable forest now opens to some of the most beautiful views I've ever seen. I'm stunned. With developers just beginning to build upscale communities on pristine mountain land, Hearty has been sitting on a gold mine. Whatever drinking buddy he's gifted with these acres will surely see the potential.

Ethan loves the land and the wildlife we spot, including a rare peregrine falcon, just coming back after near-extinction. He says the falcon's a good omen that someday the land, too, will revive, if managed well.

A bigger surprise is waiting when we go to the county seat to investigate dividing the farm. There is no will. My father didn't, as threatened, make one. In the end, despite all threats to the contrary and by default, he's left both properties to me. I like to think it was latent kindness or a sense of responsibility, but sadly, I'm almost certain it was inertia.

Bill Johnston, still thriving on the farm next door, suggests his brother, a talented carpenter, might be interested in renting the farm, and we strike a deal.

The mountain land is a question I'm not ready to answer. But already a plan is forming.

Chapter Twenty-Four

The telephone rang just as Charlotte began fishing through her handbag for the car keys. Harmony and Glenda were in Charlotte's closet with Velvet and the five gorgeous puppies that had arrived without incident twenty-four hours earlier. Charlotte had invited the young women on her duty trip up Doggett Mountain, but they had declined, enraptured by the unfolding maternal drama.

She had just fielded one phone call from a member of the Falconview executive committee and scheduled a short call for that evening to go over business, and now she was in a hurry to get away before someone else demanded even more of her time.

She grabbed the receiver as she continued to fish.

"Charlotte?"

She recognized Analiese's voice. "Reverend Ana." They exchanged the expected pleasantries before Analiese unveiled the reason for the call.

"I wondered if you were free for lunch?"

Charlotte knew the reason for the invitation. She had revealed her illness, and in good conscience, Analiese couldn't ignore it. She'd probably been waiting for Charlotte to talk to her again, and since she hadn't, she was offering lunch as encouragement.

"I'm on my way out the door. I'm heading out into the country." She glanced up at the clock again and did the calculations. She had told her renters she would be at the farmhouse by noon to collect their keys and go through the house before she returned their security deposit. The couple had already moved to Mars Hill, and it was past time to tidy final details.

"It's such a beautiful day I was hoping to entice you to eat outside with me," Analiese said.

"How about a picnic in the country?" The words were out before Charlotte realized how problematic the invitation might be for her minister. "But please, it's not a command performance. I know how busy you are, and we'll be heading straight up a mountain."

"I have to be back by four. Is that rushing you?"

Charlotte gauged the other woman's tone. Analiese sounded as if she really didn't mind coming. "Not at all. I'm dressed as casually as you'll ever see me. I'll put something together for lunch. Can I pick you up in, say, thirty minutes?"

She hung up a moment later and realized she was smiling.

The church parsonage, a 1920s Tudor in the eclectic Kenilworth neighborhood, wasn't far from Charlotte's house. When she arrived, Analiese was sitting on the porch wearing capris, a floral camp shirt and hiking boots. With her hair pulled back in a ponytail and no jewelry, she looked even less like a minister than usual.

"You have no idea how glad I am to get out of town." Analiese climbed into Charlotte's Jeep Cherokee and locked her seat belt in place. "I was just offered last-minute tickets to a ladies' tea at the Methodist church. The speaker's doing a slide show of her recent trip to the Ukraine, followed by a sing-along of Ukrainian folk tunes. They're having cabbage rolls and borscht."

"I could have gone in your place. I like cabbage rolls."

"Good, when you drop me off I'll give you the container they've promised to leave with the church secretary. I love them too much. How do you feel about borscht?"

"Not as good."

"If I put enough sour cream in it, I love everything."

Charlotte glanced at her. Analiese didn't have an extra ounce of fat anywhere. "When was the last time you put sour cream on anything?"

"When they developed the no-fat version. I bought stock I was so happy. I have to watch every bite or I'll blow up like a balloon, and I'm not kidding. As a kid I was so overweight my nickname was Dough Girl. My mother's only joy in life is cooking, and she stuffed me full of food to keep me quiet. You should have seen my father. Three hundred pounds heading toward four before he died of an overdose of apple dumplings."

This was a side of the other woman Charlotte had never seen. Analiese had always been casual, but this utterly frank woman was a ramped-up version of the one who preached Sunday sermons. She was delightful.

"So food's your enemy," Charlotte said. "You're going to see mine in a little while."

"Tell me about it."

"The house I grew up in. The land I grew up on. The community where I was the daughter of a no-good drunk and expected by some to follow in his footsteps."

"That explains a lot about you, doesn't it?"

Charlotte spared her minister a glance and a smile. "Doesn't it, though? I spent my whole life trying to prove the few people who looked down on me were wrong. Actually, I spent my whole life trying to prove the one person who *really* looked down on me was wrong."

"*You,* right? It figures. We tend to forget the eleventh commandment — Thou Shalt Not Be Thine Own Worst Enemy."

"You should have been on the mountain with Moses."

"I'm afraid I'd have been down at the bottom with the golden calf, especially since that's where the food and drink were happening. So we're going to your childhood home?"

"Somewhere between Trust and Luck."

"How so?"

"Those are the names of two local townships, and our farmhouse was right between. I'm not sure where trust came in, but I always thought it was luck that got me out."

Charlotte turned onto the Leicester Highway that would lead her up Doggett Mountain, past the kennels where she and Harmony had rescued Velvet. She began the slow climb that would eventually become steeper, narrower and turn into a series of hairpin curves.

Without asking herself why, she found herself telling Analiese about her grandmother, about her parents and the hardscrabble life she'd been born into. Also about the good neighbors, as well as the taunts at school, where her father's all-too-public antics had been a favorite topic of conversation.

"The thing is, almost no one had money," she finished. "Even those who were well off by local standards were poor by some accounts. They were like a bunch of barnyard biddies ganging up on the scrawniest, saddest chick so they would have somebody they could feel superior to before their own date at the chopping block."

"That happens in exclusive private schools, too. The kid whose father doesn't have his own jet. The kid whose mother can't claim any celebrities as friends."

"Did you grow up like that?"

"Me? Not at all, but when I was in television news I did a story about a boy who committed suicide because his parents bought him a three-year-old Lexus instead of a new one for his sixteenth birthday. The stock market's dips had curbed their discretionary spending. I remember the phrase 'discretionary spending' so well. His mother was the one who used it, like his death was just part of life's assets and liabilities. It wasn't at all clear which he'd been."

"That's so sad."

"Isn't it? I was public school all the way, but I spent the first four years of elementary school being teased unmercifully. So I can relate. And after my pediatrician and aunt banded together to make sure the extra pounds went away, I made a conscious decision never to be the butt of anybody's jokes again."

"I'd say it was successful."

The road began to climb. They chatted comfortably as Charlotte passed farms and homes, carefully taking the curves and pulling off just once so they could look out at the panorama below.

"You didn't say why you're making the trip," Analiese said as the road flattened, then began a gradual descent.

"I inherited our family property after my father died. At the time I decided not to sell it because it was worth so little. Over the years I've had this and that done to it, and it's been consistently rented. But the latest couple are now home owners, so they're handing over their keys. I have to decide what to do next."

"How long has the place been in your family?"

"It came down from my mother's side, and I think I'm at least the sixth generation."

"A real home place."

"My grandmother loved every stick, leaf and floorboard. It was all she had of my grandfather after he died, and she would have done anything to keep it."

"That makes selling difficult for you, doesn't it?"

"Except there's no reason to leave it to my daughter when I die, because she'll only sell it herself. She has no connection to it." She didn't add "or to me," although she knew Analiese understood that.

"It sounds like you've decided to sell, then."

"I missed the best chance a few years ago. Like everybody else I hoped rural property was just going to keep going up and up. So I don't know what I'll do. I want to . . ."

After a long moment Analiese picked up on her hesitation. "You have other ideas?"

"Not an idea, more like a feeling. I want

to do something to honor Gran. But this is the middle of nowhere, so I don't know what exactly. I donate to the Arthritis Foundation every year. It would be smarter to just give them more money, but this is where she lived and died, and it meant so much to her." She kept her voice light so her next words couldn't be taken wrong. "Besides, someone I respect pointed out the difference between throwing money at a problem and getting involved. I took it to heart."

"I wasn't at my best that afternoon."

"I think maybe you were. And by the way, have I told you about the kennel in my closet? Minnie would have approved." Recounting the story of Velvet and her puppies took them through Trust, nothing more these days then a dot on the map, home to an attractive general store said to serve gourmet quality lunches, a wayside chapel dedicated to St. Jude and a covered bridge that gave rise to tourist jokes about the "bridge" of Madison County, which was far removed from the novelized bridges of another state.

"The church we attended was off that way," Charlotte said, slowing and pointing to her left. "It burned to the ground fifteen years ago, and it was never rebuilt." She turned down a familiar road, and followed it slowly and carefully. Conversation stopped, since both women were too busy watching the narrow road and holding on as they jolted up a steep incline.

Charlotte finally pulled over at the base of a massive oak and turned off the engine. "Hard winters and lots of spring rain don't help a road like this one. It needs grading and new gravel if anybody's going to live here again."

"It's a beautiful, beautiful spot."

Charlotte almost felt as if she herself had been praised. Ethan had seen the beauty here, but it had taken distance and time before she could begin to appreciate what she had hoped to leave behind forever.

They sat staring out the windshield for a moment. The log house was at the top of a knoll, and the ground on either side had been terraced, with massive boulders holding top soil that must have been transported there by wagon. Now she wondered how the work had been accomplished. Had her ancestors wrenched these rocks from the woods or fields with mules? Dragged them here so the ground around the house could be leveled to plant trees and flowers? In the midst of poverty and relentlessly hard work, had they taken the time to bring whatever beauty they could into their daily lives?

Peonies flourished along one terrace, backed by lilacs and forsythia. She remembered that her grandmother had called peonies century flowers, because once planted they needed almost nothing to keep blooming. Gran had brought some into the house each spring to sweetly perfume the air with their lemony fragrance. And here they were, blooming still, pale pink and creamy white, nodding gently in the warm spring breeze.

"Every time I see it with new eyes," she said.

"How do you see it today?"

Charlotte liked the question. "There were good memories here for generations of Sawyers, my mother's family. I can feel that now. Gran told me what stories she could, but my grandfather was the one who grew up here, so she didn't know them all. I have good memories of my grandmother, too. When my father wasn't around we worked hard, but we laughed, too."

"I'm glad."

"She taught me to cook and sew, neither of which stuck, and to garden, since that's how we fed ourselves. Her tomato plants? They were ladder-worthy — tomato trees, she called them — and every single one bore enough tomatoes to feed a family of ten. She saved seeds every year. If the house had been on fire, she would have grabbed me with one hand and next year's tomato seeds with the other. I've always hated that I didn't keep them going somehow. The strain's probably lost forever."

"You must have had a lot of other things to think about."

"Like how to survive. But I still wish I'd found a way." Charlotte opened her door and stepped down. The air immediately felt familiar, crisper than in the city and, of course, cooler. She stepped out of the shade of the oak and let the sun warm her. "While we wait for my renters, let me show you the house."

They climbed solidly anchored stone steps. Charlotte could feel the strain as she hiked the path she'd run up and down at least a dozen times a day as a child. Everything was in better repair now than it had been then. She'd had a steady succession of good tenants, all willing to make improvements for a portion of the rent. During their marriage, Ethan had made suggestions and inspections, and befriended each renter. She hadn't been as willing, and in exchange she'd gotten less work and more rent. But the last couple had maintained the place well. She was relieved to see she had nothing to complain about, at least not outside.

"Charlotte, this is wonderful," Analiese said. "The setting, the house." She nodded to the right. "The outbuildings. It's a Blue Ridge postcard."

"I remember being jealous of a local family who had a manufactured house brought in. And all the while I couldn't see how wonderful this place really was."

They stepped up to the wide front porch, which housed an old metal glider with a green-and-white vinyl seat and mismatched cushions. Rockers stood against the wall, and Charlotte recognized one. "My grandfather made this." She went over to test it, rocking it with her hand. "Made it well, apparently, because it's still here." She thought a moment, then she smiled. "From the pulpit tree."

"Pulpit?"

"He made the pulpit in our church, by far the prettiest thing inside it. And this came from the same tree. I could probably still find the stump out in the woods. I'd forgotten . . ."

They walked into a living area, past stairs to the second story. The floor was wide plank heart pine that had been refinished a year before, and the fieldstone fireplace was scrubbed free of smoke and ash. A few pieces of furniture sat against walls, none of it familiar except a bench Charlotte remembered as one her grandmother had used at the foot of her bed to hold quilts in the winter.

They wandered the rest of the downstairs. The country kitchen was much updated from the one of Charlotte's childhood, but Ethan had made certain all the new carpentry fit with the character of the house. Open shelves held plates and glasses; an iron rack hanging from the ceiling next to the stove held pots and pans. The appliances were stainless, Charlotte's choice when Falconview had extras from a bulk purchase. The last tenants had painted the walls a creamy yellow, now splotched with darker areas where calendars or pictures had preserved the paint from sunlight.

"You could sit ten people in here easily," Analiese said. "That table's something."

The long table consisted of polished planks topping sturdy round legs, but it had character no furniture showroom could provide. The table had been there in Charlotte's childhood, and her grandmother had claimed it had been there during *her* grandfather's childhood, too.

"What's upstairs?" Analiese asked.

They climbed the steps and walked down the hall, peeking into three bedrooms and ending up at the largest one at the end, with large windows looking east to yet another mountain.

"This was my grandmother's." Charlotte stepped inside the room, which was empty of furniture. The heirloom sleigh bed was gone. She knew from Bill Johnston that Hearty had chopped it up for firewood one cold February. That he hadn't destroyed everything was a miracle.

Analiese joined her at the window. "She must have loved this view."

"At the end of Gran's life she lay in bed all day and looked out this window. Once I asked her what she was looking at. She said everybody has mountains they have to pass over in life, and death is waiting over the very last one. She told me she was just one mountain away."

"What do you think her final mountain was?"

"Me. She wanted to be sure I finished high school. All she could give me was my education and what little money she'd been able to keep out of Hearty's hands. She held on for that, I think, but death wasn't an enemy. She was looking forward to climbing that final mountain, and being with my grandfather and her own family."

"Her faith must have been a powerful influence on you."

"Not as much as her life was." Charlotte heard a car outside. "Let's go meet the renters."

As Analiese wandered the grounds, Charlotte chatted with the young couple, who were clearly thrilled to have bought their first home. She gave them back their deposit, and they gave her keys and a short list of repairs that needed a professional's touch.

After they drove away she saw Analiese standing up the hill at the edge of the family cemetery. She joined her there.

"Some of my family's here, including my mother and grandparents." Charlotte hesitated, then added. "I think whenever I die I'd like to have my ashes placed here with them."

"Have you left instructions?"

"Not yet, but soon."

"It's a good idea for anybody."

"On my first morning in the hospital for chemo, the social worker gave me material on things I should consider. That was the moment I realized everybody thought my survival was up for grabs. Until then leukemia was just another unfortunate challenge

I had to get through so I could work harder. But that revelation was the high point of that day. In the afternoon I had a severe reaction to one of the drugs they were using and nearly died. I was rushed into the ICU and didn't come out again for a week, but I don't remember too many details except that my whole life changed."

"I imagine it did."

"I'm not sorry."

"Not at all?"

"Well, given a choice I'd like to be thirty years younger, healthy as a horse and well acquainted with the things I know now. But seeing as that's impossible, I'll take where I am over where I was when I went into the hospital."

"What will happen to the cemetery if you sell the land?"

"I think by law they have to leave it here, but that's not going to be a problem."

"Then you're not going to sell?"

"Let me show you something on the way home. It's the best explanation I can think of, something I sold for the wrong reasons. I don't want to do that again."

They picnicked on the lunch Charlotte had bought at her favorite deli before leaving Asheville. Then, after checking the outbuildings and admiring what remained of last year's flourishing vegetable garden, they started back. They were comfortable together now. Analiese had obviously loved the Sawyer farm, not just the house but the land around it. She chatted, occasionally asking questions about the property.

Charlotte knew they weren't idle questions. "Do you have an idea for using it?"

"Inspiration comes from knowledge. I'm just putting it all together."

Charlotte didn't take the direct route back. They had time, and she was enjoying Analiese's company. By the time she turned off on a paved road lined with carefully spaced rhododendrons in riotous shades of fuchsia and purple, she had steeled herself for another encounter with her past.

They arrived at an unmanned security booth and a large carved sign announcing that they were entering Falcon View. Charlotte continued on, up and down familiar hills, past expensive but not ostentatious homes, and land still rich in native shrubbery and trees.

She parked at last, on a hill that had a view for miles and miles, and offered a glimpse of Asheville in the distance.

She got out, and without asking why, Analiese followed suit. They leaned against the hood of the Cherokee, and Charlotte folded her arms. "It's a long story. Do you want to hear it?"

"Of course."

"This land belonged to my father. When he died, I realized it could be worth a fortune. I knew if I simply sold it the way it was, I would be a little wealthier, but someone else would be a lot more so after it was developed. So over a period of months I hatched a plan — without telling my husband, who wouldn't have approved for a number of reasons.

"One day I walked into the offices of Whitestone Development Properties and asked to see the founder and president, George Whitestone. I handed the woman at the desk a portfolio I'd made that included photographs and a description of every foot of this land. Elevation, water sources, costs, transcripts of conversations with the local utility company. People from Charlotte and Atlanta were hungry for mountain homes for weekends and summers. I thought the time had come to do something about it."

"Did you have any experience?"

"I'd been studying local developers for years, and I had a degree in business management. So I knew a lot, but not enough, of course, to do anything on my own. I must have had fortune on my side. I knew just enough to intrigue George and not enough to scare him off. We sat together in his office as he looked through the portfolio. Then I pulled a folder out of my handbag and gave it to him. It contained all the research I'd done into Whitestone Development and similar firms, graphs and lists and, finally, my analysis, which showed that they were the top candidate to develop my land."

"That's extraordinary. What did he say?"

Charlotte pushed away from the car and began to walk. Analiese joined her. "I was so scared. I remember putting my hands in my pockets so he wouldn't see they were shaking. I told him what I thought the land was worth then, and what it would be worth once it was developed in two or three years. I told him that I knew Whitestone Development was working on several major projects at the present and, if my research was correct, had extended themselves financially as far as it would be wise to.

"Then I made my offer. I told him I wanted a job more than I wanted to sell the land. I wanted to work in real estate development, and I wanted to learn *everything.* I thought Whitestone Development could use a new face, someone with energy and commitment and the desire to move up the ladder. I didn't want to start at the top. I was willing to start close to the bottom as long as it was clear to everyone I was climbing steadily.

"When the time came for Whitestone to develop my land, I would sell it to the company at a bargain, as long as I was involved in every step of development. And as long as my husband, a talented young architect, would be strongly considered to help develop the site."

The view here was even better, and they stopped to admire it. "I'm sure Mr. Whitestone was impressed," Analiese said. "Not just with you, but with this land."

"By the end he agreed to consider my offer, and I gave him everything I had with me so he could explore my proposal with his team." Charlotte faced Analiese and smiled a little. "My knees were knocking so hard by the time I got to my car, I had to sit and breathe deeply for ten minutes before I thought it might be safe to drive."

"What did your husband say? You hadn't told him a thing?"

"Ethan was against planned communities and probably still is. The density's usually too high, the attention to the environment is lip service, the architecture's cookie-cutter and there's little attempt to blend into the surroundings. When we'd talked about my father's land, Ethan had envisioned dividing it into, at most, four parcels, each with a house designed to disappear into the mountainside, a residence that would be off the grid and no threat to the fragile environment that my father had already spoiled."

"Not good. Sounds like getting him to see it your way took some convincing."

"I waited until my next meeting with George Whitestone. He tried to convince me again just to sell for a nice little profit, but I knew what I wanted. A career. He agreed reluctantly, but he agreed. So then I finally told Ethan what I was up to. He was stunned. He couldn't really see I wanted to be God, to change the city and the surrounding countryside to suit my own design. I never wanted to be a poor powerless country bumpkin again."

She felt as if she had just emptied her heart, but she trusted that she'd emptied it to the right person. And she was right.

"I'm not sure what's more interesting," Analiese said. "That you did all this and worked so hard, or that you see your own motivations so clearly now."

"They're darker than I've just told you." Charlotte looked out at the view that was her father's legacy. "I think I hoped that people would fear me. I think I'd given up hope by then that they would ever love me. What was there to love, after all? So I sold this land and myself to get what I wanted. And from that moment on, my life was never the same."

Chapter Twenty-Five

The telephone rang just as Taylor put the final stitches in the hem of the skirt Maddie wanted to wear to school that morning. Today was Maddie's first day back, and Taylor understood her desire to look good, although not so much the need to pull out every single item in her closet. Of course the skirt she *had* to wear was the only one that needed repair.

Maddie grabbed the telephone with her left hand, which was still in a sling, and Taylor's handiwork with her right. "Daddy!"

Taylor watched her daughter squirm into the skirt while she cradled the receiver in the crook of her shoulder. She had been cranky and fearful all morning, waking early and eating nothing more than a few bites of toast. Now, despite the gymnastics, she was finally smiling.

"I'm leaving in a few minutes," Maddie said into the telephone. "Sam's going to take me. Mom has a class in a little while."

Sam and Taylor had carefully planned Maddie's return to school. In reality Taylor had plenty of time to drive her, but she and Sam had decided that arriving with Edna would help soothe Maddie's anxiety. She was embarrassed to face the children who had witnessed her seizure at the park, and even the get-well card she'd received from her class hadn't done much to make her feel better. Popular, diplomatic Edna would help her through her return.

"I can't wait to see you!" Maddie said. "I love you, Daddy!" She was smiling by the time Taylor hung up the phone for her. "He says Willow has a friend with horses, and I can ride when I'm there."

Taylor had to remind her heart to beat. "Did he?"

"I can't wait to go to Nashville." Maddie paused, as if she realized how that sounded. "Of course, I'll miss you."

Taylor welded a smile on her face and nodded. "Of course."

A honk sounded, and Taylor knew Sam was there. "Run along, or rather walk," she said as casually as she could. She knew better than to act like heading to school was anything other than completely normal. "I'll be here when you get home. Papa's bringing dinner tonight. We'll have a party."

Maddie did a fist bump, grabbed her book bag with her good arm and headed outside. Taylor stood in the doorway and waved, and the moment Sam's VW had disappeared, she picked up the receiver and hit speed dial.

Jeremy answered on the first ring. "Maddie?"

"Maddie's mother," she said formally. "She's on her way to school."

"She sounded excited."

"No, she's been a nervous wreck all morning." She didn't add, *But what would you know?* although she heard the sentiment in her voice.

"Look, we have to talk," she went on. "I guess I understand why you couldn't visit your daughter in the hospital."

"I talked to Maddie twice a day, Taylor. You know Black Balsam's on tour. We have one more gig, then we're done for a couple of months. Maddie knows we're going to be together soon."

"You're *not,*" Taylor said, although she had planned to work up to that more subtly.

"I'm sorry?"

"Listen, she's just gone through a trauma, and she needs to stay here, where her doctor and her medical records are. She's on new meds, and we don't know what the outcome will be. Her shoulder's healing, but she's in a sling —"

"And from what I'm told, she'll be out of it by the end of school, right?"

"But she's still healing! Did you honestly believe she'd be up to riding horseback?"

"Is that what this is about? Give me a break, Taylor. I'm going to lead her around the ring on an old nag who couldn't trot if the hounds of hell were after him. Maddie deserves as normal a life as we can give her."

"Like I don't know that? I'm the one who deals with this every single minute."

"And yet you're the one who's trying to keep me from helping, aren't you?"

She swallowed her anger and reminded herself this was about Maddie. "Look, this isn't about the horse, and it's not something I just thought of. I know you want her there. Maybe next summer —"

"Next summer will be perfect, too. But she's coming this summer, just the way we planned, just the way you and I have previously discussed, accident or no. She's looking forward to it, and I'm not going to disappoint her. I want her to get to know Willow, and she needs time with me."

He was silent for a moment, and when he continued his voice was calmer, but only as if by a huge effort. "I know this is hard for you. But epilepsy is unpredictable, Taylor. We both know it. If I wait until I have a written guarantee she's going to be seizure-free, I'll have to wait forever. I'm prepared. And believe it or not, we have doctors and hospitals in Tennessee, just in case."

"No." She couldn't think of a better way to end the conversation. "I'm sorry, but no, Jeremy. I don't feel good about letting her leave town after what she's been through. I —"

He didn't let her finish. "What's really worse for Maddie? Visiting her father in a perfectly safe environment where she'll be loved and cared for? Or staying in Asheville while her parents battle her future in court? Because this time I'm not going to sit back and let you run everything. Maddie's coming to Nashville, or I'm going to find a lawyer."

"This time?"

"Let's not go there."

"You're the one who said it."

"Okay, this isn't the first time you've tried to keep me at arm's length. But it's the last. I get that you love her. I get that you need her in your life. But I also get that she needs *me.* So she's coming. And please don't let her see how much you don't want her to.

Give her the gift of a happy farewell, okay?"

She hung up without slamming the receiver into the cradle. It was the very best she was capable of.

Harmony loved watching Velvet with her puppies. She hadn't realized how different each would be, even at this early age. They were only two days old and their eyes weren't even open, but already they were individuals.

Not surprisingly, the largest, a male, was the most aggressive. The other puppies let him squirm into place to feed without protest, as if they knew they had no choice, and in response Harmony named him Villain. Villain was a pale gold, and the other male, Valentino, was nearly as large but darker, making it easy enough to tell them apart. Valentino was less aggressive than his brother, but Harmony thought he was savvier. He didn't use brute force to get what he wanted. He waited for the right moment and found the perfect route to his goal. One of the females, Velveteen, was just as large, but she was the darkest puppy in the litter, almost exactly the color of her mother, hence the name. Violin, was good-size, too, and a medium gold with fur that rippled noticeably, as if she owed more to her poodle father than to Velvet. She was also the loudest of the litter, screeching when thwarted, like a violin in the hands of a preschooler.

Then there was the runt. The smallest female had been the last born, almost an afterthought. She was the palest, and Harmony had named her Vanilla. Vanilla did her best to find a place at the smorgasbord, but she was often shoved away. Harmony thought she was too docile and let Villain, in particular, push her around. Harmony had taken to moving Villain away from his mother and inserting Vanilla in his place. She wondered, though, if she was setting the puppy up for failure.

It was, after all, a dog-eat-dog world.

Through all the fuss, Velvet was the perfect mother. She fed the puppies; she cleaned them; she only took breaks for food, water or trips outside. Watching her exhausted Harmony, and sometimes she questioned her own fitness to do the same.

How would she do everything she needed to without a decent income or child care? The puppies would be gone in a matter of months, but a human child was a lifetime commitment.

"Velvet just seems to know exactly what to do," she told Charlotte on the way to her first prenatal examination. After much research she had discovered that she qualified for health care at Mountain Medical, a clinic funded through the public health department. Charlotte had asked to come with her, for which Harmony was grateful.

"It's not quite as cut and dried for people," Charlotte said, as she nabbed a parking space large enough for a tank.

Harmony waited until Charlotte had pulled up and back several times, ending up at least eighteen inches from the curb but luckily out of the flow of traffic.

"Did your instincts kick in?" Harmony asked. "What if mine don't? What if I have no idea in the world what to do when my baby cries?"

"You try this, you try that, and eventually they get so exhausted they fall asleep despite you. But I don't want to kid you. It's hard work."

Today Charlotte looked as if she'd been working hard herself. There were new circles under her eyes, and her skin was almost chalky. She'd been gone all morning and hadn't told Harmony where. Harmony wondered if the trip had in some way involved her daughter and granddaughter, and hadn't gone well.

The more Harmony examined her mentor, the less she liked what she saw. "Are you sure you're up to this? I mean, you look like you might need a nap more than a long wait while they get to me. It's a clinic, not an office, and I've been warned I might be sitting for hours."

"I brought a book and some papers I have to go over. I'm looking forward to sitting."

Charlotte was actually a replacement. After considering and reconsidering, Harmony had invited Davis to attend her first prenatal visit. She'd thought he might have questions the doctor could answer, but he'd sounded surprised she believed he might want to come. He'd pled a full day at work, but under it, she'd detected relief that an excuse had occurred to him so quickly.

Out of the car, she waited for Charlotte to join her on the curb. "You came because I told you Davis was too busy, didn't you?"

"This is an exciting appointment. I just wanted to share it with you."

Harmony knew better. The appointment was routine, likely to be filled with paperwork and perfunctory questions. Charlotte had come because she didn't want Harmony to be alone or disappointed there was no one to share this event with. Not the baby's father. Not her own mother.

"I just thought . . . well, you don't look

like you're feeling up to par. Maybe you ought to be resting."

"I'll sit quietly." Charlotte smiled fondly at her. "I saw my doctor this morning, so you don't have anything to worry about."

"Then you're okay?"

"He ran some routine tests. You know that's what they do best. And he sent me home with a prescription, the other thing they love to do. So it's all under control."

Harmony wondered *what* was under control, but she knew the functions of the human body weren't always that much fun to discuss.

They walked up a brick walkway recently swept clean but in need of repair. Mountain Medical was two stories and narrow. From the road she'd noted how far back it went, bordered on both sides by walkways to other entrances.

Inside she waited in a short line to sign in. The receptionist, who already looked harried, assembled a pile of papers, although Harmony had already filled out and returned a small packet she'd received by mail.

The woman handed her a clipboard. "By the time you're done with these, we'll know everything except your views on climate change. But this will give you something to do while you wait. And you *will* wait. Our director's out for the day, and we're missing two other staff members this morning. I hope you brought something to do."

"Thanks for letting me know." Harmony took the papers and made room at the window for the next woman.

She and Charlotte took seats in a corner. The room was filling up fast and there weren't many left. Harmony apologized.

"Harmony, I volunteered to be here. You write, I'll read." Charlotte opened a novel with a lighthouse on the cover and a long stretch of beach, although Harmony had expected something about real estate or global economics, complete with notes scribbled in the margins.

"Is the book good?" she asked.

"It makes me wish I'd spent the past twenty years just reading for fun."

Harmony wasn't sure what that meant, but she was glad Charlotte had something to keep her occupied.

She worked on the papers, answering questions until she was finally finished. She took the clipboard back to the window and left it, and by the time she got back to her seat, it was the only empty one in the room. She moved her denim backpack to the floor and sat again.

Someone had cared enough to make the room as attractive as paint and supersize decals could. One wall was a soft blue, the one beside it a sea green. Another was yellow, and the final wall was a pale coral. The decals were cartoon babies, smiling, playing together and sleeping. There were bulletin boards everywhere with information she probably should read but couldn't, because she didn't want to lose her seat.

At least two dozen adults occupied the room, along with almost a dozen bored children. She decided that, if nothing else, this was a chance to pick up parenting tips. Some of the mothers had brought things for their children to do, which kept them at least minimally satisfied, but others simply ignored their kids, who were climbing on tables or racing back and forth, and others reprimanded their little ones every time they whined or did anything except sit perfectly still.

She made mental notes. Always bring something for her son or daughter to do, because the two of them probably had lots of waiting in clinics ahead of them. Don't get angry with a bored child. Play word games to keep him occupied. Compliment him when he's good.

Of course now she was thinking like the

child was a boy. She wondered if Davis would prefer that. Would he find more in common with a son? Would he then be more inclined to get involved? Buddy had certainly been the favored child in her family, but Davis wouldn't be abusive, not the way her father had been. Except that, as she thought about it, she couldn't help but see similarities. Davis, too, wanted things his way, and he liked to be waited on. He didn't like noise or hassles. If he'd come today, he would probably have refused to wait.

Of course, if she was married to Davis, she wouldn't be *here.* She would be in a doctor's office with soft music and plenty of comfortable chairs. Her wait would be minimal, and the doctor and nurses would know her name. The information she needed wouldn't be tacked up on bulletin boards.

Harmony didn't want to be critical. She knew she was lucky to have a place where she could be checked and cared for. But it was hard not to compare.

Two women were called, one immediately after the other, and two chairs opened up. A young Asian couple with an adorable toddler sat down. The man was one of only two in the room, and he immediately gathered the toddler on his lap and put his arms around him, whispering in the little boy's ear. The woman was obviously pregnant, but probably months from delivery. The little boy laughed, then the mother did, too. They began to play a game with their son, something that included slapping hands and chanting a rhyme. Both parents were absorbed in the little boy's participation, encouraging him, obviously delighted in everything he did.

The mother, with a waterfall of black hair, and the child, with a darling spiky haircut, were certainly worth watching, but Harmony's attention was riveted on the father. Dressed in carefully pressed casual clothes he was here, with his family, a long wait ahead of him, but he still seemed content. Maybe he had taken off work to come today, to watch his son while his wife was checked. Maybe he wasn't employed and had taken time away from a job search, or maybe he worked for himself and only earned an income when he was on the job. Whatever his situation, he was making the most of this time with his son.

As she watched, Harmony realized that no matter what choice she made, her son or daughter would never have what this little boy did, two parents who thought he was the ace in whatever hand life had dealt them. She knew the parents had to be poor, like her, or they wouldn't be sitting here. But she thought their children, this little boy and the baby his mother carried, would be two of the wealthiest children in the world.

Harmony had been settled in a cubicle somewhere in the warren of rooms off the waiting area about ten minutes ago, and Charlotte imagined there was still a long wait ahead. She'd finished a chapter and reluctantly pulled out some paperwork she needed to look at, but the activity in the waiting room caught her eye instead.

Samantha Ferguson worked here; in fact, Charlotte thought she might even be the director who was gone for the day. She could imagine her here, and she could imagine her making changes, too. But what kind of budget did the clinic have to work with? Very little, she imagined, in a time when everyone from the government on down was strapped.

The largest problem were the children. Many of the mothers who came to Mountain Medical probably had few resources. They might be single. They might be living far from their families, or estranged from them. Whatever their stories, they had been forced to bring their other children here because no one was at home to care for them. And how difficult was that for the clinic staff? How could they do a proper exam when children were present? Did a nurse keep an eye on a patient's children while she simultaneously tried to do her job?

Her telephone vibrated, and she pulled it from her pocket to glance at the number. Surprised, she grabbed her purse and went outside to answer, since there were signs in the waiting room against making or taking calls.

"Charlotte?"

"Phil."

Phil was otherwise known as Dr. Granger, a friend from the country club who today sounded like the oncologist he was. "You have a moment?"

She knew from experience that Phil was speaking in a tone that ultimately led to bad news, and she was sorry she'd answered.

Again from experience, she knew the news would be easier if he got straight to the point. "I do have a moment, but no time at all for you prettying up whatever you called to say."

"We got the preliminaries on your blood work back."

She was amazed. "Already?" Her heart

sped up, and she was sorry now that she wasn't sitting.

"I don't like your counts. In fact, they're alarming. I want you back this afternoon for a transfusion. And I think you'll need more than one before we figure out the next phase of your treatment. We can do the transfusions outpatient —"

"We will," she said firmly, doing the unthinkable and interrupting him. "You know I don't want to go into the hospital here."

"You're going to have to let people know what's going on."

"I will when I have to."

His voice softened. "You need to ask yourself why that matters, Charlotte. Why do you care?"

"Oh, I have. Really." She was standing outside, with people passing and cars gunning engines in the parking lot. There might have been better times for this, but if she had learned one thing from her illness, it was that *this* was the time she had.

"Charlotte, are you still writing in your cancer journal?"

She was surprised he remembered. She'd told him about the journal the psychologist had suggested. He'd been pleased and said he was going to investigate for his other patients.

"I am," she said. "I've been catching up with my past."

He was silent for a moment, then his tone softened even more. "I think it's time for you to write about the leukemia, don't you?"

She was standing in sunshine, but she felt cold inside. "I will when I need to."

"You need to," he said. "If for no other reason than to stop pretending you can go through this alone."

She closed her phone, but long minutes passed before she went back inside.

Chapter Twenty-Six

First Day Journal: May 29

When Taylor is born I have no faith in myself or my daughter. When my marriage begins to fail I'm certain if I control every facet of our lives, I can bring us through the bad times. When Taylor gets pregnant I'm certain she'll listen to reason once we refuse to support her.

I'm terribly wrong in every way.

In the years after the divorce, love no longer has a place in my life. I commit fully to establishing myself and Falconview as unshakable pillars of the community. When I'm not working, I serve on boards, sure I know what's best for everyone — although the proof I don't is all around me.

One morning in the fall, I oversleep. An inventory of the past weeks tells me why. I've worked late every night. The economic downturn has kept me on my toes and given me an even greater opportunity to play lady of the manor. Telling others how to live their lives has pushed me to the edge of my own.

I decide a long weekend away will be good. I check into a spa for healthy meals, massages and sleep. Afterward I'm still tired, but functioning. I schedule more time away from work, but when I do, the emptiness of my life becomes apparent. I respond by working longer hours.

Weeks go by, and getting out of bed is even harder. I sleep fitfully and experience night sweats. My appetite disappears, and I tell myself menopause is playing tricks. I ignore bruises, telling myself to be more careful. When winter arrives I get a cold that hangs on tenaciously, but I steel myself and ignore it.

My secretary schedules my annual checkup, but I'm too busy. At last, almost eighteen months after my last one, I visit my internist, who asks why I'm dieting and expresses concern about enlarged lymph nodes. I explain about the cold that's dragged on forever. He schedules the usual blood work and gives me a lecture on slowing down.

Two days later he calls me back into the office and tells me he wants me to have a bone marrow biopsy. My white blood cell count is alarmingly high. I tell him I'm fine. He tells me I may well be wrong.

One week later I clear my schedule. Until that moment I've managed to push worry away. But when I'm waiting for the local anesthesia to take effect, as the hematologist explains what's in store, I'm forced to face the fact that this is not a test that's performed without merit.

The following week I'm back at my internist's office. His expression is grave, and for the first time I fear the worst. He tells me I have leukemia, acute myelogenous leukemia, and I will need more tests to determine how best to treat it. He talks about chromosomes and molecular testing and blood smears. I hear the word leukemia and little else.

When he suggests a local hematologist I tell him I'm calling Phil Granger, a top oncologist I know from the country club. He tells me Phil's a good choice, too, and wishes me luck. I realize as he's saying goodbye that he believes this may be the last time he ever sees me.

The next day, when I arrive for an emergency appointment, Phil's prepared with all my test results. He concurs with my internist's diagnosis, and I'm disappointed he's been influenced. I promise to make appointments for more testing, but instead I make preparations to go to Duke to begin the evaluation process all over again. I tell myself I'm lucky I can afford the best, that all the hours I've put into Falconview will finally pay off. But I can't keep the other voices in my head at bay.

If I hadn't put in all those hours, would I now have friends and family surrounding me? Would Ethan and Taylor be here to help me prepare for the inevitable? Because even as I stubbornly make my appointments and reservations, I know what the doctors at Duke will tell me.

Chapter Twenty-Seven

Between cutting up fresh strawberries and heading to the stove to check muffins, the kitchen phone rang. Harmony answered, because even though Charlotte was awake, she was still in her room and would probably ignore the phone. Harmony knew she kept a journal, and morning seemed to be her favorite time to write in it.

Harmony liked that idea, only she wasn't sure what she would say if she was keeping one.

May 29: Last week the doctor told me my due date is mid-December, and I will be able to hear the heartbeat at the next appointment. I had more questions than he had time. When I told Davis, he said I'll have a lifetime of that ahead of me if I don't marry him.

The woman on the other end of the phone sounded close to Harmony's own age. "Do I have the right number?" she asked, after she said good-morning. "Is this the residence of Charlotte Hale? Is this Charlotte?"

Harmony explained.

"This is Marilla Reynolds, Harmony. Call me Rilla. I think you and Charlotte have my dog. Velvet?"

"Oh, sure, we do." Harmony launched into the story of Velvet and the five perfect puppies and ended with: "We left a message at the kennel for your husband, but we didn't hear back. Are you doing okay?"

"As a matter of fact, I'm getting better faster than anybody expected. I'm doing therapy here at home three times a week, and with some effort I can get myself to and from the bathroom and kitchen. Brad's back at the office."

"Office? I thought he farmed for a living."

"I do the farming. Brad does the lawyering."

"Pretty handy if one of your chickens ever tries to sue you."

Rilla had a lilting laugh, and Harmony liked her immediately. "If he sues anybody it'll be the other driver's insurance company. So the puppies aren't too much trouble?"

"They're more fun than anything."

"I can't thank you enough for what you've done for us. It helps a lot to know Velvet isn't in a cage at the vet's. She deserves better."

"I've fallen in love with her, and the puppies, too."

"I wish I could see them."

Harmony hated to ask, but knew she had to. "Do you want them back? Now that you're home, I mean?"

"No chance. I've still got a long way to go. In fact, my kids are still at my mom's. She brings them here on her days off and helps around the house, but it'll be months before I'm really able to do much of anything useful."

Harmony was both relieved and sad. She hated the thought of parting with Velvet and the puppies, but she also hated hearing that this nice woman still had so far to go.

"I could bring photos," she said, before she thought the offer through. "Of the puppies, I mean. I took a whole roll with a disposable camera. They're just so cute."

"It's a long way to come just to show me photos, isn't it?"

The photos were the least of it. Harmony liked the idea of going to the country for a little while, and she suspected Rilla was probably lonely at home by herself.

"I need some fresh air," she said. "And you're not really that far away. I won't stay long and tire you out."

"You have no idea how nice it would be

to have a little company. Everybody's been great, but most of my friends work, or they're busy with their kids. I'm just lucky I'm alive and my mom can help out until I can take over again."

Harmony wondered what it would be like to have that kind of support. Then she thought of Charlotte. Her mother couldn't help her, but a stranger had taken her place. Charlotte was a pretty great consolation prize.

"I can get there in about an hour, maybe a little more," she told Rilla.

"I'll look forward to it."

After Harmony left for Capable Canines, taking a packet of photos and a loaf of zucchini bread, Charlotte considered the rest of her day. She'd been up since dawn working on her journal and an even more difficult project, the letter to Taylor. She felt wrung out, and it wasn't even ten o'clock yet. Since hearing from Dr. Granger she'd had two transfusions, and she felt better physically, but the second project of the morning had been wrenching. Now she wanted to be finished, and there was only one way to make that happen.

She took a shower and dressed carefully, although she was torn about what to wear.

Jeans were too casual, and out of character, as if she was trying to prove she was somebody else these days. She settled on a pale lime sundress and sandals, since the day promised to be hot, but she topped the dress with a thin cotton cardigan of salmon-pink.

In the shower she'd debated whether to call Ethan or simply show up on his doorstep. After the scene at the hospital, she didn't want to run into her daughter and granddaughter, nor did she want to run into some strange woman who might be spending the day with her ex. On the other hand, she didn't want to give him a chance to refuse. She wasn't going to stay, and she wasn't going to ask for anything new.

After lunch she finally made her decision. She called from her cell phone when she was only a mile from the address she'd found for him. When he answered on the third ring, she cleared her throat.

"Ethan, it's Charlotte. Do you have a minute?"

He hesitated, as if wary. "What's up?"

"I have something I need to give you, and I'm in the neighborhood. Would you mind if I drop it off now? If it's inconvenient . . ."

"Inconvenient, no. Surprising? Yes."

"I know." She sighed. "I was afraid you'd

say no, so I didn't call from home."

"You used to do this. You liked to spring things on people, but at least you usually gave them a few moments to prepare."

He didn't sound angry, and she felt herself smiling a little. "I've changed. You have a whole four, maybe even five, *minutes.* It depends on how easy it is to park near your house."

"Have you never learned to park a car?"

"I can park a car, just not to your standards."

"You mean within marked boundaries? Close enough to the curb to get there with a flying leap?"

"Your expectations were always too high."

"Come ahead. Shall I make a pot of coffee?"

That surprised her. She hadn't intended to stay that long — she hadn't expected to be invited to. "I'd like that."

"You can park in my driveway. Just don't run over my dappled willows." He hung up.

The dappled willows created a hedge along the edge of his driveway, leaves of pink, green and white on graceful stalks. The house had once been something else, a simple ranch, but Ethan had obviously done a renovation. Instead of the usual wrought-iron railings or slim wooden posts holding up the porch roof, he had installed rich dark wood pillars with stainless-steel accents. The siding was a cool slate gray, and sleek unadorned windows ran nearly from ground to roof. The landscaping was Asian in style, with a curving path to the front door of crushed white stone lined with a thick border of river stone, and studded with clumps of ornamental grasses.

The effect was masculine and spare, without being overdone. Ethan had been considerate of his neighbors, and the result was innovative, but not overwhelming.

Very Ethan.

When she was nearly to the porch, he opened the door, as if he'd been watching for her. "Not taking any chances on backing out, are you?"

All these years later, he still knew her well. She hadn't pulled in farther than a few feet from the street to save herself from plowing into a mailbox or landing in a drainage ditch on the way out.

"And I bet you got out the cream and didn't bother with the sugar. Hello, Ethan. Thanks for letting me come."

"The coffee's perking." He stood to one side so she could enter.

The floor plan was an open one, although she doubted it had started out that way. She walked directly into the living room and saw the kitchen straight ahead, separated only by a granite counter. The floors were old cherry, polished to a fine sheen, and the kitchen cabinets seemed to be the same cherry, extending to the ceiling and flanked by stainless appliances. The backsplash was tile that reminded her of piano keys.

"I bet it didn't look like this when you moved in," she said.

"It didn't look this way when Judy lived here, either. I remodeled after she moved to Chicago. It gave me something to do."

She felt a twinge, as she had the last time he'd mentioned his second ex. "And made the place yours," she said lightly.

"Want a tour?"

The house was surprisingly spacious. Four small bedrooms had been turned into three, she guessed, with the enlarged master suite stretching across most of the back. The walls were earth tones and most often bare of adornment, the furniture basic and functional, with beautiful lines. Windows looked out on small gardens, one with a tiny waterfall, or clusters of slender trees that hid the neighboring yards. Several faced the rear and a large outbuilding.

Back in the living room, she congratulated him. "It's wonderful. Simple but not stark.

And I bet Maddie loves the little bedroom with the waterfall view."

"She's my biggest fan. Let me get the coffee."

She followed him into the kitchen and took the mug he handed her. "What's in the back? I'm surprised at how much space you have out there."

"My workshop and office." He seemed to consider. "Would you like to see that, too?"

"Can I bring my cup?"

He brought his, as well, and explained what he was working on as they crossed the yard.

"I bought the bottle factory at auction and almost didn't win. After I did, I was sorry, because suddenly I realized what a commitment I'd made. That was three years ago."

"Three years?" She'd built a fifty-unit condominium in less time than that.

"I know. But the best way to develop the property is slowly. We're using elbow grease and reclaimed materials, a lot of it from the factory itself. We'll end up with six loft units, the largest with four bedrooms. The smallest — mine — will have two. I'm tired of cleaning and taking care of a yard. But the building will have simple gardens around it, so there'll be plenty of green space."

"And somebody else will take care of it.

That sounds good."

"We're leaving brick exposed, and we've opened ceilings right to the beams. We have a welding artist using old plumbing pipes to fashion stair rails, and a glass artist is taking old windows from the factory and colored glass from a neighborhood church that was demolished, and setting it in concrete for the countertops. I have drawings if you'd like to see, and photos."

"I'd love to. I would love to know if you're going to make any money, too, with all those craftsmen and artists doing the work."

"That's a very Charlotte question."

Since he didn't sound angry, she didn't apologize. "But not a Charlotte indictment. I'm honestly curious. If there's a way to have both, we need to tell everybody and make it happen."

"Mass produce it, you mean?"

She thought about that. "No. But maybe it's time we just think smaller and figure out how to do it without going broke."

"That doesn't sound like you."

"You don't know what I sound like these days, remember? We've been divorced nearly as long as we were married."

"No, we haven't."

She saw that he was watching her. "I'm

not the woman you remember, Ethan."

He smiled. Sadly. "Lulu, you never were."

Ethan thought Charlotte was honestly impressed with the factory lofts. She asked good questions, avidly examined the plans and told him what she liked best about each unit. She walked through the workshop, and trailed her fingertips over freshly sanded hickory and bundles of copper piping waiting to be carted away by the welder. She stayed long enough that coffee had become glasses of wine shared in his living room.

During the early years of their marriage they had connected over blueprints and building materials, he from an artist's perspective, she from a developer's. In the long run their mutual fascination had both kept them together and hastened their separation. In the beginning conversations about architecture and community and responsible development, like the one they'd been having for the past several hours, had stoked the fire of their romance. In the end, their differing perspectives had smothered it.

"I wish," she said, "that I had appreciated your talent more. I spent so much time trying to get you to see things my way."

He poured the last of a bottle of good cabernet into her glass. "Some of that was okay. I was a dreamer, you were a doer. I needed a shove."

"And I needed a muzzle." She smiled the smile he remembered so well from their early years and had rarely witnessed in the later ones. "You've grown into your talent, though. You were wasted at Falconview, designing houses you couldn't put your soul into. The lofts are going to be extraordinary."

"Now I'm waiting for an offer to go in on the project with me. Let Falconview bankroll the remainder and speed it up. Then you can sell the units, skimming just a *tiny* bit for the privilege."

She laughed. "You'll have a long wait. I've lost the pit-bull instinct. I'd rather just watch from afar and wish you well."

"Times are hard. We get by on long hours and dreams, but we get by. When the factory's completed, I'll probably move on to something completely different."

"That fills your well. You need the variety."

He contemplated how odd this was. He'd never expected to have a conversation with Charlotte again, much less one when she seemed to see him for the man he was and approve. He found it seductive in the most elemental of ways, as if something he'd longed for had been given to him at last. He had the curious desire to give something back, and he found himself wishing he was sitting close to her, instead of across the short expanse between sofa and chair.

Some wishes were best unfulfilled.

"Have you really changed so much? Or are you setting me up for something?" he asked.

She looked surprised, and for a moment he saw anger flickering in her blue-gray eyes. Then she sighed. "I guess I deserve that. But yes, I've changed."

"Why?"

She didn't answer for a moment, as if mulling over what answer to give, then she shrugged. "Life will do that to you."

He didn't know what she meant and didn't want to know. He knew she wanted to reconcile with their daughter. He knew she wanted access to their granddaughter. But did she want access to him? If so, she seemed to have gotten a foot in the door. She was sitting in his house finishing her second glass of wine. His own head was spinning pleasantly, but there were warning bells clanging in the distance.

"What did you want to drop off?" he asked. "We seem to have forgotten the real purpose of this visit."

"I wrote a letter to Taylor. I brought it with me."

"Do you want me to read and critique?"

"No. I'd like you to give it to her, if you will. I don't want to complicate your relationship, but I'm hoping if it comes through you, she'll be less likely to rip it up the moment it touches her hand."

He thought about that, about what an imposition this was, about the way it was bound to widen the crack that had surfaced the moment he told Taylor he'd communicated with her mother.

But he didn't say those things. He told a different truth. "Our daughter's angry at you, but you aren't the only one. She's angry at Jeremy, too. And now she's angrier because she thinks I'm taking your side."

He held up his hand to stop Charlotte's apology. "No, the point is that Taylor has problems with forgiveness, and I haven't been good about confronting her. I never was good at confronting her. I left that to you."

"You did," she said, but not as if it pleased her.

"Everybody who loves her walks a line, and if she feels they've wronged her, they're out of her life. She's forced to interact with

Jeremy, but she lashes out at him in subtle ways. She tries to keep him away from Maddie. She never gives him credit for anything. She knows, on some level, that they have to cooperate for Maddie's sake, but on a deeper level, she fights it."

"I'll find another way to get the letter to her."

"No, I'll give it to her. And I'll tell her what I'm telling you. She has to learn to forgive. Carrying this kind of anger for so long will weigh her down and keep her from moving forward. It would be different if you weren't trying to find a way to be in her life again, but you are. Now it's her turn to find a way to accept that."

Her eyes glistened with tears. "Believe it or not, I still understand her. Taylor feels things deeply. She always did, even as a little girl. So she pushes everyone who hurts her away so she won't be hurt again. I don't think it's anger so much as pain."

They were talking about Taylor, but he thought Charlotte was talking about herself, as well. Like mother, like daughter. He'd noticed the similarities between them before and hoped he was wrong. Now he knew he wasn't.

She glanced at her watch, then up at him, blinking back tears. "I should go."

He thought she was right. This intimacy was uncomfortable. It was also, like her compliments, seductive.

She got to her feet, and he joined her. "You're okay to drive home?" he asked.

"I'm fine." But she didn't move. Instead, she reached out and touched his arm, her fingertips featherlight. "Do you know what I regret?"

"Apparently lots of things."

"I was thinking of one in particular. Our lot at Falcon View. The lot we never built on."

"The land you sold right after the divorce," he said.

"The lot I bought back three years ago, after the new owners decided not to build, after all." It was the one piece of her father's land she hadn't sold, a piece she'd kept just for them.

He hadn't known. "You probably got it at a bargain."

She shook her head slowly. "I wish we had built the house you envisioned there. Every time I see that land, I think of that house."

"The one you didn't like? The dream house that was my idea and never yours?"

"If we'd worked on those plans together, we could have found a way to make it ours. I'm sorry we never did. It would have been a masterpiece."

After all the things he had expected her to say, this was a complete surprise.

"There were a lot of things we should have done and didn't," he said.

She smiled a little. "Thank you for that."

"You're welcome."

She looked as if she wanted to say more, but instead she started toward the front door, scooping up her purse on the way. She took out an envelope and set it on the entry table, then opened the door, turned and lifted her hand in farewell.

When she closed it behind her, he continued to stand there until he heard her drive away.

Chapter Twenty-Eight

Taylor was fuming, and she knew it. Yoga helped her understand the way her body and moods entwined, but sometimes she wished she could just fume, anyway. As she packed the last of Maddie's clothes for the trip to Nashville, she imagined herself in a shaded forest beside a creek. She could hear the water lapping against rocks at the edge and the splash of a waterfall just out of sight. From a nearby tree birdsong . . .

"Stupid bird." She slapped the sleeves of a striped T-shirt together and rolled it into something resembling a sausage, tucking it into a corner of the Disney Princess Wishes rolling suitcase that Maddie would probably decline to use next year when she was a grown-up eleven.

The front door opened, then slammed shut and Maddie shouted she was home.

"No duh," Taylor said, then louder, "I'm in your room, sweetheart."

Maddie came in and flopped down on the beloved lavender chenille spread Taylor had found at a flea market. "School sucks, but it's over 'til next year."

Taylor bumped fists with her. "Yippee!"

"What are you doing? I already packed."

"A bathing suit, two pairs of jeans and four pairs of shorts. I thought you might like some shirts to wear with them, and underwear, too. Just in case you need more than the pair you're wearing today."

"They have stores in Nashville, right?"

Taylor knew that wasn't a real question. "Do you have all your other stuff packed? Toys? Books? Games?"

"I packed Josefina and all the clothes Grandma made for her in my backpack. If Grandma comes to Nashville to see us, I don't want her to feel bad. And I packed three books, but I don't remember which ones."

Josefina was Maddie's American Girl doll, and the clothes Jeremy's mother had sewed for her would keep the doll well dressed for years. Taylor knew Maddie was really bringing her for comfort.

"Why don't you put in some Magic Markers and paper, and some pens? I addressed a couple of envelopes and put stamps on them so you can write me."

"I'll use Daddy's computer or I'll call."

"I would love a real letter."

Maddie rolled her eyes, but she didn't argue.

Somebody knocked on the front door, and before Taylor could respond, Maddie was racing through the house. Taylor told herself to be calm. After the phone call ten days before in which Jeremy had laid down the law, she had phoned her lawyer, who'd told her that her best and only recourse was to allow Jeremy to take Maddie to Nashville. If she refused and Jeremy hauled Taylor to court, she could face worse consequences than two weeks away from her daughter.

She heard Maddie's whoop and Jeremy's baritone drawl, and tried to block out both. She wondered if he was arrayed in Black Balsam Drifters' black jeans and black Western shirt, or if he was giving the bad-boy image a rest. Personally she thought faded overalls and chewing tobacco might be a more appropriate image for a man from the North Carolina mountains, but Jeremy's father was a banker, and his mother had a doctorate in international affairs. The Jeremy she had known as a teenager hadn't even liked to hike up to Black Balsam Knob.

She took a deep breath as footsteps approached a few minutes later, and she looked up when they stopped in the doorway. "Jeremy," she said in the friendliest tone she could manage. "We're just about packed here."

Jeremy Larsen got better looking every time she saw him. As a teenager he had been almost too thin, but since then he had grown into his incongruously broad shoulders and long legs. He had sandy blond hair and blue eyes that stood out against tanned skin. Every time she had to confront him, she noted the resemblance to her daughter, and she knew this would work in Maddie's favor in her teens.

"Willow borrowed a van, so we have plenty of room."

Taylor thought she could probably fit the entire contents of her house in a van, but she nodded. "I was hoping to meet her."

"She left to gas up. She'll be back in a few minutes."

She nodded, her gaze drifting to Maddie, who looked worried. Taylor took a breath and smiled. "You must be wiped, Jeremy. And you're turning around and going straight back? How about some coffee or something to eat?"

"We grabbed a bite about an hour ago. I'm fine. And I'd like to get there before dark, so we can settle in before Maddie's bedtime."

"That makes sense." Taylor realized she was squeezing the last of the rolled up T-shirts in her hands, the way she wanted to squeeze Jeremy's neck. She slipped it into the suitcase and zipped it closed. "I think we're set. Maddie assures me they have stores in Nashville, if we forgot anything."

"Maddie, why don't you grab anything you'd like to snack on from the kitchen?" Jeremy said. "We'll be stopping for dinner, but you might need something in the van."

Maddie looked from her father to her mother, seemed to decide it was safe to leave them in her room together and took off. Gladly, Taylor thought.

"I have her doctor's records for you, and anything else you might need. Her meds and medication reminder alarm." Taylor pointed to a blue backpack. "It's all there, including suggestions on what not to let her do."

"You mean like skydiving and mountain climbing?"

She sighed. "Okay, this is hard for me. You know it, I know it. I'm trying."

"And I appreciate it. I promise you don't have anything to worry about. We'll be careful."

"She's so excited. That's not always good."

"Has she had many seizures since the hospital?"

She knew Jeremy had done his epilepsy homework, and he'd been with Maddie when she'd had seizures in the past, so he would understand. "No complex ones. We've adjusted dosages. Maybe we're on to something."

"Willow had two years of med school before she quit to work in the music biz. She'll be a help."

"She quit med school to become a promoter?"

"She likes music better than dissecting cadavers."

Taylor made a face. "I can relate."

"I hope you can, T. I'd like all of us to get along, and Willow's the real deal for me. Once Maddie gets to know her, I'm going to tell her we're engaged."

Since Taylor had never been the real deal for Jeremy, or vice versa, she felt no jealousy. She did feel a stab of anger that she would be forced to share her beloved daughter with a stranger.

"I'm going to do my best," she said, not particularly graciously.

There was another knock, and Jeremy left to get the door. "That'll be her. Unless your dad's coming to say goodbye?"

"He did that last night."

Taylor lifted the suitcase off the bed, grabbed the blue backpack and took both into the living room as Jeremy ushered in a blonde woman who was almost as tall as he was. Her shoulder-length hair was streaked several shades of gold, and she wore more makeup than Taylor did in a month, although it was artfully applied. Apparently turquoise was her favorite color, because everything she had on, from sandals to earrings, was the same blue-green shade, which, not surprisingly, matched her eyes.

Maddie came in with a plastic bag of nuts and dried apricots Taylor had already put together for her, and Jeremy put his arm around her shoulders. "Maddie, this is Willow. Willow, Maddie, my little girl." He nodded to Taylor and repeated introductions.

Willow squatted so she could look Maddie straight in the eyes. "I'm so glad to meet you." She had a soft voice, almost out of sync with her brassy exterior, but when she smiled and her eyes crinkled in genuine delight, Taylor understood one of the things Jeremy probably saw in her.

Apparently Maddie saw it, too, because she smiled back. "Me, too."

Willow stood and held out her hand to

Taylor. "I know you're going to miss this little gal, but I promise we'll take really good care of her."

"Miss her? Me?" Taylor forced a smile. "I'm planning to eat ice cream and pizza the whole time she's gone, and watch wrestling in my bathrobe."

"Mom!"

Taylor bumped Maddie's shoulder with her fist. "I think your dad's in a hurry, sweetheart, so you can get to Nashville and see everything before it gets too dark. Give me a hug, and call when you get there, okay?"

Maddie threw herself into Taylor's arms; then, in a flurry of goodbyes and hefted luggage, they were gone.

Minutes later the telephone rang, and Taylor realized she was still standing in the same spot. She crossed the floor to answer it.

"Has she taken off yet?"

Taylor leaned against the counter, glad it was Sam. "A few minutes ago."

"Mom's keeping Edna tonight. A last-day-of-school celebration. Let's go up to the parkway and watch the sunset."

Taylor hung up after they made plans. At this moment she was supremely glad Sam had been on the other end of the line, but at the same time the identity of her caller had been no surprise. The only other person who might have called this afternoon was her dad.

She was always so busy with her daughter and with trying to make ends meet, she had no time for friends. Now she had two weeks without Maddie in the house.

How exactly was she going to spend them?

Friday night was always busy at Cuppa, and Harmony could count on the best tips of the week. This Friday the restaurant was closed to the public for a private wedding reception. She had been there most of the day to help set up and prepare food, and Stella had made sure she was well paid, since she wouldn't be needed to serve. Now she had the evening off, but not, apparently, alone.

When she came out of the ladies' room Davis was waiting impatiently by the door. She figured Stella had told him she was there.

Once they were outside, he took Harmony's denim backpack and tucked it under his arm. "It's not going to hurt you to go out to dinner with me," he told her. "We don't have to talk about the future. We can just get something to eat and catch up on our week."

Harmony knew exactly what that meant. He would tell her all about his, then his eyes would glaze over as she told him about the two visits she'd made to Capable Canines, the first to take the puppy photos, the second to drop off a casserole and an apple cake, so Brad wouldn't have to throw together dinner after a long day at his law office.

"I guess that's okay," she said, because Charlotte was attending a business dinner that night, and going home to the huge empty house didn't sound like much fun, either.

"I've got something to show you first," he said. "Have enough energy to take a little drive? It's not too far."

She had no energy, but sitting in a car didn't sound bad. "My feet are killing me. I hope you're not planning on a walk."

"No walking involved."

She slipped off her shoes once she was inside his Acura — new last year and nearly paid off. Obviously Davis was in the right firm. He was fiscally conservative, which was in line with his employers' philosophy. He didn't mind suits and ties, carefully saved his money and invested wisely. Most of all he was willing to put in long hours and play all the requisite office games. All in all, he was made to be an accountant. Had he not carelessly diddled a cute blonde waitress and gotten her pregnant, he would be almost too good to be true.

Harmony figured she had saved Davis from turning sixty-five before he turned thirty.

"Hard day?" he asked, as he pulled away from the curb.

"Kind of fun, though. I assembled appetizers for the first couple of hours. Mushrooms in filo dough — that stuff's crazy to work with, but I think I finally got the hang of it. Artichoke and goat cheese bruschetta. Edamame hummus. And I was in charge of setup. The place looked pretty good, don't you think?"

"I didn't really notice." He paused, as if he realized he'd said the wrong thing. "I would have paid more attention if I'd known you were in charge."

"It doesn't matter. I wasn't like it was *my* wedding reception."

"That would be a good place for us to have one."

"Umm . . ."

"I got a raise," he said.

"Did you?" She turned so she could see his face. "As much as you wanted?"

"Never."

They both laughed.

Davis slowed and turned into a quiet neighborhood not far from the Grove Park Inn. The lodge-style hotel had been a fixture of Asheville life since the beginning of the twentieth century, and its massive granite boulders had been hewn from the mountain beneath it. Through the years the inn's guest list had included some of the most famous citizens in America. Davis had once taken her there for a drink and the view.

Tonight they kept going until Davis turned onto a side street, following it nearly to the end before he turned again. The road curved up a mountainside, and she was glad when he stopped in front of a contemporary house with pale gray siding and a garage that jutted toward the road. She immediately liked the house, which was attached to its neighbor along one wall, liked the black shutters and paler gray roof, the big tree in the small front yard, and the quiet, tidy neighborhood of what were most likely condos.

She noted a car in the driveway. "Are we visiting friends, or are you dropping something off for a client?"

"No. We can go inside. I have the keys."

"Why do you have the keys?"

He didn't answer. He got out, and after reluctantly slipping her shoes back on, so did she, following him to the door.

"Is this the way an accountant breaks into somebody else's house? In a suit, with keys in his hand and his license plate in full view?"

"You'll like the place." He opened the door and waited for her to enter. Despite the car in the driveway, the house was empty of furniture and looked to be freshly painted. She stepped into the slate foyer and looked beyond at a stretch of pale carpet that ended at French doors leading out to a spacious deck.

She faced him. "I feel funny being here, Davis."

"You don't need to. The owners gave me the keys and told me to look around. They're moving to Sacramento and putting it on the market next week. This development's popular. They won't have a problem selling it."

"Are you thinking about buying it?"

"That depends." He rested his hands on her shoulders. "Don't you think it would be a good place for us to live? Our first house? It has three bedrooms, a master up here and two below. One for the baby, one for a home office. Let's check it out."

"But I haven't said I'll marry you."

"We're just looking around."

"You're trying to bribe me."

He smiled, and when Davis put his mind to it, his smile could be incredibly appealing. "Is it working?"

When he reached for her hand, she let him take it. They walked through the house together. Without furniture the rooms felt large, but they were probably average. The floor plan was sensible, with few surprises, but she was won over by the large pantry off a kitchen equipped with new appliances, and a lower floor only five steps down, not a full flight. The smallest bedroom downstairs, which Davis liked for the baby, was also the closest to the stairs, offering both privacy from the living area and easy access once the baby was old enough to sleep in a full-size crib. Beyond the cozy family room was a laundry area.

She had to admit this was a perfect house for a young family, just large enough to give everybody plenty of room and small enough to clean without a fuss.

Inside tour finished, Davis pointed through the sliding glass door. "I was here in the spring, to drop off their taxes, and I liked it. Come see the lower deck."

He unlocked the door, and they stepped

outside. The deck had been newly refinished, or else nobody had ever been out here. The house was the end unit of four, and the view was not of other people's barbecues, but of an open space below them with picnic tables and trees. The larger deck off the living room cast a shadow over one side, which would offer welcome shade in the summer.

"Room for some lounge chairs, and a place for the kid to play when he's old enough."

"A good place for a baby to nap," Harmony said.

"Do you like it?"

It was so much more than she'd ever expected. To go from fears of a shabby one-room apartment to this? She knew she couldn't stay with Charlotte forever. Before long she had to strike out on her own, but she hadn't expected to move to a place like this one. She imagined raising the baby here. A room of its own. Safe places to play. Good meals made in a wonderful kitchen.

"Why?" she asked. "This is a pretty expensive bribe."

"It's a good deal, and with the raise I'll need to write off more of my income. That's the practical part. But mostly? Because when I thought about it, I could see us here.

You, me, the baby. My condo's too small, and we'd be on top of each other. I wouldn't have any place to work if we made my office into a room for the baby, so I'd have to stay at work for longer hours, especially during tax season. We would hardly see each other."

She was surprised that not seeing her mattered to him. Yet the words had glided over his tongue so naturally, she found them hard to doubt.

"Are you going to buy it whether I marry you or not?"

"I hope I don't have to think about that. I want you here with me, Harmony. I know I acted like a jerk, and I'll be sorry about that forever. But when you moved out, I realized what I'd lost, and now I'm trying to make up for it. We have a baby coming, and we both need to think about what's good for him or her. I think this would be very good, don't you?"

"How are the schools?" She was hedging, but she was under the influence, not of alcohol, but of hope for the future, and that frightened her.

Davis shrugged. "Schools? I have no idea."

"We would have to check that."

"I doubt we'd be here long enough to worry. It's a starter house. We'll want something bigger down the road. But if the schools aren't good, we'll send him — her, whatever — to private school. There must be some good ones."

He wasn't thinking like a father yet, or he would have inquired. But how much time had he been given to adjust? Despite that, here he was, trying to do the right thing for all of them. Whether he'd thought about schools or not was probably inconsequential.

"I'm getting hungry," she said. "Let's get something to eat, okay?"

He looked disappointed, but he agreed. "What do you feel like?"

She was touched. Most of the time he didn't ask. "Pizza sounds about right."

"Just tell me where you want to go."

They went back through the house, but not holding hands this time. She tried not to look as if she was still checking it out, but she couldn't help noticing things she hadn't the first time. The subtle pattern in the camel-colored carpet, the silvery hardware on the kitchen cabinets, the fact that the refrigerator had an ice and water dispenser in the door.

Outside he stopped beside the car in the driveway.

"I guess they left their car here so it would

still look like it's occupied," Harmony said, aware she was probably babbling.

"They didn't leave it here. I did."

She cocked her head in question. "You did? What do you mean?"

"Do you like it?"

What was not to like? The car was a pale green SUV, a small one, which meant it performed well on hills and was still easy to maneuver in traffic, perfect for Asheville. The car wasn't new, but it had been manufactured in the recent past and looked to be in excellent condition.

"Do you need a new car?" she asked. "Are you having a problem with the Acura?"

"I don't. You do. I bought it for you and the baby. It belonged to the owners of the house, and they only want to take one car across country."

"You *bought* it?"

"I had it checked out, and it's in top condition. I had to grab it without asking you, but I was pretty sure you'd like it."

"I haven't told you I'd marry you!" She said it loudly enough that she imagined the neighbors could hear her.

Surprisingly, Davis didn't get angry. Instead, he cupped her face in his hands. "You don't *have* to marry me. The car belongs to you. Yours is about to bite the dust, and I want you and the baby to be safe, whatever you do. I owe you this much, don't you think? No strings attached."

"Oh, Davis." Her eyes filled. "I can't take such a big gift."

"Sure you can. And it's not a gift. It's a thank-you for taking care of my son or daughter, for sitting in a miserable clinic to get medical care and working an exhausting job to pay your way. Don't you deserve some of the good things in life? Here's one I can give you."

The tears overflowed. He bent over and kissed them away, then he wrapped his arms around her.

"I want to make your life easier," he said. "Why don't you let me?"

Her arms slid around his waist. He felt so good against her, and all this felt so right. Maybe he really was sorry. Maybe he really had changed. Look what he had done, just for her.

"Marry me," he said. "Let me keep making life better, okay?"

How could she say no?

Chapter Twenty-Nine

On Saturday Taylor taught an extra yoga class, and the day went by quickly enough. On Sunday she tore the house apart, scrubbed and filed. When she still had time to kill before dinner, she bundled old paperbacks to take to a library sale, along with clothes Maddie no longer wore for Goodwill.

The best and worst part of the evening came when Maddie called to tell her how much fun she was having in Nashville. Willow's house, it seemed, came with two dogs, a trio of calico barn cats and a pond with ducks and geese. Maddie's room overlooked a wildflower meadow, where the whole Black Balsam gang was coming on Tuesday for a barbecue. Willow was making her secret sauce for ribs — which Maddie said she might try to be polite.

Monday Taylor taught Pilates in the morning, and yoga at Moon and Stars in the afternoon. She liked teaching, but she couldn't imagine just teaching the same classes and postures for the rest of her life. Of course yoga was a lifestyle, not a series of exercises. She had friends who devoted every moment to purifying their minds and cleansing their bodies. Unfortunately she was afraid the things they'd willingly given up or entered into held less appeal for her.

As the day dragged on she was less able to focus. She was aware of a growing discontent, and nothing she'd learned from her yoga masters seemed to help. By the end of the afternoon she was delighted when students began to roll up mats and gather shoes, and not delighted when a couple approached to chat.

"Did your little girl go to Tennessee?" Marilee, who seemed to be the spokesperson, was just a few years older than Taylor and a single parent herself. For a moment Taylor couldn't figure out how the woman knew about Maddie, then she remembered mentioning that her daughter was leaving town. Maddie was a favorite here, and something of a mascot.

"She did go," Taylor said, trying to sound upbeat.

"Well, since you're free and my ex has my little boy for the weekend, we wondered if you'd like to party with us tonight? Nothing too out there. Maybe go somewhere and have a few drinks and listen to music. Now that you don't have to worry about a babysitter."

Taylor stared at the other woman, whose smooth blond hair showed a standard of care Taylor hadn't attempted since high school. Nor — now that she thought about it — had she attempted anything as frivolous as going to a bar to see what kind of men were on the prowl these days.

She thought about her spotlessly clean and all-too-silent house. Images of herself walking the floor with a sick infant when her high school friends were out on the town flashed through her mind. She had juggled college and child care and never attended concerts or parties. She'd even missed her own graduation. Actually, two graduations, high school *and* college.

"Wow," she said. "I'm so out of practice, I never even think about going out."

"Then take a refresher course."

Taylor couldn't say no. These were her students, and she liked every one of them. Marilee had a wicked sense of humor, and while she came to these classes to keep her weight perfectly distributed, she accepted the rest of the yoga package with good grace.

"What time?" she asked.

Marilee consulted the others, and they decided to meet about seven, at a spot downtown that Taylor knew. She smiled her thanks and promised to see them there.

She was home before the impact really hit her. She looked around the house. Furniture Maddie could flop on. A Harry Potter DVD by the television. Kid-friendly snacks in the kitchen.

Now, for two whole weeks, Taylor could think about herself for a change. She could be twenty-seven without guilt. She could laugh at tasteless jokes and make her own. She could eat what she wanted, drink as much as she could hold, assess the men who gave her a second look and even discuss their merits with other women.

If she really wanted to, she could end up in a stranger's bed tonight. Nobody would be any the wiser.

Her cheeks were wet before she realized she was crying. She stood in the middle of her living room and sobbed, and as she did, she wasn't sure for whom or what she was crying. Taylor Elizabeth Martin, a girl who had become a mother much too young? Maddie Martin Jensen, a baby who had come into the world much too early? Or the life she and Maddie had made together, a life that was now under threat from a boy who had become a man trying hard to fulfill his obligations?

Analiese wondered if Charlotte was up to her old tricks. This morning she'd gotten an invitation for something that sounded like a command performance. Of course it hadn't been issued that way. Charlotte had prefaced her plea by promising she knew how busy Analiese was and she would understand if the minister couldn't make time to meet so late in the afternoon. But then she'd followed up with such a thorough sell that saying no would have sounded ungracious and petty.

And how did anybody say no to a woman who might not live to see another year, anyway?

So here she was, late in the day in her church office, waiting for her former demon-in-residence to join her. She counted the other meetings of the day and ran out of fingers. She hoped this one went better than the one she'd just completed with her substitute organist, who had confessed to an affair with a married man — thankfully not one in Analiese's congregation.

As she waited, she strolled her study, which had been paneled in knotty pine in an age when that had been fashionable, then pickled, when that had been fashionable, too. Now the paneling was painted a restful blue, and the bookshelf that lined one wall was crowded with colorful books and mementos, including the Associated Press broadcast news award she had received for a story about overcrowding at a homeless shelter.

She stopped at the windows, gazing at the courtyard just beyond them. The courtyard was one of her favorite places on the grounds, surrounded on three sides by church walls, with a sedate fountain falling into a lily-pad-studded pond. Staring at it, she realized she hadn't been outside all day, and when Charlotte arrived, Analiese had a plan.

"Let's sit in the courtyard. I've been stuck inside, and I don't think I can stand it another minute. We have daffodils still blooming out there. Did you notice? Isn't it too late for daffodils?"

"I was on the grounds committee the year we selected the bulbs. Early and late bloomers. I guess somebody threw in late-late. I'm really glad they're a success." She smiled as if she really was. "I'd love to sit there and enjoy them."

Outside the air was warmer than Analiese had expected. Charlotte, looking tired but composed, was dressed for it in capris and a crocheted cotton top, but Analiese's long pants and blazer felt frumpy and confining.

"How are you feeling?" she asked, removing her blazer and rolling up the sleeves of her blouse.

"Glad to be alive."

Analiese knew that on the question of Charlotte's health she was being held at arm's length, but she probed, anyway. "Are you going to start the next round of chemo soon?"

Charlotte was silent, then she held up her hands in surrender. "We're working on getting my counts up, so I can. I'm kind of a tough case."

"Truer words were never spoken."

"You say that fondly."

"I actually kind of like you."

"The new me."

"Yes, and possibly the old you, too. Or at least I liked things about that Charlotte, like her energy and commitment to making things run like well-oiled machinery."

They settled on one of the benches rimming the fountain, and Charlotte leaned back and closed her eyes, turning her face to the sun. "I hope you'll like my new project. Do you know anything about Mountain Medical?"

Analiese listened as Charlotte told her about the clinic where Samantha Ferguson was the director. Analiese knew that Samantha's mother, Georgia, had once been the headmistress of Covenant Academy, and apparently not a favorite of Charlotte's. Analiese had heard that Charlotte had been instrumental in getting the woman fired.

"I'm sure every clinic is filled to overflowing these days," Analiese said. "Local clergy are always trying to find ways to assist, but there are so many people in need."

"If we can't protect our young mothers and children, we aren't much of a society. Mountain Medical's running on a shoestring. They need help, and I'm hoping we can provide it. I know the church is already involved in so many things, but the Women's Fellowship is looking for a new project. And this would be hands-on, just the way you like a project to be."

Charlotte opened her eyes, as if with effort, and went on. "Here's the thing. I was at the clinic with Harmony, the young woman who's staying with me for a while, and I noticed how much staff time is taken up with child care. So many of the patients had other children with them."

Analiese could picture it. "So what are you suggesting?"

"I think they have more room at the clinic than staff. I walked through the facility the other day. Samantha gave me permission. One of the nurses showed me around, and it seemed to me that we — Women's Fellowship, that is — could create a playroom where the records room is now. It's mostly empty, and I bet they would move records down the hall toward the back. They'd be more secure there, anyway."

"The mothers still couldn't leave their children alone in a playroom while they were being examined, could they? It might free up the waiting room, but not staff."

"Well, that's where we *really* come in. I think we could get volunteers to take over the playroom. The Women's Fellowship could sponsor it, but we could use volunteers from the congregation, too. We'd have to screen and train them, of course, but the Academy's early-childhood teachers might be willing to do the training, and I don't think we'd need licensing. The nursing staff would be right there, and so would the mothers. At the first sign of trouble, a professional or a parent could take over. Our volunteers would just be supervising the kids, sanitizing toys and handing them out, playing games or reading stories if the children wanted, but mostly keeping an eye on things."

Analiese liked the idea. And Charlotte was right, this was hands-on, her favorite kind of project because it was destined to change everybody for the better. If it worked, the volunteers might form bonds with the parents and reach out to them in other ways.

"Am I the first link on the chain?" she asked. "Or the last?"

"It didn't make sense to talk to you if Mountain Medical wanted no part in it, so I did talk to Samantha first. She thought it would be great. They've wanted a playroom, but without volunteer supervision, there were too many problems. So she's on board. And I talked to a couple of members of the Women's Fellowship board, to make sure they don't have other things in the works that would supersede this. But you're my first formal appeal."

"I'm all for it."

Charlotte looked delighted. "I promise I wasn't taking that for granted. Do you want to present it to Women's Fellowship? They meet on Thursday."

"I'd be happy to. And meantime, maybe you can get a firm commitment from Samantha. We don't want to do all the groundwork and find out they've changed their minds."

"I have some ideas for fixing up the room, but that will be up to the clinic staff and the Fellowship."

"What about the money to do it?"

"Let's see if Women's Fellowship wants to kick in some from their treasury. It'll really be theirs if they're bankrolling it, and they'll be more committed to volunteering. We need some paint, maybe tables and chairs, and plastic toys we can easily wash. I bet we can find the furniture secondhand."

Analiese watched mist from the fountain catch rays of sunlight and turn them to rainbows. The afternoon air felt warm but not humid, and a pair of cardinals called to each other from the branches of a sycamore just beyond the little pond.

Cardinals mated for life, and she wondered if these two were having a discussion about dinner plans. *Worms, dear, or beetles?*

Her own stomach was rumbling, and she realized in the midst of all her meetings today she had only managed half an apple for lunch. Time to go home and warm up a frozen dinner, but not quite. Because Analiese knew there was more going on here than Charlotte had said, which was typical and ultimately frustrating.

"Why this project?" she asked. "There are eight million projects in the naked city."

"You're too young to remember that show. I only remember it because of late-night reruns."

"My husband watched those same reruns incessantly whenever he could find them. He could say those lines exactly like the television narrator."

"I'd forgotten you were married."

Analiese *had* been, and not happily. "Have you ever noticed that all the things that happen to us are like building blocks? I had a difficult marriage, so after Greg died, I've made sure to stay off the market. Then there's you. You lost the chance to be with your daughter when she went for prenatal care, and now you're making sure other young women have the best experience possible."

"Abandoning Taylor when she really needed me is my biggest regret."

"And why you've taken in Harmony, too."

Charlotte smiled. "It's the darnedest thing. Every time I try to do something to make up for something I did in the past, I get something, too. Frankly, I don't know what I'd do without Harmony. She's like the sun rising in my life."

"And the puppies nobody else could care for? A tribute to Minnie?"

"They're so cute. You have to come see them. Bring your bathing suit and we'll swim."

"I'm not going to let you off this easy. I think something's motivating this flurry of goodwill that you haven't quite gotten to."

Charlotte watched the fountain, but Analiese could see she wasn't ignoring the query. She was considering it. Finally she spoke. "This is hard to tell."

"I know it must be."

"I've tried to write about this in my journal. I'm keeping one, delving into my past, moving at a snail's pace toward the cancer. I can't seem to write about . . ." She glanced at Analiese. "It's been a long day, and I bet you're hungry."

Analiese settled herself more comfortably, because whatever Charlotte had to tell her was more important than her next meal.

"I'm listening, Charlotte. It's just you and me and my growling stomach."

Charlotte hadn't realized she had come to see Analiese because she needed to unburden herself. She'd come — or so she'd thought — solely about the playroom. But since her illness, she had learned that much of what she did in her life was motivated by forces she never questioned. This time was no different. She needed to share something, but it wasn't an easy story to tell. So she'd pushed it into the background.

She began slowly, feeling her way. "Do you remember when I told you that after the leukemia diagnosis, I realized I needed to make amends for some of my worst mistakes?"

"A twist on the ever-popular bucket list, and a good one. Seems you're making headway."

"It wasn't quite the way I said. That was the shorthand version. The leukemia was diagnosed here, but being me, I was too busy to die and sure I just needed a better diagnosis at a major medical center. So I got an appointment at Duke, and, well, let's just say they were appalled at my stupidity, although of course they didn't put it quite that way. They told me if I wanted to live, I needed to start treatment immediately. I still couldn't believe the worst. I thought maybe I'd try M.D. Anderson in Houston, or Sloan-Kettering. If I tried everybody, somebody would tell me the others were wrong, and I really just needed rest and antibiotics."

Analiese looked as if she understood.

"Denial has its place, but that wasn't it, right?"

"Somehow I managed to drive back here, and for two days I just got sicker and sicker until I realized I had no choice. I had to go back to Duke, where I had a better chance of keeping my illness secret. So I told everybody at Falconview I was going overseas with some potential investors, then I was taking a well-deserved vacation. Of course they were stunned — still are, actually — but by then I was too sick to care. I checked into Duke with a full satchel of work and a conviction that this illness was just one more mountain in my way."

"That must have been such a difficult time for you."

Charlotte knew the answer to that was etched on her face. "They decided to use three different drugs, all fairly typical for this type of leukemia. Then, once I was in remission and doing well, they hoped to do a second round and a bone marrow transplant. They do several kinds, and the one that would be the most helpful doesn't seem to be in the cards. I'd need a sibling, or barring that we'd need to find a compatible donor — which sadly has yet to happen. But they thought if things went well after my second round of chemo, maybe I'd be a candidate for the other kind, using my own frozen cells, transplanted back later in the game."

"And is that how it's going down?"

"Nothing that complex is ever that simple. Things haven't gone as well as we hoped. Right now, unless my blood counts improve, a transplant's out of the question."

Charlotte fell silent, and Analiese didn't hurry her. She was unsure whether to continue, and if she did, how to tell the story. Finally she started the same story in a different place.

"You may not believe this, but I really enjoy the stories you tell the children on Sunday mornings. I know I came to you when you started and told you I thought you were alienating adults who didn't want to sit through story hour."

"I don't remember that."

"That's because it was just one of many things we had issues about."

"I'll buy that." Analiese reached for Charlotte's hand and quickly squeezed it. If she was surprised by the change of subject, she didn't show it.

Charlotte considered how much the human touch meant, and how the warmth of another person's hand made it easier to bare her soul.

"That was another thing I complained about," she said. "You're a very huggy person."

"Indeed I am."

"Thank you. I was definitely wrong about at least that much."

"At least."

Charlotte fumbled for a way to start the next part. "You're probably wondering what this has to do with my stay in the hospital."

"I imagine you're getting to it, albeit in a roundabout way."

"Not so roundabout as you might think."

"So let's recap. We've reached the part where you enjoy the stories on Sunday mornings, although you didn't at first."

Charlotte smiled. "The only thing I know about other religions, I learned from you. They certainly didn't teach that at the Trust Independent Baptist Church. Sometimes I'd take your stories home and huff and puff and try to figure out what possessed you. Then, about midweek, I would finally get it, or start to."

"Wow, I'm doing my job. That's nice to hear."

"Do you remember telling the story of Kuan Yin? Do you remember the details?"

"It's one of my favorites. The bodhisattva of compassion, a very powerful figure to

Buddhists and Taoists, with many different names in Eastern Asia, and many representations."

"You told us she was portrayed as male until something like the twelfth century."

"Then somebody thought that since she represented kindness and mercy, she must be female. Because those are classically female traits. So she became a goddess."

"Here's the part that really resonated for me. You said after she died, as she was journeying to heaven, she heard the voices of those still suffering on earth. She asked to turn back, to stay here until the suffering had ended."

"I've always loved that image. In a way the bodhisattvas are like our Christian saints, or even messiahs. They continually sacrifice themselves for the good of others. And Kuan Yin's journey is to show us ways to soften our hearts toward our fellow travelers and feel their sorrow so we can find ways to reach out to them."

"It's a beautiful story. And you told it right before I left for chemo."

"Ah . . ."

Charlotte knew a piece of the puzzle had just fallen into place for Analiese. "When we talked before, I told you I had a bad reaction to one of the drugs they were giving me and almost died. They rushed me to the ICU, and that's where I stayed for a week until I was no longer at death's door."

"How could I forget?"

"I didn't tell you about my roommate."

"I'm picturing all the ICUs I've been in. Isn't a roommate unusual? Especially in a situation like yours, when your immune system must have been compromised?"

"Let me tell *you,* then you tell *me* what you think. I'd really like to know."

Analiese nodded and waited.

"I don't remember how I got into intensive care. One minute I was sitting in a chair trying to get some work done while the nurse was adjusting my drip. I'd blown off the social worker and psychologist, and made sure the nurses knew that, as much as possible, I didn't want to be disturbed. I figured if I could just get the whole chemo thing over with, then I could get back to work before I had to go through the next round." She hesitated. "When work's all you have, you fall back on it, the way others fall back on the people they love."

Analiese didn't make sympathetic noises, as if she knew they would delay the story. She just continued to nod thoughtfully.

"The next minute — or more accurately, sometime in the next few days — I opened my eyes and saw shadows looming over my bed. I could hear machines beeping and wheezing, but I didn't have the strength to turn my head. I just lay there and wondered what on earth was going on. I felt like I was floating. And I wasn't afraid, not really. I kept thinking maybe I should sit up and find the papers I'd been working on. But even thinking took effort, so I went to sleep."

"Very frightening."

Charlotte lifted her head toward the sun, grateful for its warmth and grateful she was still alive to feel it. She absorbed the heat for a moment, hoping it would help as she told the next part.

"It wasn't as frightening as you might think. I was too sick to worry, and I wasn't thinking clearly enough to put facts together. The next time I woke up, there was a woman bending over my bed. She was old, older than me, although I don't know by how much, and I had the impression she was from somewhere in the East, maybe China, although I couldn't see her well. She said I'd been calling out, and she wondered if she could help. I told her I didn't have time to be sick. I remember that clearly. It took a long time to say it.

"She said she understood, because life's so short and there are so many important things to do, so much suffering to heal. I was surprised she had misunderstood so badly. I asked her who she was, and she said her name was Gwen, or at least that's what I thought. I asked her why she was there, and she said she was always in the room. I assumed she meant that every time she ended up in the hospital, she ended up in the same room in intensive care. I felt sorry for her, and I wondered what could be wrong with her that she was there so often. I fell back asleep wondering."

She stopped speaking, and Analiese didn't interrupt her thoughts.

Finally Charlotte began again.

"After that Gwen was with me almost every time I woke up, although not when the doctors or nurses were. I thought they probably chased her back to bed when they came in. I couldn't figure out how she could be well enough to get up and come to me, and still sick enough to be on that wing. But when they were finished doing all those truly awful things they do to you in hospitals and they left, Gwen would come back. I was so sick that sometimes I thought she was my grandmother, and other times I could see she wasn't. She held my hand and talked to me about my life and how I needed to be strong, because I was absolutely right, there were things I needed to do, people I needed to be with again."

Analiese took her hand, the way Charlotte had just told her Gwen had taken it, and this time she didn't let go. "And she was right."

Charlotte squeezed it. "This is so hard to tell."

"I can only imagine."

"On day five — I was told that later — I woke up and the lights were on. Things weren't shadowy anymore. Everything had cleared, and for the first time I was really aware of where I was and what was going on. A nurse was beside the bed, and she asked me some questions, like my name and why I was in the hospital, and she seemed delighted I knew the answers. It was clear I'd come through something pretty major. She started to leave, and I managed to put my hand out and take her arm. I asked her where Gwen was, and she looked puzzled. Gwen, I said, the woman in the next bed. She just shook her head and left."

"What do you think that meant, Charlotte?"

"I never had the courage to bring it up again. If Gwen really had been there, if she died and her bed was taken away with her in it, I didn't want to know. If Gwen had never been there?" She shook her head.

"You know there can be many explanations, don't you?"

"I do." Charlotte turned to face Analiese, but she continued to hold her hand. She couldn't have let go if she'd been ordered to.

She swallowed, because her throat was raw now. "Here's the explanation I prefer. Someone or something came to me and helped me face the emptiness of my life. Maybe it was another patient or a chaplain or a staff member named Gwen. Maybe it was my imagination, spurred on by your story about Kuan Yin, the goddess of mercy, that Sunday morning."

"An anonymous goddess," Analiese said. "The very best kind. The kind who would come to your hospital bed and not reveal who she was. The kind you're trying to be yourself."

Charlotte swallowed again, but this time she swallowed tears. "I'll never know for sure. Maybe it was guilt. Maybe it was the drugs I was given, or a result of being so close to death, or a way to retreat into myself during a terrible, terrible time. Maybe I was just ready for the first time to see who I had become. But whatever happened to me during that week? Gwen was the greatest gift I've ever received."

Chapter Thirty

Harmony had found a friend in Marilla Reynolds. Rilla was ten years older than she was and the mother of two beautiful little boys, but she never treated Harmony as anything but a contemporary. Also, she was a fighter, which Harmony admired and envied, since for the most part the fight had been drained out of her as a child.

Marilla wasn't yet able to do much by herself, but she never complained, and she worked so hard at rehabilitation that her physical therapist had been forced to set limits so she wouldn't complicate her own recovery. She'd graduated to a morning health care aide and was managing by herself in the afternoons, unless friends came to see her.

And friends came to see her often.

Today she and Harmony were deep in the preliminary stages of making jam in Rilla's spacious country kitchen. Harmony had picked and washed the last of a flourishing strawberry crop from Rilla's abandoned garden, passing full colanders to Rilla, who was comfortably propped at the table hulling and cutting out bad spots. A neighbor was coming later to help her prepare the jam and get it into jars.

Harmony had decided that *lively* was the best adjective to describe her new friend. Rilla had a square face, with a short nose that was most often wrinkled and a wide mouth that was most often smiling. She had a sturdy body with wide shoulders and hips, the kind that looked most at home in jeans and boots. Every thought she had showed on her face, and if it wasn't perfectly clear there, she made it clear when she spoke. Rilla was upbeat and positive, even under these difficult circumstances, but she was also painstakingly honest, as if every word had to be weighed before it was uttered.

"I can't believe I didn't put in a garden this year," Rilla said. She had brown hair that curled around her ears and over her collar, and now she brushed a spiraling strand off her damp forehead. Even hulling the berries was clearly an effort.

"You plant one every year?"

"More than one. I have a perennial vegetable garden — that's where the strawberries were — and there are asparagus, rhubarb and raspberries, too. Then, starting early in the spring in my regular garden, I put in peas, potatoes, onions, broccoli, salad greens, you know, and keep planting until midfall. I had my onion sets and seed potatoes all ready to put in, too. I bet Brad fed them to the goats."

"Goats?"

"Toggenburgs. They're so beautiful. And gentle. Like babies. When they come back, you'll fall in love."

"I don't know how you keep up with everything, even when you're feeling great. Kids, goats, garden, chickens, and then the kennel. I can't imagine how I'm going to keep up with a baby, much less all that."

"Don't forget the horses."

"Yikes."

Rilla reached over and patted her hand. "You're going to do great. You have energy and commitment, and you're a born nurturer. Besides, you'll have your husband to help you."

Harmony tried to imagine that part and couldn't. Maybe she was selling Davis short, but she couldn't picture him changing a diaper or rocking a baby to sleep.

"How did you know you wanted all this?" Harmony asked. "Did you just slip into it?"

Her own future was strictly a one-day-at-a-time affair.

"Brad and I talked about the future when he was in law school," Rilla said. "He loves the law, and he loves farming. I just love farming. So we figured he could be a lawyer and a hobby farmer, and I'd fill in everything else. It's a lot of work, but we love this life, and so do the boys."

"I love being out here. It's so peaceful." Harmony took a seat at the table and started hulling the berries in the final colander. "There's a difference between quiet like this and the kind of quiet we had at home when I was a kid. That was a tiptoe quiet, the kind when you're afraid if you make noise, something terrible will happen. This? It's a be-still-and-listen quiet. I could get into that."

"Why don't you come out again tomorrow? The boys'll be back, and you'll finally get to meet them. My mother's bringing dinner, and she won't mind a guest. Afterward we can sit out on the porch, and you can see how loud it can get in the evening with the frogs and the crickets. It's still peaceful somehow."

"I would love to, only my . . ." Harmony still couldn't say fiancé. It just didn't seem possible she and Davis were actually about to plan a wedding. “My boyfriend and I are supposed to look at rings. His firm’s having a dinner at the Asheville Country Club, and he’d like to announce our engagement there.”

“You must be so excited.”

Harmony didn’t feel excited, and she wasn’t sure why. Davis had jumped through a series of hoops to prove he was serious about a long-term commitment. She had driven the new SUV here today, and the car was proof positive. All the things she’d so worried about were never coming to pass now. She and the baby would be taken care of. Once she could leave the baby for a few hours each day, Davis even wanted her to go back to school for a two-year degree.

“Maybe Brad can give me some advice,” she said, to change the subject. “I’m thinking I might like to become a paralegal. I’d really like to be a lawyer, but that’s probably too much to ask.”

“Why?”

“I doubt Davis would like that kind of competition.” She wasn’t sure where they had come from, but Rilla just nodded.

“He likes to be the big cheese?”

Harmony was afraid he did. “How about Brad? Is he like that?”

“Not really.”

"It's not a good thing, is it?"

"Every relationship is different."

Harmony wondered. One minute she thought she'd made the right decision when she said yes to Davis, the next she wasn't sure. He wanted to marry quickly, before the pregnancy was readily apparent. People would still know the truth if they counted backward, but only the stodgiest would care.

"Why law?" Rilla asked.

"Well, if I could do anything, I'd like to find ways of protecting women. You know, from violence, from people who take advantage of them, maybe even help change the laws, so they have more recourse."

Rilla, who knew about Harmony's childhood, clearly didn't have to ask why. "Not social work?"

"No. The law can be a powerful tool in the hands of a powerful woman."

"Wow."

Harmony looked up and smiled sheepishly. "Not to say I'd be one. A powerful woman, I mean. But I guess that would be my hope. If I could live that life, I mean."

"I think you can live any life you choose."

"Maybe."

"Of course I didn't choose this," Rilla said. "I sure didn't intend to land flat on my back in the hospital. But now I'll just have to find a different route to the things I want."

"Like what?"

"First I want to get my kids back, of course. And I want to get my animals back. And my gardens back. And my life back!" She drew a breath, then blew it out. "But all in good time. I know it's going to happen. I just have to keep my eye on the prize."

An hour later Harmony thought about that as she headed into town and Cuppa. Her most immediate goal was making sure her baby was well taken care of, and once she was married to Davis, she knew it would be. But was she selling herself short? Was she selling Davis short? If they sat down and she told him she might like to go to law school eventually, would he surprise her?

By the time she checked in, Cuppa was filling up. Ray was featuring a special appetizer menu, so their happy hour crowd had grown, along with the restaurant's beer and wine list. She had already changed at Rilla's, so she went straight to Stella to tell her she was there and ready to go.

"Take over table six right now, would you?" Stella asked. "I took over for Rolfe. He was overwhelmed. If this keeps up, we may need to get you in here half an hour sooner."

Harmony hoped that wouldn't come to pass. Happy hour was a bust for tips. She washed her hands, then headed for the four-top, which was in the center of the room. She introduced herself and told them she would finish taking care of them. The group was made up of young women, older than she was, but not by much. She took an order for more drinks and promised a basket of Ray's miniblintzes. One woman looked vaguely familiar, but it wasn't until half an hour later, when the happy hour crowd had thinned and she was preparing for the dinner rush, that the young woman approached her.

"Anne Sanders," she said, holding out her hand. She was petite, dark-haired and sure of herself. "I was trying to remember why you looked familiar. Davis Austin is your boyfriend, isn't he?"

Now Harmony realized where she had seen the woman. "And your boyfriend works for the firm, too. But I've forgotten his name."

"Ricky. Ricky Brown."

Harmony took her hand, although shaking seemed a little formal under the circumstances. "Nice to see you again."

"I didn't know you worked here. I love this place."

"It's a good place to work."

"Are you going to that fancy dinner at the club at the end of the month?" Anne made a face when she asked, letting Harmony know her opinion.

"I guess we are."

"I guess we'd better, huh? I'm sure Davis is getting the same talking-to that Ricky is."

Harmony nodded, as if she understood. "You mean about showing up for events they sponsor?"

"Well, that's pretty tactful. More like showing up so they can watch us under a microscope."

Harmony wanted to know what Anne really meant, but she wasn't sure coming right out and asking was a good idea. Sometimes pretending to be in on a secret was the best way to get information.

"Do you feel that way, too?" she asked, with a conspiratorial smile.

"Well, Ricky tells me every time somebody gives him a talking-to." Anne pretended to mimic a partner with a deep, deep voice. " 'The firm's reputation in the community. The kind of young men and women we want representing us. The values this firm holds dear. The values our clients hold dear.' "

"Scary, huh?" Harmony said.

Anne ceased the imitation. "If you ask me, that's what it's all about. They represent the most traditional residents of the city, and they live in fear someone might get a tattoo or wear sandals to work or have an affair with somebody else's wife. If you ask me, they're looking to cull the herd."

"Herd?"

"Ricky thinks they need to tighten up and fire a few people here and there. They're trying to figure out who fits in and who might be a problem in the future." She lowered her voice. "He even wonders if they've hired a pro to do some checking."

"No. Really?"

"Think about it. If they get the wrong kind of person, or keep the wrong kind of person, and realize it too late, either their reputation suffers or they have a lawsuit on their hands when they try to get rid of him. And I say *him,* because if you've noticed, not very many women get moved up." Anne seemed sure she wouldn't get an argument about that.

"You're right," Harmony said, although she hadn't paid attention at the few events she'd been part of. "Does Ricky feel safe?"

"Ricky's kind of a free spirit."

Harmony got the impression this meant two things. One, that Ricky was already looking for a job where he would be happier. Two, that if Ricky didn't take on that particular task himself, while he was still gainfully employed, he might have to do it once he wasn't anymore. Probably in the foreseeable future.

Davis, on the other hand, had just gotten a raise.

"Davis likes it there," Harmony admitted.

For a moment Anne looked concerned. "Uh-oh. You're not going to say anything, are you?"

Harmony thought Anne had said too much herself, particularly if Ricky really wanted to keep his job, but she reassured her. "Not to anybody."

"I guess Davis is a pretty traditional guy." Anne paused, looking Harmony over. "I didn't think that you were."

"Apparently Davis thinks I can fit in." She finished the rest of the sentence in her head. *Particularly once we're married and our baby is legitimate.*

"Well, good luck to all of us," Anne said. "At least we can hang out together at the dinner." She gave a little wave and started toward the door where her friends were waiting.

Harmony wondered if Davis would even be seen with Ricky and Anne at the country club, or if he would avoid them in public because the powers-that-be would be watching.

Davis, who wanted to announce their engagement at the country club dinner.

Was it possible that once they were married, the baby they had mistakenly conceived could be a plus for his career? Proof he was settling into the community?

Then there was the opposite scenario. Davis, an unwed father, who was paying child support after a meaningless fling — which was probably easy to discover with a routine background check. Davis, an unwelcome addition to a conservative firm.

For the first time in weeks, all the familiar Cuppa smells made her stomach churn.

Ethan carefully bided his time until the moment was right to give Taylor Charlotte's letter. He knew Maddie's absence was like a scar on his daughter's heart. Maddie's epilepsy and Taylor's age at her birth had brought the two closer, although the opposite could well have been true if Taylor hadn't been so determined to be the perfect mother.

As it was, Taylor's world revolved around her daughter, and Ethan wanted her to have time to adjust before he broached the subject of her own mother. Now, a week into Maddie's holiday, Ethan invited Taylor for tacos, a meal that had been her favorite as a girl. He simmered a pot of black beans with garlic and onions while he chopped lettuce, tomatoes and avocados, and set them on a tray. He'd already made fresh pico de gallo and crumbled authentic *queso fresco.* The fresh tortillas came from a tortillaria on Patton Avenue, where they were sold by the kilo. Ethan wasn't above bribery to get his way.

Taylor arrived with a six-pack of Negra Modelo and the appetite of a stevedore. They set the small table that looked out on the weeping cherry tree that had been spectacular a month before.

Taylor finished a story about a night on the town with her yoga students. "So there I was, trying to be one of the gang, and I didn't have the faintest idea what to do. I was younger than anybody there, but I felt like I was their granny. A guy tried to buy me a drink, and I couldn't even say yes, because I'm not sure what that means these days."

"That's one area where I'm fresh out of advice."

She made a wry face. "Maybe I'll just ask Jeremy. He'd know."

"Does it bother you he's getting married?"

"It bothers me Willow's going to be Maddie's stepmother. I don't have anything against her except that she's sort of Dolly Parton in training, but I guess I don't want to share my daughter." She managed a wan smile. "Maddie's the only kid I'll ever have unless I figure out how to let a guy buy me a beer."

"I'll say this much, then I'm moving on, because this isn't a daddy subject. There are better places to meet guys, but you have to think about yourself for a change to find them."

"I could start hiking. That's how you met Judy."

"And look how well that turned out."

"She still calls me once in a while."

"Me, too. Friends to the end." He wondered if Taylor was edging toward a conversation about his *other* wife and hoped it was true.

"I like Judy," she said, as if she was thinking out loud. "When Maddie was little she was there when I needed her. But she really blew it when she decided to move back to Chicago. She left the best man in the world just because she missed the Midwest. It's hard to get past that."

He pulled a tortilla from its aluminum foil

packet and began to spoon on toppings. "I think you have an odd idea about what a perfect husband I was. I really wasn't. Judy and I had our issues, and so did your mother and I. Judy realized she needed a big city and a different kind of stimulation than she got here. I wasn't willing to relocate, and she wasn't willing to stay. And that says something about both of us, don't you think?"

"She met you *here.* You had every reason to think she wanted to live *here.* To me, that says she's the one at fault."

"Nothing's ever that simple."

"Are you saying you didn't try to make things work?"

"Maybe I didn't try hard enough."

"Well, you tried hard with my mother. I was there, remember? You compromised and gave up so much of what you wanted, and where did it get you?"

He stopped work on his taco and locked his gaze with hers. "Taylor, that's *not* how it was. You were young, and now you look back on my marriage to your mom with jaded eyes. But I loved her from the moment I met her, and everything I did, everything I gave in on, was less important to me than she was. That's what love's about."

"I guess we should change the subject."

"I know it's not an easy one," he said carefully, "but maybe it's time we talked about those years. Because we had some good times, honey. Not perfect, maybe not even easy, but good."

"I can tell you what I remember. My mother trying to change us both. She was never satisfied with us the way we were. She wanted us to be different, to live up to her standards and make her proud. But nothing ever would have, because her standards were impossible."

Ethan made sure she was finished before he answered. "I think she might be the first person to say there's truth in that. It's not completely true, but true in spots. The thing is, your mom was trying to make things right, not just for herself, but for us, too. Her childhood was so difficult, and she pulled herself up and out of it by sheer determination. She couldn't bear the thought you might have to go through anything like that, not ever. And so many of the things she did and said were fueled by that fear."

Taylor didn't say anything for a moment, then she shrugged. "I don't care."

"I don't think that's true. She's your mother. She held you on her lap and read you stories and walked the floor with you when you were sick. She took you to New York to see *Beauty and the Beast* for your fourteenth birthday, just the two of you, because you wanted so badly to see Broadway and Central Park and the Statue of Liberty. That was all you could talk about for months. And she bought you those beautiful diamond earrings at Tiffany's, remember? She told you the diamonds were like our love for you, one from her, one from me, pure and sparkling and always with you whenever you wore them."

Taylor rolled her eyes. "I'm not quite sure why you're defending her. You're right. She didn't beat me. She didn't lock me in a dark closet. But even that weekend in New York, I had to wear what she wanted me to, shop where she wanted to shop, eat the food she thought I should. I was fourteen, and so happy to actually have a whole weekend with her, but by the end, I was ready to come back just to get away from her."

"Which is typical of a fourteen-year-old girl. But that's not the way you spoke of that weekend, Taylor. Not ever. Are you sure you aren't twisting it now, so it won't be a painful memory?"

To her credit, she didn't answer right away. Finally she shook her head. "I'm not sure why this is relevant."

"This isn't the way I wanted to do this, honey. But somehow your mother came up, and here we are discussing our past. So I guess the time's right to tell you that she and I have talked a couple of times since Maddie's fall. She's changed. Dramatically. She's aware of the mistakes she made. The biggest, of course, was using coercion when she learned you were pregnant. But I've come to understand she was frantic, so concerned about what having a baby would do to your life that she would have done anything to protect you."

"Protect me? From my own child?"

"Are you going to tell me that having a baby at seventeen was the best thing you ever did? That it was the right time for either of you? That it hasn't impacted every single moment since? Of course Maddie's a wonderful gift, and you're a wonderful mother. But try to put yourself in your own mother's shoes. What if Maddie comes to *you* when she's sixteen and tells you she's pregnant. Will you be thrilled if she wants to keep the baby and raise it? If she drops out of high school? If all your hopes and dreams for her disintegrate?"

"I can tell you that I would never, never say she shouldn't have been born!"

"We both misunderstood that," Ethan said. "Your mother was looking at Maddie, with all those tubes snaking around her, and machines pumping and bleating, and her heart was breaking. All she meant was that Maddie shouldn't be suffering the way she was, that it was just too terrible a burden for such a little baby."

"So she says." Taylor had been holding her fork. Now she set it by her plate. "So you and my mother are talking."

"She tried to talk to *you* in the hospital."

"Where she should never have been."

"She's trying again." Ethan got up and took the letter Charlotte had written from a drawer in his desk, came back and held it out to her. "She left this with me. I told her it might be easier for you to read what she has to say than to hear it. That you might need time to think about it before the two of you talked."

Taylor didn't take the envelope. "We aren't going to talk."

"She misses you. She loves you. She wants you and Maddie in her life again. On your terms."

"My terms? *No* terms. Things are fine just the way they are."

"They aren't fine," Ethan said, putting the letter on the table beside her. "You're estranged from your mother. Maddie has never met her grandmother. It's time to heal this wound."

"This is exactly the way things used to be when you were together," Taylor said. "She talked, and you listened and then did whatever she asked. You were *always* taken in by the things she said. You always thought better of her than she deserved."

Ethan couldn't remember ever being truly angry at Taylor. He'd been upset at things she'd done as a child, and desperately unhappy about the pregnancy, but the feeling that swept over him now was very different. He waited until the first wave ebbed, then he spoke slowly and carefully.

"Perhaps I've thought better of *you* than you deserved, Taylor. Because until this moment, I honestly believed you had a kind heart and the maturity to be objective when it was called for."

"I can't believe this."

"Believe *this,* then. I know from everything I've ever learned in this life that people deserve second chances. You got yours when Maddie was born. You were given a chance to grow up and become a mother to a wonderful little girl, despite having made a pretty huge mistake by getting pregnant in the first place."

"You think Maddie was a mistake?"

"I think the *pregnancy* was a mistake, yes. A pregnancy you could have prevented if you hadn't been so busy trying to show your mother who was boss. At the time, despite the enormity, I supported you in every way I knew how, and I abandoned your mother to do it. It was the right thing, but now it's your turn."

She looked as if she couldn't believe the things he was saying. "Exactly *what* has she said to you? Because this doesn't sound one bit like you."

"It's all me. One hundred percent. You can count on it."

"She comes back into our lives, and now we're fighting. Don't you get that?"

"She comes back into our lives and now, for the first time, I see the mistakes all of us made, Taylor."

She got to her feet and leaned against the table. "I think maybe I'll go home now."

He didn't argue. "I think maybe you should. But don't leave without that letter, because it belongs to you. What you do with it is your business, but I will not be in the middle of this feud anymore. From this moment forward, how you proceed is between you and your mom. I hope you'll find a way to resolve things. And frankly, I hope you'll find the courage and kindness to let her back into your life. Because she needs to be there."

To Taylor's credit, she pushed away from the table, took the letter and stuffed it in the pocket of her jeans. Then she gave one short nod and brushed past him. He didn't turn to watch her go, but when the door clicked shut, his shoulders slumped.

"Charlotte," he said softly, "exactly when does this stop?"

Chapter Thirty-One

First Day Journal: June 11
I knew, after that first bone marrow biopsy, that my leukemia couldn't be hidden forever. Now I realize when the next round of chemo begins I must tell both friends and colleagues, so they can prepare for whatever comes next. I'm just not sure how to do it.

The last time I saw her, Reverend Ana mentioned my bucket list. Not trips to Antarctica, canopy walking in Borneo, painting coastal sunsets. I want to find ways to live after I die. I want to smile at the legacy I leave.

I'm glad I told Analiese about Gwen. She understood, as I thought she might, but I didn't tell her everything. I didn't tell her that I awake sometimes in the middle of the night, and again I feel a presence in the room. Perhaps it's only my growing certainty that I'm not alone on this journey, that hands assist and soothe me as I travel. I smile at myself because I'm a Christian who feels the presence of a Buddhist goddess in her heart and life. I marvel at how little we understand, and how flimsy are the walls we erect to separate ourselves from people and universal wisdom everywhere.

There's so much I don't understand. But I do understand this. It really doesn't matter.

Chapter Thirty-Two

Charlotte was still surprised at how quickly things could move, even when she wasn't pushing and slapping everything into shape. Less than a week had passed since she'd first told Analiese about the clinic, and now she and Samantha were watching the progress as movers wheeled the last of the file cabinets into a room at the end of the hall so that this room could be cleaned in preparation for the painters, who would arrive tomorrow.

She stepped farther to one side, so she would be completely out of the way. "I still can't believe the Women's Fellowship got behind this so quickly. I'll be honest, I think they were having something of a spat. There were two projects they'd been considering, neither of which really excited anybody. But you know how these things go. One group allied themselves behind the first, another behind the second. Along comes Reverend

Ana with a different plan, and nobody lost."

Samantha picked up papers that had slipped under one of the cabinets, gave a quick glance and tossed them in the remaining wastebasket. "However it happened, this is great. And they were okay with the apple-green the staff chose? Pink's supposed to be the most soothing color — somebody looked that up — but we were afraid none of the little boys would go into a pink playroom."

"I think it'll be great. We can paint the furniture bright colors like turquoise and purple to go with it. I'd guess the women coming in tomorrow won't get much done except priming the walls, but it'll be a start. And you don't mind being here to oversee it?"

Samantha gave one of her cover-girl smiles. "Honestly? I don't love being here on weekends, no, but I *will* love what's going to come out of it. It'll make everybody's life easier, and that will help me cope."

Charlotte was sorry Samantha had to be present, but she knew the other woman couldn't allow volunteers to be at the clinic unsupervised, not even with every door along the hallway locked.

"If you have work to do, I can clean up here by myself," Charlotte said. "I brought rags and trisodium phosphate. That's supposed to degrease the walls, so the primer goes on smoothly."

"I don't mind getting my hands dirty. And the sooner we finish, the sooner we can go home. You've noticed how hot it is in here? We set the thermostat higher on weekends to save money. And there aren't any windows worth opening."

Charlotte was glad to hear she wasn't having one doozy of a hot flash. Asheville was scheduled for an unseasonably hot day. Later in the afternoon, temperatures were supposed to get up in the high eighties, with no relief in sight until next week.

"As soon as the men are all done, I'll start scrubbing," she said.

"I'm just telling myself there's a nice cool shower waiting at home and a glass of iced tea."

"And air-conditioning."

Samantha made a face. "Not at *my* house. Turned it on last week — it screeched like a cat in heat, and that was the end. Had the landlord out. Landlord had the repair people out. Repair people had the salespeople out. Landlord had his wallet out. They'll install a new one next week."

"I know how to fix that."

"I wish, but there's no fixing that sucker. The sales guy said they're shipping it to the

Smithsonian."

"But I can fix your *evening.* You and Edna come to my house and swim. About five? We'll cook something on the grill. I'd love to have you."

"That sounds like an imposition."

"To me it sounds like a pool party. It's Harmony's day off, and if I call now, she'll invite friends and shop for dinner. Maybe Reverend Ana will show up, too. I'll give her a call."

"Well, Edna would love it."

"She ought to bring a friend, then she'll love it even more."

"You're sure about all this?"

"Never surer."

The last file cabinet rolled by, and they surveyed what remained. Dust balls, greasy shadows on the walls, holes in the wall-board.

"Lots to do here," Samantha said.

"On your mark, get set . . ."

An hour later the movers were gone, the dust was gone, too, and two walls were scrubbed clean. Charlotte needed a break. Before her illness she had been tireless. Now she had to stop and rest every few minutes. Samantha was on a stepladder scrubbing the top halves of the walls, and Charlotte was scooting along the floor on her knees doing the bottoms. They had it down to a rhythm, but it was still going slowly.

Samantha stepped off the ladder to take her own break. "My mother's dropping Edna here in a few minutes. She can help."

"Your mother?"

"No, Edna. Mom's got a job interview, that's why she couldn't keep Edna the whole day."

Charlotte wondered if Georgia Ferguson knew that *she* was here helping Sam. She sifted through possible responses for the right one. "I haven't seen your mother for a long time."

"I've told her about the playroom. She knows you're here today."

"Maybe I ought to go."

"No reason to. She's not your biggest fan, but she's not going to make a scene, either."

"I just don't want . . ." Charlotte wasn't sure what she didn't want. She finally shrugged.

"Mom's bringing bags of magazines for the waiting room that her students collect for us. She might need some help getting them inside, and I can't leave the clinic. It could give the two of you a few minutes to talk."

Charlotte knew it was well past time for

that, but she wondered if Georgia would agree.

Somebody banged on the door, and Samantha went to answer it. Charlotte got to her feet and dusted off the knees of the oldest pants she owned just as Edna came barreling in to see what they'd been doing, and greeted her with a hug. Edna saw Charlotte as a friend because she had been there to offer aid when Maddie fell. She didn't realize that Charlotte was Maddie's grandmother, though, which was for the best.

"It's yucky in here," Edna said, when she pulled away. "I'm glad you're fixing it up."

"So am I. And I hear you're going to help us get the walls clean?"

"If we work fast, we can be done fast. And it's hot in here!"

"Way too hot," Charlotte agreed.

Edna sped down the hall to see where the filing cabinets had gone, and Samantha, followed by her mother, came into the playroom.

Georgia Ferguson had shoulder-length cinnamon-colored hair and wispy bangs. She weighed no more than she had a dozen years ago, when Charlotte had last seen her, and her arms and legs were tanned and toned. Clearly, of the two of them, Georgia was weathering the storms of aging best.

"Georgia," Charlotte said. "It's good to see you again."

Georgia lifted a brow, as if to question that, but she nodded. "Sam tells me Church of the Covenant is setting up a playroom here."

"The Women's Fellowship. They're painting tomorrow."

"So she says. Don't let me get in your way." She glanced at her watch to make it clear she wasn't planning to stay.

"Charlotte said she'd be happy to help you bring in the rest of the magazines," Samantha said.

"Oh, I don't —"

"I'd like to," Charlotte interrupted. "May I?"

Georgia's hesitation was so brief it was hardly noticeable, but Charlotte saw the effort the nod that followed cost her.

"We'll be back in a minute," Georgia told her daughter. "We can do this in one load."

Charlotte followed her into the parking lot. Georgia was wearing a sage-green knit suit with a silk blouse; clearly the upcoming interview was important to her. She was behaving like a woman with no time to waste.

"So your students collect the magazines?"

"They earn service credits."

"The best kind of recycling."

They reached a Honda sedan, and Georgia pulled out her keys to open the trunk. "The two bags on the right are for Mountain Medical. The rest go to a nursing home."

"Georgia . . ." Charlotte put her hand on Georgia's arm before she could start pulling out bags. "Samantha engineered this so we could talk."

Georgia faced her, folding her arms over her chest. "Samantha likes everybody to get along."

Charlotte hadn't rehearsed what to say because she had wanted it to come from her heart. Now she wished she'd memorized a script. "Damn," she said at last. "I have so much I want to apologize for, and no idea in the world how to do it."

"There's nothing I really need to hear."

"I know you've moved on, but there are things I hope you'll let me say, for both our sakes. It all comes down to knowing how unfair I was to you all those years ago, and wishing I could find a way to make it up to you. I was instrumental in making sure you lost your position at Covenant Academy."

"You weren't the only one. Don't give yourself too much credit."

Georgia hadn't said it with venom, but

the words stung, anyway. "I know, but I could have spoken against it, and I spoke *for* it instead, and pretty loudly. I wanted you gone. I wanted a nice, traditional, safe education for my daughter, so her life would be all those things, too. The worst part?" The worst part stuck in her throat and felt as if it had been sitting there for years. "She was happy in school when *you* were there making sure she was challenged. You valued her the way she was, which was more than I did. After you left and we hired someone more conventional? She never wanted to go to school again."

"Well, we all make mistakes." Georgia turned and lifted the first bag.

"I wish I was sure of that. Sometimes I watch other people, and they make living look so easy."

Georgia straightened and handed her the bag. "You think so? You're not digging very deeply, then."

"Your life hasn't been easy," Charlotte said. "I know that. I know it was hard to find a job after you were fired."

Georgia stopped unloading and turned again. "Charlotte, I'll say it again. You're giving yourself too much credit. You didn't destroy my life. I learned a long time ago not to let *anybody* do that. You're just somebody who was on the Academy board the year they fired me because my ideas were too subversive. After that I picked myself up, and eventually I found a job teaching kids with special needs. I support myself. I still work with kids. Sometimes I even upset their parents, for old times' sake. But somehow they graduate and go out into the world and make successes of themselves. Maybe someday I'll get credit for time served and another chance to put my so-called radical ideas into play, but if I don't?" She turned her hand skyward to show she didn't really care.

Charlotte believed everything except that last gesture. "I realize I can't change a thing that happened, and I realize this is more about me and what I need, than what you do. But I did want you to know I'm so sorry."

"I'm trying to decide if that helps."

Charlotte hadn't expected anything else. "Is my friendship with Sam and Edna going to be a problem for you? Because I'll back off. I don't want to cause any more ill will between us."

"Are you spending time with them because you want to prove something to me?"

The shock on her face must have been all the answer Georgia needed. "I can tell you what Sam probably thinks. She thinks if she models grown-up behavior to both of us, maybe we'll follow suit."

Charlotte wondered if Samantha also thought Taylor would eventually follow suit, as well. "Maybe we will," she said.

Georgia took the second bag and closed the trunk.

As he waited for Harmony to call Charlotte to the telephone, Ethan heard laughter in the background. Once she answered he reconsidered his call.

"I can tell this is a bad time," he said.

"Not at all. I've been hoping you'd call."

He knew if he told Charlotte their daughter had not accepted her letter graciously, the lilt in her voice would disappear. Somehow Taylor's tantrum didn't seem like something he should explain over telephone lines.

"May I drop by sometime?" he asked. "We should talk about Taylor."

The line went silent for a moment, as if she was absorbing that. "Are you busy right now?"

"Don't you have company?"

"None you'll disturb. In fact you'll be welcome. Bring your bathing suit."

He started to decline, then his curiosity

got the better of him. "You're having a party and you're inviting *me?*"

"Nothing formal. It's just a hot day. Please come." She paused for just a heartbeat. "I'd like it if you would."

Ethan's early-warning system was finely tuned, and all his alarms went off now. Since the afternoon they'd spent together at his house, he'd found himself thinking of Charlotte too often. The barriers he'd put up were tumbling, and the good times were like vines scampering over the ruins. He wasn't sure which were more dangerous to contemplate — the good times or the bad.

"Listen, I know this is odd," Charlotte said. "And if it's *too* odd, never mind. But if it's not, this afternoon why don't we toss out the past, swim and have burgers, and after I've recovered from scrubbing walls all day, you can tell me what Taylor said when you gave her my letter."

He hung up and wondered how possible it was to toss out the past when it kept coming back to haunt them both.

An hour later he let himself into her foyer. The door had been left ajar, and from the back of the house he heard laughter and cabinets slamming. He made his way toward the kitchen, where he was greeted by Samantha Ferguson.

"You should see your face," she said, grinning. "Charlotte and I spent the day scrubbing walls at the clinic together, and Edna and I are reaping the reward in her pool. See you there." She held up a glass of iced tea in salute and headed outside.

Harmony and a young woman with tattooed snakes winding up her bare arms were at the stove. Harmony, wearing a beach cover-up with her hair in cornrows, was stirring something that smelled fabulous.

"This is Glenda," she said, "and she makes the most amazing red beans and rice. She's teaching me how. If you eat meat, we're having burgers, too. Glenda, this is Ethan."

Glenda, who had blue hair the length of toothbrush bristles, gave a short nod and went back to chopping onions.

"Charlotte?" he asked.

"She's probably with Rilla and the puppies out by the pool. Now that their eyes are open, they're absolutely capable of making for the water if somebody doesn't watch them every second. Would you like something to drink? We have cold soda in the fridge and outside, and white wine and beer."

When he turned he found a woman wearing black shorts and a bright red T-shirt standing behind him.

"I'm Analiese Wagner," she said. "Charlotte's minister."

Since he hadn't set foot in the church in the past dozen years, he introduced himself, then left her in Harmony's care and went to find his ex-wife.

Charlotte was poolside, chatting with a woman in a wheelchair who was holding a squirming golden bundle on her lap. Charlotte looked up and motioned for him to join them.

"Ethan, this is Rilla Reynolds, the puppies' breeder. And that's Violin on her lap."

Ethan squatted down to see the puppy and say hello to Rilla.

"Isn't she adorable?" Rilla asked. "The whole litter's adorable."

"Where are the rest of them?" he asked.

Charlotte nodded toward the corner, where Edna and another girl Ethan didn't recognize had set up an ersatz pen with folding chairs. They were sitting inside the enclosure with a golden retriever looking on. The dog didn't seem in any hurry to get her offspring back.

"Rilla breeds the puppies to be service dogs." Charlotte hesitated. "Some of them may be seizure dogs."

He began to get the picture. "Were you

thinking about Maddie?"

"That's how I met Rilla."

Rilla explained what had looked to be Velvet and the puppies' fate. "Then Charlotte and Harmony volunteered to take her instead, and raise the puppies until they're weaned and can go to puppy-raisers," she finished.

He had decided to quit comparing the Charlotte he'd been married to with this mystery woman beside him. "How does that work?" he said, with no comment on how strange this was.

Rilla looked happy to continue. "When they're around nine or ten weeks old, the puppies are separated and a different family takes each one. They socialize them, do obedience training and prepare them for whatever service area they're suited for."

Charlotte took over. "Rilla was just telling me that the puppies are tested along the way for things like confidence, the way they recover from loud noises or new experiences and how social they are."

"It's counterintuitive," Rilla said, "but often the bossiest puppies don't make good service dogs, because they always want to be in charge. Instead, if we can't find an area they'll fit into, they're placed permanently as pets with families who agree to give them lots of exercise and training. Quiet, fearful dogs usually don't make it, either. The testing's done on their forty-ninth day, when they're fully developed but still young enough to mold."

"Could one of these dogs really help our granddaughter?" Ethan asked.

"In a variety of ways," Rilla said, and explained that, too. "We really don't know why some dogs can sense seizures coming on. Ordinary family mutts sometimes do it on their own. We can't train for it very well, but the dogs in Velvet's family have had a fairly high success rate, although nothing like a hundred percent."

"I didn't know if Taylor would allow me to get a dog for Maddie," Charlotte said. "I just went to Capable Canines to see what I could find out."

"And look what happened," Rilla said. "By the way, I put my money on Violin here. She's the kind of pup we hope for. Villain, now? And what's the little one's name?"

"Vanilla," Charlotte said.

"Time'll tell, but I suspect those two may end up as pets somewhere."

Ethan went to visit the pen, and Charlotte accompanied him. "Rilla's husband and sons will be over in a little while," she said. "I haven't met the boys. They can't stay with her during the week until she's more mobile."

"So you took the puppies to help out?"

"That was my plan. Except they've been a delight. So I'm not sure who's helping whom."

They stood and watched the puppies and the girls. Edna liked Villain the best, and she was trying to teach him manners by pulling him away from the others when he got too aggressive. Her friend Katie, a blond-haired charmer, was checking each pup to see how good they were at cuddling. Vanilla won hands down, since she fell asleep on Katie's knee almost the moment she was put there.

"Are you going to swim?" Charlotte asked him after a minute.

"I will if you will."

At the poolside Charlotte struggled with the zipper to her sundress, and without thinking Ethan stepped over and undid it for her.

"Force of habit," he said, when he realized what he'd done.

She gave a low laugh. "I wonder if the dishwashing habit stays alive and well that long, too."

"Dishwashing gets more practice at my house."

"Too much information." She stepped out of her dress and folded it over her arm. She was wearing a two-piece suit with a tiny little skirt covering a few inches of her thighs, nothing nearly as seductive as he remembered from their past. But it suited her, revealing just enough to remind him of other times.

"That's a nasty bruise on your thigh," he said. "Are you doing your own car repairs these days? You've got a smaller one on your wrist." He put his finger just above the crook of her arm. "And another up here."

Charlotte stood perfectly still, then she looked around and down. "I didn't know. I hadn't noticed."

"You must have whacked yourself good."

"Must have. Maybe while I was scrubbing today."

"They look older."

"Are we going to jump in, or walk in slowly?" she asked.

"You're kidding, right? I jump, you walk. It's always been that way. Taylor used to time you, remember? I would be ready to get out, and you would still be inching in."

"Life's too short." Charlotte walked to the pool, sat on the edge and slipped right in. He whistled softly and joined her.

Someone switched on the outdoor speakers, and Glenda hooked up her iPod. She entertained them with an enormously eclectic playlist, which surprised everybody, since she didn't look like someone who would mix Tony Bennett and Rosemary Clooney with Lady Gaga and Mindless Behavior.

The food was just as eclectic. Everyone pitched in to get it to the table. The red beans were fabulous, and so were the burgers on whole-wheat buns. Analiese contributed German potato salad, and Rilla had brought fresh berries. Samantha and Edna brought a variety of chips and dips, and Harmony had made a green salad adorned with toasted pumpkin and sunflower seeds.

Time slipped lazily by; then as shadows deepened, people began to leave. First Analiese, who had to prepare for the Sunday service. Then Rilla and her family, because the boys were nodding off. Glenda left to attend a Jello wrestling match, taking her iPod. Finally Samantha and Edna. When Harmony began to cart puppies back to Charlotte's closet for the night, Ethan knew it was time to go, too.

Charlotte, covered from neck to toe in a white gauze beach robe, walked him through the house.

"You put on a great party," he said.

"No fuss, no bother. I always thought you

had to slave for days or pay a king's ransom to hire help. All this time it was as simple as asking people to come and let the arrangements take care of themselves."

"I had fun."

"This is the way it's supposed to be, you know. Easy entertaining. Laughter. Music. Good, simple food. Friends."

He knew she wasn't really talking about "is" but "was." She meant their years together, when it hadn't been like this very often. "Well, you're getting the hang of it."

"I am, aren't I?"

They stopped at the door. "Tell me about Taylor," she said, making it easy for him to begin.

"She's angry. We fought. She has your letter, but I haven't spoken to her since the day I gave it to her. I don't know what she's feeling."

"I wasn't trying to come between you."

He put his hand on the door and leaned against it, facing her. "You aren't the only one with regrets. I can see things more clearly now. I sided with Taylor against you too often. I was more comfortable just letting things go, and sometimes that was right. But sometimes that was lazy, or worse, a need to be the parent she could count on. I left you to pick up the slack. We got into a bad cycle, and I'm sorry for my part in it."

"Ethan." She smiled a little, then she touched his cheek. "Thank you."

She dropped her hand quickly, but he still felt her fingers on his skin. "I confronted her," he said. "She needed to be confronted, and unfortunately for me, you're not around to do it anymore. So I guess this time I had to step up to the plate."

"She has a strong will."

"Yeah, and we wonder where it came from."

"I just want . . ." She shook her head. "Even if she's still furious, I hope she'll agree to talk to me."

"I'm not counting on anything, but it's in her hands, Lulu. We just have to back off and wait."

"Thank you." And she kissed his cheek where her fingertips had rested. "For everything."

Charlotte was beyond exhausted, but she couldn't seem to stop smiling. The day had been good in so many ways. She had miles to go, but maybe she was moving forward. And being here today? With the children and the puppies underfoot, with new friends and an old husband?

She smiled at that last.

Somewhere deep in the pockets of her cover-up her cell phone rang, and she didn't even check the number, foolishly hoping it was Ethan. She snapped it open and put it to her ear. "Charlotte Hale."

"Charlotte? It's Phil."

She knew which Phil. Phil Granger, who didn't sound upbeat. She almost asked him to call back tomorrow, so she could keep this day separate from the news he was bringing. Keep it separate so that the warmth would last and see her through.

But she had learned that denial was toxic.

She carried the phone twenty yards and sank to a sofa before she answered. "It's Saturday. This can't be good news."

"I don't like doing this on the phone, but time's an issue. We rushed your last set of lab tests through, and I checked the results this afternoon. We can't wait any longer to start more chemo. I just got off the phone with your physician at Duke, and he's on board. We can do it here and continue consulting with him, the way you've asked, but, Charlotte? The secret's going to get out this time if you're doing it at the hospital. I can't believe you've kept the leukemia under wraps this long, but you have to prepare your friends and family."

"I know."

"Do you? Do you really understand? This might go well, but there's no guarantee. Your case isn't simple, if there is such a thing. There aren't any really good answers here."

She couldn't help herself. She closed her eyes and squeezed them tight, but her voice was shaky. "I get it. You can stop trying to warn me. I've looked up my odds, and I've made my will. Just do your best, okay? I'm not ready to die."

"Trust us to do whatever we can, and keep fighting. That can make the difference."

"Don't quit five minutes before the miracle."

"I'm sorry?"

She thought of Samantha. "Somebody younger and wiser told me that. I'm not done fighting. I still have things to do here."

She closed the phone and held it to her chest. And she thanked God for giving her a nearly perfect day before the storm that was coming.

CHAPTER THIRTY-THREE

Taylor wasn't a fan of self-pity. She wasn't a fan of self-congratulations, either, but silently, for years, she had patted herself on the back for the ways she had triumphed over difficult circumstances.

Now she knew she had taken too much credit. The only reason she'd been able to stand and fight was because her father had stood beside her. From the beginning Ethan had been there. On top of everything else, he'd never once reminded her what a burden she had dropped in his lap.

Now he *wasn't* there, and the fault was hers.

A week had passed since their fight, and she'd spent the early part of it holding firm to her conviction that this, too, was her mother's fault. Then, as her anger wore away and the time neared for Maddie's return, the truth crept in.

She had shown a surprising lack of respect

for the man who had nurtured and supported her. She had accused him of being a puppet, and she had actually felt a zing of pride when her carelessly launched arrows had drawn blood.

Who was she, anyway?

Without Maddie filling the holes in her life, Taylor had felt like half a person. Now, without Ethan, she felt like a ghost, someone without substance and form, someone who walked through a room and left a cold feeling of dread.

The problem was she had no idea how to make things right without agreeing to read her mother's letter. And the letter, still unopened, was in a box in her closet, where she would probably leave it until it turned to dust.

A bedtime phone call from Maddie upped the ante. Her little girl would be home by dinnertime Sunday, and ten seconds into the call Maddie wanted to know if Ethan could come and eat with them. Taylor hung up wondering how she could possibly explain their recent estrangement.

Early the next morning, when she found herself standing on Ethan's doorstop, she still wasn't sure what she should say. She had stopped for bagels and cream cheese and steaming hot coffee from a place that really knew how to make it. As a peace offering, the combination wasn't bad, but she knew the right words had to accompany breakfast for it to be worth anything.

When he opened the door dressed in shorts and a Laughing Seed T-shirt from her favorite vegetarian restaurant, she thrust the bagels into his hands. "Maddie's coming home Sunday afternoon and I'm sorry."

He still looked half-asleep and, worse, mystified. "You're sorry she's coming home?"

"No. She's coming home Sunday, and I'm sorry I said things I shouldn't have last week."

"Good news all the way around. Come in."

She followed him and set the coffee on the counter separating the living area from the kitchen. "I should never have said you couldn't stand up to my mother. Your relationship was your business, and I'll never know what really went on when I wasn't there. As a kid, of course, I always wanted you on my side, but that's the way a kid thinks. I'm sure Maddie wishes I would always agree with *her* about everything, too."

He nodded, as if he was taking that in. "Then I can assume you also realize that you didn't always see your mother as clearly as you think? That maybe the letter helped you see her a little differently?"

"I haven't read the letter, and I hope you meant it when you said this is between my mother and me now, and you don't want to be in the middle anymore."

"I meant everything I said the other day, Taylor. Including my hope that you're capable of forgiveness." He held up his hand to stop her from continuing. "But I don't want another argument. I've told you how I feel, and you've told me. The only person with no chance to be heard is your mother, and I hope someday she'll be included, too. However, that's up to you."

"It has to be. I just hope . . ." She stopped, then decided to go on. "I hope she's not going to come between us? Because, Dad, I feel manipulated. Here she gave *you* the letter —"

"A letter I suggested she write, Taylor. And giving it to me was nothing more than hope I could get it to you at the right moment. The mail's not good about that. You can't buy timing with a stamp."

She knew better than to continue. She'd learned something new about her father. He had been so good to her that for years she had thought his love and patience were endless. But she had been wrong. He had limits, exactly the way everyone else did, and he had reached them.

If she followed that revelation to its natural conclusion, maybe Ethan really hadn't been manipulated by her mother, as she had insisted. Perhaps he really had just been willing to overlook the bad parts of his marriage because he loved the good.

She couldn't push the thought away.

"I don't know what to think about all this," she said, "but I do know I love you and don't ever want to fight with you again."

He didn't embrace her, as she'd half expected. He smiled a little. "I hope there's coffee to go with the bagels."

"There is. The way you like it."

"So tell me about Maddie."

Harmony liked the way her new white blouse swished over the tops of her leggings-clad thighs, covering most of her hips. She liked the peekaboo panels of lace and the scooped neckline, and the fact that her expanding belly wasn't visible. The blouse was a splurge, not a Biltmore Village boutique kind of splurge, but a consignment shop splurge, which was a lot more expensive than her usual Goodwill finds. She thought it was appropriate to wear something nicer tonight, since she and Davis were going out to dinner, and she was pretty sure he was going to give her the ring they had picked out last week.

Although she was supposed to be working, she'd switched her night off with one of the other servers, because tomorrow Davis was busy. He had joined a fantasy baseball league made up of other young professionals, and he claimed that missing Saturday's beer bash with his new buddies was bad business. Davis was certain some of them would eventually become clients.

The time had arrived to introduce him to Charlotte. Before their engagement Harmony had always met him somewhere away from home. Now she was about to marry the man, and Charlotte was interested in meeting him, although the thought made her uneasy. She wasn't sure why, at least not exactly. But she had a sneaking feeling Davis might be too impressed with her new living quarters and attempt to charm Charlotte, who might someday need a new accountant.

The thought gave her shivers.

A few minutes before he was due she went to look for Charlotte and found her in the bedroom closet, playing with the puppies. Velvet looked relieved to have someone else attract her brood's attention, and she passed

Harmony in the doorway, as if she planned to go for a quick stretch around the house. Harmony reminded herself to let the dog out before she left with Davis.

"I'm afraid it's time to move them," Charlotte said. "They need more space, and they're so noisy at night it's hard to sleep. I thought maybe the family room. I can put up two dog gates. What do you think?"

"I think you're right. And it'll be easy to take Velvet outside from there, and the puppies, too."

Charlotte got slowly to her feet and brushed off her pants. "Maybe we can make the move tomorrow."

"Don't worry, I'll take care of it."

Charlotte led the way out, pulling the one gate they already had across the doorway to keep the puppies in. They began to yap in protest.

"I'll let Velvet outside and put her back in if she's willing to resume her maternal duties," Harmony said. "Davis should be here soon."

"Do you know where you're going to dinner?"

"He said he was in the mood for barbecue."

Charlotte couldn't cover her surprise. "What do *you* eat at a barbeque restaurant?"

"Coleslaw. Beans, if there's no pork in them. Barbecued tempeh, if I'm lucky."

Charlotte didn't have to say anything else. Harmony had been annoyed at Davis's choice the moment she heard it, but she figured since he was paying, she really had no right to object. This was Asheville, where vegans were as common as azaleas, and there was always something she could eat on any menu.

Harmony found Velvet and took her outside. "They won't be around forever," she assured the dog. "And you'll probably miss them once they're gone."

She wondered what would happen to Velvet once the puppies had been placed with puppy raisers. Without an explanation Charlotte had said she wouldn't be able to keep the dog herself, although she would like to. Harmony wanted to keep Velvet, but when she'd mentioned the possibility to Davis, he'd said a flat no. Didn't they already have enough on their plate, and weren't they going to have enough new expenses and adjustments?

She was sure Marilla would find the dog a good home, but she hated the thought that gentle, beautiful Velvet would be living with strangers.

Back inside she let Velvet into the closet,

where she was greeted with screeches of delight. By the time Harmony got back to the front of the house, Davis was just pulling into the driveway.

She ushered him inside before he knocked. He gave a low whistle, but not because she looked great — which she did — but because of the house. His gaze traveled over every feature. The staircase leading to the second floor, the dining room to the right, and the music room just beyond, with a baby grand no one ever played. He admired the art on the walls, even the ornate velvet drapes that always made Harmony think of Scarlett O'Hara and the dress she had made to impress the imprisoned Rhett Butler.

"Some place you landed," he said. "Congratulations."

Annoyance shot through her. "I had no idea what kind of house Charlotte lived in when I took her up on her invitation to spend that first night."

He seemed to realize his mistake. "I didn't mean it that way. But it *is* an amazing house."

"Come meet Charlotte, then we can leave." She couldn't help herself. "And she *has* an accountant, maybe more than one."

"What's that supposed to mean?"

"You can be your charming self for no

reason other than showing off your excellent manners."

Before Davis could reply, Charlotte came into the hallway. She extended her hand as Harmony made the introduction. "I understand you and Harmony are going to set a date for your wedding."

Davis flashed his most congenial smile. "I hope to do that tonight."

Harmony would have preferred "I hope *we* do that," but she realized she was taking offense at everything Davis said or did. She had to rein herself in.

Davis and Charlotte chatted. She told him she knew the senior partners at his firm, who conducted some of Falconview's business. He told her how much he liked what he could see of the house. She offered a tour, but he declined, saying he would love one another time.

In a few minutes Harmony was in the Acura beside him, driving toward the city. Clouds were moving in, and she was glad they'd left Charlotte's when they had, to beat the approaching storm. "I thought for sure you'd take her up on the tour."

"I knew all I needed to when I drove up. That house is worth at least a million, more likely two. And some of those antiques are priceless."

Harmony thought they were priceless, too, but only because they belonged to the woman she had come to love like a mother. "You think like an accountant, Davis. I bet you were doing Charlotte's taxes in your head."

"I'd need a little more information." He glanced at her. "You look great, by the way. New clothes?"

"New to me." They chatted until they pulled up to a restaurant with a bright purple awning not far from Charlotte's house.

The place was informal, but comfortable, with a sauce bar filled with interesting options, a wide-screen television and a menu with an entire section of vegetarian selections. Harmony began to relax.

"They've got great beer. What'll you have?" Davis asked.

If Davis had accompanied her to either of her two clinic appointments, he would already know the answer. "I'll have water with a slice of lemon," she said. "Remember? I'm going to have your baby?"

A second passed before that registered. "I must have left my head somewhere else."

He ordered a local brew for himself and the water for her, then they turned back to the menu. "Ribs are great here," he said.

He looked up and grinned. "But I know you won't eat them. The vegetarian stuff looks good. I called ahead to be sure they had plenty of options."

She smiled back and told herself that was good enough. When their drinks came, they ordered. She asked for a grilled veggie po'boy and a side salad, and Davis chose the ribs.

"I picked up something today," he said, after their server had gone.

"A cold? Your mail?"

"A certain ring." He patted his pocket.

Harmony was almost afraid to see it. She'd been in favor of something more unique to celebrate their engagement. She certainly hadn't wanted a diamond. She wasn't as political as some of her friends, but she knew that the way most diamonds were mined was unsavory, at best. She'd hoped for something mined right here in her adopted state. A ruby, perhaps, or even a garnet. But Davis had insisted a diamond was the most appropriate and had compromised by asking for one that was "responsibly sourced." The jeweler had agreed, but he'd explained the diamond would be smaller and more expensive.

Even with that caveat, Harmony wasn't anxious to wear the ring. She wasn't quite sure why.

"Well, are you going to give it to me?" she asked.

"Here? No way. This isn't the kind of place you give a girl a diamond she's going to wear forever."

Something about that sent a chill down Harmony's spine. "Well, you chose the spot, Davis. Why choose a barbecue joint, then?"

"I told you, I want to announce our engagement at the country club dinner."

"Announce it, sure, but I didn't know you were going to give me the ring there, too."

"Might as well, don't you think? It's as romantic as any place I know."

"Romantic? Surrounded by your colleagues? The partners in the firm?"

"Crystal chandeliers. Soft music. Lobster —"

"I don't eat lobster!"

"Then don't eat it, I don't care. I just think that's the right place and the right moment to make our engagement official."

She sat back, emotion roiling inside her, and despite her intent to hold it in, it escaped. "Well, you know what? I don't. If you're serious about this, then put the ring on my finger right now. Unless the pageantry and the witnesses are what it's all about."

His eyes narrowed. "What does that mean?"

"It means I'm beginning to wonder if this engagement is all for show, Davis. Maybe the big reason you want to marry me is to impress everybody at your office and show them what a model citizen you are. Wife, house, car nearly paid off. The perfect guy to move up their career ladder."

He didn't say anything for a moment. She couldn't tell if he was mulling over what she'd said or trying to hold his temper.

"I'm bending over backward here," he said. "Neither of us planned this baby. We used birth control, but it happened. So I'm trying to do what's right. If I want to do it at the country club surrounded by people I like, then what's the big deal? No, it won't hurt my career if I get married. But how can that be a bad thing? Our life will be easier if we have money. Surely you've figured that out from your own experience."

"I don't want an easy life. I want a *happy* life. I want to marry a man I love, one who's so excited to be with me he can't wait to put the ring on my finger!"

"You're hormonal."

She couldn't believe he'd said that. "I'm *what?*"

He backtracked. "You're seeing plots

where there aren't any, Harmony. It's understandable. This is huge for you, and I'm sorry if I've been insensitive."

She waited for his hand to creep up to his pocket and pull out the ring, but it didn't. He just smiled gently, as if that would be good enough.

"I want to be a lawyer," she said. "I know I have a long way to go. A four-year college, law school, all while I'm raising a child. But I think I can do it."

At the change of subject he looked like a man trying to climb a cliff with no handholds. "What?"

"How would you feel about being married to a professional, Davis? Someone with career aspirations? Someone who doesn't give in every time a decision needs to be made? Somebody who's busy and expects you to share in the housekeeping and child care?"

"I don't see why we're discussing this now. That's way in the future."

"How would you feel?" she repeated.

"Harmony, we can have a good life together, but I don't see us being a two-career family, okay? At least not two professionals. I'm going to need support to get where I want to go, a wife who can take care of the basics for both of us. And I don't see you as the career type. You love to cook and take care of people and make things with your hands. How does that add up to a career in law?"

"You keep telling me how smart I am."

"There are all kinds of smart."

She heard the message. She'd made good grades in high school, even in her advanced placement classes. Despite her terrifying home life, she had managed to rank among the top students in a large graduating class. Her high school counselor had tried to convince her to go to college, but financial aid had required cooperation from her father. In the end all she'd been able to think about was getting away.

None of that added up to anything now. Now she was just Harmony Stoddard, long-haired, tattooed, hippie chick who waited on tables and got pregnant without even trying.

"You were afraid the partners might find out you got me pregnant and didn't step forward to do the right thing, weren't you?" she asked softly. "That's why you decided to marry me. And the more you thought about it, the better a choice it seemed. Because I'm young, with nothing more than a high school education, a little stupid when it comes to what goes on in the world, easily swayed when it comes time to make decisions."

"Oh, for God's sake!" Davis slapped his hand over his pocket and pulled out the ring box. "Here's the ring. Let's make a memory. I'll get down on my knees right here on the bare floor and put it on your finger, if that's what it's going to take to make you happy!"

She stared at him, and she knew, beyond the shadow of a doubt, that nothing Davis could ever do would accomplish that. She got to her feet, stopped the server as he rushed by, told him to cancel her portion of their order and left the restaurant.

Charlotte sat on the sofa as close to Harmony as she could, because it looked to her as if her young friend needed comfort.

"It only started to rain after I was nearly home," Harmony told her.

The moment she'd seen Harmony dripping in the entryway, Charlotte had fetched towels. Now Harmony rubbed one through her hair as Charlotte pulled an afghan over her lap. "I can't believe that man abandoned you to walk here alone."

"He didn't. He caught up with me, but I told him I needed to clear my head. He even followed me in his car for a while, but eventually he drove off. It's not as bad as it sounds. The restaurant wasn't that far away."

"You must be starving."

"I'll eat whatever you didn't." Harmony cocked her head. "Did you eat anything? I left you stir-fry and a salad."

"No, I haven't eaten yet."

"You're hardly eating a thing these days. Is it my cooking?"

Charlotte rested her hand on Harmony's shoulder. "You're a fabulous cook."

"For a while I thought that might be enough, you know? Cooking for Davis. Cleaning his house. Raising our baby. And maybe it would be, but what if it's not? What if I decide I want more? That's all my mother was ever allowed to do. Davis isn't my father, but he does like to control everything, the same way my father did. How long before he started to push me around, just because I made it so easy?"

"So you aren't going to marry him?"

Harmony shook her head slowly. "Maybe I'll regret it, but you know, I'd rather be poor than sell myself short. The baby won't suffer. Davis will have to pay child support, and I'm good at squeezing a dollar dry. Maybe he'll even want visitation rights. I hope he does. But that's the only relationship I want with him. I don't think I ever really loved him. I know I don't love him now."

Charlotte felt a wave of relief. Harmony hadn't been happy since the day she agreed to marry her baby's father. There had been questions in her eyes and in everything she did.

"You know you'll be welcome here." Charlotte saw the time had come to be honest, but she stumbled over the next words. "Harmony, you'll . . . you'll be more than welcome." She stopped and swallowed. "I think you're going to *needed.* I think I'm going to need your help."

"You have such a way of turning things around so it sounds like you're the one who should be grateful."

Charlotte dropped her hand. "No, this time I'm afraid it's absolutely true. I'm . . . I'm sick. I've known for a while." She gave a shortened version of everything that had occurred so far, the diagnosis, the chemo and, finally, the prognosis.

"I'm not doing as well as we hoped I might. I'm going to need another round of chemo, but they're going to do it in Asheville this time. Things may not go well."

Harmony's eyes were wide. "Leukemia?"

"I'm afraid so."

"But they can beat leukemia these days.

I've seen specials on television about children who get cured."

"It's easier to treat in children. They've made wonderful advances. But I'm nearly fifty-three. My body's not particularly resilient, and this is an acute type that moves quickly. The first round of chemo didn't end the way we wanted it to, but it did give me this time at home. They've been trying to build me up for the second."

"Last week, when you said you were going on an overnight business trip?"

"They were doing tests and working out details. We've decided on a treatment I can do as an outpatient. But when my blood counts drop even further, which they will, I have to stay out of crowds, away from viruses and bacteria."

"The puppies?"

"I shouldn't have them in my room anymore, no. And you and Nell will have to be sure to clean up after them even more carefully than before. There'll be some point when I won't be able to be around them at all, but we can cross that bridge when it's time."

She reached over and took Harmony's hands. "I told the doctors I want to be with the people I love. And I love *you,* sweetheart. You're special in every single way I can imagine, and I'm so glad you came into my life. No matter how this ends, you can stay here, in this house, as long as you need to. I've made sure of it."

"I don't want to think about that."

"I hope this isn't going to be too much for you, but having you here while I'm in treatment could be a lifesaver. Just having someone nearby, in case I take a turn for the worse. Can you do that?"

Harmony's eyes filled, and the tears spilled over. "This isn't fair. I don't want you to be sick. I don't want you to —"

"Me, either."

"You know I'll stay. I'll do anything you need." She threw her arms around Charlotte and hugged her tight.

Charlotte thought about how good that felt, and how long it had been since anyone had held her this way. She slipped her arms around Harmony's waist, and the two women sat together in silence.

Chapter Thirty-Four

First Day Journal: June 18

During my childhood, my grandmother is many things to me, but she's not demonstrative. We rarely kiss or hug, except at holidays or during moments of sorrow. I wonder, is she afraid if she succumbs to loving arms, she won't be able to rise each morning and face what waits for her? When I sit beside the bed during her final days, she allows me to take her hand. But even then, when she most needs comfort, she wants nothing more from anyone.

When Ethan comes into my life, he's not the first man to touch me, but he's the first whose touch gives me real pleasure. In Ethan's arms I learn the joys of sex, but also the simple joy of skin against skin, a rough cheek in the morning rubbed against a smooth one, a hand across my breasts as he sleeps.

After Ethan leaves I become my grandmother. I allow no one to touch me, except in the most casual of ways. I wall off my body like a nun in a cloistered convent. At last I understand that when my grandfather died, my grandmother couldn't bear the memory of the sweet intimacies they shared. And so she made certain never to be reminded.

Divorce brings with it many sorrows, but none greater than this.

Chapter Thirty-Five

Charlotte was preparing herself for the inevitable. So far she had survived all her treatments, and there was every chance this next step in the process would, if nothing else, buy her time.

Phil and her physicians at Duke had decided on a less intensive program, which she could do as an outpatient. The hospital was nearby, and if she didn't feel well enough to drive, Nell or Harmony would take her, or she could use a car service.

The treatment wasn't optimal. The drug was most often employed for older patients, but attempting an inpatient round of stronger chemo was considered too dangerous with her recent history. And because of that, a transplant was now out of the question.

Her options were fewer and less hopeful, but medical science was constantly discovering new and better treatments. If she could hang on long enough, she might be in line for an appropriate clinical trial.

Optimism wasn't the same as denial. Even if Phil hadn't reminded her, she had known it was time to be honest about what was happening. Now Harmony knew the truth, as did Nell, who had volunteered to add extra hours if needed. Analiese had known for a while, and the next time Charlotte saw Sam, she would tell *her,* as well. She couldn't afford to spend time at Sam's clinic, not when her own immunity would be so seriously compromised. What strength she had would be needed to battle for her life.

She'd finally revealed the truth to her colleagues, as well. That morning she had called an emergency meeting of Falconview's executive committee, the colleagues who had been forced to scramble to fill in most of the gaps her absence had left in the past months. She knew they had become increasingly skeptical about her explanations, and all too frequently, when she did show up at the office, conversation stopped when she walked into a room.

The announcement had been met with silence. She'd followed it with explanations, that she hadn't wanted the staff scurrying off to find new jobs or spreading the word about her illness. She'd reminded them that the economy had already done significant damage to Falconview, and she had been sure she was going to beat this without doing more.

The explanations had been met with silence, too, at least for a minute. Then the recriminations had begun. The committee had let her know she'd sold them short right from the beginning, which was true. Then they had wanted to know what would happen to her share, the majority share, of Falconview if the chemo didn't go well.

She had admitted she wasn't yet sure, but that no matter what did happen, everyone who worked at the company would be taken care of. She had made sure of that much.

She didn't think her answer had relieved much of their stress, but it had been all she could give them.

Now, with the meeting finally behind her, another meeting in place to inform the rest of the staff, and a short visit to her attorney's office to sign new papers, she was at home in the den, lying flat on her extravagant Italian leather sofa, fully clothed in her dress and blazer. She hadn't even taken off her pumps. The day had left her nearly comatose.

As hard as everything had been, the worst encounter was still to come. More than anything, she dreaded telling Ethan, who would then have to pass on the news to Taylor. She was afraid both of them would rally to her side simply because she was ill and not because they wanted to set the past behind them. Thinking about that made it impossible to close her eyes and rest.

Harmony wandered in a little while later and caught Charlotte staring at the ceiling. "I'm sort of committed to go in a little early to Cuppa. We're giving away free appetizers to anybody who brings in five pounds of groceries for the food bank, and they're pretty sure they're going to be slammed. I told them I'd help set up, but if you need me . . ."

"I'm fine. Just tired from my meeting."

"The puppies are settled in the family room, and you can let Velvet in and out from there without any fuss. I've put down tons of newspaper, and I'll clean up the minute I get home. Don't touch a thing."

"We'll be fine. I'm just going to take a nap."

"Here?"

"As good a place as any."

Her eyes were finally closing. She struggled to keep them open a moment longer. Harmony took a plaid woolen afghan off a chair and brought it over to cover her.

"I wrote down Cuppa's number." She put a scrap of paper on the coffee table and anchored it with the cordless receiver. "If anything comes up, call, and they'll get me right to the phone."

Charlotte closed her eyes before Harmony was out of the room. She didn't need Phil's detailed report on platelets and white cells to know the time had come for intervention. She was bruising so easily now that she had to wear long sleeves to cover her arms, particularly the sites of the recent blood draws, and her thighs were bruised and sore to the touch. She had a prescription for painkillers, but she was afraid if she took them, she would never be able to get on her feet again.

She woke up when she heard the telephone. She sat up, and tried to focus on where she was and where the telephone might be. Three rings later she saw it on the coffee table and put it to her ear.

"Charlotte? Ethan."

She blinked. For a moment she was in her twenties, waiting for Ethan to come home from work and complete their little family. Then she remembered. She cleared her throat. "Hi. What time is it?"

"Five. Were you sleeping?"

"I'm glad you woke me. I had a long

meeting, and I just collapsed when I got back. If I don't get up now, I won't sleep a wink tonight."

"I'm not far away. Are you free for a little while?"

"All evening. What's up?"

"I've got something for you."

She smiled at this surprise. For the briefest of moments she hoped the "something" was her daughter, or at least a letter. Then she realized he would have told her that immediately.

"I'll unlock the door. If I'm in the shower, just let yourself in."

Thirty minutes later, showered and dressed in more casual clothes, she found him in the family room petting Velvet.

"Now I see why you're here," she said. "You just can't resist my puppies."

"I still can't believe you have them."

"They're adorable, aren't they?"

"Nothing cuter." He got to his feet. "I'm sorry I woke you."

"I'm not. Can you stay awhile?"

"I hope I can stay for dinner. I brought it."

"The surprise." She thought for a moment. "I've got a guess, but if I'm wrong, then you'll feel like you made a mistake."

"Pulled pork and all the fixings."

She clapped her hands. "Exactly what I was hoping."

"I remembered you said you missed it. I'm sure we're healthier for the vegetarians in our lives, but not necessarily happier."

"You always were the best at picking up cues. I'm really glad you picked up on that one."

"Are you hungry now?"

She wondered. She hadn't been hungry in a long time, not really. Tonight, though, might be different.

"Let's have a drink first," she said. "We can sit out by the pool — if you don't think it's too hot?"

"You haven't been outside since you got home, have you? We had a storm earlier, and it cooled the air. If things aren't too wet, it should be nice out there."

"We can always dry off the chairs if we need to, and Velvet should wander a little."

They rummaged for drinks. Ethan had never liked hard liquor, and Charlotte could no longer tolerate her favorite gin and tonic. He found a bottle of the local Highland oatmeal porter, and she poured a small glass of white wine for herself. She added cheese spread and crackers to a plate, grabbed napkins, and they took everything out to the pool, including the dog.

"Did you bring your suit?" she asked. "There's probably something around here that'll fit you if you didn't." She realized how that sounded and for some reason felt a need to correct the impression. "When I moved in I bought extra suits to have on hand. Some of them probably still have the tags."

"I'd rather just sit."

The chairs were dry, and they pulled them closer to the pool, where the sinking sun danced along the ripples on the surface. The air smelled fresh and new, the punch of ozone from the storm a welcome accent.

"The house didn't seem nearly as large when it was filled with people last weekend," Ethan said.

"The house is large enough for an army battalion. I would sell except —" She stopped. She wasn't ready to tell him about the leukemia. She wanted to just enjoy his company tonight, without anything else mixed in.

"The economy?" he finished for her.

"It's definitely not the best time to sell a house, although people with money still seem to have it."

"I'm sure the economy's affected Falconview."

"In about a million different ways."

"Half the developments that were being actively marketed seem dead in the water."

"More than half. You've done the smart thing by pulling in and sitting tight. There's always a market for beautiful craftsmanship and sensible design."

"There must be. I sold my first unit at the factory this week, and it was the biggest. So now I have money to finish my own. We've had enough repeat traffic this month that I think we'll see more sales soon."

"Then this is a celebration." She lifted her glass.

They clinked, bottle to glass. She liked the feel of that, somehow familiar and right. "What will you do with your house when you move?"

"I'm thinking about renting it. Maybe to Taylor, if she's interested. It's larger than hers, and in a better neighborhood, with more yard. Then I can continue to use the workshop."

"Plus she would have a sympathetic landlord."

He smiled. "If she decides to stay put, I thought I'd ask Sam. I'll need somebody who doesn't mind me coming and going out back."

"Sam turned into an exceptional woman." Ethan knew about the clinic playroom, so she didn't elaborate. "It's been a wonderful surprise to find her in my life."

"She's had it tough but she's come out the other side," he said.

"I'm sure her mother had a lot to do with that. I saw her last week at the clinic."

"Difficult encounter?"

She sipped her wine. "I may have over-reached again. I may have interfered where I wasn't wanted."

"Oh?"

He didn't sound too wary, so she went on.

"Last week Sam mentioned her mother had an interview, and something Georgia said to me when we spoke rang a bell, something about hoping someday she could get back into school administration. So I made a phone call. I know the school board is looking at candidates for principal at the new alternative school they're opening in September. Their choice fell through late in the spring. I heard the whole story from —" She stopped. She had heard the story from Phil Granger, whose wife was on the inter-view committee, but she didn't want Ethan to make that connection.

"From a friend," she finished. "The board's kind of in a pickle, so they reopened the search. The thing is, Georgia would be perfect. The school's for middle and high schoolers in trouble in one way or another, kids who aren't fitting in where they are, kids who need a second chance and a specialized educational experience. It's going to be small, and intensive, and they need new ways of looking at education, not the same old. So I . . ." She shrugged. "I wrote her a letter of recommendation."

"She asked for one?"

"To be honest, I'm sure she'd be horrified. But I know that was the interview she was going to, because, well, I just do."

"You have ears all over the city, don't you?"

Since it was true, she couldn't deny it. "I knew somebody on the committee that's doing the first round of interviews. I just asked if it would help if I wrote a letter for somebody who might be a candidate, and when I said Georgia's name, she didn't correct me."

"You didn't think you should consult Georgia first?"

"I've told her how sorry I am about everything that happened all those years ago. She was as polite as anyone could be, but I know she doesn't want my help. She probably assumes there would be strings attached, anyway."

"Would there?"

She looked at him and frowned. "Not even a silk thread."

"So what could you say about her? That was a long time ago."

"A long time, yes, but undoubtedly being fired continues to haunt her professionally. I said she was a wonderful headmistress, and her only sin was that she was ahead of her time. I also said I hadn't realized it at the time, but hardly a day goes by when I don't kick myself for not fighting to keep her at Covenant Academy instead of fighting for her departure."

"That sounds harmless enough."

"I went just a little further. . . ."

"I remember that tone." He mimicked her. " 'Ethan, by the way, that's not quite *all* I did today. I also bought a five-acre plot in Weaverville that I'm absolutely sure will be zoned for business and triple in value.' "

She laughed, because what else could she do? "Well, if I hadn't brought this up, I'd tell you the whole thing is none of your business."

"But you *did* bring it up. What else did you do?"

"I called some other people who had children at the Academy when everything was going on, and I asked them to write letters, too."

"Carefully choosing people who agreed with you, I assume."

"It wouldn't have been particularly helpful to choose any other kind, would it?"

"Still a mover and a shaker."

"I hope she gets the job."

He took her empty glass and held it up. "Amen. Let's dish up some dinner."

They worked together, serving up plates from the take-out containers of pork, macaroni and cheese, and beans, then heating them in the microwave. While they waited she turned on music and fiddled with buttons until she found exactly what she wanted.

When she came back in, Ethan was smiling. "Alison Krauss and Union Station?"

"I have everything they've recorded, but don't tell anybody."

"You know my tastes pretty well, don't you? They've come here, you know. Since you're such a big fan, we'll have to go next time."

She knew better than to answer that. They chatted. He told her what he hoped to do to the kitchen of his condo unit, and she told him about a revolving kitchen cabinet made in New Zealand that she'd seen at a design show.

"It takes up very little square footage but contains almost everything a kitchen really needs, including a sink. I thought of you when I saw it. Utilitarian to the core, but friendly and attractive, too. I could see you incorporating it into one of your designs."

"The hardest thing about a divorce isn't getting somebody out of your bed, it's getting them out of your head."

"I never succeeded." She turned. "If you were luckier, don't tell me. Leave me some illusions."

"I married another woman. That helped for a while." He didn't go on.

Despite herself, she was encouraged by the "a while." "I was so angry at first. Maybe if I hadn't been, we could have worked for a better solution than the one we chose."

"What solution would you have preferred?"

"At the time? Drawing and quartering had a nice ring to it. But later?" She couldn't go on.

When she didn't, he did. "Sometimes, when you let things sink too low, you can't lift them up again. We let our marriage hit bottom. If we'd tried to keep it afloat while we still could, maybe things would have been different."

"I would never have agreed to counseling, and that's what we needed."

"Why wouldn't you have gone? Were you *that* sure you were right?"

She opened the microwave and rotated a plate, then closed it before she faced him. "No, that really wasn't the reason. I was afraid if I revealed too much, if you figured out who I really was or saw how inferior I felt, you wouldn't want me anymore."

"Lulu . . ." He shook his head. "I *knew* how insecure you were. I just had this foolish idea that if I loved you enough, it would all go away and one day you would wake up and see that nothing anyone ever said about you on Doggett Mountain, including that no-good father of yours, made one bit of difference."

She hadn't wanted to lose him, but without understanding it, she had done everything possible to make sure she did. For a moment the memory was so intense, it hurt to breathe. "It's a shame we figure out these things when it's too late, isn't it?"

He didn't answer, and she knew it was time to change the subject. "Do you want to eat outside?"

"Let's. Don't forget the coleslaw."

He got another beer, she opted for water. Even the small glass of wine had dragged her down, and now she felt like a drowning woman swimming to shore against the tide. The nap was wearing off, and so was her good sense. She was saying things she didn't need to, moving too close to the time when evenings like this one had been standard fare.

She was ready to lighten the atmosphere, but Ethan plunged back in.

"Taylor came to apologize," he said. "Maddie's coming home from Tennessee tomorrow, and I don't think she wants her to know that we've been at odds."

Charlotte waited, hoping he would say Taylor was willing to take the first step toward a reunion, but he shook his head. "I'm sorry, but she still hasn't read your letter."

She wondered how much time was left before it was too late for her daughter to change her mind. "She will when she's ready," she said.

They ate in silence, and she was surprised how good the food tasted. Maybe the difference was eating outside or the familiar flavors of her past — or maybe the company — but she finished everything she had dished up.

"That was so good." She set her plate on

the table. "I haven't eaten that much in ages."

"You're thinner than I remember. Maybe too thin."

"Eating hasn't been a priority," she said, and as far as it went, it was true.

"I know it's easy to stop making meals when you're alone."

The music changed from up-tempo bluegrass to something sweet, slow and sad. She recognized the song. It was "A Ghost in This House," about a woman alone because her lover has left her.

"I remember this," Ethan said. "Someone else sang it first, a country band."

She did remember, although it had been a long time since she'd heard that version. And suddenly she could almost feel Ethan's arms around her, and hear the twang of a Dobro. Neon signs blinked in the window, and the air was heavy with smoke.

"We danced to this," she said. "At a bar somewhere in Roanoke, when we were visiting your parents that very first time."

"I remember. I had to get you away from them and all to myself." Then, without time for either of them to think, he rose, took her hand and pulled her up. "For old times' sake."

She didn't hesitate. She went into his arms

as naturally as if she had never left them. He rested his cheek on her hair and moved slowly back and forth. She could feel the soft denim of well-washed jeans rubbing against her bare legs, the warmth of his chest against her breasts. Their bodies had always fit together, and they still did. She was awash in emotion, the past and present bound together in the slow rhythm of the song and the familiar feeling of the only man she had ever loved against her.

He hummed the melody, and his arms tightened. She couldn't mistake what was happening to both of them or even pretend it was accidental. Suddenly all the yearnings she had ignored were flooding through her. She wanted to cry, but even more, she wanted to laugh. They hadn't stumbled on this moment. They had slowly glided toward each other from the day he had come to find out why she'd been watching their granddaughter. She had tried to ignore what she was feeling, but Ethan hadn't been so blind.

The song ended. He stopped moving, but he didn't release her. She turned her face up to his and waited.

"It's been some ride, Lulu. First there was love," he said. "Then anger, and now something I could almost call friendship."

She traced a line on his cheek. "Only it's not quite friendship, is it? I've never been able to forget the good times, and they haunt me."

"Maybe I should go." He didn't pull away.

"Maybe you should." She didn't pull away, either.

He lowered his face to hers and kissed her lightly on the lips. She put her arms around his neck, and the kiss deepened. She heard a soft moan and knew it was her own. Her body, so damaged and run down, was coming alive, and the feeling was exquisite.

She could feel her heart thudding almost painfully against her chest, as if it was learning how to beat again. She could feel the blood flowing through her bruised limbs. Then she felt Ethan's hands traveling down her thighs to pull her closer, and she went rigid with pain as, without realizing it, his hand settled where a bruise bloomed and grew larger each day from the last bone marrow biopsy.

"I'm sorry," he said, but she knew he wasn't sure for what.

She slid his hand to a safer place. "Don't be. I . . . I just have a bruise there."

He moved away a little. "Still? From the other day?"

"I've always bruised easily. Remember?"

He seemed to take that in, and she could almost see him processing what he knew. "And the one on your arm? You still have that?"

Her arms were now an even sadder patchwork of bruises from tests and transfusions and the effects of the leukemia itself. She tried to smile. "You won't hurt me."

Ethan looked as if he wanted to believe her, but they had been through too much together. Even now, he knew exactly what a smile meant and how to read it.

"What aren't you telling me?"

"Nothing I want to tell you right now." The spell was broken, and she could feel the change in the air around them. Twilight was no longer their friend, and the soft whisper of the pool fountain was nothing more than an intrusion on silence. She struggled to find a way to turn back time, if only by moments, but that was impossible.

"Suppose you tell me, anyway." He moved away so he could see her face more clearly.

High overhead she heard a plane, and she wished she were on it, flying anywhere, away from the truth. She wished Ethan could be with her, that they could leave their past and her future here, and live in the present together forever. That was what she'd hoped for when he kissed her, although how she'd thought she could pull it off was impossible, even now, to remember.

She wasn't sure where to start. With his eyes still locked with hers, he pulled the long-sleeved blouse she was wearing over a tank top down over her shoulders until it hung low around her hips and her arms were bare. He stared at the bruises crawling up her arms, then up at her.

"I'd almost wonder if those needle marks are from some kind of drug habit, only I know you too well. That wouldn't be your escape of choice. So suppose you tell me what's going on?"

All she could do was tell the truth, but she still didn't know how. "I'm afraid it's about as bad as it looks."

"And I'm guessing whatever it is didn't happen suddenly, say in the past few days?"

She met his eyes. "In the spring I was diagnosed with leukemia. I was hospitalized for a month for treatment. I'll start the second round next week." The next words caught in her throat, and she shook her head before she could go on. "I've only just begun to tell people. I wanted tonight without my diagnosis between us."

He looked like a man who had stumbled onto a six-lane highway, stunned, injured and slowly moving toward anger. "People, huh? I'm just *people?* How many others have you told?"

"Just a few. Reverend Ana's known for a while. I just told Harmony and the executive committee at Falconview, so they can begin preparing for the worst, if it happens. And I only told them this morning."

"Did you tell our daughter in the letter you wrote her?"

"No. No! I don't want this mixed up in that. I want Taylor to come to me because she understands I've changed and she wants us to be a family again."

"Now that's the interesting part. *Have* you changed? Because keeping secrets was a big part of who you used to be. Working behind the scenes. Manipulating people. Controlling everything and everybody."

Tears sprang to her eyes. "Ethan, please, I'm not trying to control anything, especially not you. I just wanted . . . no, I *needed* to be with you without talking about my illness. I didn't plan any of what happened tonight, but when you held me just now, I wasn't going to thrust that between us."

He spaced his words for emphasis. "You have had plenty of time to tell me."

"I couldn't. Please understand. I just wanted to be happy for a little while. Without worrying that people felt sorry for me, or were trying to be good to me so my death wouldn't come back to haunt them. Please, can't you understand?" She wiped the tears off her cheeks with her fingertips, but Ethan was shaking his head.

"I understand I bought the whole act. I really thought you'd changed, yet here you are, making decisions for all of us again. You never once considered I was better than that? That I could tell the difference between pity and love? That I could be kind to you just because you're worth it, and not because you're dying?"

She couldn't think of a reply. Finally she gave the only one she could. "I didn't want to think about dying. I wanted to be alive. Fully alive, without the shadows hanging over me. At least while we were together."

"I'm sorry, but that's way over my head. It's a lot simpler for me. You've been living a lie every time we've been together. And I fell for it, because I began to believe in you again."

He turned and started through the house. She wanted to call him back, to find the magic words to make him understand. But there were none. Even when she heard the front door close, she continued to stand and hope the words would come to her.

But if there had been words, they, like Ethan, were gone forever.

Chapter Thirty-Six

Taylor knew she was treating her daughter's imminent arrival like Christmas and a birthday all rolled into one. But she had missed Maddie so much, and while the intensity of her feelings had been instructive, she was still glad Maddie was coming home.

Late in the afternoon Maddie called on Jeremy's cell phone when they'd turned on to I-240, so Taylor was ready with fresh lemonade and cookies right out of the oven when Jeremy pulled up in the borrowed van. She watched the occupants pile out and felt a sliver of distaste that Willow was one of them. She had to jettison the attitude, but apparently today wasn't launch day.

On the front porch she opened her arms and Maddie ran into them. "I missed you," Maddie said, hugging her hard.

Taylor hugged her back, then smoothed her hair off her forehead. "It was awfully quiet without you, kiddo."

"I have a lot to tell you."

Taylor was of two minds about that. Part of her wanted to hear every detail, and part of her wasn't so sure. If the narrative included raves about life in Nashville — and she was pretty sure it would — it was going to be hard to look enthused. Try as she might, she hadn't yet conquered her jealousy. Not of Jeremy and Willow, but of Jeremy, Willow and Maddie.

"We'll have all evening," she told Maddie, and gave her another hug. Then Maddie broke loose and dashed through the house. Taylor imagined her goal was to make sure everything was exactly the way she'd left it.

"Sam brought us a bag of clothes Edna's outgrown," she called after her. "They're on your bed."

"Willow bought me a bunch of stuff, too!" Maddie yelled from the direction of the kitchen.

Taylor steeled herself, but she was almost sure her smile was frozen in place. "How nice of you," she told Willow.

"My sister owns a shop in the CoolSprings Galleria, and she let me buy at a discount. I couldn't resist, Taylor. I truly hope you don't mind." Willow, arrayed in chartreuse today, blond hair pulled up on top of her head in a rhinestone barrette, looked genuinely concerned.

"Maddie's fun to shop for," Taylor said, which was the best she could manage.

"She sure is."

Jeremy came up to the porch with Maddie's suitcase, along with a new one that probably held the equally new wardrobe. "We thought maybe Maddie could show Willow the park where she plays. She talked about it all the time."

Alarm bells went off in Taylor's head. "Why just Willow?"

"I'd like to talk to you, if that's okay. And I'd rather Maddie wasn't here."

She repressed a number of comments, all of which sounded like, *I have a telephone and you know how to use it.*

"Fine," she said. "But I made lemonade and cookies."

"We stopped for a snack a little while ago when I got gas. She'll be fine until they get back. Unless that's a problem?"

The last part sounded to her like a dare. She could have called his bluff, but she knew it was better to get the conversation out of the way, so Willow and Jeremy could get out of the way, too.

"No problem," she said.

"Half-pint!" he called.

"Half-pint?" Taylor said.

"She's addicted to *Little House on the Prairie* reruns. I told her we'd take a trip to Missouri next summer to see the Laura Ingalls Wilder house, if she's still besotted. She said she has all the books?"

"She does."

He lowered his voice. "For Christmas we're going to try to find a doll that looks like Laura. Willow says she can make clothes from the period to give her a *Little House on the Prairie* wardrobe.

Taylor knew Maddie would love that and she wondered what *she* could give her that would be half as good.

She had to stop making comparisons.

Maddie came running out and skidded to a halt. Apparently the tour had been satisfactory.

"Willow wants to see your park," Jeremy told her. "Do you mind taking her?"

Maddie looked from Taylor to her father. Taylor saw worry lines crease her forehead, and she reached out and touched her daughter's shoulder. "Go ahead, hon. We'll have cookies and lemonade when you get back."

"It's okay?" Maddie asked.

Taylor knew she had to support Jeremy. "If your daddy says it's okay, of course it is."

Maddie looked relieved. "Come on, Willow."

Jeremy waited until their voices faded before he spoke. "Let's go in and sit."

"I don't like the sound of this."

"Don't decide ahead of time. I'm not planning to run off with her, but there *is* something we need to discuss."

Inside she motioned to the sofa, and they sat, a large space between them. She tried to remember the last time a man other than her father had sat here. The resulting revelation — that it had been her sixty-nine-year-old landlord — wasn't a good one.

"We don't have a lot of time, so I can't edge into this," Jeremy said. "While Maddie was with me, I took her to Vanderbilt to have her epilepsy treatment evaluated. I was able to get the appointment a couple of months ago."

Her mind went blank. Only the last part of his last sentence resonated. "A couple of months ago? And you never said a thing?"

"Vanderbilt has a pediatric epilepsy monitoring unit, Taylor. Believe it or not, they do everything they can to make the experience fun. They had all her medical records, too. She was only in for a couple of days, and I was with her 24/7."

Maddie had said nothing about this, and

Taylor was pretty sure why. "You told her not to tell me, didn't you?"

"I told her the news should come from me. And I think you'll agree that was wise."

His words were like small explosions in her head. They continued to resound, and anger seized her. "What wasn't wise? Trying to pull this off without me! Who do you think you are to —"

"I'm her *father,* and I've been left out of pretty much every decision about her treatment."

"I've always kept you informed!"

"Do you hear the difference? You've *informed* me. You haven't *consulted* me. I needed to be sure *our* daughter was getting the right treatment for a condition that's affecting her life."

"Why, Jeremy? Can't you love her the way she is? Do you and Willow need a perfect little girl to show off to your friends?"

The room fell silent. Taylor could see him working to contain his response. Despite herself, she felt a stab of guilt.

"I'm sorry, but how could you do this without asking?" she said at last.

"I knew if I asked, you would refuse."

She tried to think about what was best here. She and Jeremy could continue to argue about their rights, or they could move on. The argument wasn't settled, but she was almost sure they were only at the beginning of his news.

"All right," she said, as calmly as she could. "What did they say?"

"Despite what you may think, I was only willing to go so far in the evaluation without consulting you. The next step will be surgery to place a grid to help them determine *exactly* where the seizures are coming from. Then they can decide where to go from there."

He continued to speak, even as she tried to interrupt. "Taylor, please, I know how this sounds, but don't panic. The news so far is really positive. The neurology team thinks surgery to correct the problem is a good option. And if they can't correct it, they'll be able to lessen the impact, so the seizures can be controlled with medication. She could be seizure-free. They'll know more after the next round of evaluations, but —"

"Next round? You mean opening up Maddie's skull so they can root around inside it?"

He fell silent again.

"She's not a broken doll, Jeremy. She's a human being, and you're talking about destroying part of her brain. What if it doesn't work, and she's worse off when they've finished experimenting on her?"

His patience evaporated. "For God's sake, this is *not* an experiment! That's why they're so thorough when they test. Every surgery has risks, sure, even an appendectomy, but do you think I'd suggest we continue on this road if she was going to be harmed by anything we do?"

"If surgery was an option, I would know. Don't you think I would know? Until now I've handled all the medical stuff."

"I think your neurologist is old-fashioned and overly cautious. I think advances are happening every day, and he's not keeping up with them. I think Vanderbilt, which is dedicated to working with kids like Maddie, keeps up with every single one. They know the moment a discovery's made and when it's safe to use it in treatment."

"No. It's too dangerous. Hers isn't an easy case. I've read —"

"*You* are not a doctor. *I* am not a doctor. We have to let doctors give us all the options, then weigh them together and make the right decision."

She was so frightened that she couldn't think of anything except no. So she said it again. Louder this time.

He stared, then he shook his head. "This

is what comes of children having children."

"I think it's time for you to leave."

He ignored her. "Neither of us had the advantage of age or wisdom when that little girl was born. We've done well, considering, but we're older now, and wisdom has to creep in, Taylor. Every hard-earned ounce of wisdom I possess tells me that we *have* to move forward."

"I'm not going to give my permission."

"Then I'll see you in court."

She got to her feet. "You wouldn't dare!"

"I would and I will. If we can't come to a decision, we'll have to ask the courts to appoint a medical guardian to study this and make one for us, because I'm not backing down."

"I'm so sick of your threats."

"And I'm sick of having to use threats to make you see reason. You know who you've turned into?" He didn't wait for an answer and got to his feet, too. "Your mother."

"What is that supposed to mean?"

"Don't you remember? You used to complain and complain to me about how your mother tried to control you. You said she worried about everything and wouldn't let you do anything you wanted. Your mother hovered over you, but who's hovering now? Maybe having a child with epilepsy is perfect for you in its own way. Because it's a great excuse, isn't it? To control Maddie and keep her at your side because you need her there? Who else do you have?"

Speech fled. She couldn't form a reply, but she didn't need to. Jeremy started toward the door, flinging his last words over his shoulder as he opened it.

"I'll meet Willow and Maddie outside and say goodbye there. You and I will talk again when and if you can see reason. If not, we can both talk to a judge."

Charlotte sat at her bedroom window and stared into the distance. She couldn't see mountains, as her grandmother had from her window. She could see her shade garden and, in the distance, the edge of her neighbor's garage. Trees formed a canopy over a brick walkway leading to steps to an outdoor patio that was seldom used. She was sorry she couldn't wish herself there, but trudging down sounded tedious and exhausting, even though it was something that wouldn't have fazed her in healthier days.

She wondered if Maddie had returned home this afternoon, as Ethan had said. She tried to imagine a life in which she could pick up the telephone, call her daughter and ask. She and Taylor would laugh about

Maddie's return, and Taylor would tell her mother that Maddie had gotten a tan, or pierced her ears. Charlotte would hang up after speaking directly to her granddaughter and promising a visit, so she could hear all the details about life in Nashville. She would arrive with a silly gift, like those stretchy bracelets she'd seen girls Maddie's age wearing.

The window seat, despite a plush cushion, felt like steel against her legs. Today had been spent either napping or sitting at the window. Ethan hadn't called, and she imagined he never would. She'd asked herself a hundred times if she'd been wrong not to tell him sooner about the leukemia. If so, which time would have been the right one? In his workshop, when he'd showed her the plans for his factory? Poolside, with children splashing and puppies yapping?

Last night, right before he put his arms around her?

Clearly she'd been wrong, yet she couldn't ferret out that perfect moment, the one she had obviously missed.

Tomorrow she was going to the hospital, so the first round of chemo could be administered and her reaction observed. If all went well, she could leave and go back each day for a week. But there were no guarantees.

There were still people who didn't know she was ill, and things to do in preparation. She was trying to formulate a plan when there was a knock at her door.

Harmony opened it.

"Sam Ferguson's here."

Samantha had been at the top of Charlotte's list of unfinished business. She wondered if Ethan had told her the news and Samantha had come to sympathize. Then she discarded the idea, because Ethan would be the last person to do her dirty work. Most likely Samantha was here to see why Charlotte hadn't showed up at the clinic today. The walls were painted now, and today the volunteers had planned to move in tables and chairs Covenant Academy no longer needed in their preschool. Charlotte knew Samantha had expected her to be there to help arrange them and see what was still lacking.

"I'll be right out," she told Harmony.

"You're sure? I could bring her in here."

"I'm fine. I'll be right there."

Harmony looked doubtful, but she left. Charlotte slipped on shoes and combed her hair, then she went to find Sam.

Samantha was in the family room with the puppies, but she didn't have Edna with her. For once Charlotte was glad not to have the little girl around. She could tell Samantha the truth in privacy.

"I hope you don't mind me stopping by," Samantha said.

"Exactly the opposite. I'm really glad you did. Would you like something to drink?"

"The volunteers brought in a five-gallon jug of ice water, and I'm floating as it is. You were missed."

She was holding a puppy — Velveteen, Charlotte thought — and now she set her down and stood.

"I'm sorry I couldn't be there," Charlotte said.

"Something's wrong, isn't it?"

Charlotte wondered if anybody had glimpsed this thoughtful, perceptive woman inside the troubled teen Samantha had once been. She guessed Georgia had seen the truth and done everything she could to be sure Samantha soared. She also guessed that she, like Charlotte, had been devastated by her daughter's early choices.

The difference was, Georgia had stood by *her* daughter.

"Something *is* wrong," Charlotte said.

"You're not well. I've had my suspicions."

"Let's sit."

Samantha joined her on the sofa, the most comfortable one in the house. Charlotte propped pillows behind her back, which seemed to ache now no matter what she did. Slowly she told Samantha the truth. What she had learned and when, what she had done about it, why she had chosen not to say anything.

"I wanted time without the leukemia hanging over every interaction," she finished. "I wanted time to straighten out my life — well, as much as I could — without people responding to me because they thought I was dying and they knew they had to." She paused, because the same explanation had fallen flat with Ethan. "But I guess that's hard to understand."

"Understand? Not at all," Samantha said. "I think it's courageous, Charlotte. Sometimes when people face a challenge, like leukemia, it brings out the worst in them. They dive into themselves, and they never surface again. But you've used your diagnosis to reach out. I hope I'll do the same if I'm ever in a similar situation."

Charlotte felt tears on her cheeks. "Thank you. Not everyone has understood."

"I'm just guessing, but I would think there are two sets of people who don't. Those who don't care about you at all, and those who care so much they can't face what might happen."

"You're such a wise woman."

"Oh, I came by it at a price, believe me." Samantha reached for her hand. "You remember I'm a nurse, right? Even if blood disorders aren't my specialty, you can always count on me to go to bat for you. You'll call when you need me?"

"I will. I'm so sorry to be opting out of helping at the clinic. I never meant to start something I couldn't finish."

"You can't be there. It's germ soup. But I'll come by regularly to give you a precise rundown." She laced her fingers through Charlotte's. "Do you want me to tell Taylor the news? Because I will, if you think it might be a good thing for her to know."

"Ethan knows. I suspect he may tell her. Would you do something else for me, though?"

"Anything I can."

"If I die and Taylor hasn't found her way back, will you tell her I really *did* understand? That I knew it was my fault the path was impassable, and that no matter what, I loved her."

Samantha looked stricken. "Whew."

"You'll do it?"

"I will. Of course."

Charlotte tried to lighten the discussion. "I may come through this with flying colors.

I might become a medical miracle."

"Don't quit five minutes before the medical miracle," Samantha said.

Charlotte managed a laugh. Then she slid over and hugged her. "You and Edna are an unexpected gift. I've treasured knowing both of you."

Samantha hugged her back. "You just keep treasuring, okay? This game's not over, and you've got a cheering section. Just don't forget it."

CHAPTER THIRTY-SEVEN

First Day Journal: June 21

The sun is just coming up, something it does slowly anywhere the horizon is rimmed with mountains, but the birds are never fooled. They begin their morning conversation well before dawn and catch up on all the news.

Gran was convinced birds are the smartest creatures in our universe, because from the very beginning, they know how to fly. No person can spread God-given wings and soar above trees just because the time is right. It's an odd thing to be humbled by birds, but this morning, as I listen to cardinals and blue jays, I'm reminded I should be.

Nell takes Monday mornings off, so the welcome fragrance of coffee is absent. I don't know what Nell does on the mornings she's not here. When she's not watching the sun come up from my kitchen, does her husband bring her breakfast? Does he pad softly upstairs, a tray with a rose against his chest, or maybe just a mug of steaming coffee she didn't have to make herself? Maybe he lets her sleep because he knows sleep is what she wants most of all.

When Ethan and I lived together, I was always in charge of coffee and Taylor's school day while he cooked. Ethan's culinary skills vanished at noon, but his breakfasts were extraordinary. I'm sorry now that I didn't eat more, that I worried about my weight or my schedule too much to sit across from him at the breakfast table enjoying his omelets or waffles. That whether Taylor's hair was perfectly combed or her homework in the right section of her backpack mattered more to me than gratitude.

I'm sorry now that before we walked out the door to start our days, I so often forgot to tell them both how much I loved them.

Today I receive my first two injections in the next stage of this battle, and I've learned I won't lose more hair, won't need an intravenous catheter. I'll receive injections for a week, then have a glorious four-week vacation before the next round.

Phil claims some patients with my particular history, genetics and chemistry have even gone back into remission with this protocol, but I know many more have not. Rising early to see the sun come up over distant mountains seems like the best tactic in the battle I'm waging. So many mornings of my life passed without me noting anything except my daily calendar.

No matter what happens next, I'll never make that mistake again.

Chapter Thirty-Eight

Analiese waited until late afternoon to visit Charlotte. She knew today was the beginning of the new round of chemo, and she'd debated dropping by. In the end she'd decided to time her visit so if Harmony was heading for work, she could stay for a while herself, just to be sure Charlotte was all right.

Her timing was perfect. Harmony was just coming outside when Analiese arrived, and they chatted on the doorstep.

"How'd she do?" Analiese asked.

"She's tired. Right now she's in the den, resting on the sofa. They gave her some medication for nausea, and it helped, but it's not perfect. I made vegetable soup. I hope she'll eat some."

"Maybe I can convince her to try."

"I won't be away long. I'm not working tonight, in case Charlotte needs me, but she asked me to drive out to the kennel to get some special kibble for the puppies. She says she'll be fine."

Analiese could see that Harmony wasn't sure of that. She was worried. "I'll stay with her until you get back, or until she kicks me out."

Harmony still looked uneasy. "If the minister of my church at home visited Charlotte, he would preach a sermon about how God sends cancer and heart disease, you know, to punish us for our sins. So if you're planning to go there, please don't."

Before Analiese could even think of an answer, Harmony tilted her head in question. "I guess you're different. Right?"

"Well, he — I'm assuming this is a he?"

Harmony nodded.

"He and I live on the same planet. We have that in common. Otherwise? Not a lot."

"Good. Because I don't want anybody making Charlotte feel worse about anything."

Analiese was impressed at how devoted Harmony was, but she realized the devotion might come at a price. Charlotte's prognosis wasn't good. What was this girl going to do if Charlotte died? She really couldn't ask. Analiese wasn't Harmony's minister, and she didn't want to inject a note of negativity into the conversation.

"I don't think God exists to make people feel worse," she said instead. "I think my job is to bring a message of hope and comfort." She smiled to make sure that didn't sound pompous. "If you ever need either, will you let me know?"

Harmony just smiled back.

Inside, Analiese called Charlotte's name and searched until she found the den. Charlotte sat up, but not quickly, and pushed a wool afghan to the side.

"I've had better days. Thanks for asking," she said.

Analiese pulled a chair closer, afraid if she sat on the sofa and jostled Charlotte, the nausea would be worse.

"I used to work the health beat on my first TV job, and I remember some tips on controlling nausea. One of them's to stay hydrated. Can I get you something to drink?"

"I have a glass of water." Charlotte waved her hand toward the table.

"Little snacks are best. I can find the kitchen."

"Is there anything in the whole wide world you don't know *something* about?"

"I don't know how it feels to be you. How does it, about now?"

Charlotte leaned her head back, so she

was staring at the ceiling. "I'm not ready for this again. Honestly, this is a walk in the park compared to what I went through at Duke, chemolite, but I got spoiled. I had some good weeks. I was hoping for more."

"You're a fighter. You aren't going to quit."

"No." She lifted her head. "No?"

"No." Analiese shook her head in emphasis.

"I've spent the past few days telling people I might die. Of course, I didn't put it that way, but they got the message."

"I'm sure that was hard."

"Ethan didn't take it well." Charlotte rested her head against the sofa again, as if it hurt to hold it up. "He's angry with me for not telling him in the first place. He thinks I was manipulating him. I'm not sure I'll ever see him again. And Taylor hasn't even opened the letter I wrote her. I wonder how I could have made so many mistakes."

Analiese knew about the letter from a previous conversation and was sorry Taylor was refusing to read it.

"Let's see . . . You're human?"

"I never wanted to be."

"I'm afraid it wasn't a choice."

"I woke up this morning all ready to face this, and now, I'm not sure I want to. What's the point? I've been trying to set things right, but when I look back on the past weeks, I don't think I've accomplished a lot."

"Of course you have. But if you expected to accomplish everything? Then that's just the same old problem, isn't it? Impossibly high expectations for yourself and everybody around you. You can't make people feel one way or the other about the leukemia *or* the way you've chosen to deal with it. There's no rule that says the moment you found out you were ill you had to tell anyone. But once *they* found out, there's also no rule that says they aren't allowed to be upset."

"I do know that. It's just . . ."

"It's just easier to be sensible and positive when you're not fighting the urge to puke."

"I'll remember that."

"I didn't just come to share my incredible store of wisdom. I have an idea I'd like to explore with you. Are you feeling up to it?"

"You're consulting me on the first day of chemo?"

Despite the response, Analiese knew she'd piqued Charlotte's interest. "I'm only going to share it if you promise to eat a little of Harmony's soup."

"I'm envisioning your last life. Do you remember forcing Israelite slaves to erect the pyramids? Weren't you the one with the whip?"

"Weren't you the pharaoh giving the orders?"

"Don't make me laugh. It doesn't help."

"The soup will."

"What's the idea about? The one you want my opinion on?"

"Your house up in the mountains. I guess there's no chance you'll want to zip up there this week and see it again?"

"I'll give you the key if you want to go." Charlotte hesitated. "A small bowl, but I do mean small. Then you'll tell me?"

"Only if you eat every single bite."

"Well? I'm waiting to see the ring," Rilla told Harmony, after a greeting hug. She'd met Harmony at the door using her walker, and she looked happy to have done so much on her own.

"No ring," Harmony said.

They moved slowly into the family room, which was aptly named, since it was clear this was where the family did most of their living. Everything here was made for comfort. Sofas wide and soft enough for naps, recliners and rockers, a brick fireplace so large that if the power went off, the family could probably cook in it and heat the house.

Rilla carefully settled herself in a rocker. "I guess the lack of a ring could mean a couple of things. It wasn't ready when he went to pick it up. He's planning to give it to you later. . . ."

"Or I decided not to marry him. That's the one to choose if you want the grand prize." Harmony flopped down onto the sofa across from her friend. "I'm okay, so don't worry. It wasn't pretty. Davis and I will be speaking through lawyers from this point, I guess. He knows he'll have to pay child support. We'll just have to work out details. I'm keeping the car, since I'd already sold my old one."

"I'm so sorry."

"You don't need to be. I was so worried about our future, mine and the baby's, I was willing to overlook everything else. Comes right down to it, I'm not even sure I like the guy, much less love him. And that couldn't be good for anybody." As Rilla listened and nodded, Harmony explained her theory that Davis had only proposed in the first place to keep "unwed father" off his résumé.

"So what will you do?" Rilla asked.

"I'm not sure. Charlotte needs me now,

but . . ." Harmony couldn't put her fear into words, that soon Charlotte might not need anybody's help, that she would be beyond help.

"You'll keep the job at Cuppa?"

"I don't honestly see how. I wouldn't earn enough working the lunch shift, and unless I luck into someone wise and wonderful who'll babysit at a bargain during the dinner shift, I can't afford to work there."

"Will you miss it?"

"It's been fun, but I'm ready to find something else." Harmony was also ready to change the subject, because there were too many unknowns in her future, and talking didn't help. "It's great to see you up and around. You look happy to be answering the door again."

"That's not all I'm happy about."

"Are the boys coming home for good?"

"They are, and we got some news last night that might be great for you, too."

Harmony didn't have a clue what Rilla meant. "How?"

"Brad and I got the insurance settlement for my accident. The other driver's company finally stopped contesting the payment. And that means now we can hire full-time help."

"Until you recover?"

"And beyond. We've needed help for a

while. Between the kennels and the gardens and all the animals, *and* the kids? Plus my plan to start marketing herbs and goat cheese at the farmer's market next summer? Well, it was just too much to do alone. So in his free time Brad was fixing up the apartment above the garage. It was pretty run-down, so we'd never even used it for guests."

"I didn't realize there was an apartment there. I figured that floor was storage."

"It's got tons of potential. He's already handled most of the renovations, except the bathroom and kitchen. Then, after the accident, he didn't have any free time. Now, finally, we can get somebody out here to finish them, then our new employee can live in the apartment as part of her compensation. And I'm thinking that person ought to be you."

Rilla's speech had been a lot to take in, and it had been delivered in only two breaths. "Me?" Harmony asked.

"You. First, I really like you, and you've already proved you're a wonderful caretaker and a hard worker. Look how you took to raising the puppies. And look how much you've helped me for no reason other than kindness. Second, I'm betting you like growing things, too, and whatever you don't know yet, I can teach you. Third, you're fun to be around. I thought of you right away when the settlement came in, but you were getting married. Now it seems like fate. A cute little apartment with plenty of privacy, no need to pay for child care because your baby can grow up with my children and be right here with you. Lots of good food in the garden. Doesn't it seem doable?"

"Doable?"

Rilla looked perplexed. "No?"

"Not doable. Heaven. You would actually consider me?"

"Not consider. I *want* you."

For a moment Harmony let herself enjoy the possibility, visions of herself right here at Capable Canines, doing all the things she loved. Raising her baby in a nearly perfect environment instead of a shabby efficiency carved out of a run-down house in town. Sharing child care with Rilla, who would know everything Harmony didn't.

Then she remembered Charlotte. "Rilla, I can't leave Charlotte yet. She needs me even worse than you do." She explained about the leukemia, and Rilla reacted with genuine sympathy.

"I'm so sorry. I was looking forward to getting to know her better. I really hope she comes through this."

"Me, too," Harmony said.

"*Of course* I want you to stay with her. I know you need to, and we have to finish the apartment first, anyway. Likely that'll take a few more weeks, maybe even a month, because Brad's just now taking bids. My first order of business is to bring the boys back, not the horses or goats. And it's too late for much of a garden this year, anyway. So at this point, I can do fine with a temporary helper during the day, somebody who'll do a little light housework and make sure the boys don't get into mischief. Brad's already checking into that."

"But I don't know how long it'll be before I could be here."

"Then we'll play it by ear as long as we can. As long as you're interested?"

"Am I!" Harmony suddenly realized something. "Could I keep Velvet? I mean, as my own dog? I could pay you for her, a little at a time. And she could stay in the apartment with the baby and me."

Rilla looked pleased. "I was never going to sell Velvet. I was going to have her spayed and find her a good home. Sounds like I just did."

Ethan wasn't sure how he had ended up at Charlotte's home place. He had decided to hike, his tried-and-true way to work off stress, and he'd driven out toward Hot Springs, then beyond, to find a good trail. The next thing he knew, he was bumping over the gravel road toward the house where his ex-wife had grown up, the house for which he'd been caretaker and landlord until their divorce.

He hadn't been back to the log house in more than a decade, although oddly, he'd kept a piece of it with him. During his renovation of the spacious country kitchen, he'd removed a cabinet door to refinish at home, then forgotten about it because later, he'd decided to turn that particular cabinet into open shelves.

When he and Charlotte had divorced, the cabinet door — natural alder under three layers of paint — had been packed up with all his other woodworking supplies and tools. He had only recently uncovered it in his storeroom while looking for wood to complete a project.

The door had been mostly stripped but never finished, so Ethan had sanded it and wiped it with the lightest of stains, then finished it with tung oil to bring out the beauty of the grain. Finally he had put it in the trunk of his car to show Charlotte when he'd visited her on Saturday. He had expected her to laugh and call him a hoarder. But he hadn't gotten around to taking the door out of the car, and, of course, their time together had ended very differently than he'd expected.

The door was still in the trunk, and now he used it as an excuse. He didn't know if the log house was rented these days, but if no one was living there, he would simply leave the door on the porch. Charlotte or her tenants could sort out what to do with it.

If Charlotte remained well enough to sort out anything.

Ethan was tired, and not from hiking, since he'd yet to get out of his car. He hadn't slept well since the scene with Charlotte, and he doubted he would sleep well tonight after wallowing in her past. Yet somehow it seemed right to be here, in the place that had shaped his ex-wife into the woman she was. He didn't want clues. He had Charlotte figured out. Maybe he just wanted to say goodbye to lingering memories.

He was nearly at the house before he saw the aging Toyota parked beneath the spreading oak at the base of the steps. He had hoped to do his hiking here, but he hadn't counted on it. He waited for a dog welcoming committee, and when none approached, he pulled up beside the Toyota and got out.

The front door was open, so he climbed up to the porch and called inside. "Hello?"

"Just a minute."

The voice belonged to a woman. He went back to the car and got the door out of the back and carried it up the stairs just as Analiese Wagner came out.

"Ethan?"

Analiese was the last person he'd expected, and he was immediately wary. "Is Charlotte here?"

"No, I'm alone."

"I'm just dropping this off. Long story, but it belongs to the house."

"Go ahead and put it inside. I'm here looking around. Mondays are my day off."

He pondered that as he carried the door to the kitchen. He imagined ministers needed time away, just like anyone else, maybe even more so. But this seemed like a strange place to spend it.

When he came back outside Analiese was sitting on a metal glider he remembered from previous visits. One of the tenants — he couldn't remember which — had rescued it from somebody's trash, sanded and painted it, and added cushions. He had always chosen handy renters.

"Join me?" she asked.

He dropped down beside her. "You never really said why you're looking around."

"Charlotte brought me here about a month ago and showed me the house and land. She wants to do something with the property, something to benefit others. I don't think she wants to sell it."

"I don't know why. There are lots of bad memories tied up in it."

"The house was in her family for a long time and meant a lot to her grandparents. Do you think your daughter might want it?"

"I'm not sure Taylor even remembers visiting here. The house was usually rented, and besides, she would have her own bad memories tied up in anything from her mother's family."

Analiese was silent for a moment, then she turned to him. Again he realized how lovely she was. She didn't make a point of it, though, like other women might have. She dressed well and took care of herself, but she was careful not to project anything other than professional detachment laced with concern.

"You're very angry at Charlotte right now, aren't you?"

"She told you that?"

"I was with her a while ago. She started

chemo this morning, and she's pretty down."

He wondered if he would ever hear news about Charlotte that didn't propel his emotions into high gear. Would he ever just think, *Uh-huh, I can see that,* then go on to whatever else was more important in his life?

"She feels like a failure," Analiese said. "And I don't think I'm talking out of turn. I'm sure she'd tell you the same thing."

"She has."

"I'm under the impression," she said carefully, "that you're angry with her for not telling you right away that she has leukemia. Angry at her for wanting to have a little time together without illness muddying the waters."

"Muddying the waters? What a delicate way to put it." He heard the anger in his voice, and despite himself, he wasn't able to control it. "Not telling me she dented a fender, that's muddying the waters. Having a disease that might be fatal? That's more like a tsunami, don't you think?"

"What do I think?" She seemed to ponder that. "I guess my own waters are muddied, because I like her. I never used to, so I know how infuriating she can be. But I've watched her struggle with her illness, and I have so much admiration for the honesty with which she regards her life and how hard she's trying to end it well."

"End it?"

"Despite the clerical collar I don't have a pipeline to the Almighty, but I've done a little research. Charlotte has an acute form of leukemia, and I doubt she'll die from something else in the far-flung future. She doubts it, too. Right now I think her final goal is to die well and leave behind a world that's a little better because she was in it."

Ethan thought Analiese's spin on this was, not surprisingly, too positive. But wasn't hope what she was paid for? Right along with faith in God and her fellow man?

He struggled to sound rational. "Maybe she's just trying to rack up points with that Almighty you mentioned."

"Really? You think so? Charlotte strikes you that way, as a woman so scared of what comes next that she's trying to hedge her bets?"

She said it lightly, but he heard the rebuke and knew he deserved it.

"She manipulated me," he said.

"Not for the first time, I imagine. I understand right now it feels like one time too many, particularly when you were beginning to let your guard down with her."

"How would you know *what* I was doing?"

"I was at the pool party, too. I saw you with her. I recognized what I saw."

His throat threatened to close. He rested his head in his hands and wished he had stayed home.

"It's very hard to take," she said softly. "It's very hard to take when somebody you love is dying."

He knew better than to let that hang between them without refuting it, but the words wouldn't come, and he was afraid if he tried to speak, tears might come instead.

He felt her fingertips rest briefly on his arm. "Any time you want to talk," she offered, "I can listen."

He didn't lift his head after he heard her drive away. He sat there, face still buried in his hands, and listened to the deep silence that surrounded him.

Chapter Thirty-Nine

On Friday afternoon the telephone was ringing when Ethan let himself into his house. Since early morning he had been busy consulting with the bottle factory contractor who would begin work on Ethan's unit on Monday, along with finishing another that had just sold.

The sale had been the high point of a week that had begun badly, but even that hadn't lifted his spirits. Now, as he hurried to catch the phone, he wondered wearily what this call might bring. More bad news about the struggle Taylor and Jeremy were engaged in? News of another injury for Maddie?

News that Charlotte had taken a turn for the worse?

Of course, he didn't really know what that last possibility might mean, since he knew so little about her disease or its treatment. She'd made sure of that by not telling him she was sick.

He picked up the phone and barked out a hello.

"Ethan, is that you?"

He relaxed a little. Judy hadn't called since early spring, nor had he called her, but the voice of an ex-wife was not a voice a man forgot.

"How are you?" he asked. "It's been a while."

"Apparently I'm as busy as you are. We really haven't made time to chat, have we?"

He asked how she was, and she asked the same. He told her about the bottle factory, and she told him about the pro bono work she was doing for legal services, in addition to her cases at her law firm. There was an uncomfortable silence, then she went on.

"I'm not just calling to catch up. I'm getting married again. I wanted you to hear the news from me."

How did a man know when a relationship was truly over? When he didn't feel a pang of regret. At that moment the only thing that came to mind was how nice it was that one of his exes knew how to be honest.

"Hey, that's great," he said. "Who's the lucky guy?"

"Somebody I met on a ski trip last winter."

"I hope he lives in Chicago." Ethan uttered the words without considering them first. Too late he realized they sounded like an indictment.

"Luckily, he does. Flying back and forth cross-country would be tough."

He seemed to remember Judy ending their marriage because flying back and forth would be *impossible,* but he knew better than to say it. "I hope this is one doozy of a love affair."

She kept her voice light. "It had better be. They say three's a charm. Luckily I think I've learned a thing or two. We'll be happy."

He couldn't help himself. "Want to tell me what you learned?"

"And bore you silly?"

He found himself shaking his head and translated that into speech. "Maybe it'll help if I get a next time."

"I'm not sure that's possible."

"You don't think there's a single woman anywhere who might be interested?"

"Of course that's not what I meant."

"Enlighten me, then."

She was silent for half a dozen heartbeats before she spoke. "You're sure you're ready to hear my revelations, Ethan?"

He frowned, because he wasn't sure he liked where this was going. "Why not give me a try?"

"Then here's what I've realized. Never marry a man who's still in love with another woman. Jay's not. He actually dislikes his ex-wife as much as he says he does."

Ethan lowered himself into the closest chair. "Would you like to be even clearer?"

"Didn't you ever realize there was somebody sleeping in the bed right between us? I know you were furious at Charlotte. I know you didn't want to be anywhere near her. But after I left, didn't you finally get that you were still in love with her?"

"I have no idea where this is coming from."

"Some people fall in love once and they never fall out of it, even if the relationship falls apart. At the worst they become stalkers. At the best they remarry and honestly try to fall in love with their new partner, but it never quite takes. Deep down, they're still yearning for the person they lost."

"I can't believe you think that was true for me."

"I *know* it's true. It wasn't the same for me. When my first marriage broke up, I was relieved, pure and simple. Then I married you, and when *our* marriage broke up —"

"I can't wait to hear this."

"When our marriage broke up," she repeated patiently, "I was relieved again, because by then I'd figured out there was nothing I could do to make you love me. Not that you didn't a little. I do know that. We had some great times. But you were never really invested in me, not in the way I wanted to be invested in you."

"Judy, come on. I'd learned the hard way *not* to be that invested in anybody again. I thought you had, too."

"You're using that to refute what I've said? Because you're as much as admitting I'm right."

She sounded like the attorney she was, and he could feel himself beginning to seethe. "That doesn't mean I was yearning for Charlotte while I was married to you."

"You never stopped yearning for what you had with Charlotte. You never fell out of love with her, or at least not out of love with the way things were when they were good."

In the space of a sentence his annoyance turned into something darker, something that until this week he hadn't even realized he had inside him.

"Well, you'll like this," he said. "Charlotte's dying. Maybe that will get her out of my system once and for all. Do you think that's what it'll take?"

As he fought back more angry words she was silent, then she said, "I'm so sorry,

Ethan. If I'd known . . ."

"What? If you'd known, you wouldn't have told me things you didn't have the courage to say when they actually *mattered?* When we still had a chance of straightening out misunderstandings and making our own marriage work?"

Now *she* was angry, too. "My God, listen to yourself. You think we actually had a prayer of being happy? Just ask yourself this. Would you be this torn up if I told you *I* was dying?"

He gathered every ounce of self-control so he could end the phone call politely. "I wish you the best, Judy, I really do. If you've figured out what you need to make your next marriage work, I'm happy. But take some advice from *me.* This time, if you think something or someone is interfering with your happiness, be sure you tell your husband while you're still married to him. Don't wait until another divorce is final."

He hung up carefully; then he kicked the cabinet underneath the telephone so hard that the phone tipped and clattered to the floor.

Five chemo treatments, with two more to go. Since returning from the hospital that morning, Charlotte had spent the rest of the day and evening telling herself she *would* get through this. Two days were nothing. Phil had increased the antinausea medication, and so far the only other side effects had been swelling and soreness around the injection sites, and a bone-deep fatigue. They were carefully monitoring her progress, and additional tests were a fact of life. If any of them had been particularly worrisome, Phil would have called.

She was alone in the house. Harmony hadn't wanted to leave for work this evening, worried Charlotte might need someone nearby, but Charlotte had made her go. The house was silent except for yips and squeals from the family room.

Today the fatigue was the hardest to bear. She could use warm compresses where the injections had been given, and if she took the meds on time, and ate and drank small quantities, she could control the nausea. The fatigue, though, was insidious. She was like a balloon with a small pinprick. The air that had lifted her above the earth to soar with the birds was slowly escaping, and unless someone found the hole and mended it quickly, she would be a puddle on the ground. Hopefully a colorful, gracefully arranged puddle, but a puddle still.

She had dozed continually. Every time

she'd tried to write in her journal, her eyelids had drifted closed, proving, she supposed, that she had nothing of interest left to say. Next she had wandered into the media room, hoping television would distract her. Over the years she had spent so little time in front of it that she didn't know what to watch, and now she felt like a voyeur peeking in the windows of people she'd never met. Even the game shows were foreign to her. She hadn't solved a puzzle on *Wheel of Fortune,* and most of the categories on *Jeopardy!* made her even sorrier she hadn't spent time just reading for the fun of it.

When the doorbell rang, she wasn't sure she'd actually heard it. The telephone had rung several times during the day, and without answering she had listened to well-wishers leaving messages on her machine. The word had obviously gotten out that she was ill, most likely through someone at Falconview, and as callers filled their allotted thirty seconds, she'd asked herself not only if they really cared but why they should.

Those questions had helped fill the time, but they had left her even more exhausted.

The doorbell rang again, and this time she imagined the UPS man with a package she didn't want. Or maybe a neighbor who wondered why Charlotte's yard service had trimmed too much off the hedge that separated them, or not enough. Staring at the ceiling, as she had for most of the day, she had come to regret all the petty interactions that filled her life. She thought doorbells were something she wouldn't miss if the new chemo was unsuccessful.

It seemed to her that somebody had designed the world backward. Facing death should come first, then slowly, after coming to terms with dying and learning what was really important, each person could begin living. Slowly, of course, picking up energy as the body grew younger and healthier. Until . . .

She didn't have that part worked out, but it had given her something to think about.

When the doorbell rang one more time, she pushed herself off the sofa and made her way through the house to the front door. She didn't even check the peephole. If masked men with assault rifles were standing on her porch, she thought she would invite them inside to end it all now.

She opened the door.

Ethan stood on the porch, jeans, dark polo shirt, hands in pockets. She thought the masked men would have been easier.

"Is Taylor all right?" she asked.

"Yes, she's —"

"And Maddie?"

He nodded.

"Then we're done here." She started to close the door, but he put his foot in the crack.

"I hope that's not true," he said, his voice a hoarse rumble over the sound of crickets and, from farther away, the clipped screech of a nighthawk.

The outside air smelled like summer, wild roses in the woods, honeysuckle beginning its perfumed reign. For a moment she just breathed it in, looking for the right words.

"I don't think I have the energy for more indictments of my character. Tell you what . . ." She took another deep breath and let it out slowly. "Put everything you despise about me in writing. I may even get to it before Taylor gets to *my* letter." She looked at his shoe, still blocking the door, then back up at him. "And as lovely as it is out here tonight, I think we're finished."

"How are you feeling?"

"Angry."

"May I come in?"

"It's not a good time." She considered that. "And I don't think there will be a good time."

"I'm so sorry, Charlotte."

She had very little fight left in her. Fight was one thing the chemo had rooted out and disposed of. If it rooted out the leukemic blasts cluttering her bloodstream half as well, she might live another decade.

"I appreciate that." She glanced at his foot again. "Ethan, if that's what you came to say, I think you're finished now."

"I don't want you to die."

She felt a flash of anger. She didn't want his pity. She didn't want a guilt-driven apology. "Here's a thought to comfort you. Ten years went by after our divorce, and I think we spoke once. So it won't be that different, okay?"

"I'd rather do this inside."

She was too exhausted to argue. She left him to decide what to do next and started through the house back into the media room, flipping off the television, then settling herself in a corner of the sofa with her feet on the cushion beside her.

He followed close behind. She watched him take in the afghan rumpled on the floor, the prescription bottles, the water glass and plate of fresh fruit gathering fruit flies that Harmony had left for her to snack on. The bananas and apples had turned brown, and the yogurt dip had dissolved into a watery layer.

"Have you eaten anything this evening?" he asked.

"You don't need to worry."

"I could make you an omelet."

Her stomach flipped, either in revulsion or hunger, she really wasn't sure. "No thanks."

"You used to love my omelets."

"I'm not up for a trip down memory lane. You've done your duty, Ethan. You've apologized, and now, if I die sooner than later, you don't have to wish you'd been kinder. I understand that impulse, believe me. I'm coming at it from a different angle, but it's all part of the same thing."

He sat gingerly on the sofa, a cushion away, but still close enough to touch.

"How's the treatment going?"

"As treatments go, not that bad. I haven't spent time in the ICU. I haven't seen strange visions beside my bed. I just feel like I've been turned inside out. And I need a lot of naps, starting now."

"You were in the hospital for a month in the spring? That's what you told me the other day."

She didn't answer.

"I can't imagine what that must have been like. And nobody knew?"

"It seemed like the thing to do."

"You weren't taking the leukemia seriously, were you? I remember whenever you came down with a cold or the flu, you just kept going. I had to drag you to the hospital to have Taylor. I think you would have worked through the delivery, if I'd let you."

She stared at him and didn't say a word.

"Did you think if you didn't tell anybody, maybe you could just ignore it?"

"Are you going to give me a lecture on facing a deadly disease? Because you have so much experience yourself?"

"I'm just trying to figure it out."

"It's not calculus. I wanted to be me. I didn't want to be me-with-leukemia. I knew I would have to tell everyone eventually. I would have told you when the moment was right."

"Right before you headed down Merrimon Avenue to pick out a coffin?"

"That's unnecessarily cruel."

"Do you know the only thing I could think about when I discovered the truth?"

"That I'd set you up? That I was leading you on? Manipulating you?"

He reached for a foot, bare and sadly in need of a pedicure. Despite her resistance, he pulled it into his lap and began to slowly massage the instep with his thumbs.

"No, what I was thinking was I'd finally

found you again, and before I could even be sure, I'd lost you for the last time."

His hands were warm against her skin, the pressure exactly right. But of course it would be, since he'd done this so often so many years ago.

She tried to pull her foot away. "That's not what you said. And stop doing that."

He held firm and didn't stop. "I know what I said, Lulu. Maybe as far as it went, the rest of it was true, too. We have a history of not being straight with each other. But here's the news flash, one I've been trying hard for years not to read. You aren't the only one who wasn't straight, and you never were. Years ago I saw things were falling apart, and what did I do? I closed my eyes. I wanted our marriage to succeed, so I refused to see that it wasn't. And I waited until everything finally exploded, then I walked out on you and everything we'd built together. Just the way I walked out on you the other night. If I don't like what I see? I guess I disappear."

This was so unexpected, she didn't know what to say. And when tears slowly filled the silence, she knew she was too tired to control her emotions.

"I am so, so sorry," he said softly, his hands still now. "For all those years ago when I didn't try to put things right. For walking out with Taylor instead of trying to find a way for all of us to stay together. For walking out last Saturday when I learned how sick you are. *That* most of all."

"You don't owe me anything. Most of that . . ." She swallowed helplessly, but the tears kept falling. "It was a long time ago."

"Time's one thing. Love is another."

"Love?"

"Apparently *I* disappear but my feelings *don't.* Tonight somebody told me I never stopped loving you, that I'm a one-woman man. And as angry as that made me, as convinced as I was that she was crazy, what was I really thinking? That you were here in this big house alone, and I could be here with you if I just dropped the act."

"I don't want your pity!"

"I *do* feel sorry for you — how could I not? But it's a small part of what I feel."

"You don't have to do this. You don't have to be nice to me. I've made it this far just fine."

"Not so fine." He slid closer, until they were face-to-face. He touched her cheek, then he pushed back a lock of hair. "I love you. Live forever, but if you don't? Let me be with you while I can."

She looked for reasons other than the ones

he'd expressed to explain why he had come. She tried to push away her own feelings, because she couldn't face another disappointment, not now, when she was hanging by a thread.

"You love me, too," he said softly.

"I've never been sure what that means."

"Oh, you know." He reached for her hand and put it over his heart. "You were always afraid to acknowledge it, but you did love me, and you've never forgotten."

She wilted. "I don't think I can survive if you walk out the door again, Ethan, so be sure you know what you're in for. I don't have the strength . . . to pick myself up and go on."

"If you don't have the strength to go on, Lulu, let me carry you for a while. Until you're better."

"I don't know that I'm going to get better." She wiped her face on her sleeve, then she met his gaze. "The odds aren't good. You need to understand what you're getting into."

He let out a long breath, and she could see something close to despair in his eyes. He put his arms around her and pulled her close. She rested her cheek against his chest, and her arms slipped around his waist.

"Then die holding my hand," he whispered against her hair. "Because I'm never going to let go of yours. Not ever again."

Chapter Forty

When Taylor and Maddie stopped by Ethan's house on Sunday he wasn't home, and a neighbor told them his car had been gone all weekend. Since he hadn't mentioned a trip out of town, Taylor was concerned, but not very. Ethan liked to hike, and sometimes he took a backpacking tent and a few basic supplies, in case he found a particularly pretty spot to settle in for the night. As a young teen she had often gone with him. She wished she and Maddie could accompany him occasionally, but she worried Maddie might get hurt on the trail during a seizure and Taylor wasn't willing to take chances.

She tried her father's cell phone, but when she got voice mail, she hung up without leaving a message and drove to Samantha's.

The day was beautiful, and she hoped Maddie and Edna could play at the park while she and Sam chatted. Except for the brief trip with Willow, Maddie hadn't been to the park since her fall. It was time for her to go back now, time to let the other children see she wasn't afraid to be there.

Samantha's VW was parked in her circular driveway. Taylor parked behind it, and Maddie skipped ahead to ring the doorbell.

Samantha, in faded jeans and a black ribbed tank top, greeted them and sent Maddie in search of Edna.

Taylor followed her daughter inside. "Feel like taking the hobbits to the park? While they're still young enough to be seen with us?"

"I'm dying to get outside. I was just trying to pay bills and replace a couple of lightbulbs first. I'm behind on everything."

Taylor had forgotten her friend had been working with a bunch of volunteers for the past few weekends. "How's your project coming?"

Samantha yelled at Edna to comb her hair and put her shoes on before she answered. "It looks great. Soon as we can get the first volunteers all trained, we'll be in business. That should be soon."

"Volunteers?"

"Ladies from the Women's Fellowship at Covenant."

"Covenant's involved?" Taylor was surprised, considering that Samantha's mother had been sent packing as headmistress of Covenant Academy.

"Nice group, too." Samantha paused just long enough to show she had to consider her next sentence, then she shrugged. "It was your mother's idea."

Taylor tried to reformat that piece of information, the way she might reformat an old computer file that wouldn't work with her new operating system.

Samantha saw her predicament. "She was at the clinic with a young woman who's living in her house, and she noticed that a lot of our moms had to bring other children with them when they came for prenatal care. So she thought of the playroom and got Covenant involved."

Taylor's reformatting wasn't working. "My mother was at your clinic?"

"Harmony — that's the woman who's living with her — is pregnant."

"She has a pregnant woman living with her?"

"Young one, too, without a lot of money. She's a sweetie. Harmony told me she needed a place to stay, and Charlotte opened her door."

The girls came running out of Edna's bedroom, so there was no more time for

Taylor to question Samantha. On the walk to the park, both girls raced ahead and back, and Taylor watched her daughter carefully. As they drew closer Maddie slowed, then inched along, despite Edna spurring her on. Once they arrived, Samantha took one look at Maddie, grabbed her hand, climbed to the top of the dome and pulled her up, too, where they sat together, cross-legged. Samantha laughed and pointed out silly things going on around them until Edna joined them. After a while Samantha climbed back down alone.

Taylor made room on the bench where she was sitting, and Samantha joined her.

"You're such a good friend," Taylor said. "Thank you."

"You're welcome."

"Should she really be up there?"

"You tell me."

"I used to have answers. Now everything just seems harder and harder to figure out."

"I can imagine."

"I used to be sure letting Maddie play here was the right thing. She deserves to do everything a child without epilepsy can. Of course, we have to be smart, but I always thought the park was safe enough we could chance it. Then look what happened."

"But she came through the fall okay,

because the dome's really not very high, which you factored in."

"Everything's a decision. What drugs she should be on. Whether I should make her go to school after she's had a bad seizure. Whether I should let her take ice skating classes after school next year. How about gymnastics? Yesterday somebody asked me why I don't make her wear a helmet, so if she does fall, she'll be safer."

"Why don't you?"

"Because she doesn't fall often enough to need one."

"Then that's one decision all taken care of."

Taylor knew what Sam was trying to do, but not every decision was that easy.

She ticked off what she did know. "No to ice skating, no to gymnastics. No to Jeremy."

"Guess what? Jeremy just crept into the conversation. All the way from Nashville."

Samantha knew what Jeremy had done. She had asked good questions but given no answers, good or otherwise. She had, as she often did, just listened.

"I guess I'm going to find a lawyer," Taylor said. "I made an appointment and talked to Dr. Hilliard. I made sure he had the records from Vanderbilt first. He looked everything over, and he still believes Maddie's best option is medication, not surgery."

"Well, you knew that going in."

"But there was new information to consider."

Samantha didn't reply.

Taylor went on. "He said there were all kinds of potential side effects after surgery. How can I take those kind of chances? This is her *brain* we're talking about."

"So you've made up your mind."

Taylor had expected Samantha to agree with her. "I guess I have." She turned to gauge her friend's expression. "You don't think I'm right?"

"Whoa, not going there."

"No, I want you to. Not just as a friend, but as a professional. I'd like your opinion."

Samantha considered long enough that Taylor grew uncomfortable. "What?" she asked, after the silence had gone on too long. "You don't want to tell me what you think?"

"It's not something you're all that fond of."

"What's not?"

"Other people's opinions, at least not once your mind's made up. What are you going to do if I don't agree with you?"

"What do you mean?"

"You don't like to listen to other people if

they don't share your views. I'm not talking about little stuff, but you're not good if it's important. It's your way or the highway. I'm not in the mood to thumb a ride."

Taylor was surprised. "I can't believe you think that."

"You're saying you don't have strong opinions and you're always open to having your mind changed?"

The question was so pointed that Taylor tried to think of a reply just as pointed. She searched for an example of a situation when she had willingly changed her mind about something that really mattered to her. When nothing presented itself, she scurried back to the root of the conversation.

"I'd like you to be honest. I *will* listen, I promise."

"Listen at your own risk then."

"Samantha!"

"I think Dr. Hilliard's old-fashioned and just plain old. Now some of my favorite doctors fit that last part, but never the first. They keep up with everything, stay fluid in the way they think, and they don't fall back on ideas that served them well years ago, unless that's all they've got. Hilliard's not one of them. He has the best bedside manner this side of *Grey's Anatomy,* and he's as genuine as they get. But he's also set in his ways."

Taylor was sorry she'd asked. "I don't see him that way."

"I know you don't."

"He's always talking about *new* meds."

"Meds are his stock in trade."

"But we talked about surgery right at the beginning, and he told me Maddie's just not a good candidate."

"How many years ago was that?"

Taylor had to admit that surgery hadn't come up as an option in years.

"They've made huge advances since Maddie was born," Samantha said. "The technology's exploded. They can map the brain and pinpoint whatever they need to know. The success rate for cases where surgery's warranted is sky-high."

"And what about the cases that aren't successful?"

"This isn't my field of expertise, but from everything I've seen lately, I'd say she wouldn't be worse for trying. Didn't Jeremy tell you the doctors in Nashville thought that even if Maddie has to stay on medication the rest of her life, the surgery and medication combination might cut the seizures to near zero?"

"It could affect her memory, her personality. Would you let somebody operate on Edna? Remove part of her brain?"

"Not if I thought surgery was going to harm her, no. But if I thought it wasn't, that it might give her a chance she wouldn't have otherwise to live a more adventurous life? In a heartbeat."

"But how do I know!"

Samantha let that die away before she answered. "You cooperate with Jeremy and give him credit for loving Maddie, too. You go to Nashville, or, if you'd rather, you go somewhere neutral. And you ask a million questions. You evaluate the program, evaluate the doctors, read everything you can about their success rate, then you make an informed decision. You don't take the word of one doctor who rarely, if ever, refers his patients to a neurosurgeon."

"How do you know that?"

"Because I've looked into it, and that's his rep."

Taylor let that sink in. "Why didn't you say something before?"

"I've tried. You weren't listening."

Thinking about it, Taylor realized that in the past few years Samantha *had* suggested second opinions, evaluation at places like Children's Hospital in Boston or Chicago, or the Cleveland Clinic. But Taylor had been certain Maddie's treatment was already the best.

"I need to talk to my father about this." Taylor's gaze flicked to Maddie, who, mercifully, had climbed down off the dome and was now playing catch with a couple of children and a brightly colored beach ball.

"That's a good idea."

Something about the way Samantha said it alerted Taylor to something behind the words. She pushed a little. "Unfortunately, that could be hard. Maddie and I went over to his house this morning, but he wasn't there. A neighbor said she doesn't remember seeing Dad's car in the driveway this weekend."

"The man has nosy neighbors."

"No, it's a good street. They watch out for one another." Taylor waited, then asked bluntly, "Do you happen to know where he is?"

"This whole conversation's about as much fun as a knee replacement."

"Why is it that you seem to know more about my life and choices than I do?"

"Because I'm nice, and people talk to me."

In a way, that was true. Samantha, because of the mess she'd almost made of her own life, was probably the best listener in Asheville. People were always taking advantage of her. Just as Taylor herself was about to.

"Where is my father?" she asked.

"I would guess he's with your mother."

Taylor hadn't expected that. It felt like a physical blow. "All weekend?"

"It's not what you're thinking." Samantha paused. "Or maybe it is. I don't want to go there."

"What are you talking about? Are you saying my mother and father are —" She couldn't even say it.

"There's a lot you don't know, and it's not my place to tell you."

"Why isn't anybody else telling me, then?"

"Really? Because you've made it a hundred percent clear you don't want anything to do with your mother, and you also don't want your father in the middle. So your relationship with Charlotte's up to you, and Ethan's doing exactly what you asked."

"What about *his* relationship with *her,* then?"

"You'll have to ask him."

"I told you, I can't find him!" Taylor put her hand on Samantha's knee, fairly sure her friend was about to bolt. "What's going on between them?"

"I can't give you details. I just know I called Charlotte this morning to see how she was, and your father answered the telephone."

Every response that rose to Taylor's lips was profane. She was on a playground with children zipping by. She knew better than to open her mouth and let any of them escape.

"Okay, look, I'm tired of this," Samantha said. "Call Ethan yourself and ask him what's going on."

Taylor ignored that. "Why did you call my mother to see how she was doing?"

Samantha didn't answer.

"Look, I deserve to know."

"Do you?" Samantha asked. "Why?"

Taylor couldn't give the obvious answer, that Charlotte was her mother, because she hadn't let that fact rule any interaction since leaving home. "Because everything she does affects me one way or the other."

"Interesting."

"Sam, please, have you taken a vow of silence?"

"You should hear this from Charlotte."

"What are the chances?"

Samantha thought that over, then she shook her head. "She's sick. Sick as in maybe she won't recover. And I guess your dad has decided he wants to be with her while she goes through treatment."

"Sick?"

"She has leukemia."

Taylor felt as if someone had punched her. Moments passed before she could breathe again. "Why didn't somebody tell me?"

"We've been through that. And since I'm being honest, I'm going to just finish up and move on. I like your mother. I know a fellow traveler when I see one. I know what it's like to wish you could make things right after they've gone terribly wrong. Charlotte made mistakes. We both know she did, up close and personal, although you know more about why than I do. I just know she's doing everything she can to try to make up for them."

"I can't take this in."

"You'll need to."

"You think I should rush to her side just because she's sick?"

"I think that's the last thing she'd want. But if you want to rush to her side because you love her? That would be a good thing."

Taylor couldn't think. Maddie, her mother, her mother and father together again . . .

"Well, she has my father," she said. "Apparently *he's* at her side." Then she thought about Sam's words. Was Ethan there because Charlotte was sick? Or was he there because, as impossible as it seemed, he still loved her?

"Maddie and I are going to head home," she said, getting to her feet.

"I think Edna and I will stay awhile."

Taylor knew she owed Samantha something for her honesty, but right now, she wasn't sure what.

"We'll talk," she said, and it was the best she could do.

"I'm not the one you need to talk to. I think we're kind of talked out, don't you?"

Taylor didn't know how to answer that, so she didn't. Instead, she went to tell Maddie her visit to the park had ended.

For two mornings Charlotte had awakened with Ethan's arms around her. More than a decade had passed since they'd slept in the same bed, but now his presence beside her felt natural and right.

When he'd insisted he was moving into her house and back into her life, Ethan had offered to sleep elsewhere, pointing out that she would rest better without him beside her. But neither of them had really wanted that.

When she had disagreed, he'd eased between the covers and gently pulled her close. Had she not been so sick, she was sure there would have been more. Despite that she found great pleasure knowing he had come to her not because she was an object of pity, but because Ethan was as hungry to find the intimacy they'd cast aside as she was. For now they just settled against each other, leg curving against leg, palm splayed on midriff, her elbow caressing the back of his hand, and found their way into each other's dreams.

On Saturday morning, while he showered, she went to find Harmony to alert her that Ethan had moved in. Harmony, eyes wide, offered to move out immediately, but Charlotte insisted she couldn't make it without her. Over a breakfast he cooked, Ethan charmed the young woman, and by the end of the meal, Charlotte could see that having him there would make things easier for Harmony, who felt the burden of Charlotte's illness more deeply than Charlotte had realized.

On Sunday afternoon after the final chemo injections, Ethan tucked her in bed for a nap and told her he would be back in a couple of hours.

"You must have a million things you need to do." Charlotte's eyelids were drooping, and her own words sounded far away.

"I need to pick up more clothes, plus

some plans I'm working on." He leaned over and kissed her. "Can I sneak in anything for dinner?"

"If I were you, I'd stop for takeout if you're craving anything other than organically grown vegetables. Harmony unearthed a juicer in the butler's pantry. She's convinced it will cure me."

"I can talk to her."

"Don't you dare. I'm not eating much, anyway. Doesn't matter . . . if it's celery or spareribs." She closed her eyes.

Sometime later she heard a soft rapping on her bedroom door. She sat up slowly, because fast movements made the nausea worse. She munched on a cracker after she called, "Come in."

"There's somebody here to see you," Harmony said. "I wouldn't have bothered you, only she says she's Samantha's mother."

Charlotte swallowed the final crumbs before replying. "Tall, reddish brown hair?"

Harmony nodded.

"Do I feel well enough to slip out the bedroom window?"

"Don't worry, I can tell her you're sleeping."

"I'll talk to her. Thanks for getting me."

She didn't change. She brushed the

wrinkles out of the knit pants she'd worn to bed and straightened the T-shirt. She combed her hair and decided nothing short of a facelift was going to make enough of a difference to warrant time and energy. She looked worse than she felt, which said everything.

She found Georgia in the living room, perched on the edge of the sofa as if she might be planning to bolt.

"I hate this room," Charlotte said.

"Did somebody foist it on you?"

"It's called a living room, but how much living can anybody really do on a silk-upholstered sofa?"

"You're asking the wrong person."

"Let's go in the den. No, let's sit out by the pool. Do you mind? Fresh air . . ." There was no point in going into the way fresh air seemed to help her nausea. "Feels good," she finished.

"Sure."

"Would you like something to drink?"

"Whatever you're having."

Charlotte stopped in the kitchen and took out two small bottles of club soda. She had set them on the counter and was reaching for glasses when Georgia rested her hand on Charlotte's arm.

"We can drink out of the bottles. Please

don't feel you have to entertain me."

Charlotte closed her eyes for a moment. "I bet you've talked to your daughter."

"Let's just sit right here." Georgia pulled out a stool at the center island and gestured in invitation.

Gratefully, Charlotte collapsed.

Georgia came back with the bottles and two glasses she'd found in a cupboard. She opened Charlotte's and poured it, then did the same for herself. "Sam thought you might be finishing the first round of chemo today," she said.

Charlotte gave a slow nod, which was less likely to send the room spinning.

"I told the young woman who answered your door not to get you out of bed. I was going to leave you a note."

"I'm glad she did."

"Why, so you can face an old foe when you're feeling limp as a dishrag?"

"I think that old saying about not kicking somebody when they're down is all wrong. I mean, if somebody's already down, kick away. What's crueler than waiting until they're happy again before you haul off and let them have it?"

"Being sick gives you lots of time to think about things like that, does it?"

"More than I'd like."

"You may not believe this, but I really am sorry you're going through this."

Charlotte thought about that. "That's nice. I'm glad, I think."

Georgia smiled. It was the first real Georgia smile Charlotte had seen in a long time. She was reminded of the younger woman, ready and eager to take on the job of headmistress. A woman filled with innovative ideas and enough enthusiasm to set every one of them in motion.

"I didn't just come for the Hallmark moment," Georgia said. "I needed to thank you in person."

Charlotte let out a breath she hadn't even been aware she was holding. Georgia had discovered the letters of recommendation.

"You're not angry at me?"

"I was for a little while."

Charlotte didn't spare herself. "I knew if I asked, you would tell me to mind my own business. And because I'm trying hard to change, I would have had to back off."

"So you worked around it."

"I guess I haven't learned as much as I thought, because I was sure it was the right thing to do, which is exactly what I thought when I tried to get you fired as headmistress."

"And succeeded."

"Unfortunately I'm persuasive."

"And a meddler."

"I'm a medal-worthy meddler. I could teach classes."

"They showed me the letters. At my second interview."

Charlotte leaned forward, nearly knocking over her water. "*Second* interview?"

"I'm in the running for the job. The committee made it clear I wouldn't have gotten this far, though, if you hadn't stepped forward. Even as long ago as that whole episode was, being fired was a black mark. Now they seem to think maybe I was just ahead of my time instead of a screwup."

"Georgia, I'm so glad. I hope you get the job. I really do."

"But you're staying out of it now." It wasn't a question.

"You're sure? My next move was blackmail."

Georgia looked thoughtful. "You laid yourself bare in your letter, Charlotte. It couldn't have been easy. And I can't think of a single reason why you did it, other than hoping to fix an old mistake."

Charlotte smiled. "And I bet you've tried."

"It's kept me awake at night." Georgia took a sip of her club soda. Then she stood. "Go back to bed. You need to rest and take care of yourself."

Charlotte stood, too. "Right now that's about all I'm good at."

Georgia hesitated, then she reached out and embraced Charlotte. Quickly, firmly, before she stepped back. "I'm praying for you."

"That's even better than a letter of recommendation."

"And every bit as successful, I hope." Another genuine Georgia smile, and then she was gone.

Charlotte listened to the front door close and thought one of her own prayers had just been answered.

Chapter Forty-One

First Day Journal: July 2

My grandmother once told me there were two things I would need to live a good life. The first was courage, and the second was fear. Now I see I'll also need them to die a good death. Courage to meet the end, realizing my death will make room so new seeds can be planted. Fear that encourages me to make my life ready for the harvest.

I wish I could hold my own granddaughter just once and tell her I've loved her since that moment ten years ago when I stood in a hospital hallway and wished she didn't have to suffer so terribly.

Chapter Forty-Two

Early in her treatment Charlotte had demanded that Phil Granger not fall back on platitudes. They had known each other long enough that he hadn't quibbled. When he'd recommended the newest cycle of chemo, he had told her the truth. It could take months before they knew if the treatment was helping. But she might not have months.

Now, almost a week since the first cycle had ended, she was beginning to feel better. Objectively she knew that was probably the side effects wearing off, most notably the nausea. She had been warned that in the next week her white cell count could drop to its lowest point, but for the time being, she was making the best use of her time.

She was just getting out of bed when Ethan came in to make sure she didn't need anything before he dressed to go back to his house. Earlier, before he'd gone to forage for his own breakfast, he had brought her tea and toast, both of which she had managed to finish; then he'd sat on the edge of the bed as she sipped, discussing whether he should set up a temporary workshop on the patio or in her garage. She'd insisted he could work in his real workshop and she would call if she needed him, but Ethan had refused.

"I like being here with you." He'd lifted her chin, the way he used to when they were much younger, and kissed her gently. "I don't want to miss a moment."

Now, when he saw she was watching him, he stretched, throwing back his broad shoulders, and smiled. "I just got off the phone. We have somebody interested in another unit at the factory."

"That's fantastic. I can't wait to see what you've done in person."

"Just as soon as you feel up to a field trip."

"Got a minute?"

He came over to the bed and sat. "What for?"

She slipped her arms around his neck and pulled him close for a kiss. "Actually, my idea might take more than a minute."

He pushed her hair off her face and looked into her eyes. He saw the invitation. "You're not feeling *that* good, are you?"

"I feel like a woman in love, but . . ." She sighed. "I'm not the greatest bargain out there, Ethan. I've looked in the mirror." Charlotte knew she was drawn and gaunt, and without her hairdresser's attentions her hair looked as thin as it really was. Her scalp was visible, and she had dark circles under her eyes.

Ethan rubbed his cheek against hers. "You're always beautiful to me, but I don't want to hurt you, Lulu."

"I think we're through hurting each other."

He lowered himself to the bed beside her. "Do you remember making love just a week before Taylor was born?"

"We didn't." She tilted her head. "Did we?"

"It was an exercise in poor judgment. We had to be creative. Very creative. You were huge."

She laughed a little. "It's coming back to me now."

She slid over so he could stretch out beside her. He turned on his side, and his hand brushed the top button of her nightgown. "I remember telling you that you could stop me any time, that if I hurt you, or you changed your mind —"

"Or went into labor . . ."

"That, too." He slowly unbuttoned the top button, then the next. "I told you to tell me to stop and I would. . . ."

"I don't remember putting that to the test."

He leaned down and kissed her, slowly, tenderly. Thoroughly.

"I'll make the same promise now," he said.

"With the same results."

Charlotte was lounging by the swimming pool later that morning when Harmony came outside, followed closely by Analiese.

"Reverend Ana." Charlotte started to stand, but Analiese waved her back into her chair. Since she was supposed to avoid the sun, Ethan had pulled a lounge chair into the shadows and settled her there before he'd left an hour ago. A warm, flower-scented breeze had nearly lulled her to sleep.

Harmony shaded her eyes and looked in the direction of the sun, as if gauging the time, although more likely she was gauging the etiquette of abandoning Charlotte. "I think this might be a good time to shop for groceries, if that's all right?"

"Reverend Ana will keep me company, and Ethan's coming back in a little while."

"Ethan?" Analiese asked after Harmony left.

Charlotte smiled at her. "He moved in."

"Well. Wow."

"Spoken like a theologian."

"Appreciation for the mystery of life is part of every theology."

"As well it should be." Charlotte motioned her into a chair. "Drinks and snacks are in the cooler on the table. Harmony and Ethan are determined to fatten me up. This morning Harmony made a special juice blend that I swear will kill or cure me. Beets, carrots, kale, wheatgrass — whatever that is. You're welcome to sample. In fact I beg you to drink it."

Before she sat, Analiese peeked in the cooler and screwed up her face in distaste. "Too bad I had an early lunch."

"For both of us."

Analiese kicked off her sandals. She'd been carrying something Charlotte had mistaken for a straw purse, but now she saw it was more like a market basket, flat on the bottom, open at the top.

Charlotte closed her eyes for a moment. "It's perfect out here, isn't it? I might just spend the whole day in this lounge chair."

"You look happy, Charlotte."

"I've been given that rarest of commodities."

"A major illness? Unfortunately, not so rare."

"A second chance."

"Ethan," Analiese said.

"He told me the two of you talked. On the mountain."

Analiese was no longer smiling. "Finding out you were sick was difficult for him, Charlotte. Finding out he really cared was more so."

"Thank you for helping him. Thank you for helping *me.*"

"In that spirit?" Analiese pulled the bag toward her, then she lifted a green plastic pot out of the depths. Inside it a fuzzy stalk with familiar-looking lobed leaves sprouted out of dark soil. "This is for you."

Charlotte might not have used her gardening skills since leaving home, but she hadn't forgotten most of what she'd known. "A tomato plant?"

"Not just any tomato plant. A miracle."

Analiese got up, put the pot into Charlotte's hands and closed her own hands over Charlotte's for a moment. "That day I ran into Ethan up at the old farmhouse, I got there first. I'd decided to look around a little before I went inside, and while I was wandering, a car drove up. It turned out to be the young couple who were your last renters, the ones who'd just moved out before you showed me the place."

"What were they doing?"

"When they moved in originally, the previous renter told them to pay attention in late spring, because they would see tomato plants coming up where tomatoes had been planted the year before. He said they should dig up the healthiest and plant them in rows in a different part of the plot. He said they would be amazed at what they had by summer's end. So they did, and they got tomato plants so tall they had to keep finding new and better ways to stake them. One year they had to resort to stepladders with bamboo poles between them."

"My grandmother's tomato trees. I can't believe they . . . ." Charlotte shook her head. For a moment she didn't trust herself to speak as memories assailed her. Her grandmother gently bending the tall plants toward her to pick the tomatoes at the top. Her grandmother in the kitchen at the woodstove placing quart jars of tomatoes in a water bath canner to preserve them.

Memories of her grandmother, who had always put Charlotte first, who had always loved her.

"I couldn't believe it, either," Analiese said, "but the young man explained. Seems these aren't hybrid plants, so they have exceptional vigor, and they're true to type from generation to generation. After you left home, maybe your father raised a few for something to eat, or maybe a neighbor came and got some, then brought a new generation back as a housewarming gift when you rented out the house."

Charlotte could see that happening. During her childhood neighbors had always shared plants. She was sure her grandmother had passed on the tomato trees to others, as swaps or gifts. And the first person Ethan had rented the farm to after Hearty died had been the brother of their neighbor, Bill Johnston. Bill had probably shared the seedlings with his brother.

"So renter told renter," Charlotte said.

"The renters who just moved out took a few plants with them when they left, but they were so busy unpacking and fixing up their new house, they didn't get them in the ground in time, and they died. They came back up the mountain hoping to find more in the garden. After they left with a couple, I made sure a dozen of the leftovers were in a nice straight row in the garden, to continue the tradition."

"And this is one of them." Charlotte caressed the pot. "I thought these plants were lost. Such a wonderful thing, gone forever."

"The seeds remained. I bet this plant and everything it stands for will continue to be passed down for generations."

"Because somebody along the way nurtured the seeds and protected them."

"The way we nurture and protect our memories of people who lived before us. The good they did? Like those seeds of your grandmother's, it doesn't die. It's passed from person to person. It lives on in other forms, in other places, but the essence of what it was at the beginning never changes."

"You can't tell a story that doesn't ring with meaning, can you?"

"I would lose my job if I tried."

Charlotte hugged the plant to her chest and reached over to take Analiese's hand. "Not if I had anything to say about it."

Ethan's car was parked in his driveway when Taylor passed on the way home from a morning yoga class, a sulky Maddie in the passenger's seat. Maddie hadn't been happy to be dragged out of bed to wait at the studio, and she hadn't kept her feelings to herself. Now she was the one who spotted Ethan's car and told her mother to stop.

When the front door opened and Ethan

stepped outside to his porch, Taylor realized she had little choice. Her father had probably noticed their car, and Maddie was already rolling down her window to call to him. She wished she had chosen a different way home.

Taylor parked at the curb and waited until Maddie jumped out to greet her grandfather before she opened her own door to follow.

Maddie had quickly launched into an explanation of where they'd been and what they'd been doing, and Ethan was listening patiently.

"I didn't even have time to eat anything except an apple for breakfast," Maddie finished. "And I'm starving."

"Because you didn't want to get out of bed when I called you," Taylor said. Then she turned to Ethan. "We have a bunch of errands to do this afternoon, so I'm taking her home for lunch first."

Maddie was pouting. "We could have eaten out."

"You're paying?" Taylor asked. "Out of your allowance?"

"You left some things here the last time you were over," Ethan told Maddie. "Why don't you run in and check your bedroom closet? I can't even remember what I stuck in there."

"Can I get a glass of orange juice before I drop dead of starvation?"

"May I?" Taylor corrected.

Maddie's eyes narrowed. "You need one, too?"

"Scoot," Ethan said, pointing. "And make sure you get everything." He waited until Maddie was gone. "That's some mood she's in."

"She got on a different schedule when she was at Jeremy's. He and Willow are up late at night and sleep late, too. Maddie doesn't want to give that up, and she's not happy I've made her." She waited, and when he didn't speak, she added some real news. "I called him last night, and we had a long conversation."

Taylor was used to her father hanging on her every word — or something close to it — but while Ethan was listening, he still seemed preoccupied.

Epiphanies happen at odd moments. Yoga was one way of seeking enlightenment, but Taylor knew no matter what she engaged in, the higher spiritual mind was a part of who she was. Sometimes that part made itself known whether she felt ready or not.

In a moment of clarity she saw how important Ethan's approval — no, not simply approval, his *adoration* — had become to her through the years. They'd been a team since the moment she walked out of her childhood home. She had counted on him for counsel, for strength, for companionship. But he was the only member of the team who had done any giving. She had unabashedly taken. And she had never worried about that unequal balance, or what it might be doing to either of them.

She had separated from her mother, not as a teenager should, gradually and gently, but with an irreparable rift.

She had *never* separated from Ethan.

"Dad," she said, "I know you're living with my mother."

"When did you stop calling Charlotte 'Mom,' Taylor? I'm trying to remember. When did she become 'my mother'?"

"When she stopped *being* Mom."

"She never stopped. She wasn't the mom you wanted or even needed at the time, but she never stopped being Mom."

"I know she's sick."

He gave a short nod of acknowledgment.

"It's . . ." She tried to give something for a change, something to show she understood, even a little. "It's good you can be there to help her." She tried to believe her own words.

"I'm not there to help her." Ethan spaced

the words. "I'm there because I love her. I've loved her since the first moment I saw her, and now I realize I've never stopped loving that woman, not the woman *you* believe her to be."

"I'm sorry, but *I'm* the one she kicked out of our house."

"A lot was said that day in the heat of the moment. It's time to ask yourself what really happened."

She was instantly defensive. "I was there. I know what happened."

"Why did you get pregnant? Have you asked yourself *that?* You knew about birth control. Have you ever asked yourself if you were trying to get even with your mom? Or trying to push the issue of who was in control of your life? You weren't in love with Jeremy. You hardly shed a tear when he moved on to another girl. And the minute you discovered the pregnancy, you confronted us with it, not with tears and not with a smile, but with a look I'll never forget. You were waiting for something, watching to see exactly what you'd set in motion."

Ethan had never asked her this. Until now, she'd never considered he might even be thinking it. She couldn't react to the things he'd implied, because she had no idea what to say. Was there truth in his words? Had she been so angry at her mother that she had thrown caution to the winds to prove she could do whatever she wanted? Be with anyone she wanted? Even have a baby at seventeen, if she chose?

This was not the first time she'd asked herself those questions, of course, but it was the first time her father had.

"We reap what we sow," he said, when she didn't answer. "Everyone in the room that day was guilty of something, and every one of us paid the price. I think I've paid my share, so I'm not paying more. I just want to be with your mother again, for as long as we have together."

"Sam says she has leukemia."

He nodded.

Again she gave him what she could. "I don't hate her, Dad. I don't want her to die."

He didn't reply, only pushed his fingers through his hair, something he always did when he was stressed. "You were telling me about Jeremy."

She was glad she could tell her father something that turned her back into an adult, after the painful foray into her adolescence.

"We talked until nearly midnight. I've

decided to take Maddie back to Nashville at the end of July. I can meet with the doctors at Vanderbilt and get a feel for the place. Jeremy and I can talk to them together. He's agreed if I'm not satisfied, we'll seek a third opinion, then make our decision from there."

"That's good news."

"I hoped you would think so."

"I know it's hard for you to change your mind and equally hard to share the parenting."

She had done enough thinking since her conversation with Samantha to realize this was true. How true she still hadn't decided.

"You're more like your mother than you realize," Ethan said.

Jeremy had told her something similar, but she still wasn't willing to accept it. "I hope that's not true."

The front door opened, and Maddie came outside. Taylor expected her father to cut the conversation short, but he added one last thought.

"I hope it *is* true, Taylor. You have your mom's strength and determination. I hope they'll serve you as well during your life as they're serving your mother at the end of hers."

■ ■ ■ ■

Charlotte would have preferred not to do any business until she felt even better, but "even" better wasn't something she could count on. When Analiese left, she propped herself up and managed a short conference call with the Falconview executive committee before she lowered her lounge chair again. As she'd anticipated, they had not been happy to learn her plans for the company, but at least they wouldn't be surprised now.

Ethan returned with lunch and set it up on the table beside her. She was touched that all these years later he still remembered how much she loved Cobb salad. He'd brought one for Harmony, too, and remembering that she was a vegetarian, he'd asked the café to leave off the bacon and substitute grilled tofu for the chicken.

Harmony cooed over the salad and the story behind the tomato plant, then promised to eat as soon as she returned from her grocery expedition.

As Charlotte and Ethan ate, he detailed everything he'd brought with him — drawers for the kitchen cabinets that needed sanding and staining, stair treads that needed multiple coats of polyurethane, a pocket door for the bedroom in his own unit.

"I was on the telephone with the executive committee at Falconview," she said, once it was her turn.

"I guess that's better than putting on a power suit and bustling through the front door."

"I think most of the staff are polishing up their resumes."

"They would leave you in the lurch after everything?"

"Loyalty wasn't something I encouraged. I made Falconview a one-woman business, and I never gave anyone much of a reason to be loyal. They knew they were always being watched and judged. Now that I'm not right there hanging over them anymore, they're snapping at one another like pit bulls, trying to see who's going to be the next alpha dog. It's my own fault."

"You don't sound worried."

"Falconview will sort itself out. Maybe the company will even go in a new direction once I'm gone. Whenever I'm gone."

"You've made provisions?"

"I've made the best choices possible. I'm confident things will work out."

He seemed to be considering what to say

next. "Taylor stopped by my house as I was leaving. With Maddie."

Charlotte knew if the news had been good, Ethan would have told her right away.

"She knows you're sick," he said. "Sam told her."

When he said no more, she realized there was no more to say. "How's Maddie?"

"There's good news there. Taylor's decided to take her back to Nashville next month and talk to the doctors who want to do the surgery. Then she and Jeremy will decide together what they should do next."

Charlotte could only imagine what a terrible burden that decision had been, and how Taylor must have agonized over it. She wished her daughter were there right now so she could slip her arms around her.

"They'll do the right thing," she said.

"You look tired. Why don't you see if you can get a little rest?"

"Right. I need a nap after all that chewing and swallowing."

He laughed and kissed her. "You ate, what? Six bites? I'm leaving the salad here so maybe you can get a little *more* tired chewing and swallowing."

He left for the garage to unload and assemble the materials he'd collected from his workshop, and she dozed on and off for most of an hour. Then, disgusted with herself for doing so little now that the worst effects of the chemo had worn off, she decided to see what Ethan was up to.

She liked the idea of the garage filling up with his things. If she wasn't yet ready to make it all the way to the bottle factory, at least she could see smaller pieces of his work.

When she stood she felt light-headed, but she'd been lying in the shade most of the day — clearly too long, if her head was any barometer. Moving around still seemed like a good idea. She stopped in the kitchen to throw out what was left of her lunch and stack her dishes in the dishwasher. Then she made her way through the house to the side door leading into the garage.

She was halfway down the hall when she realized that staying put would have been a better idea. Her legs felt rubbery, and her heart was pounding like a marching band drum line. Silently she kicked herself. She should have sat up slowly, stretched the way Velvet always did when she rose to go outside. She should have waited until her head cleared completely before she even tried to get to her feet.

As the hallway slowly darkened, she leaned against the wall. For a moment she felt confused, as if the rooms in her house had been somehow rearranged. She wasn't sure she'd been heading in the right direction, and she wasn't sure where the next doorway lay. She inched along, keeping the wall to her back, to find the doorway and hopefully a place to sit, but when she felt the wall turn to space, she wasn't prepared.

She flailed, trying to catch hold of anything, then her legs gave way just before the hallway turned as dark as midnight.

CHAPTER FORTY-THREE

Charlotte woke up to the sound of beeping. She tried to lift her head, but she was too weak. Slowly, too slowly, her eyes began to focus. She could hear voices, but she couldn't distinguish what they were saying. They were just far enough away that words were strung together in a monotone.

"Charlotte?" She felt someone take her hand. This voice she recognized.

"Ethan?" She forced herself to focus on his face. "Where . . . ?"

He squeezed her hand to show he understood. "You're in the hospital. You came in through the emergency room, and right now you're in intensive care."

She was swimming through fog to reach him. He still seemed miles away, and she couldn't focus on asking another question.

"Dr. Granger's here. I'm going to let him talk to you now, but I'm not going anywhere."

Phil swam into view, silver hair, furrowed brow. He was older than Ethan, ready to retire, she remembered. Next year?

"How do you feel?" he asked.

She really didn't know. "Funny . . ."

She couldn't put his next words together, the way she knew she should. She heard "transfusion," and "blasts," and something that sounded like "relapse."

She put together what she could and came up with what seemed a logical conclusion. "I'm . . . dying."

This time his words were clear. "I'm afraid you're very weak."

"Why . . . transfusions?"

"We're trying to stabilize you while we decide what to do next."

The fog was lifting now. She could hear and understand words. She also thought she could hear the subtext. "Trying . . ." She cleared her throat. "But probably . . . not?"

He didn't answer directly. "We have a couple of options. We can get you feeling better, then send you home in a day or two, hoping you improve enough for another cycle next month. After that we'll see where we are. Or we can keep you here and try something a lot more drastic. I won't lie to you, though — if you choose that option, the chances you'll survive the first round of the treatment are slim. In fact, I'm not even sure we can get your insurance company to agree to it."

She heard Ethan's voice. "What makes you think she can make a decision like that in the condition she's in?"

Phil's voice faded, as if he had moved to another part of the room. Silently she cheered Ethan for being her advocate, but when he came to her side and took her hand, she answered his question herself.

"Phil and I have talked . . ." She sighed, wishing this were easier. "He knows."

Ethan squeezed her hand. "What does he know?"

"I want . . . to go home. I want whatever time . . ." She couldn't finish.

Phil said something, and Ethan answered, then turned back to her. "You're a fighter, Lulu. You're sure?"

Slowly she threaded her fingers through his. "I know how to pick . . . my battles."

She could see his face clearly now, and she saw the sorrow there. She also saw that he understood her choice, although he wasn't ready to let go.

"We just found each other again," he said, so softly she had to strain to hear him.

She gave him the only comfort she could. "Aren't we blessed?"

■ ■ ■ ■

Ethan was drained when he came into the waiting room. Harmony jumped to her feet. "Ethan?"

He faced her and shook his head. "She's awake, but there's not much they can do except stabilize her for a while. The only other option's too likely to backfire and not likely to help. She's not willing to go that route."

He could see that Harmony couldn't imagine going *any* route. She was so young, and she hadn't imagined things could come to this so quickly.

He understood how she felt. Only that morning Charlotte had sworn she felt better. They had made love, tenderly, carefully, but with all the feeling he could ever have hoped for. She had eaten, dressed, spent the day lying by the pool. After breakfast she had even played with the puppies. She had felt better, seemed better, and that hadn't helped any of them prepare for what had happened.

Harmony began to cry, and Ethan put his arms around her.

"We're going to bring her home, honey. We'll be able to say goodbye when we need to. But I don't want her to die here."

"They won't let me in to see her. I'm not family."

"I'll talk to the doctor when he comes out, but for now, go home and get some dinner, please? We don't want you getting sick. You've got a baby to take care of." He squeezed her and let her go. "Promise me, okay? I can't worry about you, too."

She managed a watery nod. "I'll come back afterward."

"I'll make sure they put you on the visiting list." He found himself pushing his fingers through his hair, and he made a point of dropping his hand. "Will you do me a favor? They don't want us using cell phones on the floor. When you get home, will you call Reverend Ana and tell her what's going on? And maybe Sam?"

She waited, clearly sure he planned to say more, but he made no mention of Taylor. He wasn't going to have Harmony call his daughter. He wasn't even sure that *he* would. He didn't know what he could say that he hadn't already, and short of demanding Taylor show up, he was out of options.

When she realized he wasn't going to add a name, she nodded once more. "Would you like me to bring something back for you? I could make sandwiches and bring fruit."

"I'm only allowed to visit her for a few minutes at a time. I have time to run to the cafeteria in between and grab something. It's easier to eat there than here. I'll be fine."

She wanted so badly to do something for him, he could see that. But he was just going through the motions now, and his heart and body felt disconnected. There was nothing anybody could do.

"We're going to bring her home," Ethan repeated. "That's what we need to concentrate on now. Her doctor says he's going to try to make that happen soon. At a certain point they'll have done all they can here."

He could almost see Harmony grasping for something to hang on to, hoping this was a bad dream. "I believe in miracles, don't you?" she asked.

He told her the only thing he could.

"I do, but I also know that sometimes we see a miracle and don't recognize it. Charlotte and I found each other again. You and Charlotte found each other. How many more miracles can we ask for?"

At Charlotte's house Harmony let Velvet out and cleaned up after the puppies. She gave them fresh water and kibble, and cuddled each one. They had grown increasingly rambunctious and loved to play. They had chew toys and tug toys inside, but they were always delighted to have time in the grass, tumbling pup over pup.

Harmony loved all the puppies, but her favorites were the two that probably would never become service dogs. She thought Vanilla was the sweetest dog in the litter and hoped she went to a home where her gentle personality was appreciated. Villain, charming in his own brash way, was going to need a lot of obedience work or he would end up as somebody's junkyard dog. But his energy and enthusiasm had finally stolen her heart.

She was crying again when she stood. Charlotte adored the puppies. Until she'd gotten too sick to manage, she had handled most of their care. Now, when she died, Harmony would have to take them to Marilla's and care for them there until it was time to pass them on to the puppy raisers.

She hadn't told Charlotte about Marilla's offer of a job and a place to live, because she knew Charlotte would insist she immediately take advantage of the opportunity before it slipped away. The renovations on the garage apartment were well under way, and it was going to be adorable. Two tiny bedrooms, but what more did she need? Plenty of storage and counter space in the kitchen, room for a sofa and a couple of chairs in the living room.

Brad had consulted her about paint colors and laminate for the counters. He had asked if she wanted a shower or a shower-tub combination, and refused to listen when she told him it didn't matter, because they might need to hire someone else with different tastes.

Now she wished, more than anything, that Charlotte would still need her for months and months. She wished she could tell Charlotte about the offer, and they could laugh together because Charlotte had discovered she was going to be around for years.

But that was not what Ethan had tried to tell her.

She washed her hands in the kitchen, then she opened the refrigerator to take out the salad Ethan had bought for her. She'd come home to find an ambulance in the driveway, and she had never had a chance to eat.

The evidence of her foolish optimism filled every shelf. The refrigerator was packed with groceries she had bought on her shopping trips — organic produce for juicing, any fruit or vegetable her internet search had turned up that might fight cancer. She had driven all over town, shopping here and there and hoping, hoping. She supposed she'd been trying to plug a dike with her finger, like the story her mother used to tell about a Dutch boy trying to save his little village. But she had wanted so badly to do something.

She dished the salad onto a plate and slid the croissant that went with it into the toaster oven. Charlotte liked to tease her about her aversion to the microwave, but she saw no reason to take chances. On the other hand, maybe her fear of radio waves was like the hocus-pocus of juicing, too. No microwave equals no cancer.

She, of all people, should have known that sometimes nothing can be done for the people you love. She hadn't been able to convince her mother to leave her father, and she hadn't been able to cure Charlotte's leukemia.

But maybe, as Ethan had tried to tell her, she'd set her sights too high.

She stared out the window and considered. In the end she put the salad back in the refrigerator, turned off the toaster oven and went to find her car keys.

Taylor was working outside on the patio she and Maddie had created after moving to this house. They had discovered the flagstone at the curbside two streets away, ready to be hauled to the dump. She had painstakingly lifted block after block into her car, and by the time she had carted enough home for the patio she'd envisioned, her back had ached for a week.

The project had taken most of that summer. Marking boundaries with string. Shoveling out inches of soil. Watering and tamping the ground. Adding sand and tamping again. Then the jigsaw puzzle joys of placing stones, twisting and turning until she and Maddie were satisfied. Once the patio was done they had been so proud. When fall arrived Taylor had splurged on big clay pots, one for each corner, and ever since she had kept them filled with flowers. Bulbs and pansies in spring, trailing petunias and whatever caught her eye in summer, chrysanthemums in fall and evergreens to adorn with popcorn and cranberries at Christmas time.

She always waited until the plants were on sale and chose the healthiest. Today pansies and spent tulips were giving way to fountain grass, sweet potato vine, verbenas and English daisies. Maddie had lost interest early in the process and was in her room reading.

Taylor was so lost in thought that she

didn't hear footsteps until they crunched on her gravel driveway. She looked up and saw a tall, blonde woman coming toward her, carrying a plant in a plastic pot.

"You may have the wrong house," Taylor said, getting to her feet.

"Are you Taylor Martin?"

Taylor nodded and waited.

"Then this is the right house. My name's Harmony Stoddard." The woman paused. "I'm a friend of your mom's."

Taylor slowly stripped off her gardening gloves, examining the woman warily as she did. She remembered the name from her conversation with Sam at the park. This was the mysterious boarder, the pregnant woman living with Charlotte. She wasn't at all what Taylor had expected, younger and distinctive in a way her mother would never have approved of when Taylor was a teenager. She had a ring in one side of her nose and a tattoo. The pregnancy probably wasn't apparent to anyone who didn't know, but Taylor guessed she might be into her second trimester, judging from the slight thickening of her waist at the hem of her tank top.

"Did my mother ask you to come?"

"No."

"But you did, anyway."

"I got to thinking about something."

Harmony held out the pot in her hands. "This tomato plant? It comes from seeds your great-grandmother used to save every year and plant in her garden. Charlotte says the plants grew so tall and got so many tomatoes it took weeks to can them all. Her gran called them tomato trees, and after she left home and moved to Asheville, Charlotte thought they were lost forever."

Taylor thought this conversation was extraordinary, but she resisted asking the other woman to get to the point.

"It turns out," Harmony said, "that other people kept the seeds, or even, maybe, that every year a plant or two just keep growing and bearing fruit and spreading seeds, even when they weren't being picked, until somebody came along and rescued them. She didn't know it, though, not until this morning, when someone brought her this one." Harmony cleared her throat. "She was so pleased."

"I guess I don't see what this has to do with me."

"Your mother's not going to live long enough to see this plant bear fruit. At first I thought I'd take it to the place where I'll be moving . . . when she dies." She stopped for a moment and cleared her throat again. "Then I realized that no, as much as I wish

I were, I'm not Charlotte's daughter. And this plant belongs to her family. So I brought it for you. If you take care of it and it gets tomatoes this year, then you can save the seeds and grow them every year, like your great-grandmother did. Maybe your daughter will grow them, too."

Taylor didn't know what to say. Harmony was so earnest, so convinced Taylor would value the plant. She finally shrugged. "I don't really have enough sun here. Why don't you keep it?"

Harmony set the pot on the ground. "Would you like me to help you find a spot? Maybe in a corner you haven't considered. Or maybe out front? It looked sunny enough out there."

"You came all the way over here, found me — which must have taken some work — all because of a tomato plant?"

Harmony sent her a fleeting smile, but her eyes stayed sad. "I guess it's about roots, Taylor. About the past bearing fruit, even when something's had to work really hard just to survive. The way these plants did. The way your mother did."

"She's not the only one."

"I know."

Something Harmony had said earlier finally registered. "You said . . . she's not going to live long enough to see tomatoes on the plant? Or something like that? Has she . . . ?"

"She's in the hospital."

Taylor wanted to collapse on a bench and think about that, but she wasn't going to give this young woman the satisfaction. "I'm sorry to hear it."

"You said she wasn't the only one who had to work hard just to survive. I guess you've had to do the same thing. I know things haven't been easy for you —"

Taylor held up her hand. She didn't want to hear a replay of her life by a stranger, but Harmony took a different tack.

"My life's been hard, too. My father's a violent man, a bad man. My mother's so kind, with the gentlest heart, but he spent their whole marriage stripping away her confidence, her convictions, all her spirit. He tried to do the same to me. I had to abandon her so I could get away from him. I came here, to Asheville, and I've tried to build something like a life for myself, but it's taken a while to get strong enough."

"Look, I —"

This time Harmony held up her hand. "Your mom is the only reason I'm strong enough now to move on. I was a stranger, but she realized I was in trouble. She opened her door, and she's been with me every step of the way. She gave me time and space, and she made me feel like nothing was going to be too hard for me to find a solution. I owe her everything."

"It's ironic she could do that for you when she couldn't do it for me."

"But don't you see? She did it *because* of you. She knew she'd made a terrible mistake she couldn't fix. Not with you. When she had the chance to help me, she didn't stop to think twice."

"I'm happy for you."

"But it's not really good enough," Harmony said. "She misses you so much. She has paintings you made as a little girl in her kitchen. Pictures of you in her bedroom. She has a shelf of the books you loved as a girl in the room where I'm staying, ribbons and trophies you won for sports in a cabinet in the den."

Taylor didn't know what to say to that. She tried to imagine being part of Charlotte's decorating scheme, and she couldn't. Had her paintings been up on the walls of her childhood home? Had her mother displayed her trophies and ribbons? She couldn't remember.

Suddenly remembering seemed important. And more important? How had she so thoroughly contained all her memories? Now, as she allowed them to seep back in, the images were a flood gathering speed.

Yes, her paintings *had* been up on the walls. Their hallway *had* been covered with them, proudly framed and prominently placed, until the embarrassed teenage Taylor had forced Charlotte to take them down. Every report card had gone on the refrigerator, every school photo. Sometimes Charlotte had been too busy to see Taylor in plays or at horse shows or swim meets, but she had always taken the time to hear a blow-by-blow description afterward. And she'd always tried to take Taylor out for pizza or ice cream to celebrate. Even when Taylor's team didn't win or she didn't get the starring role.

Until the day, that is, when Taylor had decided she was too old to go with her. Sometime after their trip to Manhattan, things had changed. Charlotte's conviction that her way was the only way had moved from annoying to infuriating. Taylor had felt she couldn't breathe, couldn't move and certainly couldn't think for herself. She'd become a defiant teenager, strong-willed and angry at all the pointless rules. The harder Charlotte had tried to keep her in line, the harder she had rebelled.

Finally she had ignored her mother completely. And that was the day she began to sneak out to meet the boy who became Maddie's father.

Harmony cleared her throat. "And the puppies she's raising? They're all about you, or rather, your daughter. She hoped maybe you would let her give one of them to Maddie. They're going to be trained as seizure alert dogs. She thought —"

"Seizure dogs?" Taylor had investigated the idea, but when she'd realized what the cost would be, she had put it out of her mind.

"I'm going to be a mother a lot sooner than I ought to be," Harmony said. "My own mother told me not to call her again, that it's not safe for either of us. But every single day I wish I could, that somehow she could find the strength to break free of my father and find me here. If she did? I could forgive her anything, even forgive her for not standing up to my father, just to have her back in my life."

"Maybe you wouldn't. Maybe you would be so angry at the way she treated you that you couldn't."

Harmony moved closer; then, before Taylor realized what she was doing, she took Taylor's hand and laid it gently on the slight bulge at the waistband of her jeans.

"I'm going to be a mother, whether I planned it or not. You're a mother, whether *you* planned it or not. If you're perfect, don't tell me, because I know I can't live up to that."

Taylor pulled her hand back, and Harmony smiled sadly. "I'm going to make so many mistakes, Taylor. I gave up believing in God when our preacher stood in church and said men have a duty to keep their women in line. But I pray every night that a better God than that one will help me. Because there are going to be so many times when I don't know what to do, and so many times I'll do the wrong thing, even when I realize it's wrong. I just hope my baby forgives me."

"There are mistakes, then there are *mistakes.*"

"Maybe that's true, but I've had a good role model these past weeks. I hope I'll be like your mother and able to admit mine when I make them. If this baby's a girl, I'm going to name her Charlotte and hope she'll live up to it."

When Taylor didn't answer, Harmony turned to go. "I don't know why she let this go on so long, why she didn't try to set things right before now. Maybe it was just too painful. Maybe she didn't know how to begin."

Taylor spoke, before she even realized she needed to. "No, she called. Even after she kicked me out, my mother called every year on my birthday."

Harmony faced her again. "She spoke to you?"

"I screened the calls, and I never listened to her messages. I never told anybody she was calling, not even my dad." Taylor moved to the picnic table and dropped to the bench.

"I wasn't there when things fell apart for the two of you. I'm not trying to judge."

Taylor wondered if the seventeen-year-old Taylor, who *had* been there on that terrible night, had heard only what she'd expected to.

It was all so long ago, but maybe she really *had* looked for a way to get even with her mother for what had seemed like a lifetime of interference. Maybe, as Ethan had said, she'd even had unprotected sex with Jeremy just because she knew how much Charlotte would hate it.

"She always knew what was best for me," she said out loud. "She never wanted to hear my opinion. In the end that seemed to be all our relationship was about."

"She was *afraid* for you. She was so afraid your life would be as hard as hers was. She didn't have to tell me, because that's how *I* feel. I know that's how she must have felt, too."

Taylor understood that only too well. Hadn't she almost decided what was best for Maddie out of fear, shutting out everyone else's opinion until Jeremy threatened legal action?

Hadn't *she* refused to listen?

Just like her mother.

"We all watch and learn from our parents," Harmony said. "Now that you have something important, something healing, to learn, please don't shut her out again."

"Leave the plant." Taylor couldn't manage more.

"Your father's hoping to bring your mother home from the hospital. Maybe as early as tomorrow. He doesn't want her to die there."

Taylor closed her eyes. When she opened them some time later, Harmony was gone and the tomato plant was on the bench beside her.

She didn't know how long she sat there, but finally she went inside. Maddie was sound asleep on her bed, and Taylor tiptoed past her daughter's door before she closed her own behind her. At the closet she stood on tiptoe and felt for a shoebox, edging it toward her until she could pull it down.

She sat cross-legged on the floor and lifted the lid. Charlotte's letter to her wasn't lonely. Inside were family photos Maddie had never seen, dozens of snapshots of Taylor at different ages, and Charlotte was in every one.

Charlotte beaming over a birthday cake she had made for Taylor's fourth birthday. Charlotte building a sand castle with her daughter at the beach. Charlotte and five-year-old Taylor in matching dresses on their way to church. Charlotte taking her fairy princess daughter trick-or-treating.

Taylor had never been able to throw the photos away, even though she had tried once, rescuing them just before the trash went out. To justify her failure of courage, she'd told herself she didn't have to throw away her childhood just because her mother had shared it. Instead, she had compromised by shoving the box and her memories out of sight in the top of her closet.

For so many years she had been certain she was right, that everything that had happened eleven years ago had been Charlotte's fault, that a woman who exiles her pregnant daughter is always beyond redemption. She had worn that conviction like armor, rejecting anything that might pierce it.

But what kind of person erects barriers around her heart? What kind of person shields herself from love?

Deeply ashamed she opened the envelope, took out her mother's letter and began to read.

Dear Taylor,

The first time I saw your face, I realized how much my life had changed. I was overcome by love, afraid to breathe because of the perfection of the moment. Sadly, in the next I was paralyzed by fear. I wanted to lay the world at your feet, yet I had no idea how to begin. I vowed then that I would give you everything you deserved and more. You would lack for nothing, and for the rest of our years together, I set about making that happen. What I never realized, until it was too late, was that you had been born with everything you needed to find your own way. All I had to do was love you enough to let you. My regrets are so many I can never hope to atone for all of them. . . .

Taylor's vision blurred, and she couldn't

read the rest. Just as Harmony had reminded her, she was a mother, too, like Charlotte. How could she not understand?

She held Charlotte's letter against her chest and baptized it with her tears.

Chapter Forty-Four

Every time she awoke, Charlotte had to concentrate harder to establish where she was. She wasn't afraid. It was almost like the games of hide-and-seek she had played on clear summer evenings with the children of families who came to call on her grandmother. She remembered fireflies twinkling like stars and calls of "Ollie, Ollie, oxen freed." The sky would darken until she was no longer sure how to find her way home.

Somehow she always did.

This time when she awoke she saw she was in her own room at home, and wildflowers sprouted from a clear glass vase beside her bed. She suspected Harmony's hand in that, even, perhaps, the fields behind Capable Canines. She felt herself smiling.

"You're awake."

The voice was familiar. She turned her head a little and found Analiese sitting beside her bed. This time she was sure she smiled.

"How do you feel?" Analiese asked.

Charlotte didn't know. She took stock before she answered. "Alive. Still."

"Good call. And we're all so glad you are."

"I'm not . . . in great pain."

"There's no reason you should be. You have a good doctor, and he'll make sure of it."

"They called . . . hospice." She seemed to remember that.

Analiese took her hand. "You're all right with that?"

"Yes." Charlotte knew exactly what that meant, that now everyone was more concerned with the quality of her death than with prolonging her life. She also knew it was time. Whenever she opened her eyes, the world seemed farther away.

"What can I do for you now?"

"Raise the dead?"

"I don't think that's in my contract."

Charlotte squeezed her hand. "Thank you. For your support. Your frankness. For . . . listening."

"Charlotte, I'm so glad I had the chance to really get to know you. It's been a privilege." Analiese leaned in closer, as if she didn't want anyone else in the room to hear her. "Has Gwen been to visit you?"

Charlotte nodded slowly. "She's getting . . . pushy."

"Goddesses are like that."

"I have seen them in action . . . without always knowing. I count you among them."

"May this very ordinary goddess pray with you?"

"That would mean . . . everything."

She woke up twice more, used to finding that she was in her own room. The first time Ethan was by her side, but she fell back asleep before she could speak to him. The second time it was a woman dressed in cheerful yellow scrubs who introduced herself as the nurse who would help take care of her.

The third time when she awoke her head was clearer and the room didn't spin. She lifted herself a little, sliding higher on the pillow, and while she was ridiculously weak, she was able to move enough to take in her surroundings.

Ethan materialized out of the shadows. "Want me to prop you up, Lulu?"

She licked her lips. "I think so."

He helped her, his body warm and more solid than her own, as if his was real and hers an imitation.

"See what you . . . got yourself into?" she

asked, when she was settled.

"I'm exactly where I want to be. Do you think you could drink a little water?"

She sipped from a glass he held to her lips, proud she didn't dribble. "What time is it?"

"Dinnertime. Harmony made soup. Feel up to a little?"

She was trying to die, and they were giving her food and water, as if that would stave off the inevitable. It almost made her smile. "A few bites." She knew that would please Harmony. "But not right now." She patted the bed beside her, and he sat, then he reached out to smooth back her hair.

"Are you in pain?" he asked.

"Mostly my body feels . . . a million miles away."

"You have to let us know. But they don't want to give you more meds than you need."

She knew enough about what was coming to understand that as the end drew closer, the nurse or someone would help relieve her suffering. She was glad, though, that for now her head was clearer than it had been.

"Harmony thought you might like a puppy visit."

She imagined one of the little goldendoodles squirming on her bed, and the thought made her smile.

"Yes. Maybe . . . Vanilla?"

"I'll tell her."

He leaned over and kissed her, then got up and disappeared from view. She closed her eyes, and when she opened them again sometime later, she heard squeals and saw Harmony standing beside her with Vanilla clutched against her.

"Oh . . ." Charlotte smiled. "Sit down . . . and let's see what you've got."

"You're sure?"

"Yes."

Harmony lowered herself to the bed, and Vanilla, tail wagging hard enough to wrinkle the top sheet, dove for Charlotte and began to lick her face.

Harmony grabbed the puppy. "I'm sorry, but she's such a people dog. And she's always loved you."

"She's a cuddle dog . . . if she can't be a service dog."

"I'll make sure, no matter what, she finds just the right home, Charlotte. I promise."

"What about you?"

"I've found one, too."

Charlotte listened as Harmony explained her plan to work and live at Capable Canines.

"And I'm going to keep Velvet for myself," she said at the end. "No more litters for her. She can be my pal, and the baby's."

Charlotte felt tears on her cheeks. "I'm so glad. I made sure you could stay here . . . as long as you needed. It's in my papers, but this . . . will be better."

Vanilla jumped out of Harmony's arms and licked Charlotte's face again. Charlotte laughed and managed to wrap her arms around the puppy, although she was surprised at how leaden and unresponsive they felt as the puppy wiggled happily.

Harmony straightened her covers. "Charlotte, if I have a girl I'm going to name her after you."

"Lottie Lou?"

Harmony laughed. "Charlotte Louise, but I'll call her Lottie. I really like it."

Ethan stepped into view, and Charlotte saw an expression on his face she couldn't identify. There were tears in his eyes, but he was smiling.

"More visitors," he said.

"We'll have time later," Charlotte told Harmony. "I want to hear . . . more."

Harmony reached out to get the puppy, but Ethan stepped over and put his hand on her shoulder. "Leave Vanilla a moment, would you?"

Harmony got up. "Sure, but . . ." She turned, and whatever she saw made her fall silent. Then she stepped to the end of the bed and waited.

Charlotte was confused until she saw the reason. A brown-haired girl was coming toward the bed, blue eyes sparkling. "Oh, what a cute puppy!"

"I thought you might like her," Ethan said. "So did your grandmother."

Maddie stopped beside the bed and held out her hand. "Can I pet her?"

Ethan looked at Charlotte. "What do you think?"

"I think you . . . should probably sit on the bed." Charlotte slid a little more to the middle to make room for her granddaughter. "Her name is Vanilla."

Maddie pulled the puppy close, and Vanilla, immediately transferring her affection, licked the girl's face. Maddie squealed.

"Are you really my grandmother?" Maddie asked. "I have two?"

"I . . . really am."

"Where have you been?"

"Just waiting . . . for you, sweetheart."

Maddie looked at her closely. "Maybe you waited too long."

"I'm sure I did." Charlotte looked past Maddie, who was absorbed in the puppy again, and saw Taylor moving to her bedside.

Ethan stepped in, scooped up Maddie and the puppy without a word, and made room for his daughter.

Taylor collapsed on the bed beside her mother, put her arms around Charlotte's neck and began to cry. "I'm so sorry, Mom. So terribly, terribly sorry."

Charlotte put her arms around her daughter, and their tears fell together.

Half an hour later Taylor brushed her mother's hair off her forehead with the backs of her fingers. Maddie and Ethan were in the family room with the puppies so Taylor and Charlotte could be alone for a little while.

"Do you remember the time I was twelve and I fell off my bike on the way to school, and scraped my elbows and knees, and everything in between? You stayed home from work, even though you had a big meeting, and after lunch we lay on the sofa eating ice cream and watching soap operas all afternoon. You made me promise I wouldn't tell anybody, and you said if I did, you would deny it."

Charlotte laughed a little. It felt so good to be able to. "I release you from your promise."

Taylor smiled, and Charlotte could feel the beauty of it blooming inside her. "I think of that afternoon a lot," Taylor said.

"Even when I didn't want to think about it, it was always right here." She put her hand over her heart. "That and all the other good times. There were so many."

"You and Maddie . . . have so many moments like that ahead of you."

"And you and I missed so many these past years."

Charlotte took her daughter's hand and kissed it. "Let's be done with regrets. We learned . . . bitter lessons, but we found each other again. Some people . . . never do. I am so grateful for you." She paused, because talking was growing harder, and she was exhausted. "I am so grateful . . . for Maddie. She's everything I knew she was . . . and more."

"You're tired. You're wiped out by all this commotion, and you need to save your strength. I guess I'd better go, but Maddie and I will be back tomorrow morning. I'll bring her scrapbook. And we can set up our digital picture frame so you can watch her growing up on your nightstand."

"Technology *is* our . . . friend."

Taylor laughed, then she bent and kissed Charlotte on the forehead, adding one more on each cheek before she gave her a final hug.

On the way out she stopped in the doorway. From somewhere in the house Charlotte could hear Maddie's high-pitched laughter and the rumble of Ethan's voice. One of the puppies was yapping excitedly. The sounds of a family.

Her family.

"Maddie loves that puppy," Taylor said. "You really want her to have Vanilla?"

"For both of you. But only if you —"

Taylor smiled. "Is Vanilla *your* favorite?"

"By far."

"Then I think we'll need her with us." She smiled, but her eyes gleamed with tears. "I love you, Mom. I always have, even when I didn't want to. And I always will."

When she was gone, Charlotte fell asleep with her own cheeks damp with tears.

Later, when she awoke, she discovered that Ethan had slipped into bed beside her and gathered her in his arms. Soothing classical music drifted around them, along with the herbal scent of Harmony's minestrone soup.

He read her mind. "They'll be back first thing tomorrow," he said. "Nothing could keep them away."

"They're both . . . so beautiful."

"Your granddaughter's madly in love with Vanilla, and it's mutual. The puppy will be perfect for her. If the surgery's successful,

Maddie may not need a seizure dog, but she'll always need a pal."

Charlotte knew what she'd told Taylor was true. It was time to put all her mistakes behind her. She no longer needed them to hold her on earth. She had Taylor, Maddie and Ethan to anchor her. As long as God allowed.

"It will be easier . . . to let go now," she said.

"Did you and Taylor say everything you needed to?"

"Never, but we've forgiven . . . each other. And ourselves."

"She always loved you."

"She told me."

"She's not the only one." He kissed her hair.

"I never quit . . ."

"Loving me? Loving us?" he finished for her.

"I always loved you." Something else nibbled at her memory. She smiled again. "And I didn't quit . . . five minutes before my miracle."

"Do me a favor, Lulu. Don't quit quite yet, even if you already got yours."

"I'm going to take all the time . . . and all the miracles I can."

She drifted off to sleep again, Ethan's

arms around her, the warm imprint of her granddaughter and daughter safe in her heart.

She dreamed of Gwen, who lifted her hand and slowly dissolved into the darkness. Here, there was no more sadness to heal, no suffering to end. Dying, she promised, would be the least of it.

Chapter Forty-Five

There had been just enough time to say everything that mattered, but not nearly enough to say everything.

Twelve days after their reunion, Taylor watched as her father lowered her mother's ashes into the ground beside Taylor's great-grandmother's grave.

Georgia and Samantha Ferguson stood side by side across from her, with Edna between them. Harmony, eyes red-rimmed, stood on Georgia's left.

Reverend Analiese Wagner, in clerical garb, with a green stole with lotus blossoms embroidered on it, said the final prayer. Then, instead of dispersing the mourners, she added a personal note.

"Charlotte Hale was my friend, as well as my parishioner. I've never seen anyone face death more courageously or live the time they had left with more love in their hearts. She's now at rest in the mountains that inspired her, beside the grandmother who nurtured her and the generations of family who helped make her the woman she came to be. At the end she wasn't afraid to die, but she was sad to leave each of you. Let us rejoice in a life well lived, in a heart that overflowed with love and graced her community, family and friends, and in a spirit that is now at peace."

Maddie, who had wept when she learned her grandmother was gone, had stood solemnly through the brief service, but now she and Edna joined hands and ran toward the house, where the table on the front porch was filled with food.

Taylor wiped her eyes; then she took her father's hand, and they stood quietly at the graveside for a few minutes. The others followed Edna and Maddie and left them alone.

"Mom worked so hard to leave this place, and now we've brought her back and buried her here," she said at last.

Ethan looked tired but composed. He, Taylor and Harmony had stayed with Charlotte until the end, well past the time when she had been aware of their presence. But Ethan had never stopped believing that some part of her had still known they were there, and only when her body had been removed by the funeral home had he been willing to leave Charlotte's house.

A house that now belonged to him. That, too, Taylor thought, was an irony.

"In the end your mom came to terms with who she was and where she came from," he said. "Reverend Ana's right. She was at peace, and this is a peaceful place."

They began the walk toward the house. "I do remember coming here with you," she said. "There were chickens, and a goat."

"Some of the prettiest land in this country is some of the poorest. If good memories were built from nothing but mountain vistas, your mom never would have left."

"I hope she did something good with the farm."

"I think Reverend Ana will tell us today."

"Are you over the shock of inheriting the controlling shares in Falconview?"

Only two nights ago Ethan had learned that except for donations to charities she had supported and cash bequests to Harmony and her housekeeper — including a set of china to each of them — Charlotte's entire estate, minus the farm, had been left to him.

He gave a brief smile. "Your mom was always full of surprises."

"That was a pretty big one."

"She knew Falconview would become something very different in my hands, and I think that's what she wanted. Leaving it to me was her way of making sure the company becomes smaller and more concerned with keeping mountain vistas like these intact. I don't know whether I'll succeed, but maybe I'll have fun trying."

Taylor thought her mother had chosen wisely.

Ethan squeezed her hand before he dropped it. "You know, don't you, that everything else she left me, including Falconview, is really for you and Maddie? Her attorney told me that when they put together her living trust, she was afraid if any assets went directly to you, you might refuse."

"That was so Mom, wasn't it? She wanted to protect Maddie and me, even if I refused to let her."

"When I sell the house, that money will go directly into your account as a start. I know that's what she wanted."

"It's a lot more than I deserve."

Ethan squeezed her hand. "That's not how she felt."

"I wonder why everything we really have to know has such a steep learning curve?"

"Because once we finally get it right, it's

ours for life."

Taylor would never forgive herself for waiting so long to reconcile with her mother, but she knew Charlotte had forgiven her. She also knew what a gift that forgiveness would be in years to come.

Taylor saw that Analiese was waiting for them to join her. Later her father would come back and fill in the grave, his way of saying his final goodbye to the woman he had loved.

Ana put her arm around Taylor for a brief squeeze. During Charlotte's last days they had become close, and now Taylor, who had never expected to have anything to do with the Church of the Covenant, thought she might begin taking Maddie there for Sunday School.

"Taylor, I'd like to say something to the group after we've eaten. Do you mind?"

"I imagine Sam's staying awhile. Maddie and Edna can entertain each other."

Ethan and Taylor had scheduled a traditional memorial service for Charlotte in two weeks, when everyone who wanted to could come and pay their respects. Analiese had warned it would be a large gathering, since there was genuine sorrow for her passing at the church and beyond. Charlotte, she'd said, would have been pleasantly surprised.

At the end of her life she'd been able to see her faults, but her strengths and their impact on the community had eluded her.

In addition, Charlotte had asked for this intimate interment service on the mountain with just a few people. And, being Charlotte, she had provided a list.

Out on the porch the guests were dishing up. Harmony and Taylor had collaborated on the food, two vegetarians who'd discovered as they cared for Charlotte that they had even more in common. Harmony would be moving out of Charlotte's house next week, and not too many weeks afterward, Maddie and Taylor would visit her at Capable Canines to bring Vanilla home.

Harmony had made three different salads, and Taylor had baked the same chocolate cake her mother had always made for her childhood birthdays. They had purchased a platter of cheeses and breads for sandwiches, as well as vegetables and dips.

Everyone filled plates and found places to sit where they could face one another. Ethan started a playlist of Charlotte's favorite songs, and they listened to Alison Krauss and Gillian Welch as they ate and chatted. The midsummer afternoon was warm, and butterflies flitted from day lilies to black-eyed Susans.

Taylor cut the cake and gave everyone a slice. Harmony poured coffee from a pot she had made in the kitchen. Samantha gathered up dishes and dirty silverware. Georgia entertained Maddie and Edna by showing them how to gather "broom straw" from the yard and closest field to make their own brooms, Appalachian-style.

Ethan excused himself and went back up the hill to finish filling in the grave, and to be alone with his thoughts and memories.

Taylor sat with her cake and coffee on the steps, her back to a pillar, and watched the girls giggling and chasing each other as they hunted broom straw. "I think there must have been some good times on this porch through the years. Sitting here, looking over mountains, listening to birds. It's so peaceful. I wish we could bottle it."

Analiese, who was leaning against the wall, cup and saucer in hands, agreed. "It's a healing place."

"I think that's why Mom wanted us to come here."

"That's exactly why," Analiese said. "And I think this is the right moment to tell you the rest of it, too."

"Shouldn't we wait for Dad?"

"He knows most of it already. We'll fill him in on the rest, but this is about us."

Taylor thought that was interesting. They were suddenly "us," and she liked the feel of that. She had been close to Samantha, and even Samantha's mother, for a long time, but because of Charlotte she had quickly grown close to Harmony and Analiese. Life had a way of separating people, of barging in on relationships and insisting there was no time for friendship. She'd wondered if now that her mother was no longer alive, Harmony and Analiese would drift out of her life again. She hoped not.

Analiese set her coffee cup on the table. "At the end of her life Charlotte was able to see what a special place this farm is, too. It took time and distance, but she held on to it despite everything. For years after she left, when she hardly had enough to live on, somehow she scraped up the money to pay the taxes. I think she must have known, deep down, that keeping the farm for future generations was important."

Taylor knew she and Maddie were those future generations, the living links to the Sawyers, yet as beautiful as the land and house were, she also knew they would never live here. The house was an oasis in a complicated world, but the world was where they needed to be.

"Charlotte thought hard about what to do," Analiese said. "She brought me here to see the farm, and in the end, we came up with an idea. The thing is, it involves each of you. It can't happen without you."

"What can *we* do?" Georgia asked.

"To see that, you have to understand what Charlotte told me she'd learned. She said she discovered the only way to help anybody was to walk beside them, not to judge, not to advise, but simply to be there. She said women have always understood that offering consolation or a listening ear is what really matters, not how much money you throw at a problem — although that can help — but simply being there."

Taylor wasn't sure where this was going. She could see Georgia didn't understand, either, although she looked interested. Analiese went on.

"Charlotte didn't want to start another charity, and she didn't want a memorial. She didn't want to give this property to a charity already in existence. She wants this idea to grow organically, and for us to fashion it together our way. She wants this house and land to be a place where women come together. She and I used to talk about anonymous goddesses, those women who are always with us, behind us, in front of us, but rarely ever seen. At the end, she thought maybe this could be a place where goddesses flourish."

"How?" Harmony asked.

"She left the farm in a trust, and each of us has been named a trustee. If we want to be part of it — and the choice is up to each of us — we'll have a say in what happens, how we reach out, how we use this land and this house to help those who need it. Any one of us who doesn't want to be part of it doesn't have to be. We can add women or subtract those who need to back away. Charlotte endowed the farm, so we don't need to worry about repairs or taxes. She only asked that we each take part when we can, use our unique talents to find ways to help, then use the resources here, if we need to, to make a difference. We could use the house for retreats. We could house women who are in danger or in trouble. We could start a cooperative, grow flowers or herbs to help provide women who need it with income."

"A Goddesses Anonymous house," Georgia said.

Analiese smiled. "I like that."

"What was she really hoping for?" Taylor asked. "Because how many women can we reach that way?"

"Maybe just one at a time. But remember, there are five of us. That's ten hands reaching out. Lives might change. Our own lives, and the women we reach out to. Imagine how many of those women will reach out in turn when they're able to. We'll just be doing what women have done through the centuries, only focused. And we'll have the farm and one another as resources."

"Why did she choose us?" Harmony asked.

"Because we each have different talents and abilities. But mostly? Because she trusted us."

For Taylor, the truth was clear. Her mother had wanted something more important than a memorial. She had wanted something more than just a way to reach out to women in need, although that was certainly a large part of it.

"She wanted something for *us*," she said. "She trusts us, yes, but more than that? She wants us to be here for one another. The women she most loved or admired. She wanted this for *us*, because she can't be here herself."

"We have time to think and plan," Analiese said. "Let's each go home and decide if we want to make this kind of commitment."

For a moment they sat quietly, then

Harmony got to her feet. "Maybe this sounds impulsive, but I don't have to think about it. I know I want to be part of it."

"I love it," Samantha said, standing, too. "I'm in."

"I think it's an interesting idea," Georgia said, rising.

"I'm already in," Analiese said.

Taylor realized none of them were looking at her, but they were waiting for her to speak. As she got to her feet she cleared her throat, but her voice was husky, anyway. "I am so proud of Mom."

She wasn't sure who began the hug that followed, but as the mountain shadows deepened, they stood together listening to the song of birds and comforted one another.

Five women, and the sixth, who would always be with them.

Ethan placed the final shovelful of soil over the urn that held Charlotte's ashes and patted down the soil. Later he and Taylor would erect a headstone, but for now he placed a bouquet of roses over the spot.

When he spoke, his words were as hushed as a prayer.

"This is the hard part, Lulu. The part where I walk away for the last time. But we found each other twice, so maybe we'll find each other a third time. With a little luck, that could be the last time we'll need to."

He stood with his head bowed for a minute, then he turned, and walked downhill toward the laughter of Maddie and Edna in the field below.

ACKNOWLEDGMENTS

Many thanks to my brainstorming group, Casey Daniels, Karen Young, Jasmine Cresswell and Diane Mott Davidson, for all their feedback and suggestions along the way.

Even more thanks than usual to my agent Steve Axelrod and my editor Leslie Wainger for their enthusiasm, careful reading and recommendations from the beginning of this project.

Special thanks to Amy Challgren, who read the sections on Maddie's epilepsy to make certain terminology and details were correct, and to friend and fellow novelist Diane Chamberlain, who introduced us. Thanks also to the Leukemia and Lymphoma Society forums, where patients and family can and do share their difficult journeys. Of course, as always, if errors slipped through, they're mine and mine alone.

Finally I owe a debt of gratitude to Michael McGee, who listened patiently when I needed to vent, brainstormed with me on long beagle walks, and laughed and cried in exactly the right places.

Asheville, North Carolina, is a city I visit often. With its broad diversity and scenic beauty, it seems the perfect place to set the Goddesses Anonymous series. But fiction is not fact, and not every place I've used exists or exists in the form it does in this novel. Zambra is real and the food is delicious. Cuppa is not real, but I still wish I could try their eggplant provolone pizza. If you live in Asheville or know it well, sit back and enjoy the ride, and occasionally, the unfamiliar or slightly altered scenery.

READER'S GUIDE

1. Charlotte uses her First Day Journal as a way to get in touch with her past and feelings. The author uses Charlotte's journal as a way to connect the reader to both. Did the journal give you valuable insight that enriched your understanding of Charlotte's life?

2. Charlotte's reaction to Taylor's pregnancy creates such a huge rift that Ethan and Taylor walk out of the home the family shared. Imagine that your sixteen-year-old daughter has just told you she's pregnant and plans to keep the baby. Could you understand Charlotte's desire to force Taylor to make a different decision? Could you understand Ethan's desire to support Taylor at the cost of his marriage?

3. Early childhood research tells us that lifelong problems between parents and

children can begin in infancy. Taylor is a difficult baby and Charlotte an insecure mother. Did you believe that particular dynamic continued and influenced the events that occurred many years later?

4. Taylor insists on making all decisions about her daughter Maddie's health care. Did you admire her stubbornness and the way she put Maddie's needs first? If not, when and why did you begin to think she had shortcomings as a mother?

5. Taylor and Jeremy dated for only a short time in high school, so they really don't know each other well. Can two near-strangers find ways to successfully parent a child they accidentally created and share? Did you believe that by the end they were on firmer ground?

6. *One Mountain Away* dramatizes three "accidental" pregnancies — Charlotte's, Taylor's and Harmony's. Charlotte sees herself in Harmony, because she, too, was alone and afraid as a young woman. She also wants to help Harmony because she refused to help her own daughter. Do you believe we can make up for a wrong we've committed in the past by reaching out to

others? Do you think Charlotte tried to do enough?

7. Analiese Wagner, Charlotte's minister, has had one too many run-ins with Charlotte in the past, so when the book opens it's difficult for her to assume the role of loving pastor and reach out to Charlotte. Do you think Analiese goes above and beyond the call of duty? Do you think in the end their new relationship enriches both their lives? Could you reconcile the Charlotte Analiese knew with the Charlotte we know by the end of the novel?

8. Do you believe that childhood experiences can be so powerful that they continue to affect even the most intelligent, motivated adults? Do you know people who are still trying to make up for childhood deficits?

9. Despite all the problems in their past, at the end of Charlotte's life she and Ethan are able to find their way back to each other. Can love be so true and strong it overcomes years of separation and anger?

10. While *One Mountain Away* is the story of a woman's final months, did Charlotte's

transformation and her final reconciliation with loved ones provide a hoped-for happy ending? Are there worse things than dying?

11. Do you believe the women who knew and loved Charlotte will come together in the future at the Goddesses Anonymous house and finds ways to reach out to other women in a meaningful, personal way, as Charlotte intended? Of the "goddesses" in the final chapter, whose story do you hope to read about next?

The employees of Thorndike Press hope you have enjoyed this Large Print book. All our Thorndike, Wheeler, and Kennebec Large Print titles are designed for easy reading, and all our books are made to last. Other Thorndike Press Large Print books are available at your library, through selected bookstores, or directly from us.

For information about titles, please call:
(800) 223-1244

or visit our Web site at:
http://gale.cengage.com/thorndike

To share your comments, please write:
Publisher
Thorndike Press
10 Water St., Suite 310
Waterville, ME 04901